CW01512825

# Threads That Bind Us
## Syndicate of Fate
### Book 1

Rae Douglas

 Created with Vellum

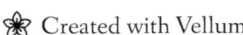

*For oldest sisters, those who find themselves in darkness, and everyone who has ever learned control by giving it up.*

*And for Rose. For inspiring Ana and inspiring me. Thank you for being the symbiotic parasite that lives inside my brain.*

# Trigger and Content Warnings

### *Trigger Warnings*

Murder (on page)
Torture (on page)
Domestic violence (between a supporting character and her
partner, off page)
Miscarriage as the result of domestic violence (between a
supporting character and her partner, off page)
Childhood cancer diagnosis (teenager, non-fatal, supporting
character, treatment as a major plot point of book)
Abandonment by mother/mommy issues

### *Explicit Sexual Themes*

Femmedomme
Pegging
Begging
Orgasm denial/control
Restraints (improvised)

Squirting

Power exchange

Public play (agoraphilia, not exhibitionism, no one is watching)

# Playlist

*Goodbye Earl* - The Chicks
*The Night We Met* - Lord Huron
*Do I Wanna Know?* - Arctic Monkeys
*Sour Diesel* - ZAYN
*Power Over Me* - Dermot Kennedy
*If I Killed Someone For You* - Alec Benjamin
*Silence* - Marshmello, Khalid
*Angel of Small Death and the Codeine Scene* - Hozier
*New Girl* - FINNEAS
*Worship* - Ari Abdul
*Lose Control* - Teddy Swims
*invisible string* - Taylor Swift

# Prologue
## Charlie

*Six Months Ago*

Fresh blood coats her arm, staining the sleeve of her shirt. Copper hair is braided against her head, framing round, flushed cheeks on pale skin. I can't see her eyes in the shadow of this disgusting alley, and that's a damned shame, because she's a vision.

She's breathing hard, still holding the bloody switchblade in a shaking grip. The man she stabbed has his hands pressed to his abdomen, blood seeping through his fingers. He's tall, unkempt, and a belligerent regular at the strip club we're behind. I recognize him from the number of times the bouncers have had to escort him out when he gets too handsy with the dancers.

Seems like that won't be an issue anymore.

The woman—I wish I knew her name—watches as her victim slumps against the alley wall, tension stringing her body tight. He sneers *fucking bitch* loud enough for even me to hear, but she doesn't seem to react. She just observes him as he bleeds out on the ground, long enough that the puddle of blood beneath him grows stagnant.

I've watched dozens of people kill with more expertise and skill than what she displayed, but seeing her press that blade into this pile of filth, watching her twist the knife, was one of the most erotic things I've ever experienced. Troubling, though maybe not surprising, considering my line of work. The jerk of her muscles thrumming with adrenaline and what must be fear, the twitch in her jaw when she thrust up into his abdomen. It was like watching a savant touch the keys of the piano for the first time.

It's clear she's a novice at this. There are places she could have stabbed him that would have prolonged his agony, or hastened his death, whatever her goal was. But she's clearly a natural. And there's something I can't explain that draws me to her.

She caught my eye in the strip club. Her outfit was out of place for a patron, too conservative to be here for fun. She scoped out the club until she spotted her target—the guy currently laying facedown on the ground. At first I thought she was pissed at her boyfriend or something, which isn't an uncommon occurrence at this establishment. Instead, she squared her shoulders and sat within this guy's line of sight.

It didn't take more than a half hour for him to lead her by the hand toward this alley. I should have stayed in the club and waited for my contact, but something pulled me toward her, and I never ignore my intuition.

I'm thankful I didn't, because missing out on this would be the disappointment of a lifetime. I keep watching as she gently pushes his body with the toe of her tennis shoe, and he slumps further into the ground. She hesitates, glancing toward the door to the strip club and down the alley where I'm lurking in the shadows. Finally, she squats down in front of him, and with the most controlled fury I've ever heard, says, "I wish I could fucking kill you twice."

It's like her voice activates some sort of current beneath my skin. A riptide of lust crashes through me at the sound of her anger. My blood hums in my veins, and I have the irrational desire to be on the receiving end of her rage.

I'm transfixed, carnal desire leaving my cock hard and my chest tight as I watch her shift her victim until she can find purchase at his shoulders and drag him clumsily toward the dumpster at the other end of the alley.

For a split second, I think about making myself known, telling her that garbage pickup happens in less than two hours, and she's not giving herself enough of a head start. That there are security cameras in the club that are going to show her leaving with him. But I imagine my presence would only terrify her.

She tucks his body as far behind the dumpster as she can, covering what's exposed with dirty cardboard boxes. After surveying her work, she glances down at herself. She's managed to keep her jeans fairly clean—a miracle, to be honest —but her t-shirt is covered in blood. I tense as she lifts it over her head. *Christo.* I try my very best not to stare at the soft slope of her pale shoulders, at the way her thin tank top conforms to her curves, at the place where it rides up at her waist.

I must let out some small sound, because she whips around and looks directly toward me. I still can't see her expression clearly, but her shoulders are tense, her head turning from side to side, searching for the source of the noise.

I hold my breath, waiting for her to calm, to convince herself she imagined the sound. Eventually she does, balling up the shirt and aiming toward the trash. At the last second she thinks better of it, grabbing her switchblade off the ground, wrapping it in the shirt, and tucking it into her bag that she'd tossed on the ground.

She sends one last glance back at the dumpster and then starts toward the mouth of the alley. I press myself farther into the enclave I'm hiding in, holding my breath again. As she passes, I get a momentary closer look. She's tall, with gentle curves and long limbs. Freckles like stars dance along her shoulders and crawl up her neck under the harsh light of the streetlamp. She's turned away from me, and I've got half a mind to make a sound again just so I can see her eyes. But in the next second, she's down the street and disappearing into the night.

It takes me a moment to process the way I reacted to her, so ensnared by something I've seen hundreds of times before. It almost pains me to admit I'll likely never see her again. I need to brush off this experience and go find Lexi inside the club, but my eyes keep flickering to the other end of the alley. To the place where I'm certain I watched her become a killer.

It's irrational, but before I know it, I'm calling Zane, telling him to coordinate with Renee and be at my location for a cleanup in twenty minutes. I find a rotting two by four and jam it under the doorknob of the back entrance to the club to avoid interruptions.

I know better than to touch anything before Renee arrives to do what she does best, but the curiosity is too strong. I yank my sleeve over my hand and shift the boxes.

His body is rolled onto its side, his face pressed into the rancid ground. I reach into his back pocket and slip out his wallet. Bryan Crankshaft. Height listed as a few inches taller than he actually is. Address in Anacostia. He's got a Metrocard, cigarette papers, two expired condoms, and a credit card that doesn't have his name on it, but instead says *McKenzie Willard*.

Renee shows up first, blocking the mouth of the alley with her car and practically skipping to my side. She's got her platinum blonde hair in dutch braids, and she's decked in a skintight black outfit with platform combat boots. She looks like a video game character, and would take such an observation as a compliment.

"Kind of messy for you, boss," she says, her voice high and lyrical as always. She squats next to the body, poking it with a manicured nail. "Out to the farm?"

I nod, and she stands up, dusting her hands off and glancing over her shoulder as Zane arrives. While Renee prepares her materials, Zane finds his place next to me. He stares at Bryan's body for a few moments before clearing his throat.

"That's not your work." He doesn't pose it as a question, and it doesn't require a response. Zane's been my driver and right hand for nearly four years, and he's seen my handiwork up close and personal too many times to count.

As Renee rolls Bryan's body onto a tarp, something catches my eye.

Tucked under the wheel of the dumpster is a watch. Its face is small and slightly cracked, and the clasp is broken. The band is black leather, impressed with a snakeskin pattern, and even though it's dark, I can tell it's soaked through with blood. It could be anyone's. It could have been here for weeks before tonight. But despite the blood, it seems fairly clean, and for some inexplicable reason, I reach down and snag it.

It's pretty. Vintage. Delicate in design but sturdy in structure. I slip it into my pocket, rubbing my thumb over the pattern in the leather.

Zane and I leave Renee to her work, and as he drives us out of the Navy Yard, I stare out into the starless night, thinking about fate and copper hair.

# Chapter 1
## *Gwen*

I'm scribbling furiously on the notepad balanced on my knee, with its *Children's National* logo emblazoned in red across the top, a little gray teddy bear waving at me. Cheerful little asshole. On my right, Ana is squeezing my hand so tightly that both of our fingers are turning white, but I don't shake her off. I want to grab and hold her. I want to sob together. Whatever the oncologist is saying is literally life-or-death important, but I can't focus. My attention flits to the uncomfortably happy photos of sick kids on the walls, to the old carpet and heavy furniture, to the bright wallpaper and sleek computer, overwhelmed by the weird hospital time capsule vibe of the room. I'm disoriented, and maybe it's a physical reaction to the impossible words coming out of this doctor's mouth.

"Surgery is our next step," she says, her eyes kind and voice soft. I know it's probably because she's done this so many times that she knows how to stay composed, but I wish she would yell. Be angry at the cancer with me. "But I want to make sure you understand, Morgana. Stage 0 DCIS means the cells are pre-cancerous—it hasn't spread. You're incredibly lucky that we caught this so early. Treatment is relatively short, and if everything goes according to plan, your long-term risk of invasive cancer is incredibly low. This is treatable and survivable."

Ana's face is blank as she nods, but I can feel her sweating against my palm. It's not like we didn't see this coming; a fifteen-year-old doesn't make it into this room without a horrifying number of tests and needles and scans. We've been overwhelmed with meetings with social services and family support liaisons and so many people who are trying to prepare me to be the twenty-seven-year-old caretaker of a kid with cancer.

Dr. Beldiah, the annoyingly pleasant oncologist, continues talking about timelines and treatments and *next steps*. She explains how I can schedule everything with a family assistance specialist who will call me tomorrow. I'm writing every word down because I'm currently running on auto-pilot, and I think Ana's hand in mine is the only thing stopping me from crumbling.

"Gwen, could I possibly speak to you in the hall? A nurse is going to come in to take Morgana's vitals and give her some information." Dr. Beldiah picks up her phone and presumably dials whatever nurse she's referencing.

For the first time in over twenty minutes, I turn fully toward my favorite person in the entire world. Her auburn hair is twisted into a bun at the nape of her neck, messy and frayed. Her jaw is clenched, and her nostrils flared. But she's not afraid. I've seen this look on Ana before—she's angry. And fuck, doesn't she deserve to be?

Her hand grips mine so tightly I've lost feeling in it, but she doesn't turn to me. I know that expression too, because I know all of them. She doesn't want me to leave.

"I think I'd rather stay with her for now, if you don't mind,"

I breathe out, feeling like I'm talking through a straw. "You can say what you need to say here. She deserves to know everything." I turn back to Dr. Beldiah. "She can handle it."

Her eyes flicker between me and Ana, and she's saved from answering by the click of the door opening and shutting. An older man with speckled hair and wire-rim glasses kneels beside Ana and wraps her free arm in the blood pressure cuff. A little pulse monitor goes on her finger. Dr. Beldiah leans toward me.

"Someone from the billing office will call you sometime this week to set up an appointment. There are financial aid applications, and they can answer questions about your insurance coverage. It's a lot to handle, I know, but there's support here."

I wince and glance at Ana. The doc was right—she doesn't need to hear this. I grimace as the nurse tells her they're going to need to do her blood pressure one more time and she should take some deep breaths.

"Thank you, I'll keep that in mind." I say the words, but I'm not really sure what I mean. My little sister has been on my insurance since the day my first plan kicked in, about a month after high school graduation. I couldn't remember the last time she'd seen a dentist before then—our mother has never been particularly skilled with paperwork or appointments or parenting—but ever since, I've made sure she's the absolute picture of health. Teeth cleanings and eye exams and physicals before joining the softball team. And when she took a line drive to the chest during practice, I got her to the emergency room, thinking we could handle whatever was coming. My biggest worry was that she broke a rib and she wouldn't be able to play in the winter league championship.

And now here we are, one CT scan, two MRIs, a biopsy,

and countless blood tests later, and I have no idea how much this will cost. I've created a comfortable life for us, but my tips keep us afloat, and the insurance isn't *this* good.

Eventually, her blood pressure settles, and Dr. Beldiah sends us off with a folder stuffed with pamphlets and forms. As we leave the hospital hand in hand, Morgana doesn't say a word. We've had nine years of it just being the two of us. We know each other inside and out, left and right, and I'm certain Ana needs to be the first one to break the silence. She needs to exert some small amount of control in this situation.

She doesn't let go of my hand until we're standing directly in front of our neighbor Jimmy's blue two-door I borrowed. It's probably ridiculous, but I had a nightmare last night that we took the Metro to this appointment and the red line shut down, and we were trapped on the train until the cancer took over Ana's entire body. I wasn't tempting fate.

When we're both settled in the car, the winter cold stinging our noses with the engine still off, she turns and looks me right in the eyes.

"How the fuck do you get breast cancer with no boobs?"

I am so taken aback by the question, I actually laugh. For a fleeting moment, guilt swallows me, but then Ana laughs too, the sound full of disbelief.

"Where is the cancer even hiding? What tits exist for it to live in?" She huffs bitterly into the frigid air, still turned toward me in her seat.

A pained smile pulls onto my lips in response to hers.

"Don't say fuck, and don't say tits," I laugh, my reproach lacking any sort of authority.

"I think I've earned the right to say tits today."

She's right. She's earned it.

"Okay, fine, but still don't say fuck." I turn the car on and navigate toward the exit. Ana is still smiling, but it feels strange now. Like how she smiled when Danny Whicker un-invited her to prom freshman year because a senior girl had shown interest. Pained, but in a way where she's mad at herself for allowing it to hurt her.

"Are you hungry? Boob cancer earns you dinner pick of the night." I thread the car through the streets of Columbia Heights, scowling at the college kids and Hill staffers as they mingle outside restaurants and hidden gardens. I usually love this city. But today, it's the city that saw my sister get cancer, so I'm pretty irrationally pissed at it.

As Ana's smile melts into something more natural, she leans back into her seat, kicking her shoes off and tucking her heels against her thighs. She's always balled herself up, especially when we're in the car. It makes her look so young. Today more than ever.

"Do we have pad see ew left in the fridge?" she asks, unwrapping and rewrapping her hair in the bun at the base of her neck. The traffic picks up as we inch our way toward Adam's Morgan.

"You can have fresh pad see ew tonight. We can grab it on the way," I offer. She rests her chin against her knees.

"Ginny, I think tonight's going to be the last normal night for a while. I kind of want to pretend it's a regular Tuesday, you know?"

The fact that she used her nickname for me—the one only *she* uses—settles my pulse a little. I can do that. I can do normal. I can *so* do normal. I'm not on the edge of panic. I don't want to scream, to cry, to rage against this threat I know I can't fight. I'm not terrified.

I'm normal.

"Okay, but I'm having someone deliver ice cream because I ate the last of it before my shift yesterday. Don't yell at me."

Her look of mock shock and chagrin is so classically

Morgana that I think maybe she's right. We can have one more night of normal.

It's not until late that night, after we've moved the chaises around to make the couch into a giant bed and eaten until we're nearly comatose, that I realized I never asked if she was okay. But maybe neither of us are ready for that answer, anyway.

## Chapter 2
## *Gwen*

"And you're the legal guardian of your sister?" the guy from Children's National's billing office asks for the third or eleventh time. I take a deep breath.

"No, technically, my mother still maintains parental rights. But Ana is my dependent. She's covered by my insurance policy." It had taken quite a bit of assistance from a pro-bono family attorney to figure out how all of this worked nearly nine years ago.

"Unfortunately, it seems your policy didn't cover a significant portion of the lumpectomy, and it doesn't look like it will cover much more of Ana's radiation therapy." He clicks his tongue twice. "And to apply for financial assistance, you must be her legal guardian, regardless of the insurance policyholder information. Could your mother possibly join this call?"

I nearly laugh out loud. Sure, once I figure out what continent she's on.

I'm fucking exhausted. Ana's surgery—the lumpectomy to remove the little clump of pre-cancerous cells in her chest—was almost a week ago, and she was a fucking champ. But when the bill hit my inbox yesterday, I nearly went into shock. Hence, this phone call.

"She hasn't seen Morgana in over four years. I wouldn't know how to get her involved in this process," I say, slipping farther down the wall outside the club employee break room.

I shift my feet to get blood flow to my legs and crack my neck. The guy—David or John or something biblical like that—sighs into the receiver. "Look, I understand you're in a unique situation. I would encourage you to file for termination of parental rights based on abandonment and adopt your sister legally. Until that happens, I don't see how an application can be submitted."

I know I'll regret my next question, but I can't help it. I'm a glutton for situational awareness and punishment.

"Be honest with me here. What am I looking at?"

The line is silent for a moment.

"Costs vary widely, but based on what I'm seeing in her treatment plan and your coverage, you're looking at between sixty and eighty thousand dollars."

He keeps talking, but I can't hear anything through the whooshing sound in my ears. Jesus Christ, those are some very large numbers. We have *broke your arm at practice* emergency money, but nothing that could cover what this is likely to cost.

I interrupt Judas and ask if he can email me the information I'm not paying attention to, and he agrees. But I already know I need another plan.

Kenzie, my best friend and fellow overworked waitress, peeks her head out of the breakroom door to check on me, her long dark hair whipping around her face.

"Hey, what's going on? You look sick." She slides against the wall and sits on the floor next to me, resting her head on my arm.

My natural inclination is to shrug it off, pretend it's nothing. Kenzie's been through too much, and I never want to add to her stress. But the stress is starting to eat me alive.

"Apparently, our health insurance is even shittier than I thought," I sigh, resting my cheek on top of her head. She groans beneath me.

"Preaching to the choir on that one. I swear last summer would have cost me less if I had no insurance at all," she says, and my chest squeezes.

"Man, this fucking sucks," I admit, and she hums in agreement. "They won't let me apply for financial aid without Isabelle, and honestly Kenz, who the fuck knows where she is now?" We sit in silence for a few moments, Kenzie snuggling closer to my side. "If the financial aid was guaranteed, maybe I'd put some effort into finding her. But for all I know, she's married into oil money again, and then what happens?"

"I wish we could help more," Kenzie whispers, and I'm already shaking my head.

"You guys do enough, hanging with Ana when I have to be here," I say, waving over my shoulder toward the kitchen.

Kenzie may be my only true friend of the group, someone I'd trust with my secrets, but everyone here has been more than decent to Ana. Thanks to them, she knows how to say *go fuck yourself* in four languages.

"Wish we had half the fucking money people drop on these dinners," Kenzie mutters, and I can't help but agree.

"A tenth," I joke, nudging her with my elbow.

"You kind of get why your mom husband-hopped at places like this, you know?" she laughs humorlessly, shrugging me off and pushing to her feet. She reaches for her side instinctively, flinching as she stretches. Even half a year later, her body's still recovering. And as much as I hate seeing her in pain, the knowledge that she's safe soothes the feeling. That I made *sure* she is.

That thought should comfort me, but my brain finally catches up to her words, piecing them together until they hit me in the chest like a brick. A sickening feeling settles in my stomach as I realize I might, in fact, have another option. Suddenly, I need to drop my elbows onto my knees and breathe deeply. I'm pretty certain this is a terrible idea. But I can't leave any option unexplored when it comes to Ana. I can try for her. I can do this for her.

THREE DAYS LATER, I'm standing on the MARC platform half a block from a mid-tier restaurant that I have a six-thirty dinner reservation for. I left Ana at a weekend sleepover with her best friend Gray, and I absolutely did not tell her where I was going. I don't expect Ben to have any desire to spend more time with Ana, but I'll cross the *tell your baby sister you asked her absent father for her cancer treatment money* bridge when I come to it. My nose stings from the cold as I hustle down the street, hoping to get this painful situation over with as quickly as possible.

Ben is wealthy, but easily bored and incredibly manipulative. For all my mother's flaws, she was very careful not to get pregnant with her soup du jour's offspring after she had me, but Ben wanted control. My theory is that he liked to prove he could manipulate every boundary a woman had before he would let her go. Tell her to dye her hair, leave her husband, lose weight, get a boob job, quit her career, stop using birth control.

He left the day he found out my mother was pregnant with Ana, and I haven't seen him since.

I don't expect that he's turned over a new leaf regarding his daughter, but maybe he's decent or self-centered enough to care if his genetic offspring makes it into her twenties.

I force myself not to vomit at the prospect of Ana not having a twenty-first birthday and smile at the hostess I've landed in front of. It's mechanical and fake because, not for the first time, I'm paralyzed by the spiraling fear that keeps me up at night. Of Ana being one of the few who doesn't survive this. Of too-small coffins and memorials at softball games.

The hostess leads me to a tiny two-top in a secluded corner, and I'm surprised to see Ben already there. He's handsome in the way men who model for stock images are handsome, in a blank, vacant, and mildly unnerving way.

When the hostess pulls my chair out for me—a bit of a show for a place where nothing on the menu costs over forty dollars—Ben glances up from his phone and does a double take. For a second, it's like he's seen a ghost, and then his expression morphs into something between amusement and a challenge.

It's quite the curse, looking so much like my mother. Most people would assume it's the dark copper hair that's our most obvious shared trait, but we look cloned in almost every aspect. Both of us are tall, with long arms and legs, wide hips, and small chests. Her hazelnut eyes are just a shade lighter than my dark brown ones, but the freckles scattered from nose to temple are shockingly identical.

I've been on the receiving end of the look Ben's giving me a few times. The shock and intrigue, like an unaging ghost from their sexual past has come to haunt or fuck them. It's all I can do to force myself to ignore the obvious question in their eyes—*exactly how much like her mother is she?*

"Gwendolyn, how are you?" Ben asks, and I hold back a massive eye roll. My name, in fact, is Guinevere. Guinevere and Morgana, childhood friends and future conspirators in King Arthur's court. Our mother's odd obsession with the fable forced us into some early nickname decisions, hence Gwen and Ana. It's not lost on us that, in the tale, Morgana eventually murders Guinevere, but Isabelle's not a stickler for details.

"Gwen is fine, Mr. Mattherson, and I'm..." I stumble a bit. How am I? There is literally not enough time in the day to explain. "I'm doing okay, all things considered. How are you?"

"Wonderful, now." He smiles at me from across the table.

The lighting from the cheap battery-powered candle on the table casts an ugly shadow across his face, giving me full body chills. He picks up the red wine in front of him, and I can see his teeth through the glass as he drinks, which requires me to plaster my face still in order not to gag. This is for Ana. For Ana.

"You're very kind," I say as naturally as I can while forcing actual bile back. I grip the water glass sweating in front of me and take small, practiced sips. "How is your work going?"

That question alone is enough to get Ben rolling. It's shocking how easy it is to get people like Ben to talk about themselves at length. Usually, with Ana and her friends, or co-workers at the restaurant, I love hearing people get ramped up about something they love. For Ana, it's early 2000s vampire media, including an anime called *Vampire Knight*, whose two seasons we have watched an unholy number of times.

But when people like Ben talk about themselves, there's no passion. They're not doing it because their devotion to their work is so unbridled they can't help but go on and on about what they love. No, they talk to maintain relevance.

It's boring and trite, and I smile and nod through the conversation like I do with every table of men who want to impress their waitress. It's nearly twenty minutes before Ben shifts the subject.

"So, Gwen, do you want to tell me why I'm here tonight?"

It feels harder than it should to open my mouth and ask for

money from this monstrosity. He should feel obligated to help his own child. But I've got this sinking feeling that Ben has never felt obligated to anything but his own dick.

"I'm actually here to ask a favor," I start, putting a soft, simpering smile on my face. *Play the part, Gwen.* His eyebrows raise slightly but gives nothing away. "It's about Ana."

I truly should have expected the blank look I'm getting right now, but it somehow shocks me.

"Ana. Morgana. Your daughter?"

He laughs once, a bark turned toward the ceiling that raises the attention of the surrounding tables. He's cradling his wine glass, and the urge to break it against his face is consuming.

"Of course, Ana," he says, a little too loud. "How is she?"

I'm going to lose it, I really fucking am. Only the image of Ana doing treatment *alone* because I had to pick up another shift for the money keeps me from falling victim to my poorly-managed temper.

"Ana's actually not well at all. She's recently been diagnosed with early stage cancer. She's had surgery, but she also needs radiation therapy and the costs are incredibly high. I've been raising Ana on my own for a while now, and haven't been able to get ahold of Isabelle in a few years. I'm coming to you hoping, as her father, you'd be willing to assist with the cost of the treatment."

I withheld as many non-pertinent details as possible, but I can see Ben's brain working. Piecing together my level of desperation, my commitment to Ana, my lack of options. He's obviously surprised by the news, but he doesn't seem particularly affected.

The waitress drops another glass of wine for him, and tops off my water. When she departs, he seems to have come to some sort of conclusion.

"How much are we talking?" he asks, and I'm almost

relieved. He's considering it. Holy shit, this might have all been worth it.

"I'm still working through some insurance information, but the estimate is up to eighty thousand dollars." I resist the urge to cringe at the number. Ben is the beneficiary of generational wealth, and is involved with some very lucrative and relatively shady shit; the amount wouldn't go unnoticed, but it wouldn't truly affect him.

"And what do I get in exchange?"

I should have known. I should have *fucking* known. I grip my hands together in my lap, trying to stave off the anger rising again.

"What do you mean?"

"An investment needs a return, Gwendolyn," he responds, and I'm shocked a real human smile can look so cartoonishly sickening. "What is my return?"

"The life of your daughter?" The response comes out biting, but I can't help it. I had thought prepubescent rage fueled my teenage hatred of Ben, but looks like thinking he was a fucking rat at eleven years old was pretty fair.

"I don't know Morgana. She doesn't reach out and doesn't seem to want to be a part of my life." I barely cover my disbelieving scoff with a cough. Apologies that your child didn't pick up the phone and call her absentee father, you bastard. "But maybe *you* can give me that return."

## Chapter 3
### *Gwen*

Fuck absolutely everything.

Fuck Ben and his wine stained teeth, and his money, and his offer. Fuck Isabelle, and her inability to settle down when she had a child. Fuck the American healthcare system for bankrupting people when children get cancer. And most of all, fuck the cancer itself.

Ben's willingness to write me a one-time, personal check in exchange for an open-ended agreement to be his mistress sits heavy in my stomach. Eighty thousand dollars in exchange for my conscience. After Ana's treatment concludes, my vagina and other orifices would be beholden to him. *I'll call you whenever my wife is out of town or busy*, he said. Wouldn't want to schlep it to the city for his pay-per-lay and risk running into his flesh and fucking blood.

Separate and compartmentalized, I can deal with each individual aspect of this agreement. I knew making a deal with Ben would require some sort of extended contact with him. Infidelity is not the worst thing I'd considered doing for the money; I've done far worse for people I love far less. Sex work is work, and something I would have considered if starting a new career wouldn't take more time than I had. But it's the fact that Ben is forcing my hand in all of this when he should do this *for his child.*

Working through my rage, I make it as far as Union Station, the MARC and Amtrak passengers huddling together against the wind, scurrying toward the terminal with its shops and gorgeous ceilings and deep-seated smell of fast food. I'm on autopilot, a lifetime of navigating busy crowds keeping me from bumping into anyone. By the time I make it out to the grand entrance of Union Station, the dome of octagon windows reflecting murky skies through their glass, I feel like sinking into the floor and disappearing forever.

I can't go home right now. Ana's at Gray's until Sunday morning, and I cannot be alone with my thoughts. I think about calling Kenzie. She'd rally the good waitresses, the event managers and sommeliers, and the bartenders who best toe the line between complimentary and creepy. They'd make me laugh, tell me how to be a bad lay so he cuts the deal off early and I still get my money.

But the impending doom is sinking into my bones, and I feel like I'm living the last night of my life as I know it, and I don't want them to witness it. They're the closest thing I have to family other than Ana, and as pathetic as it sounds, I don't want to explain this.

I know my answer already. There's no question, no hesitation. For Ana, I would do much worse.

I just need to mourn.

I'm staring at the ceiling like a fucking tourist, trying to summon strength from the pretty architecture. *Just give yourself one night to grieve the life you thought you could live. One night to be selfish.*

I'm making my way out into the cold before I really know where I'm going, wandering aimlessly around the lamplit streets until I stumble into NoMa. It's a neighborhood I rarely visit, but maybe that's a good thing. There are no memories of Ana and I here.

I pass crossroads tucked with coffee shops and tattoo parlors and restaurants, busy for a weeknight, but still so much quieter than the neighborhood around our apartment. I want the calm to be reassuring, to give me peace, but all it gives me is space to think. I try to keep walking, to rush through residential streets to get to the next busy corner quickly, but it's not enough. My brain keeps humming the same tune.

*Just like her. You're. Just. Like. Her. Sure you have your reasons, and maybe you think they're better than hers were, but what do you know? In the end, you're making the same choice.*

I'm about to give up and make my way to whatever Metro stop is closest when I'm halted by the sounds of whooping. Loud, frat-boy level whooping. I hear the telltale signs of a group of girls cheering before downing shots.

That sounds like an escape.

I make my way up the street and am greeted by the beautiful sight of chaos. Neon signs blending with the harsh light of street lamps. Sweaty, barely legal bodies slamming against each other. Someone in a large purple hat wandering around a corner to puke in a bush. *Catalina's* is emblazoned in red neon cursive over the entrance. It's perfect.

I show my ID to the bouncer and wade through the sea of people jumping up and down to some eighties rock song. The band is so loud my teeth rattle, and I'm indescribably relieved to be here. My bummer expression persists, and I'm not exactly going to get up and dance, but it's nice to have the noise chase everything else away.

I make it to the bar at the back of the room just as a group of people in pink leather dresses get up from their stools at the very end of the bar. I take a seat, and the faded blue velvet is surprisingly comfortable.

There's only one bartender, and he's swamped at the other end of the room, so I swivel around and observe the bedlam that is Catalina's.

The ceilings are tall, and from corner to corner, the walls are filled with music paraphernalia. The popcorn ceiling is painted with huge arcs of color, intersecting and blending through the texture.

There's no formal dance floor, but between the yellow leather booths and black high top tables, people are jumping and dancing and swaying to whatever beat they can find. The band in the corner, whose banner is unreadable in the dim light, plays with the bass too high and the speakers too loud, and everything melds into one continuous thump of voices and guitars and scraping chairs and drums.

A tap on my shoulder pulls me out of my enamored stupor, and I turn to see the bartender smiling at me. His hair is bleached so blond it's nearly white. Through his right eyebrow are three silver rings, making his bright green eyes practically sing. He's got a smile like the Cheshire Cat, and I already want to be his best friend.

"How ya doin' tonight, Baby Red?" The deep Boston accent surprises me, but all I can do is smile wider.

"I'm here to do better," I reply, fishing my card out of the bottom of my purse and handing it to him with raised eyebrows. "A French 75 on an open tab, if you can."

Without missing a beat, he leans across the bar, snatches my card out of my hand with his teeth, and turns to one of the registers dotting the back counter. I try not to stare open-mouthed, a giggle caught in my throat. Even though there are tons of people here, no one seems to be annoyed that there's a bit of a wait for drinks.

"You don't have someone helping you out?" I ask as he slides my card back to me and grabs a bottle of gin from the case.

"Everyone who comes to Catalina's knows you wait for your drinks, and you party while you wait." He drops the bottle onto the counter and flings his arm to point at a sign behind a register. "Get rowdy, get rough, but don't get rude." He reads it like a command, which it probably is. I salute him, and his face splits into that grin again.

He mixes my drink, pours it into a champagne flute, and places it in front of me with a flourish. When I go to pick it up, he takes my hand straight out of the air and shakes it.

"I'm Sammy, Baby Red, and it's wonderful that we've met."

"I'm Gwen, Sammy baby, and it's already been a delight," I respond as he lets go of my hand.

I lift the drink to him and he blows me a kiss as I take a sip. Sweet and tart and bursting with bubbles, the drink is lemony and sugary and perfect. Seeing my look of pure bliss, he takes a bow, winks, and skips the other way down the bar to tend to more customers.

Sammy's energy is infectious, and the good feelings brought on by the bubbles and the smiles make me want to chase happiness as far as it will take me. From the depths of my wildly disorganized bag, I pull out a book I've been dying to finish. There is no actual plot, no real structure. I lean my arm against the bar, tucking myself away from anyone who might want to engage in conversation, and sip on my drink as I enter another world.

An hour slips by as I page through my book. My glass stays full, Sammy swinging by now and then to top me off and peek over the top of the pages. But as the words start to blur, and the story winds down to its inevitable happy ending, my chest feels tighter and tighter. These two gorgeous vampire ladies get their happily ever after. I want that for me. And it's not going to happen.

Even four-ish drinks in, I know I'm overreacting. First, Ana is worth it, one million times over. She's my best friend, and my sister, and sometimes feels like my own kid. She's my everything. I know I'm going to say yes. The rest of my drink goes down without me really tasting it.

And I also know it's temporary. Ben's offer is to sleep with him—*gag*—not marry him. Eventually he'll get bored, as he always does, and then I can move on. Try to wash the memory of saying yes to my own mother's ex off my body. Still, I know I won't be the same person after, and I'm already grieving the person I am at this moment.

I don't want to be like Isabelle. For so many years, I hated her for chasing after men with money, men who barely cared about her, while I was desperate for her attention. I never fully understood why she acted like she did, doing ridiculous things to secure the fleeting affection of whoever she was dating. Maybe she was incredibly insecure, or selfish, or just wanted things we never had. But every time one guy dropped her, she would dust herself off and find someone new to prove how desirable she was, showing her with gifts and trips.

At least this is different in one way. I'm not abandoning my personal sense of morals for attention and affection. I'm doing it for Ana.

My mind is racing again, and the music and booze are no longer beating the anxiety into submission. I want to take off my shoes and run through a forest until my body hurts so much I can't think about anything but the pain. I want to drink myself to sleep at this bar.

Instead, I do something far worse.

I make a pros and cons list.

I find a pen tucked into a pocket of my bag and turn to the

last page of my book, drawing a line down the center, marring the page forever. Annotating is one thing, but this is blasphemy. I probably could have asked for a bar napkin. Or grabbed one of the four notebooks also available in my bag. Too late now.

My fingers fumble for my drink until I realize the glass is empty, but I don't look up. I scribble *pros* on the left side of the line and *cons* on the right, underlining them with the heavy ink. Okay. I can do this.

The first one on the pros side is easy.

*Ana Lives.*

That's the ballgame, really. But I feel like I'll get some sort of catharsis out of going through the rest of this exercise. So I start on the cons side.

*Fucking Ben.*
*Helping a man cheat.*
*Letting Ben touch me.*
*Being like Isabelle.*

There's a lot more. I keep jotting them down until I've filled the cons half of the page with reasons that would keep me from saying yes to this under any other circumstance. There's only one other thing I can add to the pros.

*This is temporary.*

I stare at the page, anger building up in me again, but this time it's aimed at myself, for not saying yes immediately and needing time to process. I reach for my drink again, hoping for the comfort only your favorite cocktail can provide, only to remember it's empty.

"God, are you gonna get me another drink or not?" I demand, not at all slurring and definitely not yelling.

Tears sting the corners of my eyes, and I need another French 75 to fix that, damn it. When I yank my gaze from the scrawled notes in the back of my book, I'm looking not at Sammy, with his cat-got-the-canary smile, but at something else entirely.

His hair is tousled and messy. His eyes are dark and pretty and almost familiar. He's got a little more than a five o'clock shadow dusting his tanned skin, and the cut of his jaw makes me want to drool openly. And that's all before you get to whatever's happening from the neck down, which I physically cannot look at or I'll evaporate on the spot.

He's also looking at me with the kind of intensity that should feel scary. Like he's seen a ghost, and he's thrilled about it. Like he wants to consume me.

*Oh my god, this is the hottest man I've ever seen.*

"That's a very kind compliment," he says in a voice that might kill me. It's quiet, low, and tilted with the slightest Mediterranean accent. Greek? Italian? Who cares? There's a glimmer of something almost disbelieving in his eyes.

*Also, he can read minds, which is crazy.*

"You're actually just saying all of that out loud," he replies, and the little smile he's sporting makes me break out in a cold sweat. Jesus Christ, when's the last time I got laid?

"I'm not even sure how to apologize for that."

Although I really do want another sparkly drink, I'm pretty sure assuming the hot bartender can read minds means I need to switch to water. Ana's old enough that I rarely worry about having a drink or two while she's out with friends, but I haven't been this drunk in ages.

"Actually, a club soda and lime is probably a good idea," I amend, sliding my empty champagne flute toward him. He glances over his shoulder at Sammy, who's busy chatting up three dudes in boat shoes and salmon-colored shorts, before shrugging, filling a glass with ice, and hunting for the soda nozzle.

When he finds it, he clicks a few of the buttons before filling my glass and setting it in front of me. I cock my head at him.

"Are you new here or something? Or new at bartending?" When he quirks an eyebrow, I take a sip of my drink and grimace. "You gave me Sprite. Is this your first time using a soda nozzle?"

He slides the glass from my hand, the back of his fingers grazing my palm in a way that feels intentional. I can see a hint of pink at the tip of his ears that makes me want to smile like an idiot.

"New bartender, yeah. Something like that." He fills another glass, this time with the right setting, and places a little bowl with an entire lime's worth of slices in front of me. His hands grip the bar, and I seal my tongue to the roof of my mouth so I don't accidentally blabber about how fucking hot his hands are. What is it about hands? Clean nails, but calluses and scars. And tattoos. I can't make out all the details in the low light, but there are delicate bird wings on his left, and a snake wrapped around some sort of staff on the right. I'm mesmerized by both the art and the canvas. Maybe it's because I can imagine how they'd look against my body. Something I certainly shouldn't be pondering about a stranger while he's at his place of employment. I'm still examining his hands when he reaches across the bar and grabs my book before my brain can catch up.

"What's this?" he asks, running his unfortunately sexy

fingers over my writing. I try to grab my book back and nearly knock over my glass, which he catches before it can tip.

"I can't be the drunk girl at the bar telling my sad life story to the hot bartender. It's cliche, and despite being drunk off my ass, I'm still too sober for that."

I clasp my hands together and shove them in my lap, hoping he gets bored quickly, or has more customers that he needs to talk to, or a meteor falls from the sky and kills us all. But instead of any of those things happening, he continues to study my little pro-con list.

"I can't help but notice there are a lot of cons here," he muses, leaning against the bar in a way that seems purposefully nonchalant. Do hot men practice that move? Do hot dads teach their hot sons how to lean against things? This should be a study in the American Journal of Medicine or something.

"It's not the absolute number of pros and cons that matter," I say, reaching toward the book. He holds it above his head, and I huff back into my seat. "Each item is weighted, and in this instance, the items in the pro category are weighted more heavily."

He looks back and forth between the list and me, making some sort of calculation that my very sad, kind of drunk, and weirdly horny brain can't deduce. Then he closes the book and slips it into his back pocket. Before I can protest, he turns around and grabs another champagne flute.

"We'll come back to the book, but I think you deserve one more drink. What were you having?"

I should be annoyed that he's stolen my list. Instead, the pleasant buzzing from the liquor has been intensified by bantering with a hot person, making me much more amenable to pushy tattooed bartenders sticking their nose in my business.

"If you insist, a French 75 please," I say, letting myself flirt just a little.

He stares for a second, smile still barely there on his lips, before his expression goes blank. He looks around for a minute, turns in place, moves towards Sammy, and then seems to give up.

"I've got a confession," he says, placing the flute on the lacquered wood in front of me.

My smile grows.

"You don't know how to make a French 75?"

"I'm not a bartender."

My jaw drops a little, and I wave my hands in his direction, half accusatory and half defensive.

"But you're standing back there! Behind the bar!" I'm yelling at him a little, but I'm also laughing, and he seems embarrassed and oddly pleased. Color tinges his ears again.

"One bartender at Catalina's, remember?" he asks, gesturing toward the sign Sammy showed me earlier. "Sammy's a friend. I was just visiting."

This guy and Sammy seem like exact opposites. I've known them collectively for like twenty minutes, but where Sammy is gregarious and fun and easily likable, this man seems more reserved and calculating. Like he wants to know you before you know him.

"If you're just visiting, why'd you serve me the club soda?" I accuse playfully, running my finger over the rim of my water glass. His eyes flash as they follow the motion, and I can feel myself flush at the attention.

"Not sure." He shrugs, backing away to where Sammy is now gawking at him. "But I'm going to keep serving you."

# Chapter 4
## *Charlie*

I can't fucking believe it.

It's physically painful to rip my gaze from her, but I turn to make my way toward Sammy, calculating the odds of her showing up here. I feel almost euphoric.

Even though I never saw her face clearly, I know it's her. The freckles, the hair, the same inexplicable pull in my gut toward her. It's been months, but I think about the woman in the alley almost every day.

When I finally yank myself back to the present, Sammy's staring at me like I'm a ghost, which, considering the month I've had, isn't unreasonable. I haven't felt like myself in weeks, but something settled in my chest the moment I laid eyes on her.

I wrap my arms around my friend, hugging him even though he's still frozen with a bottle of tequila in his hand. Patrons are staring at me solely because of the state of shock Sammy's in, and I laugh as I let him go.

"Da quanto tempo," I say, shaking his shoulders. Something in him snaps, and he drops the bottle on the bartop to throw his arms around me.

"Carlo Costa, as I live and breathe!" He pulls away to grasp my face in his hands like my Nonna did when I was a kid running around Bari.

"I am going to kill my sister for telling you that," I grumble, shaking him off. No one calls me Carlo in the States, not even my parents. I've been Charlie my whole life, save for time I spent with Clara and our cousins under our grandparents' tutelage in Italy.

"Better stock up on silver bullets, or wooden stakes, or whatever kills something as terrifying as Clara," Sammy responds, turning back to the bar to pour the shots he abandoned. "Speaking of terrifying things, you look at least seven times more menacing than the last time I saw you. What the hell happened?"

Hard question to answer. Sammy vaguely knows who I am, *what* I am. He knows my line of work creates monsters. It's a testament to our friendship that I don't bristle at the question. People have lost tongues for less.

"You mean the tattoos?" I ask, my hand automatically moving to the olive branches I had inked into my throat last fall. I glance over my shoulder to catch my redhead staring at my ass, and sparks light under my skin.

"Amica," Sammy starts in a bad Italian accent, "your ink cannot surprise me at this point. No, you look more... serious?" He pours a mug of some local craft beer and reconsiders. "No, determined. And for a man of your inclinations, determination is worrisome."

"Only for the other guy," I say, trying to make a joke of it. But he's right. The last few weeks have changed the way I see myself, my future, and the fate of the family.

Sammy slips down the bar to take a few more orders, and I take the opportunity to look back at her again. She's turned on her seat and propped her elbows on the bar to watch the crowd, and the neon lights flash against her skin like watercolors. I grab her book out of my back pocket and raise my eyebrows at the cover. Two lingerie-clad women, covered in blood, their bodies pressed against one another, sharp teeth exposed. Intriguing, but not really what I'm here for. I flip open the back page.

The list is a little depressing. Whatever the situation she's contemplating, it's clear she's got strong feelings about both Ana and Ben. It's also obvious she's backed into a corner. And that she's already made up her mind.

I've spent my entire life reading body language, unintentional signals, truths and lies we can't help but reveal. When I watched her from my post behind the bar—and I had been watching her for far longer than she realized—I couldn't see indecision. She wasn't considering; she was *confirming*. It was in the set of her shoulders, and the way her eyes narrowed at the page instead of wandering or closing in thought.

I want to slither into her mind. To lay my head in her lap and listen to her tell me about every decision she's ever made. To know if she made a similar list before she killed the man in that strip club alley.

"Reading Baby Red's book?" I nearly jump out of my skin at the sound of Sammy's voice.

Gesù Cristo, I'm distracted. Even in this busy bar, I should be able to sense someone approaching me from behind. I recenter myself, concentrating on the way the air feels against my skin, and the energy of the room pulsing against me, before slipping the book back into my pocket.

"I'm expanding my taste in literature." I reach for a champagne flute among the clean glasses at the back of the bar and hold it up to my friend. "Teach me how to make a French 75?"

His shit-eating grin has a wattage that could light up the fucking Washington Monument.

"Reading her books and making her favorite drink? Just propose, why don't you?" he jabs, grabbing the glass and pulling ingredients. Without giving me time to react, he recites instructions as he pours and shakes. When the drink is done, he places the flute in my hand, turns my shoulder, and smacks my ass to get me moving toward her.

She's facing the bar again when I reach her, but refuses to look at me. Which is fine. I place the drink on the napkin in front of her and wait to release it until she drags her eyes from my hand and finds my eyes.

I lied—it's not fine. I would prefer it if she didn't stop looking at me for the rest of the night. Maybe longer. Definitely longer.

"Thank you," she murmurs, ducking her head to hide a small smile. I think she's grateful, if not a little embarrassed, and I find some kind of strange pride in the fact that I navigated her correctly.

She's contemplative as she drinks this time. The anger she had while writing in her book and the humor she had while chastising me are both absent. Her eyes are dull, glazed over, and lined with repressed tears. My instincts—the same ones that tell me when crosshairs are aimed at me and when a friendly face has become a foe—warn me to push, but gently.

"How'd you hear about Catalina's?" I ask, finding safe ground to get her talking. She looks a little surprised by the question, but a tiny grin pulls at the corners of her mouth.

"Actually, Catalina's found me," she answers, propping her chin on her hand and taking a long drink. Being a gentleman and not a fucking creep, I look away as she darts her tongue out over her bottom lip. "I was wandering around, trying to find a distraction, and the glorious choir of drunk college kids answered my prayers."

I can't believe I'm about to give thanks for *Dollar Shots for Seniors Night*. Sammy instituted the tradition of once-a-semester nights to, quote, *reward those idiots for making it through another term without quitting.* Never mind that the dates, in February and October, make absolutely no sense relative to the local universities' calendars. I'm about to sponsor a special summer session.

Because this can't be a coincidence. Twice now fate has brought me to her, and I'm determined to find out why.

I'm drawn to her, and it's not just because she's gorgeous, though I'm not fucking blind. Smooth, long hair, like burnished metal. Full, dark lips tilted into a reluctant smile. Earth-brown eyes that I was so desperate to see. She reminds me of what I imagine sirens would look like. Seductive, alluring, and deadly.

"Well then, I'm glad the esteemed young men of Sigma Alpha Epsilon could help you find your way." I reach across the bar and hold my hand out to her. "It's wonderful to meet you..." I trail off, nearly calling her Baby Red, like Sammy did.

"Gwen," she responds, placing her hand in mine.

"Short for anything?" I ask. It's a simple question, but her face lights up as she nods.

"Actually, yes, it's short for Guinevere," she says, resting her chin back in her hand. "My mom had a weird Arthurian thing, so I'm Guinevere and my little sister is Morgana." Her expression shudders a little, and I think back to the book. *Ana lives.*

"Doesn't Morgana murder Guinevere?" That brings her smile back.

"Details, details, bartender man. Your turn." Her voice is still a little slurred around the edges, but it feels like an equal mix of alcohol and entertainment.

"Charlie," I reply, pushing myself forward against the bar as Sammy comes sprinting toward me, only to grab a bottle of grenadine, wink at me, and run back to the other end. Sammy seems to usher patrons toward him at the other end of the bar, keeping them far from me and Gwen. Meddlesome little fuck, I missed him.

"Short for anything?" When I glance back at Gwen, she's got a grin on her face almost as genuine as when she was laughing with Sammy. She thinks she's teasing me, and although I rarely give the information out freely, I want to upend her expectations of Charles.

"Actually, yes, it's short for Carlo." Spinning her words back at her feels intimate in a way that makes my skin flush. That pretty mouth pops open a little.

"I actually think that's long for Carlo, not short, but nice to meet you, Charlie."

Before I can say anything, she glances at her bag and then hauls it into her lap. An excavation that would rival archaeological digs occurs in front of me as she scrambles through her belongings and finally pulls out her phone. Her brow furrows as she swipes across the screen, taps away, and then places the phone with the screen face up on the bartop.

I'm not even going to pretend I don't want to pry.

"Everything okay?" I ask. Gwen runs her fingers through her hair and then shakes it out before tapping the screen of her phone to life, and then immediately clicking it off again.

"Yeah, just my sister, Ana." She glances up at me and back at her phone. "Morgana. She's at a sleepover at a friend's and is almost out of antibiotics."

Her face flashes like she's caught herself saying something she shouldn't.

"She okay?" I ask.

Gwen's phone lights up, and she swipes at it quickly, cracking a smile at the screen that loosens the weird feeling in my chest.

"Yeah, she'll be good through the weekend. She's just wondering why my current location is a fantasy card game store called The Jade Salamander."

I had completely forgotten what this building was before

Sammy bought it. She tips her head back and looks at the god-awful painted ceiling again before turning back toward me.

"Why is this place called Catalina's, anyway?" she asks, sipping her drink. Before I can respond, Sammy materializes like she literally summoned him with her question.

"Because I own this bar, and Catalina owns my heart, and so everything I have and am is in honor of her." Sammy is yelling in this lyrical way he does when he talks about Catalina, slipping under the bar to sit next to next to Gwen on the faded blue stools. He sighs deeply and slings his arm around her shoulder, making her giggle.

"Shouldn't you get back here and serve your customers?" I rib, grabbing a bar towel and whipping it toward him. He only scoots closer to Gwen, laying his head on her shoulder and rolling his eyes at me.

"You've got it covered."

"I do not work here." But he doesn't hear me, because he's already launched into his *Catalina Monologue.*

A plotless and over-exaggerated story of unrequited love that was not at all unrequited, seeing as Catalina has been enamored with him from the moment they met. Gwen seems entertained, so I lean into my new bartender career and hurry down the walkway, praying that people order beer on tap and pouring what have to be terrible drinks when they don't. I recognize Gwen's laugh over the music and I think about stealing her away to somewhere I would be the only person who could hear it. She's only known me for twenty goddamn minutes. *Pull yourself together.*

It's another half hour before I finally make my way back down to where Sammy and Gwen are chatting, Catalina having joined them at some point. She's nestled between Sammy's legs, leaning toward Gwen with four different tubes of lipstick trapped between her fingers like joints. Gwen's cheeks are flaming red. Actually, her chest and neck are too, and I have to physically force myself not to reach for her, desperate to feel the heat beneath her skin.

"Are you sexually harassing your own customers again, Catalina?" I ask, pressing my hands against the bar top and ignoring the dude waving two entire dollar bills at me halfway down the bar. Gwen's eyes sweep over my hands and arms before halting and turning back to Cat.

"I'm not sexually harassing anyone, and she's not my customer. She's Sammy's." Cat keeps her focus on Gwen's lips, which coincidentally are now what I'm focused on too. They're parted and a little pouted as Cat opens one tube with her teeth, swirls the little wand around, and paints the tiniest dot of bright purple.

"No, it's too blue!" Cat declares, running her finger across Gwen's lip to remove the paint. She blushes even harder. "I know people say redheads shouldn't wear orange, but I think a terracotta color would look really pretty on you. Oh!" Cat snaps, shoving the makeup into Sammy's hands before turning back to her prey. "What color are your nipples?"

It takes me a solid minute of coughing to right myself. Every inch of Gwen's skin is lit up, and Sammy is pulling Cat backward to nuzzle into her neck.

"My love, people find it rude when you ask them to expose their nipples in public, remember?"

She grips him by the hair and lifts his face from her body.

"I didn't ask her to flash us, I wanted her to *describe* her nipples. They say the shade of your nipples is the best color for your lipstick."

"Is there any amount of money I could give you to get you to stop saying nipples in my presence?" I ask, trying to take the attention off Gwen as she pulls herself together. Catalina turns

39

her sharp eyes on me and gives me a smile she could have only learned from Sammy.

"I'm sure I can find a dollar amount that can convince me..." she starts as Sammy leans forward and whispers something in her ear that makes her cackle. Unabashed glee shines from her eyes, and I realize I may have made a mistake turning her attention on me. "My lovely Sam has also reminded me that we take payment in the form of sexual favors. Remember that thing you did last time with the silk and the—"

"Okay, yes, Catalina, thank you for the very explicit reminder. I think I'll just deal with the nipple thing." I'm trying not to look at Gwen, but I can feel her eyes on me. I'm not ashamed of my sexual history, especially not where Sammy and Catalina are concerned, but it is something I like to ease strangers into. "You two would do well as carnies."

I have no idea how that worked, but Cat twists in her seat and grabs Sam by the face.

"Charlie is so right, babe. We would be excellent circus performers." She kisses him, and he kisses her back, and I roll my eyes at their ridiculous zeal for life, for each other. "Let's go join the circus, my love."

He slides her off the seat and stands, only to pick her up and wrap her legs around his waist. There is not enough room for this kind of behavior, so her ass ends up perched on the bar top right in front of me, and I back away with my hands in the air.

"Fuck that, baby, I'll sell this bar and buy you a circus and name it after you." He kisses her forehead, ducks under the bar flap, and pops up next to me so quickly I'd have whiplash if I hadn't done this song and dance with the pair of them a thousand times before.

"But not tonight, because Charlie is a shit bartender, and I need to fix the mess he's made. Tomorrow I'll buy you a circus."

Once Cat disappears back into the crowd, I turn back to Gwen. She looks like she's just been electrocuted, which honestly isn't an unfair reaction to spending that much time with my friends. Her mouth is open in shock, punched up into a crazed little smile. Her eyes are wide and don't know where to settle until she sees me looking at her.

"I won't apologize for Sammy and Cat, but I will for not warning you before they got going." I run my hand through my hair, for some reason worried about her reaction.

"I think I might be in love with Catalina," she mouths at me.

"Don't tell either of them that, or you'll end up learning the finer mechanics of erotic aerial suspension," I wink at her, and she blushes deeply again.

"They seem like the kind of people who could convince me."

My brain does whatever the human equivalent of skipping a record is at her words. I can't tell if that's an admission of a kink, her flirting, or just the last lingering bits of champagne bubbling up to the surface, but all I can think is *I want to find out.*

Bleeding through the brain freeze is the realization that Gwen's not annoyed or overwhelmed by my friends, nor does she seem to be affected by their relationship structure and the part I've played in it.

I don't know what makes me do it. This is the wrong place in the conversation to change the subject, but something forces me to reach into my pocket and slide her book back across the bar. She looks down, but doesn't reach for it. Despite the fact that we're both looking at ostensibly one of the least safe for work novel covers I've ever seen, I can tell by the way she sighs that we both know what I'm about to ask.

"Ready to talk?"

# Chapter 5
## *Gwen*

I shouldn't want to tell him. He helped make tonight exactly what it was supposed to be. A distraction. Fun. A farewell. I can get a rideshare, set my alarm, fall asleep, and wake up tomorrow ready to accept Ben's offer, because I had tonight.

But there's something about the way Charlie gave me space without leaving me alone that makes me feel like I'm not about to drunkenly blubber at the annoyed bartender.

So, I tell him. About Ana's diagnosis and surgery, about Isabelle's constant absence, about insurance and cost estimates and financial assistance, about Ben and his wine-stained teeth and his offer. I can't meet his eyes, so I keep my gaze on the cover of my book, letting everything flow out of me like an exorcism. And it feels kind of nice.

I don't really have confidants. Not to say that I don't have friends. Kenzie is the best, and she's great with Ana, but it never feels fair to burden her with my life when I've been her protector ever since we met. My other coworkers are nice. Gray's mom is sweet and caring. Though Ana is not technically my child, I do sometimes feel like a parent, and parenthood is incredibly isolating. Especially when the people who would usually be your confidants, namely other parents, are constantly throwing us judgemental glances. I hear the whispers. *What happened to the mother? Can she really care for her? I bet she was just a young teen mom and doesn't want us to know.*

So instead, Ana is my best friend. And I do everything in my power to make sure she doesn't get parentified like I did, which means I keep a lot to myself. I'm honest with Ana about as much as I can be, and then I make sure she never sees me sweat.

And that means tonight is probably the first time I've cracked in my adult life. I feel like I'm a runaway train on a downhill slope as I spill everything. It pours and pours, and yet somehow I don't feel lighter. A burden isn't lifted. I just feel like I'm digging myself further into a grave, and I don't know if it's mine or Ana's. How could I feel better? The cancer's still there. I still will have to suck the dick of a man who probably hasn't flossed in his adult life. Talking about it won't change it, so why should it make it easier?

"So tomorrow I'm going to get up, swallow my pride, and call her father and agree to his terms," I finish, slumping over as I rest my arms on the bar top and drop my chin onto my folded hands. "Every single part of this situation is ass, but there aren't many other guaranteed options, and I need a guarantee when it comes to Ana."

The beat of the music around me, the singing and yelling and movement, the cacophony of noise doesn't obscure Charlie's voice one bit.

"Gwen, look at me."

His hand brushes over my arm, and warmth rushes through my body as I glance up, even though I'm a little afraid of what I'm going to see. I'm basically admitting to premeditated adultery, so outright disgust wouldn't be unreasonable. But Charlie doesn't look disgusted, or like he pities me, or even confused. There's something more resolute in his eyes, almost like pride? Or determination? But I'm pretty terrible at reading people, and also still a little buzzed.

"There are people in this world who say they will do anything to protect the people they love, and there are people who actually will. You are the latter."

He moves some half empty drinks and soaked coasters so he can raise the bar flap and slide into the stool next to me. The bar is starting to settle, patrons laughing and singing as they spill into the streets, leaving room for us to stretch under the dim lighting. I turn my head so I'm facing him, my cheek pressed to my fingers.

"I know it's the right decision to make. And I know even if it was the wrong one, I'd make it anyway." I close my eyes on a sigh. "I just wish there was a less horrifying option."

We're both silent for a moment, and I appreciate it. Because I *do* wish there was a better option. But everything else I've thought of—changing my line of work to something more lucrative, stealing a really fancy piece of art, starting a heart-wrenching social media fundraiser, calling my mother—isn't guaranteed to work. And I will not hope with Ana. I will be certain of her outcome.

"What if I could give you one?"

His voice is quiet but clear, maybe a little hopeful, and at first I'm not certain he's talking to me. But when I turn, he holds my gaze with this strange, determined light in his eyes.

"What if you could give me one *what*?" I ask, hesitant. A little ball of anxiety and apprehension builds in my stomach.

"A less horrifying option. Or, at least I personally think it would be less horrifying." He opens my book to the little T-chart in the back, and drifts his fingers over my words. "You wouldn't have to commit adultery. Not even close, actually." His eyes lift to mine and then shift back to the book, ears red again.

"I'm open to anything at this point," I say, trying to rein in the flicker of hope burning in my chest. He could suggest something I can't do. Or something somehow worse than Ben, which may seem impossible, but I don't doubt the limits of men.

"You could marry me."

Technically, I heard the words he said. But the part of my brain that processes sound into cognitive action has apparently flatlined, because I cannot figure out what he means. Marry him? Like the institution of marriage? Like legal documentation and rings and uncomfortable garter tosses? That can't be what he's suggesting. We don't know each other. Maybe marriage has a definition I'm unaware of. I got a *needs improvement* in fourth grade reading comprehension, so that's probably it.

I'm staring blankly at the side of his face, but he's still looking at the book. He reaches over the bar, snags a pen from a checkbook, and creates a second T-chart on the page next to mine.

"Pros," he starts, labeling the columns in neat, thin penmanship that should not be attractive because penmanship is not a thing modern society determines attractiveness on. "First, you wouldn't need to be a mistress. Or—" he squints at my writing. "—deal with the scent of musty cheese? I didn't know cheese could be musty." He adds lines to his list, and I try to mentally catch up to the reality unfolding in front of me. "Of course, most importantly, Ana lives. But in the cons, this wouldn't be temporary. Not sure how much weight that holds for you, but probably a lot? Also, you'd have to deal with being a Costa, and that should probably be weighted pretty significantly. Want to add anything to the chart?"

He looks at me while he holds the pen out, but I'm still a little too stunned to grab it from him, or make a sound, or blink.

"What do you mean, marry you?" I finally choke out, feeling like I'm talking underwater.

I don't know this man. He's charming and a level of handsome that should be investigated, but he's still a stranger proposing marriage to me in a bar. I should run. I should slap him. I should throw my near empty-club soda in his face and stomp away.

But maybe we really all do become our parents in the end, because I stay seated.

"My work is a family business. And with family comes tradition." He twists the pen between his fingers. "Circumstances with my parents have changed, and my sister and I will be taking on more responsibility soon. Which means we'll be held to tradition younger than we expected. Part of that is to continue the family name."

His gaze goes distant as he stares at our lists, and I try to contemplate what kind of family business requires marriage to strangers in bars. Certainly the bookshop owners and mechanics and butchers of D.C. do not.

"What are you, in the mob or something?" Genius question, Guinevere. Like he would fucking tell me if he was in the actual mob. Kill me for asking, more likely. But a tiny smile ghosts at his lips, like he finds the thought funny.

"Not exactly, but you're closer than you probably think." Goosebumps break out over my skin as he takes a deep breath and turns to face me fully. "I'd like to tell you more. Give you a proper choice. This wouldn't be short term, and there are other negatives you should consider, but I can also offer you more than he can. Monetarily and otherwise."

I can feel my face flame and I open my mouth to say something—what, I'm not totally sure—when he stammers.

"No, sorry, that came out completely wrong." He's cringing, staring down at the book again. "I meant protection. And long-term support. You'd have more than the bare minimum. This would be a lifetime of ensuring that you and Ana were taken care of. Food, housing, softball cleats, college tuition. Neither of you would want for anything."

I can't seem to organize my thoughts. The voice reminding me I do not know this man is persistent in the back of my mind. But honestly, do I really know Ben? And the parts I do know, I fundamentally hate. I barely saw him when he and Isabelle were together, and he was out of our lives in less than a year. How much less do I know the man sitting in front of me than my sister's father?

Another part of me, a part that I resent, can't help but crave that stability. I wouldn't come out of this worrying about the cost of physical therapists or long term treatment. I wouldn't wonder what happens if Ana needs more support than my crappy job can provide. Even more, college? Ana would have a future of dorm rooms and keg stands if she wanted it. I've been banking on her getting a softball scholarship, but to not even have to think about it?

Does that make me like Isabelle? Does taking this choice—to marry someone for that stability—make me more like her than taking Ben's offer does? Does it matter?

I also know that there must be some massive caveat if this is his proposition. He might not be in the mob, but if he has the money he's implying, and is willing to offer it to a stranger, there must be some pretty significant strings attached. Illegal, possibly immoral, strings.

"What in the world makes you think that I'd be willing to marry a stranger I met in a bar?" I ask, incredulous.

The world seems to come to a stop as he reaches into his pocket, never taking his eyes off mine. When I look down at the bar top, I freeze, every last bit of oxygen leaving my lungs.

"Because you're not a stranger to me, Gwen." His tone is too soft for the threat he's making, but I can't lift my eyes.

Because sitting in front of me is my grandmother's watch. The only relic I have of my father. He wasn't a great guy, and he didn't stick around very long, but his mom wanted to leave something to her only granddaughter.

I wore that watch religiously, despite the fact it made me feel childish, holding on to an artifact of a family I never had. But I lost it that day.

I tried to convince myself I had taken it off before I went to the strip club. That I left it in Kenzie's hospital room and someone had accidentally trashed it. Or that I took it off at work while cleaning dishes and forgot about it.

But deep inside, I knew. I was so afraid that night—not because of what I'd done, but because I could get caught and leave Ana with no one who cared for her. And it wasn't until I was home, bleaching and burning my clothes, that I realized my watch was gone. And I knew I'd left a tiny piece of evidence behind.

I forced myself to believe it was okay, that because I never purchased the watch, there was no paper trail connecting me to it. But I was still terrified someone would find Bryan's body, connect him to Kenzie and her hospital stay, and connect me to her. And the little timepiece in front of me would be proof.

The face is broken and dried blood is etched into the crevices. Still, the hands move, the ticking sound the only thing I can hear.

It feels impossible to breathe, panic flooding my senses as I spiral. How did he find me here tonight? Has he been stalking me? Waiting for the right moment to reveal what he knows? Is he going to turn me in?

I brush my fingers over the band of the watch, unable to help myself. He trails a tattooed finger over my hand, but I'm too in shock to flinch.

"I'd like to tell you more about my proposition, if you don't mind?" His words are soft, lulling, almost gentle, but the meaning behind them is clear.

This is blackmail.

I try to steady my heart rate. Freaking out won't do me any good. I need to keep my mind clear. I glance up at Sammy, but he's not guaranteed to be any help. He's Charlie's friend, not mine.

"What do you want?" I ask, refusing to meet his eyes, even with his hand still on mine. I hate my body for its reaction, for the warmth that spreads from his touch.

"Just the opportunity for you to hear me out." He laces his fingers through mine, his touch so tender.

I swallow hard, thinking of what else he could know about me, about Ana. More than what I told him tonight? Does he know about the McCallums, where they live, where Ana is right now?

I have to buy time to figure out a plan. Right now, he's asking me to listen to him, and while this could get a lot worse really quickly, I need to appease him until I can be sure I can guarantee Ana's safety.

I nod, afraid to trust my own voice, finally lifting my eyes to meet his. His gaze is searching, and whatever he sees on my face causes him to knit his eyebrows together. Concern flits across his face, and this time I do flinch when he reaches to touch my face. His expression is so open, so clear, that I can almost feel the sting from the rejection.

What the fuck does he have to feel concerned about? He's the one in control of this situation—of my life—right now. My chest tightens as the anger I'm so terrible at controlling crawls up my throat, burning me from the inside out like it's always done.

"Gwen, what's—" Charlie starts, but I cut him off by yanking my hand from under his.

"Just tell me what you want me to do," I whisper stiffly, trying to tamp my fury down and not make this worse for myself. Charlie balks, seemingly stunned by my reaction. I want to ask him if the other people he blackmails acquiesce more easily.

His eyes search my face, and I have no idea what he could be looking for. Even if he doesn't know me at all, I've given him enough information about my dedication to Ana that he must know I'd never risk leaving her helpless.

"Why don't we find somewhere more private to discuss," he says, his voice tilting at the end of the statement, almost framing it like a question. "I would prefer to handle this privately."

Of course he would. I know I shouldn't leave this bar, that I shouldn't be alone with him, that nothing good happens at secondary locations. But, predictably, my rage is eclipsing all logic. He's already got all of the leverage; what's a bit more?

"Fine," I agree, grabbing my bag and reaching for my wallet. He reaches out to stop me, but I yank my arm away before he can touch me.

"I covered your tab," he says quietly, cocking his head at me slightly.

I suppress a roll of my eyes. He can't possibly think he's being chivalrous right now.

"I can pay for my own drinks," I quip, not sure why I'm fighting this. His gaze softens as he observes my reactions, probably trying to calm me.

"I offered you marriage, Gwen, and I intend to show you what it would be like to be my wife. I cover your tab, I hold your door, I support you in any and every way." His eyes are so dark, so serious, and the conflict of emotions in my chest is disorienting. If he's just going to coerce me into marrying him, why would he act like this?

"Archaic," I mumble, though I want to say much more. A small smile pulls at the corner of his lips, and I wish it wasn't so pretty.

"Maybe, but to be fair, there would be expectations of you as well."

My heart stutters unpleasantly, nausea turning my stomach at his words. Of course, I just told him all about Ben's offer, and now he's got ideas of his own.

He offers me his arm as we stand, but I start toward the exit on my own. If I'm about to walk into a nightmare, I'll do it on my own.

# Chapter 6
## *Charlie*

Something's wrong. She's sitting in the back seat next to me, but she's shrunk herself so much it feels like there's a chasm between us. I can see little white half moons where she's dug her nails into her own arms, clutching herself tightly.

I replay the way she almost looked hopeful when I gave my offer. Shocked, yes, but there was a little spark in her eyes, like she could see the potential the same as I could.

But she completely shut down as soon as I laid her watch on the bar. All the anger and hope and wit I'd seen completely vanished.

"I disposed of his body properly," I say, jarring us out of the tense silence. Her anxiety is so thick in the air that it nearly kicks in my ingrained instincts to push, to harm, to get her to break.

But I don't want that. Even more than being desperate to have her hear out my plan, something about her turns off that need in me. The last thing on the planet I want is for her to yield to me, and it's a strange sensation.

She says nothing, her lips pressed together so tightly I'm

afraid she's going to split the skin with her teeth. I try to soften my expression.

"My team erased the security footage in the strip club as well. No one even filed a missing person's report on him." Her brows are furrowed together, and she's breathing deeply through her nose.

"Why didn't you come find me right away?" Her voice is soft and tight, like she's terrified of my reaction. I don't really understand her question, but maybe talking will calm her down.

"I never looked for you. I found some basic information about Bryan to ensure no one would come looking for him or his body, but I never tried to find you. Seeing you tonight was —" I stop myself just short of saying *fate*. "It was a coincidence."

She scoffs, the sound too shaky to be unphased.

"So what? You hold on to all of this information just in case you stumble upon the girl you want to blackmail?" she demands, anger leaching through her fear.

Blackmail? Is that what she thinks this is? That I'm going to use what I know about her to what? Force her to marry me?

For a moment, I consider it. It would probably work. I could threaten to take the evidence that doesn't exist anymore to the police. It would solve my problem and hers. It wouldn't be the first time a Costa spouse was coerced into the family business.

But my stomach tightens unpleasantly at the thought. Not only would my sister likely kill me if she ever found out, I don't want to force Gwen's hand. I want her willingly, or as close to it as I can get.

She doesn't know that the collected anger, the vicious calm I saw in her that night was like a siren's song. That this isn't blackmail, it's *proof*. Proof that she can walk in our world. All I want is an opportunity to show her I can also provide what she needs. An explanation pours out of me without any organization of thought.

"Gwen, no, please," I say, removing the watch from my pocket and holding it out to her. She eyes it warily, but doesn't make a move to take it. "I wasn't clear. I didn't explain." I'm scrambling, still holding the watch out in front of me.

"Didn't explain what? How you told me I should marry you and pulled out evidence that I killed someone?" Her voice is stronger now, fury replacing despair rapidly. "You don't fucking know anything. He nearly fucking killed her." She chokes on her words for a moment, a grimace stealing over her features. "She got pregnant and when she told him, he beat her so badly she miscarried. Broke three fucking ribs. She was in the hospital for days. And I just knew if he came back, he'd kill her. And I wasn't going to let that happen."

Her fists are clenched, and once again she looks like an injured animal backed into a corner. But before I can even respond, she loses all trace of apprehension.

"No matter what you think you know, I'm not letting you blackmail me into fucking you." She takes a deep breath, steadying her shoulders. "You just told me you erased all the evidence against me. And I'll fuck the devil I know before the devil I don't, but thanks so much for the offer."

I've never felt like this before. Panicked and swimming in guilt, my chest so constricted I feel like I'm drowning. I was so caught up in the threads of fate I saw spinning us together that I didn't even imagine this scenario from her perspective. And it was *cruel*.

"I apologize," I say, because I mean it. I'm sorry I frightened her. I'm sorry that she got into this car, from her perspective, under duress. "First and foremost, I'm not proposing the same arrangement as Ben. You are under no obligation to sleep with me."

I rub the back of my neck, mourning the fleeting memory of her flirting with me in the bar. But I can wrangle my attraction. Fate ties people together in many ways, and I should be thankful if it gives me a partner who might understand me and my work. I shouldn't wish for more, especially when she so clearly doesn't want that from me or Ben.

"I didn't know why you killed him, but it didn't matter. I wasn't planning on coercing you into anything with me. You asked why I thought you would say yes to my proposition, and *this* is why. Because when I saw you that night, I knew you understood the cost of a life, and the weight of your decision." I swallow hard, imploring her with my gaze, begging her to see the truth in my words. "There are few who can understand me, my family, our decisions and actions. I think you could be one of the few, and we could establish an agreement that benefits both of us."

She's silent, her anger simmering lower and lower until confusion mingles with it in equal spades. Her fight-or-flight reflex is still in overdrive, and I swear I can hear her heart pounding.

"Please," I say, holding out the watch. "Take it. I don't need it."

She reaches her hand out gently, her fingertips brushing against mine as she takes it from my hand. She's still shaking slightly, but she holds the watch in her lap, staring at the shattered face.

"I'm having a hard time understanding what's going on," she whispers, the war of emotions clear in her voice. The adrenaline of fear is starting to recede, and I watch her slump against the door, body exhausted.

"There are some things I would like to explain to you, and

the conversation will be long and confusing and exhausting. But let me be clear, I am not going to force you into anything." I steady my breathing as she finally looks away from the watch and locks eyes with me. So beautiful. "I want to provide you with an option that would be beneficial to both of us, and regardless of if you choose me or Ben, I will never say a word of what happened last summer."

She's silent as her eyes map my face, looking for deceit. But she won't find it. It's an uncomfortable sensation, but I force vulnerability into my expression. I let her read everything, from guilt through sincerity, and I feel myself tug on the string I know connects us.

She must feel it, or at least believe me a little, because she leans fully into the door, closing her eyes and tilting her head back so her throat is exposed. I practice pushing down my attraction to her, settling into the warm comfort of knowing that this is, at a minimum, a bit of trust between us.

"You really could not have made this whole situation more threatening if you tried," she says, her laugh incredulous.

I throw a rueful smile at her, feeling the muscles in my shoulders finally relax.

"I truly am sorry for scaring you," I reply, watching her stifle a yawn. She's about to hit a massive wall from the adrenaline drop, judging from the drooping of her eyes.

"More pissed than anything else," she mumbles, and I think that's half true. She glances out the tinted window of the sedan. "Probably should have asked this earlier, but where are we going?"

"I asked Zane to drive us around so we could talk," I say, lifting a hand toward the closed divider. She yawns against her hand again. "Though I'm not sure if tonight's the best time for that now."

"I can stay awake," she protests weakly, her eyes slipping

closed once again. I suppress a laugh as she settles into the seat more comfortably.

"We can talk in the morning," I say softly, knocking lightly on the divider and directing Zane to reroute home.

"Morning," she mumbles.

I watch her sleep as we make our way toward the house, her face relaxed and unburdened.

## Chapter 7
### *Charlie*

I carry her into the house without rousing her. More guilt needles my chest as I realize she'll likely wake up uncomfortable and afraid.

I take off her boots and coat, leaving them on the chair by the door, and put her phone on the spare charger that Bea left in the bathroom. I'm itching to soothe the alarm I already know she'll feel in the morning, so I leave her some pain medication, a glass of water, and a few notes to orient her before I finally leave her to sleep.

I should rest, too. I've been on planes for the better part of two days, and I took a fair fucking beating before that, so my body needs to recuperate. But I can't stop thinking about ends and beginnings, about choices and options.

When I left Trani last week, I was unnerved. Clara and I both were. Our mother taught us the skills she thought would serve us best in our future roles; Clara got her strategizing, long-term vision, and quiet, merciless calculation, while I got her penchant for swift and violent justice. Clara rarely gets her hands dirty, saving her particular brand of violence for personal ventures. But I have been steeped in blood for as long as I can

58

remember. Dissecting the eyes of corpses with my mother in my preteen years to learn how to blind someone with a blade without puncturing the brain. Late nights with Uncle Mauricio as a teenager, exchanging blows and learning the finer art of how to hit to break bone. Viciousness has become almost second nature.

I'd be a fool to think any of us are invincible, especially in our line of work. But seeing her burned and scarred in that bed was a stark reminder of mortality, both hers and mine. She's been the head of the Costa family for almost forty years. One wrong turn, one moment of misplaced trust, and we nearly lost her.

All our lives, our parents worked to ensure we had the time they didn't to acclimate to our futures. We were given the opportunity to become confident in our inevitable roles, with Clara as our matriarch, and me as her right hand. We could find life partners that walked in the same circles, or could learn to, without pressure. No arranged marriages in our early twenties, like they had. But with our mother weakened and our enemies so strong, there are few options left on the table.

As far as I can tell, Clara doesn't see it the way I do. She—focused on patterns and long-term consequences—thought only about shoring up our alliances, projecting strength, and ensuring that the vicious tide we keep at bay does not creep while our mother heals.

But I saw it in my father's eyes. It was time for us to adhere to tradition, to do what was asked of us as Costas. Step into our own futures.

And as a family business, *family* is crucial. Not only to carry on the line of Costas to do this work, but also to maintain a meticulous image. An interconnected web of blood and legal relatives to uphold the justice we are committed to. A problem, of course, for a thirty-one-year-old who had purposefully avoided commitment, for more reasons than one.

And my solution had walked through the door of Catalina's.

Gwen won't add to the Costa network of connections throughout the world. As far as I know, her family doesn't rub elbows with arms dealers, own surveillance companies, or take part in international politics. But really, that's Clara's role more than it's mine, though I imagine she'll disagree once she finds out my plan. It's the gift of being the youngest, perhaps, that you have more choice. A monarchal spare, only tasked with being the sword to the queen.

I do feel slightly guilty, using Gwen's situation to my advantage. People think that empathy runs thin in a world like mine, but the Costa family acts according to a strict set of moral boundaries. If we were religious, we'd likely say we were the hand of divine justice. Instead, the family acts as a council of judge, jury, and executioner for the evils of the world. I'm not sure how my mother would feel about leveraging the victimization of the United States healthcare industrial complex for my benefit, but I suppose those are decisions I need to make on my own now.

And it does seem that Gwen shares our idea of justice.

I realize I've been standing outside the spare room door for quite some time, and try to shake off this sensation of serendipity. The right person, who was the right level of desperate, at the right time. The solution isn't perfect and will require much more digging, which isn't my strong suit.

I walk to my office and sit in the heavy chair behind my desk, running my fingers over the keyboard to wake up my computer. I have no doubts that she will accept my proposition. It's insurmountably better than the one Ana's cretin of a father is offering. And her willingness to build her own moral compass, to seek vengeance when an opportunity is offered to her, is evidence enough for me to try.

Which, tragically, means I need to call Emily.

There are extended Costa family members all over the world, but there are few who are integral to our operations, who sit on the council. Emily is one of them. Despite being twins, Clara was the eldest, if only by a few hours. As a result, she was always separated from the rest of us. But Bea, Emily, and I trained together. And there is a trust that's built when you learn to spy, torture, and kill together.

But trust doesn't equate to affection, and Emily might be one of the most irritating people I've ever met. Part of it is that she's smarter than all of us combined. I'll never understand the way her brain maps out problems, sees solutions that only she can. She also challenges me the most, pushes me to justify my actions when most people, even those we're related to, worry about turning my attention their way.

I also think that the three of us growing up in such close quarters, being pushed to our physical and psychological limits in each other's presence, means we know more about each other than anyone in the world, including our own parents. And we're all a little uncomfortable with that truth.

Unfortunately, Emily is a better researcher than me, and I need answers quickly. Usually, I'd employ one of the distant cousins who work in cybersecurity or surveillance to collect information on a target, but this feels different. I don't want anyone outside of the council knowing too much about Gwen.

I pull my phone out of my pocket and dial Emily. Last I checked, she was in Southeast Asia helping resettle victims of a typhoon, while simultaneously conducting research on box jellyfish stings. Genius fucking freak.

"You better be actually dying." Her voice breaks through as

a groan, and I check the time on my watch. Three-thirty in the morning here should be late afternoon for her.

"Is playing with fish so exhausting that you're relying on mid-day naps now?" I ask, wedging my phone between my cheek and shoulder as I open our secure search engine.

"I got back from Laos like a week ago, you asshole. I'm in New York." Fuck. I was in Trani, and then a horribly remote area of Russia for a bit, so I guess it's been a while since I've checked in. "Also, sea jellies aren't fish."

The less groggy she becomes, the more likely it is that she's going to release some sort of genetically modified venomous micro-bug into my shoes. I've sunk this ship already tonight, so might as well give her something to appease her.

"Welcome back to the States. My apologies to the sea jellies and for the early wake up call. As an olive branch, I'm about to hand you personal information about myself in the form of a research inquiry." I start typing information that I know about Gwen into the search engine as I wait for Emily to answer. She's quiet for a bit longer, and then I hear her shift in her bed.

"Fine, fair trade. Who's the target?"

I bristle at the word, which is a strange reaction. Everyone is a target to us—friends, enemies, lovers. Gwen being my future wife doesn't change that. Even if I inexplicably want to shoot Emily for saying it.

"Guinevere Byrne," I say, recalling her last name from the card she left on her tab at Catalina's. "Daughter of Isabelle Byrne, second parent unknown. Going to need a full background on her and her younger sister, Morgana Byrne." I can't imagine the fifteen-year-old cancer patient is up to anything particularly nefarious, but thoroughness is key.

Emily starts typing in the background, which likely means she's tucked onto her couch with her laptop balanced on her knees.

"Good for mom, giving her daughters her last name," Emily starts, the clicking ramping up to fake hacker movie levels. I'm about to correct her when she starts again. "Well, nevermind. Seems like that's the last thing she gave those girls. How deep do you want me to dig on mom of the year?"

"Deep. Gwen and Ana need to be vetted at levels that will meet the family's standards."

That gets her attention. The clicking abruptly stops, and I can almost see the look she'd be giving me if she were sitting in front of me.

"Do my ears deceive me, or should I search for bridesmaid dresses?" Her voice is teasing but sharp, and I know the weight that comes with it. Bringing someone into the family isn't a choice any of us make lightly, although I might be throwing caution to the wind a bit here.

"Don't start choosing flowers yet, Emily." But my scolding has no bite. I promised her personal leverage, and she's getting it. "But I'd like to see if she can keep up with us. And I need you to be a helpful little bookworm and make sure the skeletons in her closet won't fuck us over."

There are few things that I truly couldn't handle, but if she was blood-related to one of our enemies there would be complications. Better to be prepared.

"How'd you meet the new Mrs. Costa?" Emily asks, her typing ramping up again. Seems she's gotten past the shock.

"Does it matter?" I shoot back, pulling up a photo of Gwen and Ana in a middle school newspaper.

Despite the obvious similarities—the red hair, the freckles—the two really couldn't look more different. Ana is thin and gangly, not just in the awkward pre-teen way, but in the way where you know she'll be tall and lithe forever. Her nose is long and her jaw is sharp, and I wonder if she looks more like Ben or Isabelle.

"You telling me that you've purchased yourself a wife isn't enough information for me, dear cousin. Give me the story while I start building their files."

I'm barely listening, scanning Gwen from head to toe in the photo in front of me. It's from four years ago, so she's about twenty-three, according to the birthday on her license. She's obviously tired, but clearly thrilled for Ana, who seems to have won some sort of prize. She's got her arms wrapped around her sister's shoulders, their faces pressed together with massive grins. Her hair is wrapped into a tight bun on top of her head, and there's a pencil stuck through it like she ran to this competition from work. Despite the exhaustion, she looks happier.

No shit. She's not dealing with cancer and Ben, and murder, and whatever the fuck else in this picture.

"I didn't buy her," I finally say to Emily. She scoffs, but I keep pushing. "And I met her at Catalina's."

"Cristo, I've been out of the loop. You haven't even been in D.C. for over six months, and you're just now getting a background..." she trails off, and I think she's finally figured it out. "You're telling me that, instead of the delightful friends I've set you up with over the years, you've decided to marry some girl you met less than twenty-four hours ago?"

"How do you know how long I've been back?" I ask. She ignores me. This is predictable.

"What happened to Luan? His mother does great document work for us, and he's gotta be at least six-four. Or Chantrea? They're doing more expressionist art stuff now, and their half-sister is already on our payroll."

I know Emily's not trying to talk me out of Gwen, she's trying to understand my logic. I'm one of the little puzzles she likes to do to keep her brain fresh, like she's a retiree in a group home.

And while Luan was handsome and Chantrea was engaging, my instincts never pushed me to commit more than a few nights. Perhaps it's because I was looking for connection, for compatibility, when that's all but impossible for someone like me. I should have been aiming for coincidence and mutual goals. But we're here now, and I can't ignore this pull toward Gwen. Though, for some reason, I don't want to share that with Emily.

"Timing's everything, right?" It's a bad lie and she likely knows it, but she seems to let it slide.

"Just make sure you tell Clara about this when I'm in the opposite hemisphere."

# Chapter 8
## *Gwen*

I know immediately that I'm not in my bed. My mattress has never once been this comfortable. There's a memory, half dream and half nightmare, pulsing at the back of my mind with the beat of this fucking headache. I don't want to wake up, because I know I'm about to face something less than ideal. But I can feel the warm sun on my face, and I know it's only a matter of time before I have to confront reality.

With all the enthusiasm of getting a tooth extracted, I force open my eyes. Light filters through the curtains, gently illuminating what is most certainly not my apartment. I'm tucked under a plush comforter of muted olive, the sheets just a shade lighter, all buttery and soft against my skin. I sit up, clear my eyes, and take in the rest of the simple bedroom—dark wood furniture, decor in camel and green.

Simple, pretty, and calm.

Three adjectives that could not be used to describe me at the moment.

I clutch the sheets in my hands and try to piece together last night. I remember meeting with Ben and getting to Catalina's. There are a few moments from the bar that are blurry, but I vaguely recall a bartender reciting a sonnet? I definitely remember Charlie, and the tattoos, and the feeling of his eyes on me. The fear that flooded my veins when he placed my watch on the bar top.

Shame rakes through me. Getting into Charlie's car, whether or not I thought I had a choice, was the most idiotic thing I've ever done. He could have turned me in. Blackmailed me. *Killed me.* And what would happen to Ana then? Doesn't matter that he seemed genuinely shameful that he scared the ever living fuck out of me.

Reckless. Fucking reckless.

I wallow in my anger, searching for my phone to check the time and make sure Ana hasn't called when I see water and pain medication on the nightstand. Well, that's considerate. He could have laced either with something, but if we're being honest, there were dozens of times Charlie could have drugged and murdered me last night, so playing the bit out this long would be a little ridiculous. Or that's what I convince myself as I down three pills and chug the water.

Under the glass there's a small envelope, with thin, neat writing. I pick it up and stretch as I read.

*You fell asleep in the car last night, so I brought you here.*

*The cabinet under the sink has towels and toiletries.*

*Make yourself at home.*

*Again, I apologize.*

*-C*

He could still be playing some sort of horrific mind game, but the longer I think about it, the less likely that seems. Wouldn't someone who wanted to manipulate me into complying with his demands use my vulnerable state to his advantage? I grab my coat from the chair in the corner of the room and fish in the pockets for my phone, coming up with only another little envelope.

*I put your phone on the charger in the bathroom.*
*-C*

A *chivalrous murderer, fantastic.* I step into the ensuite and snag my phone from the counter, a voice in the back of my mind reminding me that I am *also* a murderer and can't be all that judgemental.

It's nearly eight in the morning, but I guess I shouldn't be surprised. Knowing how late it was when I left Catalina's, there's no way we got here before three in the morning. There's a few texts from Kenzie checking in on Ana's radiation therapy appointment times and offering to cover my shifts. A slew from Ana, letting me know Gray's parents are taking them to one of those medieval jousting performance things in northern Maryland. I text her back, telling her to be careful of her stitches and to call me if she needs anything.

ANA

She lives!

When's the last time you slept in past 7?

ME

In the womb, I think. You sure you're feeling okay?

The little typing bubble pops up, disappears, and starts again. She's typing for a long time, but when the message comes through, it's short.

ANA

Yeah, I'm all good.

Obviously that's not true, but pushing her now while she's out with Gray will not help. She's been a little withdrawn since the surgery, but that's to be expected, right? She may be upset right now, but she's safe. I trust Linda and Paul with her more than anyone other than myself, and they'll keep her distracted and cared for.

In the meantime, I've got a proposition to hear out.

I take less time in the shower than I want to, but invest a significant part of my time under the hot water trying to compartmentalize all my emotions. The confusion, the hope, the anger, the fear, and the tiny thread of lust wrapping them all together.

When I step out of the shower and reach for a towel under the cabinet, my hand lands on another little envelope.

What is this, Clue?

*Extra clothes in the dresser.*
*-C*

Short and less than sweet, but I'm not looking a gift horse in the mouth. When I'm dried off and my teeth are brushed, I open the drawers of the dresser in the bedroom.

They're all empty, save for the top center one, which contains what looks like a men's t-shirt and sweatpants, a camisole top, and a pair of thick socks.

Strange. Mildly creepy. Are these the clothes of his

previous victims? If Dr. Spencer Reid has taught me anything, it's that some people go through some serious rituals before they commit crimes.

Guess there's only one way to find out. I drag on the clothes and gingerly peek out the door.

There's noise coming from the end of the hallway, soft scraping and the rattling of dishes. I pad down the hall until I can see into the living area.

Charlie's standing in the kitchen, his back turned toward me, and I can see a complex design of butterfly wings tattooed on the back of his neck.

I force my eyes to the ceiling, trying to will away the desire to trace my fingers over the ink.

Last night at the bar, before I was scared half to fucking death, it was fun, feeling this little attraction to him. But now? He already has the upper hand between us, and I hate the idea of giving him even more leverage, even if he never knows about it. I shake myself, trying to fortify my resolve. I can compartmentalize.

I clear my throat and move toward the kitchen slowly, trying not to startle him. But he only throws a slightly reserved grin over his shoulder, turning back to the stove.

"Good morning," he says quietly, placing what looks like omelets on two plates. "I hope you slept okay, and weren't too unsettled when you woke up."

"I mean, I'm as settled as I can be, all things considered," I mutter, the last remnants of annoyance about last night seeping into my words. Charlie turns fully now, sliding the plates onto the peninsula, and something in his gaze flashes as he assesses me.

"I made breakfast," he says, and I know how flushed my cheeks and neck are. Being a redhead is a curse.

"Um, okay?" I say in place of a thank you, because I really don't know how to react.

I perch myself on one of the stools tucked under the counter and pull a plate toward me, eyeing Charlie hesitantly. He seems to fight a sly smile, and I'm pretty pissed at my body for somehow losing its fear instinct overnight, because all I feel is a low simmering in my belly.

"Ana doing okay this morning?" He's leaning his hip against the counter, eating his eggs, like this is the most normal thing on the planet.

I tell him she's got plans with friends, that she seems to be feeling okay, as I beg my brain to find the fear, the panic. To have some sort of logical response to whatever's happening here.

When I finally bite into my food, I try not to show my shock. I'm not a picky eater by any means, but this is my favorite breakfast. Fluffy eggs, sauteed mushrooms, sharp cheese, onions, but no green peppers. Judging from the way Charlie's eyes shine with something bordering on glee, it's not a coincidence.

I shrug my shoulders and dig back in, and Charlie lets out a laugh under his breath.

"So, I agreed to hear a proposition," I say, gesturing between us with my fork. "So, you know. Proposition me."

A full smile blooms across his face. I pretend it doesn't make my heart skip.

"Straight to business," he mutters under his breath. He turns around and reaches on top of his refrigerator, pulling out a paperback.

Not *a* paperback. *My* paperback.

He slides it in front of me, and a tense silence settles over the room. Not because of the wildly not-safe-for-work cover, but because we know what's written in both of our handwriting inside.

"You have a problem that needs resolving," he starts quietly, flipping open the back cover and folding the pages down, creasing the spine. "And right now, you have two options. First, Ben."

My jaw twitches, but I stare at my little pro-con list. It's not pretty, but it's known.

But my eyes are drawn automatically to Charlie's list, a mirror to mine. It looks like he's added a few more items to each side, and I lean forward to see them more clearly.

"I know I didn't make myself clear last night," he says, circling the peninsula and sliding into the stool next to mine. He keeps a safe distance, giving me room to breathe. "But I think we can offer each other something that we both desperately need. Support. Financial, logistical, familial, and emotional. I'd like to explain more fully, but you have to know that hearing this, even if you don't agree to my proposition, will change your life. Even if you decline my offer, The Syndicate will monitor you for the rest of your life, ensuring that you never reveal any of the information I'm about to tell you. And if you do, I won't be able to control the consequences."

The intensity radiating off him raises the hairs on the back of my neck. In any other circumstances, a name like *The Syndicate* would seem ridiculous, cartoonish even, but it's clear how serious he is. I swallow thickly, considering the risk. It's unsettling, sure, but I know how to keep a secret.

"I'm listening," I say finally, leaning back in my chair and crossing my arms over my chest.

He assesses me for a few beats, his eyes coasting over my face, my hands, my shoulders. There's something weighty behind his gaze, like he's searching for a sign that I'm ready to cross this line.

But I'm not afraid of what he's about to say. Despite the way I reacted last night, today I feel like I did last summer, where fear wasn't even a consideration. Maybe it's delusional, or my mind trying to protect me, but I know there's nothing he could say that would make me more afraid than I am of Ana's diagnosis. And he must realize it, because he matches my posture before he begins.

"There's a long and drawn out history. My family and our work go back centuries, to Isabella of Aragon and the Black Plague. We've survived the rise and fall of empires, and it's a story I'm happy to tell you one day. But what matters for tonight is that The Syndicate of Fate is the Costa family's—*my* family's—legacy. The full network spans thousands of people, in their own silos, employed to do what we need to find justice. And my family sits at the center, directing our priorities and determining what sins we address."

He pauses for a minute, and I take a moment to process. In any other circumstance, my automatic assumption would be that he's making this up. It's too outlandish, like a plot from one of Ana's comics. But I can't seem to doubt the way he's looking at me.

"And exactly what kind of justice do you find?" My voice is a little hesitant, and his mouth ticks up into a soft smile.

"One I'm sure you can appreciate." He passes his thumb over his bottom lip and huffs a little laugh. "We've developed our own moral code of sorts. The focus shifts depending on who is in charge. My mother, for instance, has been intent on breaking up human trafficking rings. Stories of drug runners lacing their product with cheap and deadly additives particularly affected her father, so The Syndicate spent a significant amount of time hunting down those who were intentionally causing harm." He drums his fingers against the table, shoulders tight. "There is a lot of evil in the world, and almost every definition is based on perspective. We're powerful, sure, but we are small relative to the sea of potential targets."

I shouldn't believe him. I shouldn't even engage with this. But instead of following that logic, I open my mouth and ask another question.

"I imagine you also have to stay relatively under the radar, right?" I ask. "Can't disrupt governments, give anyone a reason to look too closely?"

He shrugs, his casual demeanor about this doing nothing to cool the simmering in my blood.

"Sometimes, yes. Although we would be naïve to think that we're not on the organized crime watch list of most countries' investigative agencies. We're careful and selective about our targets."

"I can only imagine. Even Capone got caught."

It will one day be evidence against me in a court of law that I'm bantering in this situation.

"I pay my taxes." The deadpan rebuttal earns him a little laugh, but I'm already spinning my next question.

"So what exactly is your role, then?"

"Technically, I am Clara's spare, in case anything happens to her or her future children. But I'm also her sword. If I was bitter about it, I'd call myself her attack dog." He seems to find that funny. "She tells me to kill, I kill. I go on whatever missions she assigns me, or follow her on ones she wants to attend to personally. Theoretically, she could assign me to any position, but I'm good at..." he trails off, glancing up and then back at me, resolution settling in his stare. "Well, to be blunt, I'm skilled at torture. At information extraction. My mother taught me, and I use it sparingly, only when necessary, but it's my speciality."

Anticipation and a little worry flash across his expression. He can't seriously be concerned that this is the admission that will get me to bolt, right? The irony would be astounding.

I try to sort through the emotions swimming through me, but the overwhelming one is understanding. He and his family have obviously professionalized the concept, but I've proven to both of us that cruel retribution is a response I can sympathize with.

There's also something less professional heating my blood beneath the surface. But I shove it down, refusing to name it. This is essentially a business agreement, nothing more. I keep my face as smooth as possible as I respond.

"And the reason you need a wife?" I ask, and I can't help glance at his mouth, his tattooed fingers lightly stroking his bottom lip.

He's made it clear multiple times. This is a job offer. A partnership. Any tension I feel is one sided. Plus, I nearly ripped his head off when I thought he was suggesting something more. I can't have it both ways.

"It's tradition for those taking generational positions in the organization—really, just Clara and I—to be married before we take our permanent roles. My parents had an arranged marriage. They were confident in the match and found love and respect over time, but they wanted to give Clara and I more autonomy over the decision. But my mother's been hurt. Severely." He stares over my shoulder, his gaze distant and pained. "She will live, but she won't be able to lead us anymore. So Clara and I need to fulfill our duties, and part of that is finding spouses."

I move without conscious decision, and suddenly I have his hand tucked in mine, my fingers slipping under his palm and my thumb rubbing calming circles against his skin. His eyes snap to where we're connected, crawling up my arm until they settle on my face. Empathy rolls through me like a wave.

"I understand," I say, squeezing his hand lightly. "You're

the kind of person who would do anything for your family. I get it."

The recall of his own words to me last night loosens his tense shoulders, smooths his furrowed brow. He doesn't pull his hand from mine, and I try to ignore the way his touch radiates throughout my body.

"And between you and me." I let go of his hand and wave mine between us, avoiding his eyes. "Are there expectations…"

"No," he cuts me off, his voice harsh and final. "As I promised last night, there are no expectations like that between us." The heat continues to spread until I'm fully flushed, though embarrassment is driving it now. Why the fuck did I ask that? "There will be a contract." He declares, looking a little flustered himself. Probably appalled that I even implied anything different. "You can suggest changes, and it can be amended over time. But it'll include the expectations of both of us, okay?"

I collect myself as much as possible, breathing through my nose and trying to will the blush from my face. It would actually really help to see this all written out, to lay expectations on the table, to be sure I know what I'm getting into.

"Yeah, a contract would be good," I nod, and as both of us relax back into our seats.

Maybe I'm certifiable for considering this. Maybe the safe, predictable route is to accept Ben's offer, pay for Ana's treatment, and close my eyes and pretend I'm anywhere else while he fucks me. Maybe the person I was before last summer would have made that choice.

But I haven't been her for a long time. Charlie is witnessing whoever this version of me is, and he's not balking. He's giving me a chance to embrace it, to find my footing, to immerse myself in it. All while caring for me and Ana for far longer than we could have ever hoped.

The vision of her happy, healthy, without a worry in the world, is what makes me close my eyes and nod.

"Okay."

My eyes are still closed, but I can almost hear him cock his head to the side.

"Okay?" He asks, and I nod again.

"Okay, I'm in."

# Chapter 9
## *Gwen*

I'm sweating again, and not because of the temperature, as I knock on the McCallum's door. Charlie offered to take Ana and I to her appointment, but when I insisted on slow-rolling Ana into this, he nearly demanded I let Zane drive us. Which is why I've got a twenty-two-year-old shadow who, and I quote, *has a history of evading police helicopters*, hanging out against the sedan.

"Hi, hi, hi, Gwen, come on in," Linda sings as she opens the door, throwing her arms around me and dragging me inside.

Gray and Ana's footsteps on the floor above complement the musical tones of some kid's show on the living room television. Gray's little sister, Maddie, sits with a bowl of dry cereal in her lap, attention rapt on an animated family of dogs.

"Thanks for having Ana for the weekend," I say as she lets me go and ruffles my hair with her fingers.

She's in her early thirties, and despite having a teenager and a toddler, she always looks frustratingly put together. Even though it's Sunday morning and my sister and her son have probably run her ragged for the past two days, her dark hair is pulled back in a slicked back ponytail, her makeup is done, and she's in a matching lounge set that probably costs more than my mattress.

Linda and her husband Paul have always been kind and compassionate to both me and Ana. Part of it is because Ana and Gray have been inseparable since kindergarten, and stayed friends even when his family moved into the suburbs. Another is that Linda and I bonded over being the only teen moms in Ana and Gray's entire class—although obviously under different circumstances.

But most importantly, Ana didn't balk when Gray transitioned. He walked up to her at school one day when they were twelve and told her that his name was Gray now, and Ana told him she was happy he didn't choose Kevin.

Linda and Paul didn't balk either, because they're decent and loving humans, and I think they appreciated that Ana made Gray's life easier when a lot of other kids made it harder.

I don't know if Linda is my friend, but she's definitely a mom-mentor, and that's appreciated.

"Are you kidding me? Gray spends so many weekends with you, I should pay you child support." She grabs Maddie's bowl of cereal just as she's about to dump it all over the couch. "Plus, if Ana didn't come over, I don't know what would motivate my child to clean his room, so please don't thank me."

Before I can respond, a scuffle of careful footsteps come down the stairs, and the kids enter the living room with their faces covered in blue paint.

"Jesus fucking Christ," Linda whispers, but it's not quiet enough, because all three of the minors in the room scream *swear jar* at the same time. Linda fishes a dollar bill out of her wallet on the kitchen counter while I turn to Ana.

"If this is some sort of anime thing, I might lose my mind," I say as I lick my thumb and drag it across her cheek. The paint comes off easily, thank god. Ana rolls her eyes at me, which in any other situation I would scold her for.

"We're testing out our Crespallion cosplay," she replies like I'm the biggest idiot on the planet, rummaging in her bag until she pulls out a giant makeup palette with multicolored cream foundations. "It's just makeup."

"Okay, so it *is* an anime thing?" I grab the palette from her and flip it over, breathing a little sigh of relief when the ingredients look thoroughly washable.

"Crespallions are from Doctor Who, Gwen, not an anime," Gray says, smiling at his mom. "The theater makeup did the trick, thanks mom."

I glare over my shoulder at Linda, who looks appropriately shamed as she slinks behind the kitchen counter. I cannot have a conversation about Cresp-whatevers while I'm trying to figure out how to explain Baby Driver outside to my sister.

"Okay, well, I appreciate your dedication to your craft, but we have to get to your appointment, so please go wash your face."

I spend the next ten minutes watching cartoons with Maddie and waving off apologies from Linda as she packs Gray's lunch for theater practice. Honestly, they're fifteen. They could be joyriding or in prison or avoiding my calls, and they're preparing for Comic-Con, so I'm thankful for face paint.

When Ana comes downstairs, a ring of blue in her hairline, my stomach churns. I hate lying to her, but there's no way around it. I have to lay the foundation for Charlie being in our lives now, and I have to build a backstory.

I take her backpack so it doesn't bump against her incision and fiddle with the zipper as she thanks Linda for letting her stay. When we're standing in the foyer, Gray and Linda distracted with a discussion about nut allergies in his theater troupe, I grab onto Ana's shoulders.

"Before we go outside, I have something to tell you." She raises a blue-tinted eyebrow at me.

"Did you crash Jimmy's car? because I'm not lying and saying it was me."

I pinch her nose and she shakes me off.

"No, I don't have Jimmy's car." I take a deep breath, readying myself to purposefully lie to the most important person in my world. "Actually, my friend sent a car to pick me up this morning. His driver, Zane, is outside."

Ana stares at me, her mouth slightly open and her brows pressed together, like I've spoken a riddle she's supposed to solve.

"A friend? Sent a car?" Her voice is incredulous and teasing, a hint of hurt lacing her words.

"He's more than a friend, I guess. But yes, I've been seeing someone, and he offered to have his driver pick us up." I take another deep breath through my nose and try to steady my heartbeat.

"How have you possibly been dating someone without me knowing?"

I knew she was going to ask this. Not only because we spend nearly every waking second together, but also because hidden under that question is, *how did you keep this from me?*

"We've kept things low key because I didn't want to introduce you to anyone before I was sure they meant something serious to me. But it's serious enough now." The lie tastes bitter on my tongue, a sensation that only gets worse when Ana's eyes soften and she grabs my hand.

"You didn't have to hide something that made you happy just because of me."

In any other situation, her words would have me pulling

her against me and telling her she's being uncharacteristically sweet. But the guilt beats down any chance of that. I have to repeat *Ana lives* over and over in my mind to remind myself why I'm doing this. Doesn't make me feel any less like throwing up.

"I promise, I hadn't even thought about it before last night. It just wasn't the right time, and now it is." At least that is, in some twisted way, true.

Ana reaches for the door handle and turns to me before she opens it.

"A driver is pretty cool, though."

"Okay Banana, how are we feeling?"

That's what the radiation oncologist, Dr. Mya, has taken to calling my sister. *Banana*. I'm pretty sure Ana hates it by the way she cringes every time they say it, but she doesn't correct them.

"Good. I feel like I'm ready," she replies, nodding her head against the crinkly paper cover of the exam bed.

She's got her arm gingerly stretched over her head, and the oncologist presses around the incision, checking the scarring flesh again. They nod and pull their gloves off to type something into the workstation next to them.

"Good to hear. You can get dressed, sweetheart."

Ana pulls her camisole back down carefully, and I know it hurts more than she's saying.

"Can she still take painkillers for the incision during radiation?" I ask, my notebook cracked open in my lap once again.

"Yeah, that should be fine, if she needs them." They look

up from their workstation and raise an eyebrow at Ana. "Are you in pain?"

Ana blushes and shoots me a glare. "Only a little, when I stretch too fast or have to lift my arm," she says as she drags her cardigan carefully over her shoulder.

"Well, you don't have any swelling or anything like that, and your stitches dissolved nicely, so I'm not worried about infection. Some residual pain is normal, so take over-the-counter medications if you need to." They shut down the computer and move to Ana as she sits up. "You're going to do a great job, Banana. Keep your head up, okay?"

We leave the office and stop by the lab for one last blood draw before we're finally out the door. It's only midday, and Kenzie took my shifts for the next two days, so we're free to do whatever Ana wants.

"What's on the schedule, Banana?" I ask, wrapping my arm around her shoulder as she zips up her coat. The intense eye roll confirms my suspicions about the nickname.

"I hate that. Bananas are gross," she says, bumping my hip with hers. She thinks for a few seconds before an evil-looking grin spreads across her face. Pure joy lights her eyes.

I'm terrified.

"I want to meet the boyfriend," she demands. I navigate us around the parking lot toward the bus stop, staring at her in disbelief.

"What? Why?" I don't even give her time to respond. "Don't you want to see a movie? Eat until we puke? Go to the comic book store?" I'm bribing at this point, and she knows it.

"Nope, I want to meet Charlie. That's his name, right? I wouldn't know, since you've hidden me from him for the last six freaking months." She's saying it like a joke, but I heard the slip. She doesn't think I hid him from her, she thinks I hid *her* from *him*. I grab on to her shoulders as we hit the bus stop and look right at her.

"Hey, no way, girlfriend," I shake her, and she giggles, but there's a little bit of hesitancy in her eyes. Oh, fuck. "You think I hid *you* from him? He knows all about you, seriously. You're the coolest kid in D.C., I barely ever shut up about you."

She smiles a little brighter, her shoulders relax an inch, and the clenching feeling in my gut dissipates a fraction. Truth is, Charlie probably knows more about her than he does about me.

"Okay cool, then you should have no problem introducing us," she smirks, rocking back on her heels. I glance at my phone and down the street, praying for the bus to show up and give me a few seconds to think.

"He does have a job, Morgana," I deflect, watching the bus turn the bend of Michigan Avenue and sending a thankful prayer up to whoever is cutting me a break.

"Oh, does he? I wouldn't know, because I know *nothing about him*," she stresses, pulling her phone out of her pocket. "Also, it's Sunday."

"Attitude," I reprimand as we tap our phones against the reader and scramble toward the back as the bus jolts forward. "Yes, he has a job. He works for a foundation." That is, in all technicality, true. "And foundation people work on weekends sometimes." I'm reaching.

"Great, does he get a lunch break? We can bring him something." She slips next to the window and I sit beside her.

"There's no way I'm getting out of this one, huh?"

She shakes her head, nearly bouncing with joy.

"Shouldn't have asked me what I wanted if you didn't want an honest answer," she taunts, peeking over my arm while I pull up my texts with Charlie. I turn the screen away and shoot her a glare, but it doesn't dim her smile.

This was going to happen eventually. I just thought I might

have more than twenty-four hours to process all of this. Apparently not.

> **ME**
>
> On a scale from one to ten, how busy are you right now?

The bubbles pop up, disappear, and then reappear.

> **CHARLIE**
>
> Is everything okay?

I laugh, and Ana tries to sneak another peek before I pull her hood over her eyes.

> **ME**
>
> Yeah, no emergency. Ana's just asking to meet you.

> **CHARLIE**
>
> Oh.
>
> Yes.
>
> I mean zero. I'm not busy. That's fine. Good.
>
> Are you on your way home from the hospital?

I stare as the strange cadence of texts rolls through. What is happening? Does he not want to meet her and feels obligated to? Is he uncomfortable? He seemed completely fine with discussing Ana's presence in my life yesterday.

> **ME**
>
> If you'd rather wait it's no big deal, I can tell her you had work.
>
> Seriously, no worries.

His reply is immediate.

CHARLIE

No, I want to. I was just surprised. I'm in the Navy Yard but I'm leaving now. Why don't we meet at that cafe on Belmont and 18th?

Let me know when you get off the bus.

Also, why are you on the bus and not with Zane?

I roll my eyes and change my settings so he can see my location.

ME

If you wanted to stalk me you could have asked nicely.

And I told him we could get home on our own.

CHARLIE

That's not the deal. Support, remember? Comes with the territory of being my wife.

Even via text, that word—*wife*—makes my chest feel tight and my limbs feel loose, like I'm swimming a little too deep for comfort and enjoying it.

And as much as I want to protest, the selfish part of me craves this. I try to justify it, convincing myself that it's better for Ana, that she can stay at school a half hour longer because we don't have to jump on the Metro and a bus. Shame makes it hard to swallow, but I type out a response anyway.

ME

We'll discuss it. See you in a bit.

"He's going to meet us near home for lunch. Does that work?"

Ana puts her head on my shoulder.

"Thank you."

♡

BY THE TIME we've hopped off the bus in Columbia Heights and made our way downhill toward our neighborhood, Ana's lost her bravado. For all her big talk, she's a pretty reserved kid when she's not putting on a performance.

Cosplay? Easy, she's behind a costume and makeup. Softball? No problem, she's got a role to play and a team with her. But one-on-one, she tends to be an observer, and hesitant to trust.

Man, our parents fucked us up.

I do my best to quell my own nerves as we head into the cafe, sweat dripping down the back of my neck despite the temperature. Like a magnet, my eyes land on Charlie sitting at a back table, and he grins when he sees me.

"No fucking way," Ana whispers, and I smack her on the back of the head lightly before helping her gently take her coat off. "No offense, Ginny, you're pretty and everything, but come *on*."

My face is on fire, I can feel it, but I hope it's being played off as flush from the walk over. I lean down next to Ana's ear.

"Don't be a weirdo and hit on my boyfriend."

Ana gags dramatically. "Ew, he's old enough to be my dad, you freak. I can just objectively tell who the reacher is here." She snags her coat from my arms and fishes her phone out of the pocket.

"Real nice, Ana. Thank you so much for the assessment," I bite as we navigate around the tables to the back of the restaurant. She scoffs behind me.

"Don't know why you were hiding this guy. If it was me, I'd be renting out billboards."

Jesus Christ, this was a bad idea. Also, when did she start talking like this? I should start paying attention to the books she's reading.

"Behave, please," I whisper as we get up to the table.

Charlie's already standing, and when we reach him, he grasps my elbow, pulls me forward, and presses his lips against my cheek. It's the first time he's touched me like this, a fact that my brain is blasting like a tornado alarm through my skull. When he pulls back, I'm sure I look like I've been electrocuted. Sure as hell feels like it.

"Hi, missed you," he whispers. He's so good at this. From the outside, with the casual touches and soft smile, it has to look like we really are enamored with each other. He chuckles at my expression and turns to Ana. "You must be Morgana."

He puts out his hand, and Ana glances at it, and then me, before shaking it.

"Yeah, Ana is fine," she says, hugging her coat closer to her body but keeping her face neutral.

Charlie pulls out a chair for her and takes her coat to drape it over the seat next to him. He does the same for me, so I'm sitting beside Ana, and it feels intentional. Like he doesn't want to separate us.

"It's really nice to meet you, Ana," he says, pulling up the sleeves of his sweater. The left one catches on a bandage wrapped around his arm. When I raise my eyebrows at him, he covers it back up and winks at me.

*Christ.*

"Nice to meet you too, *finally*," she says, and her attitude has me elbowing her in the ribs, but only because it's her good side.

"Hey, it's not his fault—" I start, but Charlie cuts me off.

"No, it's okay, you're allowed to be upset." He unrolls his silverware from the napkin, and it feels like he's trying to find something to do with his hands. "I'm sorry we haven't met earlier. Gwen made it clear that she wouldn't bring anyone into your life that wasn't serious about her, and I didn't do a good enough job of convincing her I was." His eyes flash to me with a quick smile before turning back to Ana. "That's my fault, and I'm sorry."

I don't know what's more shocking, the way the lies slip from him so easily, or the sincerity with which he says them. I guess I can't really be upset—I'm deceiving Ana just as much as he is. But it's still hard to school my features.

Ana takes a beat, staring at Charlie with a contemplative frown.

"So you didn't decide to clue me in so you can help the charity case?"

"Is that what you thought?" I grab Ana's hand. I hate how close to reality she's hitting without knowing it. Even more, I hate that she sees herself like that. Despite my grip on her, she keeps her eyes locked on Charlie. It feels like she's assessing him, reading for a weakness or a lie.

"No, I guarantee you that's not what's happening. I care about your sister, and I want to be a part of your lives."

My stomach is churning. I feel like I'm sinking, like I'm failing her.

But like a light switch, the atmosphere changes as Ana pulls her hand from mine, picks up her menu, and starts browsing the brunch options.

"All right, I believe you," she says, and Charlie's fighting a grin as he mirrors her.

I'm staring open-mouthed at both of them.

"Ana, I promise I didn't—" I start, but again I'm interrupted, this time by her.

"I didn't think it was you, don't worry. Just wanted to make sure GQ over here wasn't looking to get on your good side by pretending to care about the cancer kid."

"Why would you even think that?" I ask, picking up my sticky plastic menu without looking at it.

"Because men are gross," Charlie answers, and Ana looks over the top of her menu with her brows raised. "I know saying it doesn't win me points."

He can't see, but behind the menu, a small smile takes over her face before she neutralizes it.

"Correct."

We spend the rest of lunch talking and, to my genuine surprise, laughing. Ana badgers Charlie with questions about his work, his family, his tattoos. I'm learning just as much as she is about him, which is both comforting and disorienting.

He hates orange juice. As a kid, he was terrified of snakes, but got the tattoo on his right hand when he overcame the fear. He's the Chief Operations Officer at his family's foundation, which helps victims of human trafficking resettle, either back in their homes or here in safe havens and shelters. A lawyer by training, he went to the University of Chicago for law school.

I have no idea how much of this is true, and seeing how easily he lied about our relationship, I try not to put too much stock into his words. But for every question he answers, he asks one of Ana back, tossing me a few along the way.

Everything about this is so normal, and while part of me is relieved, I'm also racked with guilt. It's all a facade, and every moment from here on out will be too. I didn't even stop to consider the fact that it's not just me that has to have a relationship with Charlie. Ana's going to build trust with someone based on a lie. *My lie.*

Ana excuses herself to the bathroom, and I double check

that she's feeling okay before she heads toward the other side of the cafe. When she's out of earshot, Charlie grabs my hand.

"You doing okay?" he asks, his thumb rubbing soothing circles against my clammy skin.

I can tell he's trying not to look worried, his smile a little too fake for comfort.

"Yeah, just a little hard to lie to her, you know?" I take a deep breath through my nose.

"You mean about how long we've been together? I thought we agreed on that?" His question seems genuine enough, and I shrug, downing half my glass of water with my free hand.

"And all the stuff about your personal life. I think it's just hard for me to imagine her getting to know someone and it not be one hundred percent real, you know?" I'm staring toward the bathroom, still worried that maybe she's in pain or nervous about tomorrow, when a squeeze of my hand brings me back to Charlie.

"None of that was fake, Gwen," he says, the crease between his eyes deepening with concern. "There are things we can't tell her, of course. But I really do hate orange juice, and I'm allergic to blueberries, and I think Revenge of the Sith is criminally underrated." He grins a little, like he's encouraging me to do the same, and I roll my eyes in response. "We're in this for the long haul, right? Partners, hopefully friends. That means being as honest with Ana as I can, and hoping both of you can trust me to take care of you."

It hits me then just how sincere he was yesterday. He meant it when he said *friends and partners.*

A little piece of me I didn't know was out of alignment settles. Sure, I was worried about turning into Isabelle, about marrying a man who doesn't care about me just for what he can provide. But I had no idea how something as simple as true, earnest friendship would settle that fear.

All I can do is smile and nod, but Charlie seems to understand. When he pulls his hand away, I notice the bandage peeking out of his sleeve again.

"Are *you* okay?" I ask, gesturing to his arm as I try to finish my soup. It was the only thing I thought I could stomach when we ordered.

"Yeah, just a little scratch," he replies, brushing it off. "Work, you know?"

I wait silently for him to continue, but he nods his head toward the bathroom. Logically, I understand why we shouldn't talk about it here. But even the mention of his work has my heart rate picking up.

I shouldn't be intrigued. Understanding? Sure. But interested, fascinated, maybe a little more? I try to shake the inclination, but as soon as he told me about The Syndicate, it felt like a part of my soul I had tucked away since last summer was suddenly illuminated, and I don't know how to switch it back off. Don't know if I want to, either.

"You're going to have to tell me more about that one day." I try to say it casually, but I think he hears it in my tone.

"Thinking about joining the family business once you become a Costa?" His tone is almost flirtatious, like he half expects me to say no, and half hopes I don't. It has my pulse racing in a manner that is wildly inappropriate for the topic.

"Thinking about it."

His eyes widen a bit, but he doesn't have time to respond because Ana's making her way back to the table. Her face is a little pale, and I'm immediately consumed with fear.

"What's wrong?" I ask, putting the back of my hand against her forehead as she sits down. Her smile comes out as a grimace.

"I took the stupid antibiotics on an empty stomach this morning, like an idiot." She leans away from her empty plate.

"Do you have those ginger nausea pills?" I'm reaching into my bag before she even finishes the question.

"Yeah, of course. Did you get sick?" I ask, fishing through my bag for Ana's meds.

"Ew, Ginny, no. If I got sick in a public restroom, I would have texted you." She pops the ginger pills in her mouth and dry swallows, but I push my water at her.

"Drink, it'll help." She rolls her eyes at me but complies and then glances over at Charlie.

"Sorry, I'm kind of gross."

I want to argue with her, tell her not to self-deprecate, but Charlie's laugh cuts in.

"No problem, I got my appendix out at fourteen and acted like I had the plague for weeks. My sister nearly killed me, she was so annoyed. You're not even scratching the surface of acceptable grossness."

I toss him a thankful smile, rubbing small circles on the back of Ana's neck like I used to do when she was little. It seems to help, but her face is still a bit pale, and Charlie takes it as his cue to distract her.

"Why'd you call her Ginny?"

Despite her furrowed brow, Ana cracks a smile.

"I couldn't say *Gwen* when I was a baby. Something about the *W* sound that really tripped me up. So I called her Gin, and that turned into Ginny." She turns toward me, her face relaxing a little. "I think I'm the only person who calls you that."

I don't know what parents feel like, but if it's one tenth of the feeling I get when Ana says shit like this, I get why they think the sun shines out of their kids' asses.

"Yeah, just you." I squeeze her shoulder, breaking the contact with her when it seems the ginger has started to abate her nausea.

She picks up her juice and takes a tentative swallow.

"I like it. It fits you," Charlie teases, winking at me.

I roll my eyes.

"Don't get any ideas. That's only for Ana."

"I don't know, maybe I'll give him permission," Ana quips, glancing at Charlie like they're conspirators. "We'll see how he does."

# Chapter 10
## *Charlie*

My breath comes heavy as I roll my shoulders out, trying to ignore the stinging pain in my left forefinger. Rookie mistake, angling the blow the way I did, catching my hand like that. It's a testament to how distracted I am.

It's unfortunate that my hands will look like this, freshly bruised and broken, when I get to the hospital. Normally, I prefer blades. The precision and control are more comfortable. But there has been something particularly fulfilling about killing those that played a part in my mother's harm with my bare hands.

A soft sob comes from the man tied to a chair in front of me, and I refocus. He's held out longer than I thought he would, especially considering I don't need anything from him. This isn't information extraction, it's revenge.

I'll admit, I'm impressed by his resolve. He had to know when he woke up here that he was going to die, had to realize what he was paying penance for. He could have succumbed to the encompassing darkness almost an hour ago, let himself slip into unconsciousness, but he forced himself to stay lucid. Perhaps it's pride, or dedication to his mission. Both of which I can respect.

But, as they always do, he's beginning to break.

I press my fingers under his chin, where shattered bone shifts under my touch. An involuntary cry slips from him.

"Aleksander, I want to thank you for this gift," I say, forcing his gaze to meet mine. His face is so battered that his own mother wouldn't recognize him, and I don't know if he can truly see me. "It is rare to find a traitor who can withstand this much torture. I haven't had this much fun in years."

I think the look he gives me is supposed to be a snarl, but it's weak. He's almost there.

They always break. They always submit.

It's a trial-and-error thing, learning how to bring someone beyond their limits without killing them. When I was a teenager, my mother would let me watch her work, talking through the decisions she made based on the subject's heart rate, response to blows, reaction to cuts. She'd have me slice into my own thighs to learn where arteries and muscles were, noting every flinch of pain as a failure. I studied other's weaknesses, not only to exploit them, but to ensure I didn't have them myself.

Aleksander's head hangs down when I let go. Another blow across the face, but he can only groan. One more, and he can barely turn his face back toward me. I shake out my hand.

"Turning on the Costas, who have supported you and your family for generations, is the height of cowardice and shame. What would your daughters think about their father if they could see him like this?"

And that's how I know how far gone he is. He doesn't react. Three daughters, and he doesn't lift his head to ask if I've gone after them too.

Pathetic.

"No, please don't beg," I say, my voice heavy with disgust as I circle him. "The Costas do not punish children for the sins of their parents. They will remain safe, if not cut off from the comforts they experienced under our protection."

He doesn't move—doesn't say anything.

I think about prolonging this, if only for my own personal retribution. He may have only played a small part in the ploy that nearly killed my mother, but I've had little time to seek out the larger actors. Aleksander is getting a disproportionate burden of my vengeance.

But before I can land another blow, a rap comes at the door. There's only one person it could be, so I call for Zane to come in.

"We've got to meet the girls in two hours," he reminds me, leaning against the door frame.

Zane may mainly act as my driver, but he's no stranger to the activities that happen in this room, so he barely glances at the man in the chair.

"I'll finish this, thank you Zane," I say, and as he closes the door behind him, I grab my hunting knife off the table on the other side of the room.

"Lucky for you, I don't have the time to make you feel all the pain you deserve." I press the knife against the side of his throat and slice, severing his carotid. "I have somewhere much more important to be."

After I shower and change, I lock the basement behind me and meet Zane in the foyer of the farmhouse.

"Text Renee and Nickolas and have them clean this up before the end of the day."

Zane nods and pulls his phone out as I slip into the back seat of the sedan. The garage door rolls up, and we slowly make our way past the acres of central Virginia farmland belonging to the Costas, home to hundreds upon hundreds of pigs.

Useful animals, in my line of work. Hungry, thorough, and undiscerning with their meals.

The dirt road leads into a forest of red maples, and Zane takes the turns smoothly as I stare at my phone, seeing nothing.

I know I'm an obsessive person. When I saw my mother burned in that bed, the need to plan our retribution over-whelmed me. I fixated on the path that would ready me to take over my inherited responsibilities.

Now, I feel myself obsessing over Gwen. Maybe it's natural, considering the way the universe seemed insistent on pushing us together. But what I didn't expect was wanting to know more than just how she would affect me and my family. I just beat a man near to death, and all I could think while I was doing it was, *I wonder what Gwen is doing right now.*

I thought this persistent tug toward her would be relieved once she agreed to my proposal. And why wouldn't it? I needed someone to play a part, to act as a piece in a larger puzzle, and she fulfilled that. Box checked.

But I already know Gwen is more than that, even if it's difficult to admit. My attention is consumed with what I could do to make her more comfortable in our arrangement during the entire drive to the city. We make a few stops before the hospital, filling a backpack with everything Emily recom-mended based on her research into DCIS and her deep dive into Gwen and Ana's spending habits: socks, books and manga, one of those massive reusable steel water bottles, the speciality lotion a bunch of blogs recommended, and endless snacks. The kid eats a shocking amount of Takis and Twizzlers.

Gwen insisted that, for at least the first few sessions, she and Ana commute to the hospital as they normally would. I know it's to avoid overwhelming Ana, but something about not having her in my car sets me on edge. Perhaps it's my predisposition to hypervigilance. I can't protect her, both of them, if they're not near me.

Zane drops me off, handing me the backpack and a thick envelope through the window. It's colder today than it's been, the bitter, quick wind biting at my face but soothing my bruised hand. I flex it, allowing the pain to ground me as I make my way through the sliding doors.

I haven't been to many children's hospitals in my lifetime, but the odd discord between the cheerfulness of the decor and the worried faces of families milling around the lobby is unsettling. Hot air balloons in multiple colors and patterns hang from bright blue ceilings over people huddled with their loved ones, staring at their phones and glancing at their watches. I can only describe it as surreal as the receptionist at the long check in station waves me forward.

"Hi there, welcome to Children's National Medical Center. Who are you here to see today?" Her tone is pleasant and professional, but I see the way her eyes flicker over my tattoos, her nose scrunching.

"My girlfriend's sister has a radiation oncology appointment today, and I'm here to meet them," I respond, laying the accent on thick. It has its intended effect. I'm not sure why Americans are put so at ease by a Mediterranean accent, but I use it to my advantage.

"Last name of the patient?" She asks, her smile brighter.

I give her Ana's information, along with my ID, and she prints me a sticker to wear, directing me to the elevator bay after a security guard checks the backpack.

There's no preparing for the terrifying nature of the child's voice that announces the elevator is *going up*. It's like a line from a horror film, and it actually makes me shiver.

When I exit the haunted elevator, there's another receptionist who directs me down a labyrinth of doors and hallways, all color-coded and animal-themed, until I finally reach the radiation therapy waiting room.

Gwen looks up as soon as I round the corner, and something settles in my chest when I see her.

She gives me a soft smile, and Ana glances up from her phone and waves.

"Hey, Charlie, you didn't have to come to this," she says, pulling an earbud from her ear. Despite her words, she seems happy to see me, but from the way she's glancing between Gwen and me, I think she's more happy for her sister.

"Wouldn't miss it. Plus, I heard you might need post-appointment distractions." I hand her the backpack as Gwen raises her eyebrows at me, but keeps her lips sealed.

"Oh awesome, Demon Slayer!" she nearly yells, pulling the manga out of the backpack and flipping through them. "This is so cool, thank you!" She flashes me a grin that I can't help but return.

"You're welcome."

The words are barely out of my mouth before a staff member in pink scrubs opens the door at the end of the hall and calls Ana's name. She starts to get up, and Gwen grabs her hand.

"You're good?" she asks, and Ana nods, only looking a little scared. "You've got warm socks? And your playlist?"

"They let me play whatever music I want over the speakers the whole time," Ana explains to me, leaning around her sister.

Gwen shakes Ana back to her.

"You're going to be fine, okay? It's less than an hour." It's clear Gwen's convincing herself more than she is her sister. Ana leans down and hugs her gently.

"First few are the easy ones, save the nerves for when I feel like ass." Ana pops a kiss onto Gwen's forehead and takes off toward the waiting tech before Gwen can respond.

She seems to be frozen as she stares at the door Ana disappeared behind.

"She shouldn't say ass," she whispers to herself, clasping her hands together tightly.

I bump her shoulder gently with mine to try to loosen her up.

"She probably says it a ton when she's not around you."

Gwen rolls her eyes at me, a smile slipping over her lips.

"Yeah, but I pretend that's not true," she says, tilting her head back and resting it against the wall. Her eyes are closing when she speaks again. "She's right. You didn't have to come. She'll be fine."

I consider brushing it off, but the truth is, I want Gwen to realize how much I meant it when I proposed a friendship.

"I think Ana couldn't care less if I showed up. I'm here for you," I say, settling back as well, my posture mirroring hers. She opens her eyes to give me a look that's half surprised, half annoyed, before closing them again.

"I'll be fine too," she murmurs.

We sit in silence for a bit, the quiet only interrupted by the sound of footsteps occasionally passing by. I have no baseline for how busy a pediatric radiation therapy unit usually is, but it seems fairly empty today. A blessing.

After a bit, Gwen cracks her neck and sits forward, running her fingernails through her scalp and shaking out her hair.

"She's right, though," she finally says, turning toward me in her seat and crossing her legs so her whole body is jammed into the little chair. That cannot be conformable. "Everything I've researched says the first few weeks are pretty easy with the side effects, but eventually she'll start feeling terrible. Ana needs vegetables, and more calories, but we're supposed to avoid antioxidants? And she'll be dehydrated, so I bought like five cases of that stuff you put in water to boost the hydration? I don't even know if that works."

Gwen's babbling, but she's also staring at me like she's desperate for validation that she's doing this right. And she is, because she'd do anything for Ana, and that's really all that matters.

I reach around her, grab the backpack I brought off Ana's chair, and unzip it for Gwen. She peers into it tentatively.

"I got a few recommendations. Lotions and body washes for when her skin gets irritated. I was also going to suggest we find somewhere new to get dinner after each appointment, so she's got a reason to look forward to meals. If I can't be there, Zane will take you, or have it ready to go when her session is done." She picks through the chips and sweets, staring into the backpack. "We'll figure it out."

I might be pushing it. Gwen has figured it out on her own for so long, and accepting financial support doesn't necessarily mean she's ready to accept emotional support, too. But it feels important to me.

I saw the way my parents were. They didn't love each other when they got married—they barely knew each other. But they have spent every day supporting and caring for one another, and found the most steadfast love I've ever seen along the way. And even though that won't be the result for us, I still want her to know that she can rely on me.

She swallows hard before looking back up at me. Her expression is guarded, but she nods once, zipping the backpack up and placing it at her feet next to her bag. Her movements are careful, like she's thinking too hard about them, and I wish I could say something to convince her to trust me.

She eyes the envelope tucked under my arm, and I hold it out to her.

"Our contract," I say as she turns it over in her hands. "You don't have to review it now, but it proposes both of our roles and responsibilities in this partnership, as well as a tentative timeline for major milestones. I've flagged some areas for your feedback, but please leave commentary wherever you see fit."

She pulls the small packet out, neatly stapled and littered with yellow flags.

"Most romantic proposal I've ever seen," she murmurs. Heat crawls up the back of my neck and I try to grab the file back from her, but she turns away from me. "I'm just teasing."

"I know it's a little clinical," I admit, my knee bouncing. "I just thought that would make things easier."

Our eyes meet, and the flush that crawls over her skin has my hands itching to trace its path. This is what I meant by *easier*. If the contract is detached and analytical, it won't give her any reason to blush like that. Which means I won't imagine what the rest of her body looks like flushed, under wildly different circumstances.

"Easier, yeah," she mutters to herself, digging a pen out of her bag. "Well, I've got nothing else to do right now."

It's not particularly long, but it is detailed. Sections on our roles within the Costa family, as members of The Syndicate, as voting parties on the council. She adds a few notes here and there, and when I try to look over her shoulder, she hisses *no peeking*.

I resign myself to listening to her flip the pages, scratch her notes, hum to herself. That is, until she hits the timeline section.

"Moving in next week? Seems a little fast, doesn't it?" she grumbles, scratching out the clause in bright green ink.

"We've been dating for six months already, remember?" I argue, but she just rolls her eyes at me.

"And that's supposed to be long enough? I can't imagine

living with someone before we've been dating for at least a year." Her eyes continue scrolling down the page. "Though you've got us married by that time."

I can't help the laugh that slips from me at her tone.

"While I appreciate the societal norms here, I do also have a schedule to keep." She bites the inside of her lip. "Tradition holds that I can't take my role officially until I'm legally married, and while I'm willing to wait some time for Ana's sake, my family also needs me."

I think of my mother, unable to speak to us, fighting every day to heal when the nature of her injuries begs her to succumb. Of my father, looking at her like he nearly lost his sun.

"You're right," she whispers, resting her shoulder against mine. "I can agree to engagement within six months if we can push back the move-in to six weeks, just to give Ana time to adjust."

We negotiate back and forth a bit more. She's quick to agree to quit her job, but would like to become more involved in the Costa family work once Ana is back in school. There's a lot more to that conversation, especially considering the way the memory of her killing has me playing out some elaborate fantasies in my mind, so we table it for the time being.

She asks a little about what her friends—mostly Kenzie—are allowed to know, about how much people like Sammy and Catalina are aware of. She pushes back on Ana being given a trust. When she flips the page to the last one, her hand stills.

"This is something we can discuss in the future, if you'd like," I say, trying to gauge her level of discomfort or possibly panic.

Bold of me to just throw the heading *offspring* onto the last page and leave only a tab with a question mark, but I had no idea how else to address the subject.

"Is that something that's required?" she asks, keeping her eyes on the page.

"No, not at all. Clara is required to have an heir, but even she's not expected to have children biologically if she doesn't want to. There are no requirements of me here." I want to see the look in her eyes, to be sure if my words are soothing her, but she doesn't look up at me.

"And if children were something I theoretically wanted in the future?" she asks.

Now that she's said it, my imagination runs away with itself. My body on top of hers. Feeling her arch underneath my touch. Begging her to let me fill her.

I'm barely able to stem the upswell of possessiveness that hurdles through me. She's not asking for that. She explicitly stated so.

"Obviously, we wouldn't go about it in the traditional way." She cringes, and I rush to make sure she knows I didn't include this as some creepy ploy to get her to sleep with me. "There are plenty of safe in-vitro methods, or we can discuss adoption. There are some moral quandaries we'd have to think through, bringing a child into The Syndicate. But yes, if co-parenting is something you wanted, I would be open to it."

My pulse is racing and I feel like I've just run a marathon. How do you explain to someone that you're not pressuring them to have children, and most certainly asking them to sleep with you in order to achieve that goal, but also impress that you're not opposed to fatherhood, all in a marriage contract you typed up on your phone in bed?

She's tense and quiet for a few moments, scribbling bright green flowers into the corner of the page. She finally takes a deep breath and writes below the heading *open to the possibility*.

She reviews the last section on security for her and Ana,

making a few small edits, before passing the document back to me.

"Let me know if you're amenable to those changes," she says, and her voice is almost teasing, even if her smile's a bit tight.

I'll take what I can get in this moment.

"We'll make it work."

# Chapter 11
## *Gwen*

I should have waited to worry until she felt like ass. Ana was right.

It's been three weeks, and every day has gotten harder for her. She's just a little more tired, a little more sore. She's kept up a good front until this point—joking and rolling her eyes and insisting she can still watch softball practice. But when I tried to wake her up today, she just rolled herself further into her covers and muttered that she felt like she hadn't slept at all.

I brush the hair off her forehead, watching her face scrunch and relax in her sleep. Tears well, but I blink them back, wishing I could take this away from her, to trade places. The never-ending nausea intensifies, bile clawing at my already-raw throat as I think about what I should have done differently. What I could have changed. Less fast food, more fresh vegetables. Cutting out blue dye, or maybe it's supposed to be red. Moving her to the countryside where she could breathe fresh air. Throwing out those nonstick pans when they started to flake. I'd give anything to go back and change it all, but I can't, and she's suffering for it.

I stand there for what feels like hours, wishing for impossible things. And when she finally settles into a deeper sleep, I step into the hallway to call her school and let them know she'll be out for at least the next two weeks, promising to keep them updated as her condition changes.

Back in the apartment, I stand in the middle of the space, turning in circles. I feel like I should do something productive—cleaning, or prepping food for Ana, or *anything*—but there's nothing to do. Even though Ana's treatments have taken up a significant portion of our afternoons, she's still been going to school three days a week until today. And for the first time since I was fifteen, I don't have a job. Which means I've filled every waking second with deep cleaning the kitchen and washing sheets and fixing the leaky shower head.

I pick at my nails, suddenly anxious. I don't know the last time I actually had nothing to do. Sure, I've taken time for myself while Ana's been with friends or I had a random morning off from the club, but I always had a running to-do list gnawing at me. The emptiness is disorienting.

I'm saved from considering cleaning the bathroom grout by the buzz of my phone against the kitchen counter. When I slide it open, I'm confronted by a very long text message from my landlord with a passive aggressive reminder that if I'm going to pay my rent in cash, it has to be hand delivered to him, not left in an unmarked envelope in his mailbox. Which is a little rude, seeing as I *didn't* pay my rent in cash. I dropped a check in the mail three days ago, like I always do.

Confused, I switch over to my bank app, wondering if he meant to text another tenant, or if my check got lost in the mail somehow. When my account finally loads, I drop my phone on the counter, staring at it in shock.

I haven't checked my bank account in a while. Charlie's been almost annoyingly insistent about paying for dinners with me and Ana, sending us groceries, and covering all of the small things that I've barely swiped my card over the past few weeks. But there's no way on god's green earth I should have over fifty thousand fucking dollars in my bank account.

I tentatively pick my phone back up, swiping through the activity history. There's no rent withdrawal, but there's a notification for a canceled check, and a one-time transfer of a number with four zeros before the decimal point.

There's not even a question of where this came from. I pull up our text thread, feeling like I'm having an out-of-body experience. My teeth are set on edge, irrational anger pulsing through me.

ME

Take it back.

I flip back to the bank app, ensuring I didn't hallucinate while I wait for his response. It doesn't take long.

CHARLIE

Good morning.

Take what back?

I take a deep breath, glancing over my shoulder at Ana bundled up under her covers, sleeping as soundly as she can.

ME

I swear to god, Carlo Costa, I'm not in the mood to be fucked with.

Please take back the money you deposited in my bank account without my approval.

I watch the little typing bubbles, my irritation not abating at all when another realization crashes into me.

ME

> Also, did you pay my rent? Because that
> wasn't part of the agreement.

The bubbles disappear and then start up again, and I click my nails against the counter, counting the seconds until his response pops up.

CHARLIE

> Yes, Guinevere Byrne, I did pay your rent, and
> yes, you did agree to it. The contract explicitly
> states that I will fully financially support both
> you and Ana. Since we agreed to a modified
> move-in date, I covered your housing costs.

I grind my teeth together again, frustrated with myself that I didn't consider how my insistence on waiting to move in would change things. Even though I logically know the rent for this dingy apartment is a drop in the bucket for him, my chest still tightens in discomfort. I asked for support, signed a fucking contract for it, and it still makes me nauseous to think anyone needs to take care of me.

ME

> I have savings and a plan. We would have
> been fine.

A tiny voice in the back of my mind reminds me we wouldn't have been fine for long. That if Charlie hadn't paid the bill for Ana's surgery, I actually don't know if we would have been able to make rent, even if I kept working. That my savings could cover our expenses for a few months, maybe, but after that we'd be screwed.

CHARLIE

I'll say this as many times as you need me to.
I have no doubt you could figure this out on
your own. But we agreed to support each
other, and this one way I can support you.

I hate this. I hate that he's right. I hate that the way he frames it calms my heart rate down. I hate that I needed someone else to come in and save Ana. I hate that I can't be enough for her.

Accepting his offer didn't make any of this easier. It being the right thing to do just made me madder at myself.

ME

And the transfer?

CHARLIE

In case I'm not around to pick up the tab.

I scoff and roll my eyes, dropping my phone back on the counter. Charlie has kept his promise from that first day of Ana's treatment. Once I finally gave in and agreed to let him help with our commute to appointments, he's taken us to almost every single one. On the few occasions he couldn't be there, Zane's dropped us off and picked us back up, always with dinner and a note from Charlie about the restaurant he found. He's fit into our lives seamlessly, like he was always meant to be there. It's unnerving, and I shouldn't enjoy it.

Ana's still got her guard up a little, but I can tell she enjoys having him around. They're both leagues smarter than me, and she likes talking with him about the things she's learning, asking him questions about college and law school that she knows I can't answer. He treats her like an adult, as much as I do, and I can tell she appreciates not being babied while she's going through this.

Instead of answering Charlie, I snatch my phone back up and text Kenzie.

ME:

You working today?

KENZ

Not until 3, thank god. Want me to come over?

Please. I haven't seen you in ages.

She sends a gif of that old lady from the Titanic, and I roll my eyes.

KENZ

Is Ana home? I can bring bagels from the bakery by my place.

ME

Yeah she's home, but don't worry about it, she's sleeping.

I'll grab them anyway, she can eat when she wakes up if she wants. I'll grab coffee for us too. I'm only half awake.

I stare at the screen, my brows pinched together. Kenzie is the best kind of friend—she used to pick up Ana from school when I couldn't change my schedule. She gives excellent pep talks, and she's the sweetest person alive. But she doesn't offer to buy things, especially over the past six months. The hospital bills from her assault have been taking over her entire life, so much that she had to leave her apartment in the Navy Yard and find a room for rent in Columbia Heights. I don't want her to stretch her budget for breakfast, but I also don't want to seem ungrateful. Instead, I just send a little heart emoji and trust she's got it covered. I can always stick a twenty in her bag when she's not looking.

A HALF HOUR LATER, Kenzie's letting herself in with her spare key, balancing two massive iced coffees on top of three boxes of baked goods. I rush to grab the drinks from her before they tip over, and she pecks me on the cheek.

"Sorry," she whispers, glancing at Ana's tightly shut bedroom door. "Couldn't reach my phone to text you for help."

She slides the boxes on the counter and opens the top one, peeking inside and then moving it to the fridge.

"I saw these little fruit tarts that looked so good, and I know how much Ana loves raspberries, so I just had to get them." She's bouncing on her toes as she opens the lid so I can see inside. They're adorable, tiny and glazed, and she's right—Ana will love them.

"There are bagels and cream cheese in the bottom one. I assumed you had butter for Ana." She yanks her hair out of its ponytail and flips her head over, putting it back up again. "And I got some random pastries too, just in case she's craving something else."

Kenzie has always been the most energetic person I know. She talks a mile a minute, keeping everyone around her laughing and entertained. I love how she fills a room, how you never feel alone when she's near. Her joy is infectious, and one of the worst parts of seeing her with Bryan was watching that light fade whenever he was around. It never fades anymore.

"Jesus, did you walk all the way from Columbia Heights with this?" I ask, snagging the cream cheese out of the bottom box and sticking it in the fridge. Kenzie peels her scarf and coat off, hanging them on the hooks by the door.

"Oh, fuck no, I took a rideshare," she laughs, opening the last box of pastries and digging out a chocolate croissant.

A rideshare? Kenzie? There have been times where she's walked home from the club because she didn't want to spend the two dollars on the Metro fare. What is happening?

"You really didn't have to do all this, Kenz. I appreciate it, but you didn't have to go out of your way." We both know what I actually mean is *you didn't need to spend the money*. There's a flush on her cheeks as she smiles through a mouthful of pastry.

"Actually, I kind of have some news. I know there's a lot of other stuff to talk about, and I didn't want to drop it on you right when I walked in. But, well..." she trails off, swallowing hard and looking a little embarrassed.

I wish I could tell her that, no matter what she's about to say, it's not as unbelievable finding someone in a bar to pay your sister's medical bills in exchange for your hand in marriage.

"Everything okay?" I ask, grabbing her hand as she leans back.

"Yeah, actually, everything's better than okay. Apparently, there's this charity fund at George Washington, and when I was there, I signed up as a potential donation recipient. I don't really remember doing that, but there were a ton of forms, so I must have. Anyway, apparently one of these *guardian angel* rich people paid off all of my medical debt." She takes a deep breath, and there are tears welling in her eyes as she beams at me. "It's gone. Like, all of it. They paid it all off."

Before I can even react, she launches herself at me, wrapping her arms around me and crying into my shoulder. I choke out a laugh, burying my face in her hair and holding her close to me.

"Holy shit," I gasp, shaking my head. She nods against me, tears of relief seeping through the sleeve of my shirt.

"Do you know who donated?" I ask, pulling back and wiping the tears from under her eyes. I know her answer before she even opens her mouth.

"No, they said it was anonymous. Something about medical privacy or whatever."

I'm not naïve enough to think it's a coincidence. And even though I was livid at Charlie barely an hour ago over finances, I can't find it in me to be upset. Kenzie deserves to be free of every memory of her heinous ex, especially the financial burden he caused.

Kenzie grabs our coffees and snuggles into the couch cushions as I pick up my phone.

ME

And Kenzie's medical bills?

It's not until I'm half way through my second cinnamon bagel that I get his response.

CHARLIE

I take care of what's mine. That includes everyone they love.

ANA WAKES up a few hours later, still a little fatigued but feeling better. She snuggles up with Kenzie and they talk about their favorite subject—reality television cooking shows—as I make Ana a plain bagel with butter. I'm happy her appetite hasn't waned too much, though our meal schedule has been indefinitely screwed by our regular four o'clock post-treatment dinners.

They turn on some show that requires contestants to bake under the most ridiculous conditions I've ever heard while I shower and get myself ready for her appointment. When I step out of the bathroom wrapped in a towel, I hear Ana and Kenzie giggling together.

"Seriously, he's obsessed with her. I've never seen someone pine so hard for someone they're already dating," Ana laughs, pulling her socks on.

I tap my phone and realize we've only got about fifteen minutes until Charlie will be here to pick us up.

"Ugh, jealous," Kenzie groans, flopping her head back on the couch. I squeeze into the only corner of my bed nook that you can't see from the couch and shimmy into my jeans.

"Is there a couples cooking show now? Because I thought you two had bled every streaming service dry of food-related reality TV," I yell into the living room, throwing a sweater on and hunting for socks in the mess that is my nightstand drawer.

"I'm talking about you and Charlie," Ana scoffs, getting up from the couch as I come back into view.

"What? Why?" I ask, finding my tennis shoes in the coat closet and slipping them on. "Also, can you grab your bag? I repacked it last night, it's in your room."

She stretches before throwing me a smile and heading into her bedroom while Kenzie packs up the leftovers from this morning, tucking them into the fridge.

"Because I haven't met him yet, and I am begging for crumbs of information from your fifteen-year-old sister." She bumps me with her hip, and I roll my eyes at her. I've told her a little about Charlie via text, but I've kept the details to a minimum. "You're happy though, right?"

I don't know how to answer that. Happiness really wasn't a

consideration when this whole thing started, and now there are a lot of confusing emotions involved.

"He's a good guy," I hedge. Honestly, that's not even completely true. But by conventional standards, I'm not a good person either.

"As long as he's taking care of you two," Kenzie says softly, her smile small and understanding. I grimace a bit, backing away from her touch.

"Kenzie, I..." I start, but she cuts me off with a wave.

"Gwen, you never have to explain yourself to me." She takes a dish towel and wipes down the tiny counter of crumbs. "You're always the person doing whatever you have to do to take care of the people around you. And you know what's best for her," she says, gesturing toward Ana's room. "I just want you to be happy."

We're silent for a minute, and it's a weighty feeling, knowing how honest Kenzie's being.

I don't think she knows what I did that night. She's never mentioned anything about Bryan not coming back, about him never calling. But there are moments where I wonder if she suspects. Like when she told the cops who interviewed her at the hospital about her injuries that I was with her the entire time she was at the hospital, even though I know she remembers me leaving. Or when she talks to me like she's doing now.

It's that feeling that makes me whisper, "I'm not sure if I made the right choice here, Kenz. I don't even know if a right choice exists."

She swings her arm around my shoulder and kisses my temple like a sister would.

"I don't know what your options are, but I do know this. You deserve a little peace, Gwen. So if this choice brings you peace, I think you've made the right one."

# Chapter 12
## *Charlie*

I'm about to do something I definitely should *not* do.

I have a feeling, if it works, Gwen's going to be pretty fucking pissed at me. But I'm coming to learn that I like her angry. Getting under her skin is the closest I can be to getting under her without going back on my word. And even if I didn't enjoy the way fury tinted her skin, I'd push my luck just to get her in my home faster.

Ana's packing up her bag after treatment, more exhausted than usual, hiding yawns behind her hands, and I seize my opportunity.

"How about I make you two dinner at my place tonight so we can all rest," I suggest, holding my hand out for the backpack.

"Your place?" Gwen asks, her eyebrows raised.

"Yeah, my place," I reply, mirroring her expression. If she wants to make this seem out of place in front of Ana, that's her choice.

"We can't go to your place," she scoffs, holding Ana's coat out for her.

"Why can't we go to Charlie's place?" Ana asks, glancing between the two of us cautiously.

I don't blame her—this sounds like the beginning of a fight to me, too.

"Because Charlie lives kind of far away. And by the time we cook and eat and clean up, it'll be late, and you'll be tired, and then we'll have to drive all the way back home," Gwen says, stepping between me and Ana to pull her sister's hair out of her collar. But Ana's eyes catch mine and I take my shot.

"You could stay the night," I say with false nonchalance, watching Gwen's shoulders stiffen instantly at my words. "I've got spare rooms and toothbrushes, and I have the ingredients to make that lemon pasta we had last week in Georgetown."

Ana's eyes flash with the first sign of energy since I picked them up, and she was giggling with Kenzie. She turns to Gwen, whose teeth I can hear grinding.

"Can we go?" she asks, bouncing on her toes a bit. "I really like that pasta."

"You sure you're okay with this?" Gwen asks, combing the ends of Ana's hair with her fingers. "Staying the night and everything?"

Ana just rolls her eyes. "I would have said no to him if I thought it was weird."

A pinprick of guilt needles at me for manipulating Ana like this, but I brush it off. Moving them into my home is safer for her, too.

Gwen lets out a sigh of defeat, and I know I've won the first battle of the night. When she turns and leads Ana down the hallway toward the exit, she shoots me a glare over her shoulder that crackles in my chest like a firework.

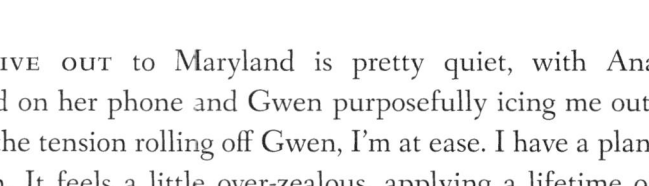

THE DRIVE OUT to Maryland is pretty quiet, with Ana distracted on her phone and Gwen purposefully icing me out. Despite the tension rolling off Gwen, I'm at ease. I have a plan, a mission. It feels a little over-zealous, applying a lifetime of training to something as low-stakes as getting Gwen to change her move-in timeline. But the pattern is comfortable, familiar, like an equation that you slide the variables into.

The thought keeps me in high spirits as we pull through the manned gate and onto the long drive almost an hour later. Ana perks up in the back seat, slipping her earbuds out and peering through the window at the dusk-covered view. My home isn't anything grand, just a single-level ranch, but the property is fairly large. Native plants and grasses stretch over the dips and valleys of the yard, stretching around the house for almost three acres. It's too dim to make them out clearly, but the shadow of a few buildings is barely visible at the edge of the property. From the outside they look like old barns, but they house weapons and motorcycles, and panic rooms, all connected to the house via tunnels.

"Do you have, like, animals?" Ana asks, shoving her shoulders between Gwen and me, lifting off the seat to see further before her sister pushes her backward.

"Seatbelt on until the car is off," she mumbles, clearly still fighting her anger at me. The more I can get Ana on my side, the more Gwen will want to feed into her enthusiasm.

"No animals," I say, parking in front of the small garage attached to the house. "My cousin, Emily, loves researching native plants, and she was visiting when I was looking for a house. She said I had to buy this one because it was basically a nature preserve of Western Maryland wildflowers."

"That's pretty cool," Ana agrees, which is about as high of praise as I can expect from a teenager.

"They're all dormant right now, but in the spring, the whole yard looks like a prism. Colors everywhere."

Ana hums appreciatively as I get out of the car and open her door for her. I hear Gwen's door open and close behind me, and a huff from her as she follows us toward the house. A bubble of laughter climbs its way up my throat, but I suppress it. Sure, Gwen's affection is a lost cause tonight, but I don't need to test my luck any more than necessary.

I try to be as subtle as possible, unlocking the door with my code and thumbprint, but Ana's standing right next to me with her eyebrows raised.

"Safety first," I say lightly.

She looks at me with teenage incredulousness, but follows me inside anyway.

I close the door behind Gwen and reach for her coat instinctually, helping her slide it off her shoulders. She shoots me another glare that fills me with warmth before I move to help Ana.

"Make yourself at home," I say, turning to hang everything up, letting Ana slip off her shoes and explore.

I can tell Gwen noticed at least some differences from the last time she was here, because she can't seem to settle on any part of the room. Decorative pillows and blankets are thrown around the cushions of the conversation pit. A projector screen hangs on the wall over the fireplace. There's a brand new dining table, just big enough for the three of us to eat at, between the living area and the peninsula where Gwen and I came to our agreement. Art and decor hang on the previously blank walls, all purchased by Bea when I told her I needed my home to look more *lived-in*.

This thing where Gwen avoids my gaze has become my new favorite game. I like how she simmers, how she lets her anger build, how she tries to control it. Even more, I'm addicted to how she loses that control and just *has* to aim her fury at me. I pretend gravity is forcing her toward me the same way it makes her the center of my attention.

It feels so different from all the times I've gotten victims to submit to me. Because I don't want her to break. I want her to detonate, for her anger to burn so hot it consumes me, too. I want her to turn all that passion toward me, in whatever form she'll give it.

"This is the coolest living room ever," Ana says, walking around the edge of the sunken couch. She seems hesitant, but not scared, almost like she doesn't want to intrude.

"Who needs a normal couch when you could have a movie theater, right?" I joke.

She smiles at me, her eyes flashing to Gwen, who's doing her best to seem like she's in a good mood. Ana can tell something's up, based on the worried look in her eyes.

"You want to pick out a movie while I cook, or help me?" I ask, moving to the kitchen and turning on a few more lights. The few times we've eaten in at Gwen's apartment instead of trying a new restaurant, Ana's insisted on leading in the kitchen.

"Can I take a raincheck on the cooking? I really want to learn more, but..." she trails off, and I wave her off.

"No problem, kid," I reply, gesturing at the coffee table. "The remote is there somewhere. Pick whatever you want."

She smiles tentatively and walks down the little stairs, sitting on the edge of the sofa. Gwen stands near the dining table, watching her sister with her arms crossed over her chest. I don't want to seem like I'm hovering, so I get to work, pulling out ingredients and watching them out of the corner of my eye. After a few minutes, Ana settles on an old Star Trek movie—I bought every single sci-fi and fantasy movie and TV show available to download—and Gwen finally gives up and joins her.

Her frown softens as Ana snuggles up next to her, chattering about 1980s cinematography and the evolution of special effects. Gwen still throws glares over her shoulder at me, but they're more annoyed than flat-out pissed.

I'm sure that's about to change.

It takes me less than an hour to finish dinner. I'm not much of a chef, but I followed an online tutorial and practiced three times earlier today. Ana's still tired, but she seems more at ease as they pause the movie and sit at the table, a throw blanket still draped around her shoulders.

Something in my chest warms at the domesticity of this. Ana is still talking about classic movie makeup. Gwen asks her questions, referencing inside jokes that make them both giggle. I grab Ana one of the vitamin juice things a pediatric cancer blog recommended and pour Gwen a glass of Valpolicella.

"Is that what you want to do in college?" I ask as Ana digs into her dinner. Gwen pushes her food around a bit, but seems pleased that Ana's hungry.

"I really like makeup design, but I think I love costumes more," she says, hiding a mouthful of pasta behind her hand. "There's a lot of cool programs in theatre and movie costume design that I want to check out this summer." Her eyes flash to Gwen quickly and then back to me. "But there are also schools close to here, too."

Gwen's eyes meet mine for a moment, and for the first time all night, she's not mad. She looks almost relieved.

"You have to make a list of the out-of-state ones so we can

plan our summer," she says, finally starting on her dinner. Ana is poorly suppressing her excitement, the gleam in her eyes clear.

"Some of them are kind of far away," she hedges, but before she can get too dejected, I jump in.

"What's your dream school? The number one program you have to check out?" I ask, leaning back in my chair. I don't have personal connections at many universities in the States, but Emily knows everyone in the biomedical research field. There has to be a connection somewhere.

It's Ana's turn to push her food around her plate, hesitating to answer.

"It's a little crazy. I don't know if I even have the grades to get in, and definitely won't be able to get a scholarship," she says, her voice tight.

I kick her leg gently under the table, and she glances up at me.

"Come on, dream a little," I say.

I can feel Gwen's gaze on the side of my face, but I don't look away from Ana. She blinks a few times before swallowing hard.

"Carnegie Mellon," she whispers almost reverently. A little sparkle lights up behind her eyes. "It's one of the best programs you can get into, and everything they do is amazing. I've watched, like, a billion videos online."

"I guess we've got a trip to Pittsburgh to plan, then," I reply, nodding my head at Gwen. "If you guys don't mind me tagging along, of course."

Ana seems surprised by the offer, but turns to Gwen, her expression hopeful.

"Can we just go see it? I promise I'll apply to community college too," she begs, nearly bouncing in her seat.

Gwen looks back at me, and maybe I don't just enjoy seeing

her angry. Maybe I just crave any moment where she puts her emotions so clearly on display, like she's doing now. It's gratitude, and it makes me feel alive.

"Yeah, of course," Gwen replies, reaching across to tousle her sister's hair a bit. "Charlie's going to have to help you with applications, though. That's not my area of expertise."

She's extending an olive branch, forgiving me for forcing her into dinner here tonight. The look on her face, the feeling thrumming through my veins, is almost enough for me to give up my earlier plan. To sink into this little peace.

But I don't know how to turn that part of my mind off. Even though part of me no longer wants this and wishes I could deviate, the plan is set, and there are too many decades of habit forcing me down the path I've laid.

"I'm sure your sister will be much more help when you're writing your statement of purpose, though," I say, picking up my fork. "But we can pick nights after school to do ACT and SAT prep, too. I think you'll probably take them for the first time in a few months, right?"

"I was going to wait until May, just so I had more energy to study. But I can take it any time during junior year if I need to," she says, her treatment so normal to her now that she doesn't so much as cringe at the mention of its effect on her life. I don't know if it's forced or just Ana's natural state of rolling with the punches. "But you don't have to come all the way into the District to help me study."

Gwen's going to fucking kill me.

"I don't mind, but you're also welcome here whenever you'd like," I say cooly, gesturing toward the hall. "I think I have old test prep books in my office, but they may be from the LSAT. We'll pick up some new ones. But my home is your home."

I can feel Gwen's demeanor change without even looking at her.

"That's very kind of you, but obviously Ana needs to be close to school," Gwen says tightly, her glare cutting.

Ana's eyes flash between us, worried again.

"Of course, it's only an offer. You know I only want to spend as much time with you as possible," I say, putting on an affectionate expression that isn't difficult to find.

"Do we not spend more time here because of me? School and appointments and stuff?" Ana asks, her brow furrowed. She looks a little wounded, and I wonder how much she worries that her needs affect her sister.

"No, that's not what I meant," Gwen huffs, plastering on a patient smile for Ana while still trying to shoot daggers at me. "Charlie's house is far away from my work, too."

"Yeah, but you don't work there anymore," Ana points out, and Gwen grits her teeth a bit.

I didn't ask how she explained her sudden abundance of free time to Ana, but it's clearly a sore spot for Gwen.

"We have a life in the city, Ana," she says, her tone suddenly much more maternal than sisterly. But Ana's not following suit.

"*I* have a life in the city. But you don't. You have Kenzie, but I know she's not the reason we don't spend time here. It's me." There's a defiance I've never heard from Ana. A little bit of her sister's temper shows itself in the flush of her ears.

"Hey, attitude," Gwen chides, putting down her fork and crossing her arms over her chest. "If I decide to not spend time up here so I can get you to school on time like a grown up, that's my decision. That doesn't mean it's your *fault*," Gwen says with determination.

"Yeah, but first you hide me from Charlie because you don't want to *change my life* or whatever." Gwen starts to interrupt, but Ana talks over her, almost yelling. "And then you avoid seeing someone you like because it's far from my stupid cancer appointments? Tell me how that's not my fault."

I'm frozen in my seat, not knowing how to react. I wanted some sort of conversation like this, sure, but the pain in both of their eyes makes my chest ache. Because this moment is my fault.

For the first time in my life, I regret my training. I wish I knew any other way to get to the solution I needed. I suddenly understand Clara and her incessant need to strategize.

"Something being *because of you* doesn't mean it's your fault," Gwen responds, her harsh tone laced with empathy. "That's just life, Ana. Charlie and I have it figured out, don't worry."

Both sets of eyes turn to look at me, Gwen's a warning and Ana's a demand.

"Did you want her...or us...to spend more time here?" Ana asks, swallowing the nervous tilt to her voice. "Did she say no because of me?"

I meet Gwen's eyes. This is it. I have the opportunity to be on Gwen's team. To tell Ana no, that I'm also busy with work, that Gwen never limited our relationship because of her. Gwen's eyes beg me to make that choice. Some quiet part of my heart does, too.

But it's no use. I've found my opening, and I free fall into it.

"I..." I stutter, and I wish it was manufactured for effect. "I offered to have you move in here."

Gwen's expression turns to ice, betrayal the only emotion I can sense. Ana's jaw drops a fraction in shock before she turns back to her sister.

They go back and forth, angry and hurt. Ana demanding to know why Gwen refuses to live her life, using her as an excuse. Gwen repeating that it's her decision, that her sister isn't a burden, that she doesn't regret her decisions. By the time dinner has gone cold, they're both huffing, arms crossed, refusing to look at each other.

"I want to go to bed," Ana announces, pushing away from the table. Gwen and I both stand, but she cuts me a look that locks me in place.

"I'll show you the spare rooms, okay?" Gwen says quietly, walking down the hallway, Ana following a few steps behind.

"Ana," I say before she can leave. Both sisters turn toward me. "I'm sorry. I didn't mean to start all of this. Your sister loves you so much. All she wants is for you to have everything you want."

Fury is rolling off of Gwen, and I can't blame her. All I've done in this moment is position myself as the good guy.

"It's okay. I just want the same thing for her, too."

Ana walks past Gwen down the hall, disappearing from my sightline, but Gwen's rooted to the spot. She stares after her sister, and I wish I could live inside her mind again.

It takes a few moments, but eventually Gwen follows her down the hall without a second glance at me. Their muted voices travel through the walls, soft and a little apologetic, and I clean the kitchen. They'll repair this little rift in their relationship soon, maybe even tonight, and now I've planted the seeds to make Ana comfortable with the idea of living here. And Gwen might agree to it, if only to prove that Ana's needs don't limit them.

The familiar thrill of winning, of executing a plan, of getting the outcome I wanted, pulses through my veins, but it's not as sweet as it normally is.

I'm nearly done loading the dishwasher when I hear the door to Ana's room shut. There are no footsteps, no sign that Gwen's returning to the living room, but I'm not fooled. She's probably standing in the hallway, doing her best to contain the anger boiling in her chest.

Finally, I hear her approach. Muffled steps, steady breaths, so much control.

"Ana get settled okay?" I ask, even though I know it will set her off. Usually, I enjoy taunting my prey, especially after I've already won.

Maybe that's the problem. Maybe I don't want Gwen to be prey.

"What the ever loving fuck was all of that?" she demands, each word clipped and laced with venom.

"What do you mean?" I ask, even though I don't want to. I'm pushing further than I need to, and a little voice in the back of my mind that sounds suspiciously like Bea tells me to stop.

But this is what I do, it's who I am. I find someone's weakness—be it physical or psychological or emotional—and exploit it. I use what I know and get them to break, to submit, to give me what I want. And Gwen's weakness, ironically enough, is the fortress of fury she's built around herself. So tall and wide she doesn't see the cracks in its foundation.

It's second nature to keep searching for faults I can take advantage of, to push for one more slip up, one last break. To show her I can slither into those cracks. Bea's voice taps at the back of my mind again, screaming at me that Gwen is not a target, not a victim. That there are other ways to get what I want, to work with her, to have her on my team.

Partners, maybe friends.

But the sensation is so familiar it's like muscle memory, my body and mind slipping seamlessly into this version of myself. When she finally walks up and stands next to me in front of the sink, I smile at her, and it feels wrong, too cruel. This isn't the smile I gave my redhead in the bar. It's the one I give to my victims.

"Inviting us over here without clearing it with me first? Using Ana to get me to move up my timeline? Manipulating every fucking second to get what you want?" Her voice shakes with fury, and my smile falters. She's angry, sure, but she's also teetering on the edge of some break, pain and sadness thrashing through her eyes.

"Gwen, I..." I don't even know what I'm about to say, but she doesn't let me find out.

"Don't you fucking dare. I agreed to your fucking terms. I wanted to ease Ana into this because I don't want her feeling like a prop in my relationships. Like she's going to meet some new guy who wants her sister to upend their lives and make her leave her home every six fucking months." She's whispering, maybe because it's the only way she knows not to scream.

Possessive rage crashes over me at her words.

"She will not meet anyone else," I say, resisting the urge to touch her. "I'm yours."

Her eyes flare for a moment before she starts washing the dishes in the sink, movements jerky.

"That's not the point," she seethes, scrubbing a plate with such vigor that I worry she'll break it and slice her hand open. I think about taking it from her, telling her she doesn't need to clean, but I'm a little afraid to interrupt. "I'm not putting her through the shit Isabelle did, changing her whole life, her school, her friends, just for some fucking guy. Especially not in the middle of treatment."

The comparison hits me like a brick. It hadn't occurred to me that she'd feel like her mother, but I also failed to consider how it would frame me in Ana's mind. Does she remember enough about Ben and the men like him to worry I'll be the next version of them?

Shame nips at me, but I try to brush it off. Gwen is safer, more cared for, more supported, under my roof. So is Ana. I grip the edge of the counter and look at the ceiling with a hard breath.

"You being here is for the best."

For a second there's silence, before a splitting pain radiates through my hand. I'm so shocked I choke out a gasp, and grip the counter harder as my gaze catches on a fork standing upright from the back of my hand.

"You have no idea what's best for us," she says, voice quivering, and I don't know if she's going to cry or scream.

I meet her eyes, and her emotions are so painfully obvious, written across her face like she's screaming them at me. Betrayal, pain, fury.

The pain brings a sense of clarity I haven't felt since the night began. That tangled knot suddenly unravels, and I'm faced with the reality that I did this to Gwen, to Ana. That I took the woman in the alley who I couldn't forget and turned her into another target, a mission.

Her brain seems to catch up to her actions, because her eyes fall to the utensil in my hand. One prong sticks almost directly out of the eye of the snake inked there. She breathes out a heavy sigh.

"That may have been an overreaction," she says reluctantly, releasing her grip on the fork.

A smile pulls at the edge of my lips, humor crowded out by remorse.

"I don't know, I've done worse for far less important reasons," I whisper, watching blood pool in little bubbles on my skin. It's not too deep, and she miraculously didn't hit any bone, though I don't think that was purposeful. I hold my breath as I pull the fork out with my opposite hand.

"Do you have a first aid kit?" she asks sheepishly.

I look sideways at her and catch her gaze before rolling my eyes with a smile. She grimaces, and I reach into the cabinet over the refrigerator to grab the kit, tossing it on the peninsula.

"You were right," I admit, unzipping the case and finding the antiseptic. "Everything I did tonight was out of line. It's not an excuse, but this is what I'm used to. Manipulating everyone around me to fit my plan. It's something that I don't want to do with you," I say, glancing up at her as she leans against the counter. "But you're allowed to keep stabbing me until I learn to handle myself better."

A smile kicks up at the corner of her lips, but she rolls them between her teeth to squash it. There isn't too much bleeding, but I rifle through the kit again, looking for bandages.

"Let me," she says, suddenly in front of me. She takes my hand, skin so soft and smooth against mine.

There's an electric current where we touch, igniting my whole body. I swallow down the feeling, hoping if I don't react, she won't let go.

She finds a larger bandage and unwraps it, carefully placing antiseptic on the pad and smoothing the sticky ends around the contours of my knuckles.

"You will not treat either of us like that again," she says quietly, the threat seductive and lethal as she runs her fingertip over the edge of the bandage. "You will figure out a way to appropriately negotiate our contract, to communicate with me, or you will find out what happens when someone wrongs me twice. Do you understand?"

Our gazes lock, and despite the malice in her question, her expression is almost sweet. I want to taste it. I want to taste all of her.

But I just nod, and she smiles before dropping my hand and heading toward the hallway. The part of me that lacks self preservation begs me to ask her to stay in my bed. For appearances, of course. But I somehow keep the words from pouring out of me as she makes her way toward what I can only assume is the guest room Ana's not sleeping in.

Right before she disappears around the corner, she looks over her shoulder.

"Oh, and now that timelines are up for negotiation, I'm making some requests," she says, her tone light and airy. "I'm looking forward to learning the family business, Charlie."

# Chapter 13
## *Charlie*

At first I thought I'd won this little exchange. Sure, I might be bringing Gwen into the family business a little early here, but it seemed like an easy concession if I got to have her under my roof sooner. She'd eventually learn that her taste for violence is what drew me to her.

As I watch her walk down the stairs behind the glass door, I realize I was very, *very* wrong. Because the last time I watched her kill someone, I could barely contain my attraction to her. And now I'm about to witness it again, and I can't fucking touch her.

I don't pray—what god would listen? But I mutter a request for strength to the universe as Gwen hits the landing. I told her to dress comfortably, in clothes she didn't mind incinerating. Hair pulled back, in a form-fitting, long-sleeved shirt and jeans, she looks like she could be running errands. Like joining me in bleeding my enemies dry is almost domestic. I can't seem to remove my hand from over my mouth.

"Hi," she says simply as I open the door for her, her breath puffing in front of her lips. Her cheeks flush from the cold.

Or maybe the flush is from something else entirely. I wish I was imagining the way her eyes travel down my frame and back up, the hint of something carnal in them. It's fuel to the spark lit between us, and I try my best to dampen it as I take her arm and lead her carefully to the car.

I want nothing more than to lean into the feeling, stoke the flame, see if it consumes her the way it does me. But even if we share a mutual attraction, I can't push. I'll never know if she's only reciprocating because she believes she has to in order to take care of Ana. And even if, somehow, I could be certain, she'd never want the version of me I crave to be around her. Not with what she's about to witness.

The drive to the farm is long and quiet. Dusk is settling over the treetops, pinks and purples flashing over Gwen's skin as she leans back against the headrest, staring at the world whipping by. I still can't tell if she's nervous, but I know she'll talk when she's ready.

There's no music, but she doesn't seem to mind, and neither do I. I love the sound of the road under my tires, the soft hum lulling me into imagining what it would be like to drive down these roads on my motorcycle, with Gwen wrapped around me.

That image keeps me occupied until we're finally pulling through the gates of the farm. Gwen perks up, her eyes wide as we make our way up the winding dirt road. I feel her gaze on the side of my face when the pigs come into view, and I keep my eyes forward despite the smile pulling at my lips.

Emily's car is parked near the front door, sleek, clean, and out of place against the rustic setting. When she offered to be here for Gwen's first introduction to our work, I was hesitant. I wanted this moment to be between the two of us, to be intimate. But Emily was right—I'm not always the most self-aware when I become this version of myself, and I don't want to scare Gwen.

Once the engine is off, I turn toward her. She's got her arms crossed under her chest, nails digging her into her own skin. She's avoiding my gaze, and that just won't do anymore.

"Gwen," I say softly, breaking the bubble of silence we created. She takes a steadying breath through her nose and turns to me, her jaw clenched and her eyes guarded. "Emily, my cousin, will be inside, and she's going to help me explain some things. Then you and I will go downstairs." I reach out and grab her hand, smoothing my fingers over the indents she's made in her arm with her nails. "At any point, you can go upstairs. There is no shame in not being able to handle what's about to happen. Torturing someone is very different from what you experienced last summer. It takes longer and it's exhausting, physically and psychologically." I brush my thumb over her hand and her eyes flicker down to the motion before meeting mine again.

"I understand," she says, swallowing hard.

Her guard is still up as I search her expression, and I haven't yet learned how to read her well enough to unearth what she's hiding. I want to dig, but I have to trust her to know her own limits, or to be willing to learn them.

I nod, unbuckle my seatbelt, and slip out of the car, opening her door before she can do it herself. She follows me into the main house, our footsteps disguised by the distant noise of hungry pigs.

Emily's sitting on the old couch, her back against the armrest and her feet propped up on the cushions. Unsurprisingly, her laptop sits open on her thighs, and she only looks up when the door closes behind us.

"Holy shit, you actually brought her," Emily says, closing the screen and standing. She's barefoot and in men's workout clothes—her standard attire for when she's holed up researching—and she stretches before making her way across the room.

"Gwen, this is Emily, my least favorite and smartest cousin," I introduce as Emily sizes her up. I don't know why I expected Gwen to cower at all, but her spine is steel and her expression is unreadable as she assesses Emily.

"And you're Gwen, the magical murderer," Emily says, her dry humor landing only for her. There was no getting around telling her about Gwen's escapade with Kenzie's ex, and now she's taken to some creative nicknames. "Talk about coincidence, huh?"

"Still not convinced he didn't stalk me for six months," Gwen barbs back, and Emily's eyes crinkle at the corner as she smiles.

"Not his style," she turns back to the couch and plops down unceremoniously, opening her laptop back up. "He likes to believe the universe speaks to him," she taunts, wiggling her fingers in the air with her eyes locked on the screen.

"I do not believe the universe *speaks* to me," I argue, gesturing for Gwen to sit on the loveseat across from Emily as I take the armchair. "I just think everything happens for a reason."

"Sure, whatever," Emily waves me off, uninterested in a conversation in which she knows she can't change my mind. "Do we want to talk about our friend downstairs?"

Gwen shifts forward, her posture tense but not fearful. I watch her out of the corner of my eye as I motion for Emily to continue.

"Kayden Thorne, which is a fucking crime of a name, by the way," she recites, lazily scrolling her trackpad. "Twenty-six, American born, living in Mogilev, Belarus, and doing low-level intelligence gathering under Zia Gia's team. He was recruited two years ago after his dad helped Gia with some issue with imports in southern California. Suspect that he got swayed by Konstantin's team of arms runners about four months before Lucia's attack. I don't think he's high enough up in Konstantin's organization to know anything useful, but it would be nice to know who approached him, if you can get that out of him." She flicks her eyes up to Gwen, who doesn't look like she's breathing, and back down at her computer. "I can't imagine why you wouldn't be able to."

I crack my neck, the familiar feeling of calm concentration creeping into my veins. I glance at Gwen, who's already got her head tilted in my direction. Her brows are slightly furrowed, but she just looks a little confused.

"Gia is my other cousin, Beatrice's, mother, and Lucia is mine. We're fairly certain that Konstantin's team is responsible for her attack, but we have no idea how he knew she would be in Ankara. Clara, my sister, is working on a top down approach with the Russians back in Trani, but we're trying to catch small fish and see what they can give us."

It's so natural, this feeling. Like slipping into your most worn jacket. Without conscious direction, I'm already positioning slices and blows in my mind. Maybe Emily's right, and we'll only confirm his involvement with the Russian arms dealers who've been trying to eradicate The Syndicate since we cut off their North American arm nearly a decade ago. But the most seemingly insignificant information could have outstated impact. I need to know what he told them, so I can find our weaknesses and seal them like a tomb.

Emily clears her throat, and I realize I've been staring at Gwen. I still can't sense fear from her, but her eyes are mapping my face like she doesn't fully recognize it.

"How did you find out he had flipped to the Russians?" Gwen asks, shifting her gaze to Emily.

For what it's worth, Emily doesn't take Gwen's question as

an insult to her intelligence gathering. She likes people who probe, because *she* likes to probe.

"He missed a few check-ins, and his reporting became more and more vague," Emily replies, clicking through something at a rapid rate. "He was supposed to be working some leads we had on fake advertisements for models and actresses in eastern Europe that end up being trafficking hooks. We were initially concerned that he got turned into a customer by a ring, but then we started tracking him leaving the country, and pieces started to fall into place. We got confirmation from our team in St. Petersburg last week."

Gwen rests her elbows on her knees and asks more questions, and I observe her. The resolve that feels manufactured in her eyes. The way her fingertips whiten from how tightly she clasps her hands.

I remember wishing I could see her eyes in that alley, but now I'm not sure it would have made a difference. Because even after weeks of watching her emotions written plainly on her face, I still can't read her right now.

"How long until his sedation wears off?" I ask when their conversation lulls, rolling my fingers against the arm of the chair.

Gwen's watching me again, and it puts me on edge. I know this is who I am, and I want to see if she can handle it, but something in my chest rages against her seeing me like this. It will only reinforce the idea that this is the core of who I am—controlled and manipulative.

But I've backed myself into this corner.

"He should be up any minute now," she replies, kicking her feet up on the coffee table. "He's a big dude, but I don't think Zane gave him the full dose when he got him off the plane."

I stand up, cracking my neck again, a habit I should quit.

Gwen glances between me and Emily, a little more hesitant as she rises.

"You're not coming down too?" she asks my cousin, who snorts.

"Research and development is more my lane. Plus, I'm not patient enough for Charlie's line of work. I prefer a more direct approach." She glances up and meets my gaze, a challenge there. "He's got this handled."

Since we were kids, Emily's never questioned my abilities. She's pushed me to my limits, made me better. But the way she's looking at me right now, it's like she doesn't believe for a moment I *have this handled.*

But she's wrong.

"Stay behind me as we go down the stairs. There's a table in the far corner of the room that you can observe from. If you'd like a closer look, let me know before you approach." My instructions to Gwen are harsh and tactical, but this is the reality of the job.

Gwen nods, even though her eyebrows have shot into her hairline again. I turn toward the cellar door, and I hear Emily whisper behind me.

"Do what feels natural. That's how he learned, even if he's forgotten."

The words sting a little, but I compartmentalize them like I do everything else. My concern for my mother's health. The sound of the refrigerator humming in the background. My lust for Gwen. Every stimulus, internal and external, falls neatly into a file, tucked away to be reopened after I leave this house.

We make our way past two locked doors and a railless staircase, and I keep close track of Gwen behind me as I open the door.

Kayden is very much awake. The room is soundproof, but as soon as I crack the door, his muffled screams fill the space.

He's sweating, but he hasn't pissed himself, which is a minor miracle.

I can feel Gwen like a tether is attached between us. I don't turn to watch her, but I know she goes to stand at the table like I told her. Kayden's eyes flicker back and forth between us.

"Good evening, Kayden," I say calmly, rolling up the sleeves of my shirt. "I hope your flight was restful."

He starts screaming again, and I doubt the words would be clear even without the gag. His fear is like a noxious gas, spreading through the room and permeating my nervous system. I hate the metaphor of predator and prey, but it's fitting, the way my subconscious starts cataloging his weaknesses.

It's unlikely he's dedicated enough to Konstantin's team that anything more than a little roughing up will be necessary. But I have a student today.

"I'm sure you won't mind," I say over his screaming, nodding my head back to Gwen without looking at her. I don't know why, but I can't. "We're using tonight as a learning opportunity for a friend. You're amenable to that, aren't you?"

Spit is dripping down his chin, his muscles bulging against the restraints holding him to the chair bolted to the floor. He has his eyes locked on Gwen, and his noises turn pleading, like he's begging for her to release him. My blood simmers under my skin.

"See, I knew you'd be understanding," I say as I reach out and grab his chin, forcing him to look at me. "I hear we have a lot to talk about. I do hope you'll be forthcoming."

Terror still pulses through him, but anger, too. I've found that people don't just go through the stages of grief when someone they care for dies, but when they know their life is about to end as well. He's not yet accepted his own impending demise, and that works in my favor. He'll offer more in exchange for a life he can no longer bargain with.

I hold his chin through his thrashing, his attempts to break free, but Zane has perfected this particular art. I wouldn't have brought Gwen down here if I thought for a moment our victim could get loose from his restraints.

"Now, I'm going to take out this unseemly gag, and we're going to talk a little bit about what you told Konstantin's men," I say calmly, wiping his spit from my fingers onto the side of his face. He doesn't look shocked—it's impossible that he doesn't know who I am and why he's here—but his expression hardens a bit. "If you're forthcoming, I'm sure this will be a pleasant exchange."

I hear Gwen shift behind me, but I still can't force myself to look at her. Am I afraid of what I'll see in her eyes, or what she'll see in mine?

I reach behind Kayden's head and untie the cloth gag, and immediately he's yelling and thrashing again. I roll my eyes, tossing the fabric into the corner of the room and stepping away to let him wear himself out. He's screaming for help, for me to fuck off, that he *didn't fucking do anything*, his voice quickly growing strained.

"It's instinctual for them to rebel like this, especially if they haven't received any training to the contrary." I raise my voice so Gwen can hear me without taking my eyes off Kayden. I hear her shift again, but don't feel her come any closer. "Generally, they wear themselves out in a few minutes, but the body will sometimes produce intermittent bursts of adrenaline throughout the process, which is something to keep in mind if you ever decide to loosen a victim's restraints."

She only hums in response, but something about the sound of her voice settles in my mind. It doesn't draw me out of the moment, but acts like a window into a world outside this room. I've killed with others before—family members, Zane, the occasional external partner or extended Syndicate member—but I've never experienced this sensation.

I place the question of *why* in another little compartment and file it away, even if I continue to bask in the small comfort I've found with her here.

As Kayden's struggling becomes less enthusiastic, I move so I'm directly in front of him and squat down so we're eye level with each other.

"Okay, Kayden. Why don't we start easy? Who from Konstantin's team approached you in Belarus?" I ask, my tone almost patronizing.

"Man, go fuck yourself," he spits, breathing heavily from exerting himself with useless struggling. I roll my eyes.

"That is not what I'd call forthcoming," I say, patting him on the side of the face firmly. He flinches away at the touch, and I can't help but laugh. "Let's try that one more time, yes? Who approached you?"

"I'm not telling you jack fucking shit," he sneers.

Cocking my head at him, I track his expression, his breathing, the set of his jaw. I realize he's not refusing because of his dedication to Konstantin, but because of *pride*. This exchange has bruised his ego.

What a fucking idiot. I crack my neck again and step back again.

"Unless you're working with someone trained to withstand torture, a little motivation is all someone usually needs," I instruct Gwen again, listening to her take a few tentative steps forward. She keeps her distance though, as I slam my fist against Kayden's face.

"Fuck," he nearly screams, breathing hard through his mouth as blood trickles from his lip.

"Normally I would move straight to blades," I inform

Gwen, latching on to that little window in my mind. "But I don't think our friend here is going to need much convincing."

Kayden sneers, blood coating a few of his teeth.

"You don't know fucking anything," he says, before I land another blow across his face. His cry is choked, like he's holding it back.

"Konstantin's people run weapons to some of the most vile people on this planet. Is that the glory your father wanted for you?" I say, striking him again, this time across the right side of his jaw. He spits blood at my feet.

"You think your family is any fucking better?" he yells, and the way his anger ratchets fuels me. Every inch less controlled he becomes, the more I sink into my skin, the steady familiarity of this work.

More than fists and blades, reading people is the most important part of what I do. What will get someone talking—silence or responses, threats or blows, anticipation or onslaught? Kayden's pride makes him more likely to argue, to prove he's right, and I'll use that to my advantage.

"I think we have a set of morals that we adhere to, and you sell your loyalty to the highest bidder." I'm not even through the sentence before he's laughing.

"Morals? Fuck you, man. You're not any different from the rest of us," he chokes on the words as I strike him again. This time, he takes longer to recover. "You don't fucking know anything," he repeats.

I step back and let him recover a bit, biding my time. He'll give me Konstantine's contact. They always break.

There's a few beats of silence, cut only by Kayden's heavy breathing, before I hear Gwen's hesitant steps.

"Charlie," she nearly whispers. The window in my mind brightens a little more, illuminated by the sound of her voice. "Do you mind if I ask him something?"

It takes a shocking amount of effort to turn and meet her gaze. She's still guarded, her wall still high. I have the same impulse I did at Catalina's—to crawl into her mind, under her skin, to be so close to her she can't help but reveal her every thought to me.

I had expected her to just observe, but she doesn't look afraid. Her eyes still map my face, but she seems resolved, so I nod.

Her movements are careful and calculated as she steps around me and squats in front of Kayden. I have to remind myself that he's restrained, that if he could have gotten free he already would have, that she's safe. That even if he did somehow release himself, I wouldn't let him fucking touch her.

Her knees rest on the ground, droplets of Kayden's blood soaking into her jeans. She tilts her head up, locking eyes with him.

"Why do you think our family is no different from anyone else?" she asks, her voice kind and empathetic.

The words *our family* echo through my head like a prayer, like a hymn. I'm so captivated by them I almost miss the way Kayden's eyes flash with fear before icing over again.

Gwen stares at him a moment longer, contemplative, before turning over her shoulder to me.

"Teach me."

There's something alive inside of me, attempting to crawl its way out through my throat to consume her, to *be* consumed by her. It's a lust I've never experienced before, so natural and dominating that it might be in my blood.

The little window is the only thing that reminds me to rein in this sensation, that she doesn't feel this, that I *promised*. I control my expression the best I can, more difficult than any training or torture I've experienced, and turn toward the steel table.

It's easy, choosing a blade. It's the same one I learned with, nearly two decades ago. Warm and familiar in my palm, I turn it over, making my way back to her.

I don't look at Kayden, even though I hear him struggling again. I'm captivated entirely by her gentle determination, the empathy that I now think was not for our victim, but for me.

I kneel beside her and slide the handle into her palm, adjusting her fingers on the hilt and encompassing her hand with my own. Together, we tilt the edge of the blade against Kayden's thigh.

"Press here, mia filettatura."

## Chapter 14
### *Gwen*

The blade is so sharp it slips through Kayden's pants and skin with ease. I register his screaming, but my senses are overwhelmed with the feeling of Charlie's hand on top of mine, his breath at my ear.

"Gently," he murmurs, pulling our hands back and removing the knife. There's a thin slice like a filet in Kayden's leg, blood seeping from it in a steady, uneven stream. "This area here," he drags his finger over the center of Kayden's thigh up toward his groin, smearing the blood like paint, "is where the femoral artery is. Good for a quick death, but not if you're looking for information. Puncturing larger veins can lead to bloodletting too, but they're harder to avoid. You'll learn with time."

He maneuvers our hands, his fingers now laced through mine, so the tip of the knife is pressing into Kayden's knee, who whimpers above us.

"The kneecap tends to be particularly effective, and painful," Charlie says, and when I start to push forward, I feel pressure on my fingers.

"Give him a chance to answer, mia filettatura," he chides softly, and I can hear a smile in his voice.

It's the second time he's called me that, but I'm afraid I'll break the moment if I ask him what it means. Instead, I turn to the man writhing in the chair above me. His pale face is nearly gray, blond hair sweat-stuck to his forehead.

"What did you mean when you said we were no different?" I ask again, my voice a lot stronger than I actually feel. And it's not fear or revulsion making my heart pound in my throat and my bloom hum. I feel almost like I'm disassociating, having an out-of-body experience. Only potent desire is grounding me.

Kayden doesn't answer, his bloody lips pressed together in defiance, but still shaking. I lock eyes with him as Charlie and I press the tip of the blade into his kneecap together.

"Fucking psycho bitch!" Kayden sobs, the words coming in broken breaths.

I feel Charlie shift, plunging the knife deeper, under the bone of his kneecap, and Kayden's screams become more frantic.

"You don't fucking speak to her like that," he commands, his voice deadly, the smooth flirtation I detected earlier gone.

The hairs on the back of my neck raise, and I nudge my knuckles against his on the handle.

"The artery goes behind the knee, right? We need more time with him."

Charlie releases a long breath behind me before he loosens his grip.

"Thank you," he murmurs, his lips a hair's breadth from the skin of my spine, and a flush crawls up my chest.

"One more time, Kayden," I say neutrally, putting just a slight amount of pressure on the blade to tilt it up. He screams, and his blood flows thinly down the weapon to my wrist. "Explain what you meant."

"Fucking stop!" he begs, animalistic sounds tearing from his throat.

"Fucking answer," I reply, holding the blade still.

Charlie's not guiding me now, just brushing his fingertips over my knuckles gently. The logical part of my brain knows it's concerning that I can feel that touch *everywhere*, but something instinctual is taking over.

The feeling I had in the alley—the control, the vindication —is nothing compared to this. It's like I've only known the surface of myself my entire life, and now that I've dived below, I've discovered a riptide. The sensation is magnified one thousand-fold by Charlie's warm body hovering behind me, his eyes tracking my every movement, his skin *so close* to mine.

Kayden has his head thrown back, his eyes pressed shut and leaking tears. I shrug.

"Suit yourself."

But before I can move more than a centimeter, he's screaming.

"No, fuck, stop," he pleads, his voice cracking with agony.

I still, looking up at him with raised eyebrows and a placid smile.

"Something to contribute to the conversation?" I ask.

Charlie huffs a laugh behind me.

Kayden pants hard, watching the blood seep out of the gashes in his leg, and I wonder if everyone looks like this when they know they're conceding to their own death.

"No one from Konstantin's team approached me," he says, and Charlie's hand finds its place on top of mine again. Kayden must feel the pressure, because he whips his head up to stare at me. "I fucking swear they didn't. Someone told me in April that I was reporting to a new handler. They started giving me more money, telling me I was working on higher-profile shit, that I shouldn't worry about the girls and the trafficking." He chokes on some of the blood still filling his mouth.

"And at what point did you realize you were no longer reporting to The Syndicate?" Charlie asks from behind me, voice condescending and authoritative.

"You don't fucking get it, dude. I *am* working for The Syndicate. You just don't know what's going on in your own fucking house."

Charlie grasps my hand tightly and pushes the blade, shoving it further into Kaden's body than before. His scream is piercing, agonized, but Charlie doesn't flinch, even as my hand pulls back against him.

"How about you start from the beginning, huh?" Charlie's tone is so light and carefree you'd think we were having this conversation over a pleasant dinner.

Kayden pisses himself, and I wrinkle my nose.

"The new handler," Kayden sobs, straining against his restraints. "She gave me cash, said I'd been switched to a new team. Guns, not trafficking. I thought I'd be checking in on small arms dealers, since you guys are so high and fucking mighty about your *greater good* shit. But I just passed information, facilitated deals. Arms into Estonia and Lithuania. Smoothing over shit at ports."

Kayden's panting now, sweat sticking his t-shirt fully to his chest, shivering from the cold. I wonder if he's going into shock, but Charlie doesn't seem concerned.

"And you didn't think to ask any questions? You just trusted that this new handler was truly from The Syndicate?" Frustration coats Charlie's words, like he's annoyed by Kayden's stupidity.

Can't say I blame him.

Kayden glares down, his eyes glazed over in pain, his skin ghostly white.

"Number one rule of working for your fucking family is to not ask questions you don't need the answer to," he chokes out, his eyes rolling back in his head a bit. "Plus, she had the dove."

Charlie stills, his body frozen behind me. It doesn't even sound like he's breathing.

"She showed you her sigil?" He asks, and it's the first time I've ever heard him sound unsettled.

Kayden closes his eyes, nodding once as he shivers.

There are a few beats of strained silence, cut only by Kayden's labored breathing, before Charlie moves.

The sudden absence of his body behind me feels like being dropped into the frigid ocean. I barely have time to turn around and look for him when he's back, looping some kind of strap around Kayden's injured leg. It takes me a few seconds to realize he's putting a tourniquet on him. I can't get my body to move the way I want it to, to do anything at all, as I watch him rachet the band tighter and tighter as Kayden screams. The little stream of blood that was flowing from Kayden's leg peters out, and Charlie turns back to me.

He doesn't say a word. Just holds his hand out to me. My body feels frozen though, my limbs heavy, and my brain is two steps behind whatever is happening. Charlie doesn't seem upset or surprised, though. He just kneels down again, lacing his fingers through mine, and guides my body up.

I don't look at Kayden as we leave. I'm not sure what's happening to me, but the sudden shift in energy is making me feel weak and unmoored, and not in the pleasantly erotic way I was feeling with Charlie guiding my fingers on his blade. The stairs seem uneven and twice as long as they did on the way down as we head back to the main house.

As soon as the door clicks behind me, it's like the blood that was pounding through my body suddenly stops moving at all. Stars dance in front of my eyes, and I don't even have the wherewithal to be embarrassed as a cold sweat breaks out over my skin.

Charlie's still silent, gripping me around the waist as I slump against him. He navigates me past Emily on the couch and through a little archway. I barely realize I'm about to throw up before he gently helps me to the floor, holding my hair back and away from my face.

I empty the contents of my stomach into the toilet, sweat pooling at the nape of my neck and dripping down my back. I grip the side of the bowl, trying to forcibly steady myself as I heave again and again. Every part of me feels raw and feverish, chills weakening my limbs and making me see double.

It's a few minutes before the muscles of my abdomen stop twitching, and the haziness at the edge of my vision starts to dissipate. I cough, wipe my mouth, clean myself up, all while Charlie rubs soft circles on my back.

As my senses come back to me, the humiliation I was missing before comes flooding in. I shrug Charlie's hand off of me and force myself to stand.

I don't even know how to explain what happened in that basement. The overwhelming feeling of rightness. The way my body seemed to know what to do before my brain did. The intimacy.

I can still feel Charlie's touch against my skin, the thump of his heartbeat against my back, his breath so warm and close that his lips had to be nearly touching me.

It's bad enough I was *that* turned on by his hand wrapped around mine, guiding the blade into Kayden's skin. But to project that feeling onto Charlie? To imagine he wanted to be closer, to close my eyes and pretend this little lesson made him feel the same?

He told me he's not interested. He's made it clear. For

fuck's sake, *I made it clear*. I grip the edge of the bathroom sink and shake myself. I'm so fucking frustrated. In a few weeks, I've gone from pissed at the thought of him blackmailing me into fucking him, to reluctantly attracted to him, to this? Wet and feeling like a live wire from nearly killing a man with him?

There's something seriously wrong with me. What's worse, I have absolutely no urge to fix it.

I snap my head up at the feeling of Charlie's tentative touch against my back. When I find his eyes in the mirror, they still hold the same unforgiving hardness as they did when we walked down the stairs, but there's something different at the edges. I'm too overwhelmed to read it, though.

"It's okay," he murmurs, his eyes tracing my reflection. "It's a normal reaction."

My stomach turns at his words, and I can feel a flush crawl up my chest and neck. Suddenly, it's impossible to meet his gaze. Was I really so obvious? Could he tell how intoxicated I was by not only his touch, but what we were doing together?

Could he tell that wielding that knife to exact what I wanted felt like foreplay?

"Everyone gets sick their first few times. Even after years of experience, sometimes the adrenaline drop is just too much for your body to handle. It doesn't make you any less capable."

Of course. Of fucking *course,* that's what he means.

I try to swallow down the relief that he couldn't see my desire, and the disappointment that he doesn't *want* to see it. I turn on the faucet, splashing water on my face and rinsing out my mouth.

"Yeah, okay, thanks," I stammer, pulling down my hair and retying it. I can feel his eyes on me, but I'm not brave enough to see the pity in them.

"I mean it, Gwen," he says, and the heat of his body grows

closer. I busy myself with washing my hands. "It happens to all of us."

"Charlie puked on a ski lift two years ago because my method of gutting someone didn't settle well with him," Emily calls from the living room, and I take the opportunity to slip away from Charlie, walking toward her voice.

"I thought this wasn't your thing?" I ask, my voice rough and scratchy. "Research and development, right?"

Emily's got her feet kicked up on the couch's armrest, her laptop resting against her thighs. She's watching some sort of surveillance video with her arms crossed behind her head.

"I said I didn't have the patience for Charlie's line of work," she replies, sending a cruel wink my way. "I tend to be a little trigger-happy. More of a *shoot first, talk never* kind of girl."

"Speaking of patience, you're going to have to stay here a little longer," Charlie says from behind me. "We think our friend has more to say."

I take a seat as Charlie relays the information we have so far to Emily. Her expression becomes more and more serious, and she shuts off her video and sits up straight on the couch as he finishes.

"I was really fucking hoping it was bad luck and a coincidence," she groans, rubbing the back of her neck in small circles.

"I don't understand why this is so significant," I say, crossing my legs and resting my elbows on my knees. "So Kayden was recruited to Konstantin's team from someone else inside The Syndicate. It shouldn't be that hard to figure out who, right?"

Charlie glances at me and then turns back to his cousin.

"The problem is, The Syndicate is structured so that this *shouldn't* happen." She blows out a breath and meets Charlie's eyes, who nods for her to continue. "We have lots of low-level people doing small things for us—translating, passing information, surveillance. For the most part, they don't even know they're working for us. They're hired as contract workers by shell security or data processing companies. A few who show promise, like Kayden, are given a little more information so they can look into specialized targets. But above that level, every single member of The Syndicate is hand-picked and monitored by voting members—basically just us and our parents. It's why our teams are so small."

"So if Kayden was introduced to Konstantin's team by someone within The Syndicate who had information about my mother's whereabouts, then we have a much bigger problem," Charlie interjects, looking down at his hands. "Do we tell Bea? Or Gia?"

Emily hesitates, her fingers pressing harder into the back of her neck.

"I think we need to have more information first. Kayden may not know the names of The Syndicate members who are working for Konstantin, but if he could see the fucking sigil, he's got to know more than he's letting on."

"The sigil?" I ask, glancing between the two of them. Charlie doesn't look up, and after a beat, Emily answers.

"The dove tattoo. We've all got one." She lifts her hip off the couch and inches down her shorts so I can see the ink covering her hip bone. It's smaller than Charlie's, but the design is nearly identical. "It's unique to the upper echelons of The Syndicate—a dove with tears of blood. Something about the blindness of fate, the sacrifice of upholding it. Fucking dramatic, in my opinion, but we've gotten them for generations. If the woman he talked to showed him one, she has to be important to us."

I watch Charlie rub the wings tattooed onto his hand absentmindedly, nodding along with Emily's words. I convince myself that the urge in my chest to soothe him is completely platonic. After a few beats of silence, Charlie looks up at me.

"You up for another round?"

# Chapter 15
## *Gwen*

na's hair is soft under my touch as I comb it with my fingers. We've been on Charlie's couch—well, *our couch*, now—for the entire morning and early afternoon, watching the animated Star Wars show she loves. She's got a pillow propped under her side so the sensitive skin on her chest doesn't rub against anything.

I hear the door click open and shut again, gruff voices carrying in boxes of our clothes and the limited mementos we wanted to keep from the apartment. My stomach clenches.

"Are you sure this is what you want?" I ask, scratching the crown of Ana's hair. Her eyes are barely open, but she manages to roll them anyway.

"You promised not to ask that again," she quips, giggling at something happening on the screen.

I swallow hard.

"I know, but this is really fast. We can wait longer." My throat is tight as she shifts to look directly at me. Glare, actually.

"You spend all your time doing everything for me. Putting your life on the back burner to take care of me. We're doing this

157

because you love him, and he loves you, and this is what it takes to prove that you're not turning into a weird hermit because of me."

She turns back to the TV, and I nearly choke on the instinct to correct her. I know it's logical for her to assume that we love each other, but it's the first time I've heard that word in the context of our relationship, and I nearly break out in a cold sweat.

I don't love Charlie. Lust after him, maybe, after the events of this weekend. Trust him, albeit a little blindly.

But if Ana believing I love him makes this move easier for her, I'll let her think that. My stomach turns at the thought that eventually, Charlie and I will have to start saying it to each other, if only to keep up appearances. It shouldn't matter that it's a lie, but it does.

I turn over my shoulder as the door opens again. This time, the guys moving our stuff in are carrying a large box, grunting under the weight of it, which is strange. We left the vast majority of our furniture to be picked up for donation, and most of our things were cheap and flimsy, anyway.

Charlie enters the house behind the movers, observing their work with his hands in the pockets of his jeans. It's not like I haven't seen him dressed casually, but something about jeans and a t-shirt looks so domestic on him it has me in this weird, hormone-induced trance.

He catches my gaze, a soft smile pulling at the corner of his lips as he pulls the door shut behind him. I feel heat creeping up my neck and turn away without smiling back.

I had really hoped whatever insanity had overcome me while torturing Kayden would be contained to that room. But while it isn't as potent, I still feel his fingertips dragging over my knuckles when I'm trying to fall asleep.

I focus on the show, not understanding half of what's going on, as Charlie joins us on the couch.

"What's with the boxes?" I ask.

*Partners, maybe friends*, I remind myself as my skin buzzes with his proximity. It's been like this every time we're anywhere near each other this week, and it's driving me fucking insane.

"A surprise, for later," he replies, and when I look over at him, he smiles and nods at Ana, who isn't paying any attention to us. She seems to be caught up in her own mind, which is fair, seeing as it's her last day of treatment.

Even though it'll be a few months before we do follow-up scans and confirm that the treatment worked, her oncologist has been optimistic. And being done with radiation feels like something to celebrate.

Ana's exhaustion has only gotten worse, though, and she's barely wanted to eat after treatment, much less do anything fun. But her spirits seem up today.

She has a small grin the entire drive to the hospital, her fingers tapping to the beat of the music blasting through her headphones.

"You're staring at her," Charlie whispers as we turn off the highway. He's been quiet the whole trip, but I could feel his eyes on me.

"Yeah, I know," I reply, watching Ana close her eyes and lean her head against the window. Charlie's hand squeezes mine in my lap.

"You did a really great job," he says.

My answering smile is a little pained. "She did all the hard work," I argue.

"I didn't mean with the treatment, though you handled that well, too." He squeezes my hand again and I finally tear my eyes away from my sister. "I meant with raising her. She's a good kid, and that's because of you."

I barely hold back the tears welling in my eyes as I look back at her in the rearview. She's strong and funny and brilliant, and while most of that was the luck of the draw, I can't help but to be proud of my part in the person she's become.

"She could have been raised by wolves and would have turned out this good," I say, brushing off the compliment. But Charlie doesn't let it go.

"She's got someone in her life who loves her so much, they would go to the ends of the earth and back for her. That's not nothing, Gwen."

Charlie pulls into the closest parking space we can find, and Ana barely waits for the car to stop before she's opening her door.

"Ready for your finale?" I ask, looping my arm around her shoulders and pulling her tight against me. She wraps her arms around me, nearly tripping over my feet.

"As long as there's no encore," she sighs.

When we get checked in and upstairs, Dr. Mya is standing in the waiting room, a huge smile plastered on their face. I haven't seen them since Ana's last pre-treatment appointment, but they've been sending me updates on Ana's progress.

"Banana!" they call out, and Ana huffs a laugh under her breath. "Congratulations on your last day!"

The other techs and nurses I recognize from the last few weeks gather around Ana, telling her how well she did and how proud they are of her. Charlie and I hang back, letting her have this moment with the people who took care of her.

I notice a few of the staff giving Charlie a double take, glancing at him when Ana's preoccupied with someone else. Without thinking, I take a step toward him, angling my body so we're nearly touching.

160

"Territorial," he says under his breath, putting his hand on my hip and gently pulling me closer.

Heat climbs up my chest, but I scoff, trying to play it off.

"I am not *territorial*, it's just rude," I argue, but he's not wrong.

It strikes me that Charlie and I have absolutely no agreement about seeing other people. That he could be getting these kinds of looks from any and everyone, entertaining them, looking at them with desire. I hate myself for caring.

"They don't know that this is fake."

Charlie's hand freezes on my hip, the soft touches suddenly still. I try to turn, to figure out what's wrong, but he holds me in place, fingers digging in softly.

"Wouldn't want them to wound your pride," he says, his voice a little harder than before.

I want to argue, but what the hell do I even say? He might be right.

The staff dissipates, and Dr. Mya leads Ana back to the treatment area. She looks back at us, bag slung over her shoulder, and she smiles like she really is happy.

Ana's last appointment goes by quicker than any have before. When she returns from the treatment area, a radiation tech holding her hand and her jacket already around her shoulders, I can see it in her eyes. She made it. And even though we're not out of the woods yet, the feeling of relief is overwhelming.

People keep coming by, wishing her luck with her scans, making jokes about how they hope they never see us again. Charlie gets a few more lingering glances, but each time his hand finds its way around my shoulders, or onto my knee, and I curse myself for feeling comforted by the motion.

She's chatty the entire ride home, telling Charlie and me about the playlist that one of the nurses made for her based on the music she played during treatment. She's still exhausted, and based on Dr. Mya's latest message, she likely will be for weeks, but she seems hopeful.

Traffic is light, and we make it back relatively quickly. When we walk through the front door, Charlie turns to take Ana's coat.

Ana hovers in the entry a bit, rocking on her heels, and I realize that this is the first time we've walked into this house as our *home*. In the apartment, she'd kick off her shoes and launch herself onto the couch, or claw through the pantry for cheese crackers. But neither of us knows how to act.

Charlie must have been prepared for the awkwardness, because after hanging up our coats, he turns to Ana.

"This is *your* home now, okay? Leave your shoes in the hallway, decorate the walls, do whatever you want. Both of you," he says, glancing at me. "I know it'll take some getting used to, but I want you to be comfortable here. So, I've got a little surprise."

Ana looks to me, but I've got no answers for her, so I just shrug and let Charlie lead us down the hallway. When we land in front of the door to Ana's new room, Charlie steps back and urges her forward.

"Go ahead."

Ana cracks the door open, leaning in hesitantly. But all nerves seem to disappear as she sees what's inside.

It's the same bed I slept in on my first night here, but the olive green sheets have been replaced with pale blue ones. Pictures that used to be pinned to her bedroom wall with thumbtacks—of her softball team, of her and Gray in cosplay, of school events and championships—are hanging in frames above a small desk. But it's clear what the star of the show is by the way she beelines to it.

There's a second desk on the wall across from her bed, quite a bit bigger than the other one. Small rolls of fabric are stacked in open shelves under the tabletop, and books on costume design and fashion are lined up in color-coordinated rows along the back. Gold fabric shears, black charcoal pencils, rotary cutters, and other tools of the trade sit in pretty acrylic containers. A peg board hangs precisely on the wall.

But nothing stands out more than the shiny new sewing machine sitting in the center of the desk. It looks professional grade—dark blue and massive, with a fancy computer screen on the front. It's way nicer than the one Ana uses at the public library, or even the one Gray has.

"Holy shit," Ana whispers, running her shaking hand over the top of the machine.

I should tell her not to say shit, but *holy shit*. I've looked up how much these things cost, and it's in the hundreds, maybe thousands. This is way too much.

But as I watch Ana sit at the chair in front of the desk, peeking under the table and searching through the swathes of fabric, I can't chastise Charlie about how much he spent. Because if I'd been able to, I would have done the exact same thing.

"This is really mine?" Ana asks, swiveling around in her chair. She looks on the edge of tears, which has me swallowing back my own.

Goddamnit, I cry a lot lately.

"All yours, kid," Charlie says, crossing his arms and leaning against the door jam. "We've got to get your applications ready, right?"

Ana smiles so wide it's got to hurt her cheeks. She spins

around in a circle in the chair, the joy radiating from her like sunshine.

"Thank you, Charlie," she says, but Charlie shakes his head.

"Thank your sister. She's the one who made this happen."

Sometimes when I look at Charlie, I can't read a thing. He's so disciplined that every emotion is locked in some sort of safe I can't crack. But there are moments like this where it seems like he's unlocked it for me, letting me see everything written there.

An inside joke, a thank you, a gift. A moment where we're on the same team.

Ana collides with me, and I avoid touching her left side as I hug her back.

"Thanks, Ginny," she whispers into my shoulder. "For everything."

As EXCITED as she is to tear into new projects, Ana's also exhausted. The burst of adrenaline she got from her surprise is quickly dwindling, and we make quick work of the pho that Zane drops off. We eat on the couch, Ana curled up under a blanket with her bowl on her belly, as Charlie asks about the projects she wants to work on for her portfolio.

"All right," I say, stretching and grabbing her bowl from her lap before it spills. "Time for bed."

Ana just nods, flinching as she accidentally brushes her side with the blanket. Charlie grabs the bowls from my hands and nods.

"I got this. You guys go ahead."

I try to let all the gratefulness I feel seep into my smile before I help Ana up off the couch.

"Come on, let's go find our pajamas," I say, letting her lead me down the hall toward her room. When we get to the two doors at the end, she turns toward hers and I start to open the second spare.

"Where are you going?" she asks, standing under her doorway with a look of sleepy confusion on her face.

I look at her, and then into the spare room. It's got the same high-end yet basic furniture that Ana's room had when I stayed in it that first night.

"Umm..." I start, trying to figure out what in the world possessed me to think that my belongings would be in the second spare room.

Ana laughs, sparing me from coming up with a response.

"You don't have to pretend you sleep in separate rooms. I'm not that naïve." She turns and shuts the door behind her. "Don't be weird about it, though!" she calls through the door.

Charlie's chuckle from the end of the hall startles me, and I turn to him, a little shell-shocked.

"I have no explanation for what just happened," I say, arms raised in defeat.

Charlie just laughs again, and the sound settles like something warm and familiar.

"You can sleep in the spare room, if you'd like," Charlie says, a small, slightly sad smile on his face. "Or I can switch the office to this side of the hall and you can make your own room next to mine."

The offer is sweet, and I nearly laugh at the fact that this is the same man that I thought was blackmailing me into sex weeks ago.

"No, it's okay. She'd figure it out in a second if we weren't in the same room. If you're all right with it, I'm sure we can figure out how to share."

There's a quick beat, a flicker of some sort of strange cama-raderie, and for a second my desire seems manageable. Because if I'm being totally honest with myself, most people aren't lucky enough to have someone in their lives who is in their corner. And Charlie's in mine.

He clears his throat, crossing his arms and looking at his feet.

"I've got a surprise for you, too," he says, his ears red and voice nervous.

"You really did enough, more than I ever could have asked for," I reply, trying to repress my smile. I don't think I've seen Charlie anything other than confident and self-assured since that first night at Catalina's.

"Come on," he says, tugging at my arm and leading me down the hall toward his room—*our* room.

My pulse climbs, thinking about him lying next to me in bed, nearly touching, but not close enough.

But he doesn't lead me to the bedroom. Instead, he pushes open the door to the office and steps aside. The room looks split in two. One side has a desk against the wall that's covered in neatly organized files and folders, a laptop open on the edge. Bookshelves line the walls to either side, filled with the memo-rabilia of dozens of stories, faded photos of a group of kids near a glimmering ocean, books with well-worn spines. A heavy chair sits behind the desk, dark leather faded, with a checkered blanket draped over the back.

The other side has the same furniture, same layout, but everything is empty. The leather on the chair is crisp and new, and the blanket is the one that used to be draped over the end of my bed. But otherwise, it's identical.

"What's this?" I ask, stepping into the room. The last bit of sunlight is peeking over the rooftops of the outbuildings through the window. There would be a beautiful view of the wildflowers from here in the spring.

"Our office," Charlie says simply, standing next to me, arms nearly touching. "I know so much about Ana. Her dreams and her ambitions, what she likes and hates. And I feel like I know so little about you." His voice is calm, comforting, like the sound of rainfall on a roof. "At first I thought I hadn't been listening, or asking the right questions. And while that's part of it, maybe you don't know those things about yourself either."

I try to make my expression incredulous when I turn to him, but I think he can see the vulnerability in my eyes, how close to home he's hit.

"You have been Ana's sister, her mother, and her protector for so long. You've spent so much of your time making sure she has the world. I think you've lost sight of yourself. So I wanted to give you the opportunity to find yourself again." He gestures at my side of the office, but I can't look away from his face. "Take classes, become a potter, or a gardener, or a blacksmith. Fill the shelves up with pictures, or books, or those creepy porcelain dolls. Try a thousand things and hate them all until you love something. And then tell me about it."

There's this tightness in my chest that borders on pain. I love being Ana's sister, her parent-figure. While I've never resented her for even a second, there have been moments where I wonder who I would have been if I'd had the time and freedom to find myself. Now I'm standing here, in this office, being given the opportunity to do so. And I don't know how I got this lucky, stumbling into a frat-filled bar on a random Friday night.

"I apologize if I overstepped," Charlie says, taking a step back and giving me some space.

I realize the tears I've been trying to hold back all day are finally falling, and I wipe them away with a laugh.

"No, you didn't," I promise, taking a step closer to the desk.

A few of my personal belongings lay on top. A framed photo of me and Ana at her thirteenth birthday party. The mother's day card she made in the fifth grade that had the word *mother* scratched out and replaced with *sister*. The shot glass, one of a pair, that Kenzie and I stole from the fancy nightclub in Baltimore on my twenty-first birthday.

My grandmother's watch, cracked and bloodstained. My vampire book.

"This is a very kind gift, Charlie," I say on a breath, turning back toward him. "It means a lot."

He smiles, and I feel it sink into my bones.

# Chapter 16
## *Gwen*

The last two weeks have been hell. I feel like I'm descending into some sort of madness.

No matter how early I get up, Charlie's always gone, and I have no idea how he leaves without waking me. I'm tempted every single time to reach across this massive bed, to touch the indent in his pillow and see if it's still warm. But I don't, because I'm neither in a Hallmark movie nor fucking insane.

Ana's been home, joining her classes virtually whenever she can and sleeping as much as possible. I spend a lot of time trying to give her space, sitting behind the desk Charlie set up for me, staring at the empty shelves.

When Ana's done with school, and when she's feeling up for it, I text Zane and he takes us wherever we ask. Movies, walking trails, less popular Smithsonians we've never gotten around to visiting. Or we sit on the couch and scroll through the seemingly endless movies and shows Charlie's downloaded.

There's something so normal about our routine that I would be just fine if it weren't for the evenings.

It's like Charlie's proximity fucks with my cognitive function. He walks through the door sometime before six every night, and suddenly I'm reminding myself to blink at a normal rate. He and Ana cook together, she tells us about school, he talks about lawyer things I barely understand, we eat, I act like an alien trying to convince everyone they're human. I've taken on cleaning up after dinner while Charlie and Ana do SAT and ACT prep and review the Carnegie Mellon application. I brainstorm ways not to be in the same room as him until after he falls asleep.

It's so fucking ridiculous. You get horny while torturing someone with a guy *one time* and all of a sudden you can't function around him?

Charlie hasn't brought up the night at the farm again. We went back down into that basement three times. I mostly observed, watching how Charlie evaluated Kayden, the strategic way he timed his blows. After, he passed information to Emily, and they discussed strategies to suss out how far up in the organization the rot had climbed. But when we finally left, Emily half asleep on the couch, Kayden was very much still alive.

I doubt that's the case now.

I find myself thinking about it constantly. The feeling of balance with that knife in my hand. The calm control it gave me, so different from the rage-fueled decision to kill Bryan.

Ana sometimes says that when she's sitting in front of a sewing machine, the world around her disappears. Every sound other than the quiet, rhythmic hum of the machine fades into the background, and her hands move without conscious instruction. She just *feels it*.

I think I finally understand what she means.

And I'd probably be able to handle that, process what this

means about who I am, if it wasn't for whatever the fuck is happening to my nervous system.

Ever since that afternoon, I've been a string pulled too taut, a rubber band ready to snap. It's not fair to him at all—it's not like he knew teaching me would have this effect. But now I can't help but read into every touch, every glance. I catch him looking at me in the mirror while I brush my teeth, and my brain spirals, convincing myself there's longing in his eyes. We lay in his giant king bed, an empty space double the size of my body between us, and I have to remind myself the tension is imagined. That every slight movement he makes isn't meant to bring him closer to me. That he doesn't *want* my touch.

The passing attraction I felt for him when we met at Catalina's used to be manageable, especially considering how advantageous our agreement is. But now it's tormenting me.

I'm exhausted, and I know Ana can tell. I've done everything in my power to make sure she knows it's not her fault, but it's not like I can explain the truth.

I'm convinced that's why she's begging me to send her back to school.

"I've missed so much class right before AP testing, I don't even know how I'm going to pass. And what if I don't make softball captain next year? My resume is going to suck for Carnegie," she whines, pushing her food around her plate.

"Your resume isn't going to suck," Charlie says, kicking her gently under the table.

She rolls her eyes with a tiny grimace but keeps staring at her plate

"Admissions committees are understanding of circumstances like this," I add, but it doesn't seem to help. Ana doesn't say anything, but her jaw clenches and her cheeks burn. I feel lost, like I'm navigating this all wrong.

"I just don't want you to push yourself so hard that you hurt yourself," I say cautiously, setting down my fork.

"You're always telling me to listen to my body, that I'm the only one who knows what it's saying," she shoots back, her lip quivering a bit. My chest clenches. "Does that not count here?"

The room is silent, none of us moving an inch. I catch Charlie's gaze across the table, and his eyes are filled with pity that I'm pretty sure is for me, not for my sister.

"Look, give it two more days of going to class all day virtually," I acquiesce. Ana snaps her head toward me, a hopeful look in her eyes. "Two entire days, Ana, no skipping any periods or mid-day naps. If you can make it through and you don't feel completely awful, you can go back on Thursday, okay?"

She's so excited that she shovels the rest of her dinner down, throws her plate in the dishwasher haphazardly, and nearly sprints back to her room, presumably to call Gray.

My anxiety about sending her to school, the fear that she only wants to go back because she thinks she's burdening me, is enough to distract my reactionary nervous system from Charlie's presence.

For a while.

But soon, despite my spiraling thoughts and busy hands, the one-sided tension can't be ignored. I hate that I've been so fundamentally changed by that one experience I can *feel* where he is in a room, even when I'm not looking at him. It's like I'm attuned to him.

Torture.

"We need to discuss her protection," he says quietly as he joins me at the sink.

I hand him a freshly washed baking pan, he dries it, I build a domestic fantasy in my head that revolves around lazy kisses in dark kitchens, I want to die.

"Right," I say with a heavy breath, trying to focus. "You think she's in danger?"

"No, but I think people will take an interest in her, in both of you, especially as you're seen in public with me more and more."

I nod and scrub a plate that could definitely go into the dishwasher.

"So, how does this work? Does she need a bodyguard or something?" The thought seems ludicrous; some muscled-up dude in sunglasses following around Ana and her little gaggle of friends as they complain about their statistics teacher and sneak off campus for lunch.

"Not exactly," Charlie says, reaching over to pluck the overly-clean plate out of my hand. "Ana's school district has a security services department. I'll place someone I trust—her name's Lily—in their office. She won't follow Ana all the time, but she will have to have a geo-locator in her backpack so Lily can find her in an emergency." He takes a breath. "Ana doesn't even have to know."

My stomach clenches, but I know he's right. There would be too much to explain. Another secret I have to keep from her.

We're silent as we finish the dishes, my body and brain caught in separate chaotic spirals. When we're done, and the kitchen is wiped down, Charlie heads to the bedroom without a word.

Two days later, I have no choice. Ana made it through her entire school day both days, and even insisted on going out afterwards. She passed out right after dinner, but she held up her end of the bargain, so I have to hold up mine.

Charlie's up before I am, as always, and drives himself to work—which work he's going to, I never know. Zane's waiting for us by the car when Ana and I are ready to head into the city. Ana gives him a bright, excited smile, which seems to take him a bit by surprise. But Ana's sunshine cannot be dimmed today, and some of my fears are abated by how happy she is, for the first time in a long time.

On the forty-minute drive, Ana tells me about everything Gray's informed her has changed since she's been away. Melissa Bulwarke, the girl who sits behind her in history, shaved her head in *solidarity* with Ana's diagnosis, not knowing that Ana wouldn't need chemo. Mrs. Layman, the chemistry teacher, had to explain multiple times how radiation therapy wouldn't make Ana radioactive. Gray's taken to calling her *the most popular freak in school*, a title apparently previously held by the kid who's double jointed in his elbows.

When we pull up to the school drop-off zone, I want to ask her a million times over again if she's sure, if she doesn't want to rest for a few more days. But I don't want to stifle her joy. I'm hiding so much from her, and even if she has no idea, I need to show her I trust her completely with something.

"You call me if you need anything, okay?" I ask, because I can't help it.

She kisses me on the cheek as Zane opens her door.

"Thanks, Ginny," she says, and she bolts out of the car.

The ride back is so much longer than the one there. By the time I get to the house, I want to collapse. I'm physically and emotionally exhausted.

I planned to run errands, distract myself for the rest of the day until I could get into the pickup line obnoxiously early, but nothing felt right. So I told Zane to drop me off, hoping maybe I could lie on the couch with my phone on my chest, waiting to sprint out the door if the school office called me.

I didn't expect Charlie to be home. I assumed he'd be out for the whole day, like he's been every other day since we moved in, but I can hear the shower running in our room.

I was going to change before making myself another coffee and hunkering down in the living room, but I hesitate. The few times he's showered while I've been in the bedroom, I've had to recite the Gettysburg Address by memory to avoid imagining him dripping wet.

I need to get a fucking grip. I can't act like this forever.

Exposure therapy, right?

When I peek inside, I can see the bathroom door is cracked. Steam and light trickle into the dark bedroom, and Charlie is silent, so I cross my fingers that I didn't disturb him and make my way into our closet.

I shuck off my blouse and pants, wondering why I dressed like an office manager to drop Ana off at school, and grab loungewear from the built-in drawers without turning on the lights. I nearly trip and crash into the wall pulling on my running shorts, but steady myself at the last second, straining to hear if Charlie noticed me.

I can hear something that sounds like his voice, but the shower is still running. Quickly pulling socks on to muffle the sound of my feet, I lean out of the open closet door.

Was that...a grunt? Is he hurt? Or maybe it was a cough? I move out of the closet and start reaching for the bathroom door before yanking my hand back. What am I going to do? Walk in there while he's soaked and naked and check to see if he has a cold? What the ever loving fuck has come over me?

I turn, intent on burrowing into the couch and pretending I've been there the whole time, when I'm frozen by the sound of a long, low groan.

Holy fuck. This cannot be what I think it is.

No, absolutely not. I will not think about this. I will not react to this. He thinks he's home alone, and this is a massive violation of privacy.

But I can't move. His breaths are coming louder and faster over the shower spray, and my imagination runs away with itself. Despite the fact that I'm wracked with guilt and embarrassment, I can't help but think of slick skin and panting breaths, to wonder if this is what he'd sound like with his hands on me, with his body under mine.

My pulse is racing so hard I feel lightheaded. All the one-sided tension from the past two months is finally breaking, and the need that fills me is indescribable. The memory of every little touch, every platonic moment of contact, is overwhelming as I stand in the middle of the room, listening to him fuck his hand in our shower.

I can feel the flush crawling up my chest, my neck, my cheeks, my whole body feeling like magma. His breath catches, and he's silent for a moment, and I hold my breath.

"Fuck, Gwen, please."

For one millionth of a second, my body freezes, terrified that he caught me standing here listening to him. Until reality hits me like a train.

*My* name. He said my name. Groaned my name while he came. He's coming in our shower and he said my name. Gwen.

The words reorganize themselves in new orders a thousand times over as I listen to him pant. They don't seem real. *This* can't be real. It's got to be a figment of my imagination, the madness of unresolved horniness manifesting in a delusion-filled break. My hands twitch, desperate to touch myself, to feel how wet I am, to come while he says my name over and over.

The sound of the water turning off shocks me back to reality. I rush out of the room, trying to shut the door behind me as quietly as possible. Grabbing my purse, I'm texting Zane before I even have my shoes on. I need to go to the least sexy place I can think of.

ME

Can you take me to the Botanical Gardens?

# Chapter 17
## *Gwen*

"**O**pen mine next!" Kenzie sings, snatching her gift off the coffee table and tossing it into Ana's lap.

She giggles and carefully peels open the wrapping, preserving the paper as best as she can. Inside a glittery gold box are little tester sizes of a million different skincare products, from cleansers to moisturizers to sunscreens.

"Look, I love that you do the cool special effects makeup, and you're incredible at it. But if you're gonna put that shit on your face, you have to take care of your skin afterwards." Kenzie leans over and picks a few things out, handing them to Ana. "We'll try different things out and see what works for your skin, and then whatever you like the best, we'll go get full sizes together, okay?"

Ana sets the box back on the coffee table and throws her arms around Kenzie.

"Thanks, Kenz, you're the best," she says, and Kenzie squeezes her tight.

"Anything for my favorite kid."

I lean against the dining table, letting the comfort and joy of this day settle into me. Gray's sitting next to Ana, peeking over her shoulder while Kenzie explains the utility of oil-based cleansers. Linda and Paul are across from them, entertaining Maddie and watching the kids laugh with soft affection. Ana's *happy*. Really, truly happy.

"You feeling okay?"

Charlie bumps his shoulder into mine as he settles next to me, arms crossed. He nods at the hand I have cradled against my chest and I flex my fingers automatically, feeling the pull of the bandage on my skin. The cut isn't deep, but it hurts like a bitch.

"Yeah, it's nothing," I say, trying to brush it off.

Embarrassing enough that I slipped when Charlie pressed his fingers against my wrist to adjust my grip the other day. I will not let him know both the injury and my ego still sting.

Charlie just raises his eyebrows, like he knows I'm lying but is letting it slide, and I try not to blush. It's been a month of training, not just with him, but with other members of The Syndicate as well. Sometimes Lily, Ana's shadow, will have Zane cover her so she can teach me hand-to-hand combat. Zane walks me through restraints, both how to make them and how to get out of them. He even lets me drive every once in a while, showing me how to handle a car when it's running over one hundred miles per hour. Once, Charlie joined us at a tiny airstrip in the middle of a cornfield where Diego, The Syndicate's resident fleet expert, offered to teach me to fly a prop plane.

Some time over the past four weeks, I've learned to manage whatever the fuck happens to me around Charlie. It helps that I have a release valve now. I can blame the intimacy of learning how to kill and maim for the way my body thrums around him. And then, when we leave that little room, I can compartmentalize.

Or at least, that's what I tell myself. I don't have many other options.

There's a small part of me that I know is not convinced. It's fed exclusively by the memory of Charlie's voice coming from that shower. When I'm laying in bed at night, listening to his steady breaths next to me, it seeps into my mind like poison into water, permeating every inch of the insulation I've built.

We watch as Ana opens the envelope from Linda and Paul —tickets to Awesome-Con, their standard gift for the past few years. Ana thanks them, and she and Gray talk about their cosplay plans in a level of detail I will never fully comprehend.

"You think she's going to be up for tonight?" Charlie asks, watching Ana hide a yawn behind her hands.

She's been back at school for almost a month, and while her energy levels seem to get better every day, she still passes out right after dinner almost every night. But she slept in today, knowing we have evening plans for her birthday, even if they're a surprise to everyone but Charlie.

"You've amped her up too much. She'd tape her eyes open before she missed this," I reply.

"Hello? Can I open yours?" Ana asks for what sounds like not the first time, staring at Charlie and me with her eyebrows raised in annoyance.

I shake myself again and join her on the couch, squishing between her and Kenzie.

Ana carefully unwraps the paper and lifts the lid of the box I hand her. Her hand stills over the top.

"You don't even know if I'm going to get in." Her voice is tight, breaking a little on the end, as she picks up the sleeve of the vintage Carnegie Mellon sweatshirt. The edge is embroidered with the year she'll graduate.

"I've never been more sure of anything in my life, kid," I say, pulling her under my arm and tucking her head under my chin. She squeezes around my ribs, and I hope she can feel how much I believe in her.

An hour later, Kenzie takes off for her shift, and the McCallum family piles in their car to follow us to whatever surprise Charlie has planned.

"You're still not going to give me any clues?" Ana asks Charlie as Zane pulls the SUV around.

Charlie opens her door for her and narrows his eyes.

"You're not getting anything out of me at the last minute," he taunts, closing her door and walking around to the car to open mine. "She's not big on surprises, is she?"

"She's a control freak," I say, and Ana sticks her tongue out at me.

"Wonder where she gets it from," Charlie laughs.

Once Charlie's in the passenger's seat, Zane takes off, ensuring the McCallum's car is following close behind. Ana only lasts for a few minutes before she's trying a new angle.

"Hey, Zane," she says, meeting his eyes in the rearview mirror. "Do you happen to know what the surprise is?"

"Ana," I scold, slapping her arm lightly as Charlie laughs again from the front seat. "Don't try to get insider info a half an hour before we're there."

But she doesn't even look at me. She's staring down Zane, a challenge in her eyes, and I wonder how he'll hold up to her.

"Unfortunately, I've been sworn to secrecy," he says, nodding his head toward his boss beside him. "But I promise it's really fucking cool."

She laughs, and I lift my arms up in defeat.

"Can we watch the language around the minor?" I implore, shoving her arm again. All she does is laugh and look down at her phone, obviously texting Gray.

"Sorry about that, Miss Byrne," Zane says, but I catch his smile in the mirror.

A half hour later, we're pulling into a small artsy community in Reston. There are gallery spaces with warm lighting and wine bars with their outdoor seating covered in tarp to keep the ice away. Zane pulls us through a few blocks before idling in front of what looks like a large fabric studio.

We all get out of the car, Gray scrambling to catch up with Ana as his parents wrestle Maddie out of her car seat. Charlie hits the intercom, letting whoever's inside know we've arrived. I can't help but be impressed by the wall of fabric rolls lining one of the walls inside. It looks like art, the way they're stacked, creating a chromatic grid across the whole space. The big, open windows let us see a few long, high tables with drawers underneath, and I wonder if we're at some sort of upholstery shop.

I hear a whispered *holy shit* from Gray as a stunning woman in her thirties and a shorter, curly haired man around the same age appear from a back office. Paul turns around to give Gray a look, but he doesn't even notice because both he and Ana are staring open-mouthed at the studio.

"I'm assuming you know these people?" I stage whisper to Ana, and she turns to me incredulously.

"You've watched her YouTube videos with me. She's only like, the most famous cosplay designer of the last decade." Ana turns back to the studio as her apparent idol unlocks the door. "I think I might be dreaming."

Ana and Gray are nearly vibrating out of their skin as the designer shakes hands with Charlie and introduces herself— Jessica—and her co-designer, John-Michael. They usher our group inside, and the kids are shown to a table where they perch themselves on stools, watching in awe as their cosplay heroes start to unravel fabric and teach them things that go way over my head.

The adults, plus Maddie, stay back a bit, while Zane stations himself at the door like a sentry. When she gets squirmy, I swing Maddie onto my hip and walk her around the studio, and we point out all the colors that she loves.

I watch Charlie and Linda and Paul continue to chat quietly while John-Michael instructs the kids on some sort of intricate stitch that has them both smiling from ear to ear. I can't keep my eyes off Ana, though. It's such a hard emotion to place, this mix between joy that she's so clearly enjoying herself, and grief that I'm not the one who gave this to her. It feels selfish to even care about that when she's so happy, but I don't know how to turn it off.

The front door chimes, and I watch Charlie exit the building, his phone pressed to his ear. His brow is furrowed and his shoulders are tense as he leans against the side of the building, staring at the cracks in the sidewalk.

I bring a half-asleep Maddie back to her parents, watching Ana out of the corner of my eye as I wander toward the exit. Zane positioned himself between me and the door, and I don't know what he would do if I tried to leave. But I don't need to. The glass isn't thick enough to keep out Charlie's voice completely.

"I'm not sleeping with her, and I have no plans to do so. Gwen's proven that she can handle our work, and we negotiated an agreeable arrangement, like generations of Costas before us." The words are a little garbled, but they hit me squarely in the chest as I stare at Ana and Gray, pretending I'm not listening. "I'm doing my duty."

He's quiet for a bit, nearly motionless as he listens to the person on the other end of the phone.

"Are you asking as my sister or my boss?"

Clara then. I grip the edge of the table, wishing I hadn't walked over here, and knowing I needed to hear this.

"It won't be a problem. Gwen and I are a means to an end for each other," he says with finality. I don't turn to see if he's hung up, just plaster a smile on my face like I've been watching Ana and Gray the entire time.

The door chimes again, and I feel Charlie's warm presence slide next to me.

"Sorry, that was Clara," he mutters, keeping his voice low to not disturb the lesson.

I nod, angry at myself that I feel so betrayed. He didn't say anything I didn't already know, but it's still painful. Evidence that I'm not nearly as good at compartmentalizing as I think I am.

"We've got an event tomorrow night," he says, his body still tense. "A charity dinner. I'm sorry for the last minute notice."

I clear my throat, trying to swallow past the lingering disappointment, the words *means to an end* on repeat in the back of my mind.

"That's fine. I'll be with Ana and her class at the nature conservatory all day, but she's spending the night at a friend's after to finish their project. Her mom will take them to school in the morning."

Lucky timing, I guess. I would hate to leave Ana sitting alone in that house so soon after her birthday.

"Thank you," he says, and he sounds like he means it.

I refuse to look at him, watching Ana's face light up as she pulls a swath of fabric off the table.

"Thank *you*, for doing this for her," I whisper to Charlie next to me. I feel his fingers tap the back of my hand, almost like he wants to lace his fingers through mine. But he doesn't. And I'm grateful. Because I can't take being any closer to him.

"You did this," he whispers back. "I told you, you're the kind of person who would do anything for the people you love. You found a way to protect her and give her the world."

I swallow hard and watch Ana, her brows furrowed in concentration as she studies a seam Jessica is showing her. And, even though it does nothing for my self-preservation, and only half of me actually wants to do it, I reach out and take his hand in mine.

He doesn't let go.

# Chapter 18
## *Charlie*

I'm in the shower when I hear Gwen knock on the bedroom door.

"Hi," she calls, clearing her throat loudly. "I'm going to get changed while you're in there, if that's okay?"

I turn the shower as cold as I can.

"Of course," I reply. "Dress is on the bed."

I try to focus on *anything* except the sound of her pulling off her clothes, of her unzipping the garment bag Zane picked up. But it's impossible. I shouldn't think about her nearly naked in the room next to me. Shouldn't wonder which parts of her skin have freckles and which don't. She's never in anything more revealing than bike shorts and t-shirts around me. I'm desperate to see more of her.

I spent the morning with Sammy, helping him unload crate after crate of booze into the inventory room, praying that the manual labor would keep me from thinking about Gwen.

It didn't work.

I give it a few minutes after the noise of her changing seems to quiet and turn off the shower, drying off and wrapping a towel around my waist. Part of me hopes she's gone into the living room, so I can delay the inevitable. But when I open the door, water still dripping from my hair onto my shoulders, she's standing with her back toward me.

There's not a word for how incredible she looks. The dress, made of sapphire blue silk, drapes around her body in waves. The straps are thin and the zipper lays open to the small of her back. I feel indecent even looking at her, the lingering cold of the shower doing nothing to temper the heat crawling up my chest. The fabric ends just below her knee, but a generous slit exposes her thigh as she tosses a camel-colored coat on the bed. She's slipped into beige heels, the straps meant to circle her ankles still undone.

It takes every ounce of control I have to school my expression as she turns over her shoulder. Her cheeks heat immediately as her eyes drop to my bare chest, and against my better judgment, I allow myself to read her flushed skin as attraction instead of embarrassment.

I'm so incredibly fucked.

"You look beautiful," I say.

The word is too small, but it's as close as I can get in English, maybe in human language. She's been stunning since the moment I saw her, but there's something about her dressed to *feel* beautiful—not for the practicality of doctor's appointments or errands or torture—that has me nearly speechless.

"Thank you," she replies quietly, clearing her throat and shifting her eyes back to mine. "Mind helping me with the zipper?"

I should put on clothes first, or take another cold shower. But I just nod, and she pulls her hair over her shoulder and offers me her back.

She has freckles along her spine. Tiny, almost translucent ones, not nearly as prominent as those on her shoulders and nose and temples, but still there. You'd never see them unless you were as close to her as I am now.

Goosebumps erupt across her skin where my fingers drag as I pull up the zipper. There's no longer a string pulling us toward each other. There are magnets. Impossibly strong ones, demanding I touch her more, press myself against her.

I force myself to take two steps back.

She whispers a soft *thank you* without turning around, and I move to the walk-in closet, taking the opportunity to put some distance between us and recenter myself.

I dress without paying attention to my movements, focusing on slowing my heart rate and calming my raging hard-on, trying to think about work or who will be at the fundraiser, or literally anything but the constellation of stars that decorate Gwen's spine. But it's no use.

It's been impossible to focus on anything else since my call with Clara. I knew my sister thought my decision to bring Gwen into the family was impulsive. I never in a million years imagined she would threaten to vote against our marriage.

For a marriage of a council member to be legitimate in the eyes of The Syndicate, there has to be a vote. My parents and Clara, as well as my cousins, aunts, and uncle, will all have a say in whether Gwen is the right person to join our efforts. There hasn't been a rejection in generations, and although the Matriarch or Patriarch technically holds veto power, I've never heard of it being used.

I tried to downplay my feelings on the phone, to prove to Clara that I was acting responsibly and following a well-laid plan, but the mindless panic I felt when my sister made her threat shifted something fundamentally.

There's no use in denying how much I need Gwen. The pressure in my chest, the primal need for her, is terrifying. It's getting harder and harder to refuse myself those moments where I read into her flush. Where I wonder if I've made a mistake, keeping her at an arm's length.

When I'm decent, dressed, and as put together as I fear I'll be able to manage tonight, I return to the bedroom. She's sitting on the edge of the bed, one leg crossed over the other, leaning over to secure the strap around her ankle. Her copper hair falls over her shoulders in large, soft waves, obscuring most of her, but I still get a glimpse of the bodice of her dress pulled tightly against her breasts, forcing them to spill over the top.

Before I can recognize the terrible idea for what it is, I'm kneeling in front of her, brushing aside her hands and placing her foot on my knee. Her jaw drops just a fraction, pupils dilating and breath caught in her chest. I watch my own fingers intently as I fasten the clasp, trying to ignore what's become obvious. It wasn't embarrassment, or intrigue, or gratefulness, or even me projecting my attraction on to her. The look she's given me constantly, since the afternoon at the farm, is desire.

I can feel the heavy beat of her pulse inside her ankle as I fasten the second shoe. I wonder what she would do if I pressed my lips there. If I dragged my mouth up the inside of her leg, under her knee, between her thighs. Would she open them for me, arch her back and hook her leg over my shoulder? Lace her fingers through my hair and pull, or push me closer? Would she do it because she wants to? Or because she thinks she has no choice?

I don't know how long it is before Gwen clears her throat, but it's too long for this to be interpreted as anything innocent, with my thumb rubbing circles on the inside of her calf. She crosses her leg but doesn't unclench her fingers from where they're curled into the comforter. I need to stand, to move, to not be on my knees in front of her, but if I do, all pretense will be thrown out the window. She'll see how painfully hard I am, just from the thought of tasting her.

She whispers her thanks again, seemingly able to collect herself better than I am, shifting her legs to the side and slipping off the bed.

"Going to finish getting ready," she mutters, and it's not until the door to the bathroom clicks closed behind her I'm able to stand.

We both have a better grip on ourselves by the time we get into the car and head toward D.C. Zane's playing bodyguard outside Ana's friend's house, and while I could have pulled another driver, something about the feeling of the wheel beneath my hands is steadying.

The drive is tense in a way it's never been between us. I ask about Ana's field trip, and Gwen asks about Sammy, but both of us seem lost in our thoughts, trailing the ends of our sentences and humming non-committal responses. There are a few moments where I feel her almost break. She works herself up, pressing her fingernails into the skin of her hands, and opens her mouth to say something. But every time, she seems to talk herself out of it.

Despite the unbearable need to hear what she wants to say, I know it's for the best. There's already so much happening tonight. Neither of us can handle whatever we can feel simmering between us.

The unease means that I don't warn Gwen about anything that's about to happen at this event, which I realize as we're pulling up.

"I'm sorry," I breathe out, reaching into the center console to grab the valet key and trying to avoid touching her. "I should have told you about the event."

A smile flashes across her face as she smooths over the indents she's made in her hand.

"It's okay. I assumed I'd just follow your lead." She gives me a tight, nervous smile that has my chest clenching.

The valet lets me out of the car, and I wave off the second attendant so I can open her door myself. When she slips her hand into mine, a shudder runs up my spine.

I hold her coat out to her, the evening unseasonably cold for the beginning of summer. With her back to my chest, and her scent of lemon and amber surrounding me, I lose all sense of reservation.

"I trust you," I whisper, lifting her hair from where it's trapped under her collar. "And I think I'd much prefer following your lead."

It's a stupid risk, ramping myself up like this before an event where we'll be surrounded by people. But it's worth it when Gwen glances over her shoulder, her cheeks rosy and eyes round with surprise, and only hesitates a moment before reaching behind her and slipping her hand into mine.

The ballroom is packed to the brim with people laden with luxury, sipping top shelf liquor and chatting around high top tables. Despite the bodies moving around the room, the air is chilly, and Gwen tucks herself closer to me, shivering without her coat, which we left at the check. I slip my arm around her shoulder as we step into the fray.

I notice familiar faces—other foundation and non-profit executives, high-level government officials, donors with pockets far deeper than mine. We may have been invited to this dinner, but the price of a seat is well more than the value of most people's cars.

"People recognize you," Gwen whispers as we make our way through the crowd. A few eyes flicker our way, some with nods that I return, some avoiding my gaze completely.

"The Costa Family Foundation is well known in these circles," I say casually, snagging a glass of champagne from a passing waiter and handing it to Gwen. We find an empty table, and I find it difficult to remove my arm from around her shoulder so she can sip her drink.

"Some of them look afraid of you," she says, almost like a question rather than an observation.

"Afraid of *us*," I rebut, winking at her.

She rolls her eyes, but the corners of her mouth pull into a smile around the rim of her glass.

"I thought your family's work was a bit more...discrete." Her eyes flicker around the room, many of the guests averting their eyes as soon as hers land on them.

"Most of them are only aware of the work of the foundation, but the legacy of The Syndicate is well known among those whose families have crossed our paths in the past. Even if they don't know why they should fear us, their parents and grandparents have warned them to stay in our good graces, or to stay invisible." I smile and nod over Gwen's head at the man waving at me, who starts making his way toward us. "But don't worry, tonight should be filled with more allies than enemies."

Gwen starts to respond, but the Administrator cuts in.

"Mr. Costa, so good to have you here. Your mother was too kind, sending a donation and her son in her absence. I hope she and your father are enjoying their anniversary trip."

Clara's been busy spreading rumors, it seems. There's a pang in my chest, the memory of seeing her in the hospital for the first time etched into the back of my eyelids.

"Good to see you. And I'll pass on your well-wishes. They both seem to be enjoying themselves, to the point that they forget to check in with us." Dr. Loden laughs, and I slip my arm back around Gwen, finding comfort in the soft skin of her shoulder under my hand. "Let me introduce you to my partner, Guinevere. Gwen, this is the Administrator of the Federal Aviation Administration, Dr. Christopher Loden."

Gwen holds out her hand and he shakes it, smiling widely at her.

"Nice to meet you, Dr. Loden," she says, sweet and unphased.

"Lovely to meet you, Gwen, and wonderful to see you settled down, Charlie," he laughs, shooting me a look over Gwen's head. "We thought you might be an eternal bachelor."

"Just had to wait for the stars to align," I reply, unable to suppress my smile at how true the words are. "Are we going to be blessed with the company of your husband tonight?"

Dr. Loden rolls his eyes and turns over his shoulder, searching the crowd.

"He's here somewhere, probably annoying the DEA staff like he enjoys doing so much," he says, his smile indulgent and amused, before turning back to us. "I hope you don't mind if we talk a bit of business over dinner. The Secretary has been asking about local non-profit organizations that have international arms to assist trafficking victims identified at airports, and few have as far of a reach as the Costas."

"We'd be happy to discuss." I glance down at Gwen, who already has her eyes on me, some indiscernible look in her eyes.

Maybe it's the overt affection throwing her off—this is the most we've touched each other since meeting. Again, I'm reminded of what I don't know—does she want to touch me as badly as I want her, or is this simply an obligation?

Suddenly, the doors at the other end of the ballroom open, and the Secretary of State walks through, his wife and son a few steps behind.

He thanks the room for their attendance and generous donations to the resettlement non-profits benefiting from tonight's fundraising, and after a round of applause, invites us into the adjoining room for dinner service.

We all filter slowly out of the opulent ballroom, event staff leading us individually to our seats at round tables draped in white linen. Gwen and I are seated with other non-profit executives, most of whom greet me personally.

There are polite introductions with congratulations on promotions and inquiries into kids' college applications. Gwen keeps up easily, smiling and chatting, her hand easily falling to my shoulder when she laughs at a joke someone made. We share glances and smiles, and at one point I pick up her hand and press my lips to her fingers, just because it feels right.

"You're very good at this," I whisper to her when she recommends a wine to one attendee hosting an oyster tasting event, whatever that is.

"You'd be surprised how much I'm relying on a decade of waitressing," she says under her breath, and I can't help but laugh.

As dinner is served, speaker after speaker makes their way to the small stage at the front of the room, presenting awards and thanking attendees. Videos meant to pull at our heartstrings and empty our wallets are played on giant screens. All the while, Gwen and I seem pulled toward each other, our chairs moving closer together as I lean in to whisper an explanation for a story someone tells, or for her to ask about someone's reaction. I stretch my arm to rest over the back of her chair, and after a moment of hesitation, she rests her hand on my knee under the table.

I'm not paying any attention to what's being said on stage. Because all I can think is, *what if?* What if this isn't acting? What if fate really was this kind to me?

Under all the hope is a final, well-buried level of fear. That all the *what ifs* are true, and it's because she wants the version of me she sees when we work together. Someone who controls every moment, every movement.

I swallow past the sinking feeling in my stomach. Maybe

for her, I could be that. I'm realizing I'd do almost anything for her. Maybe I can do this, too.

Gwen's hand squeezing my knee brings me back to the present, and most of the table is looking at me with their eyebrows raised.

"Mr. Gao asked how we met, and I thought you'd like to tell the story," she says, obviously suppressing a laugh. I can't look away from her. She seems so *happy*. Relaxed, giggling, smiling at me like we share an inside joke, because we do.

"If you'd believe it, we met at a bar," I say, winking at her and watching her blush rise as a smile splits across her face. "She mistook me for a bartender and she was so beautiful, I couldn't correct her until I had to admit I didn't know how to make her favorite drink. Haven't been able to look away from her since."

Her expression softens, and she lifts her hand to my face. I press a kiss into her palm.

"Well, you two are quite the pair," a younger guy who I don't recognize pipes in, reaching to grasp the hand of his partner. "Seems like we finally know which of the Costa crew will get married first."

Clara, Emily, Bea, and I have always known our marital status was a topic of conversation among our peers and colleagues. It's the way of the world when you have the generational wealth and legacy of the Costa family. Still, it can be frustrating to have people speculate on something so critical and personal, especially with what marriage signifies in our family.

But when I look back at Gwen, I don't feel irritation. All I can feel is a sureness that goes far past any arrangement we've made.

"I'd bet on it," I say, mostly for her.

She leans forward slightly, and I nearly dip my head to kiss her before I stop myself, pulling back a bit too abruptly. Gwen's eyes flicker to my mouth, and hurt flashes through her eyes for a moment before she seems to shake it off, leaning into my shoulder and smiling at the table.

"He's not much one for public displays of affection," she says, covering for my reaction. There's a few awkward chuckles, but a man I don't recognize laughs louder than everyone.

"Ah, man, you can kiss your wife in public. I think we're all adults here," he exclaims too loudly, earning us glances from the surrounding tables. His partner winces a bit when he leans over and plants an enthusiastic kiss on their cheek, but gives him an indulgent smile when he pulls away.

Gwen glances at me from under her lashes, and my pulse starts racing. I could brush this off, give us an out, but I don't *want* to. Now that I've been presented with the opportunity, my whole body craves her lips against mine, her body closer than I've ever allowed us to be.

"Not my wife quite yet," I say, slightly quieter, trying to ask her a question with my eyes that I can't ask out loud. *Is this okay? Do you want this? Please?*

Her eyes search mine for a moment, and maybe there is some thread tying us together, because I know she understands.

"Oh, soon enough, though. No need to split hairs."

Her pupils are blown wide, probably a mirror of mine, as I lean into her. Her hand squeezes my knee so tightly, I don't think she's doing it consciously. I leave the last millimeter of space for her to close, needing one final confirmation that she's choosing this.

Kissing Gwen can't be explained. Every cell in my body is humming at some new frequency as she sighs into me, relaxing her grip on my leg and opening her lips ever so slightly. My hand grasps the back of her chair like a lifeline, to stop myself from slipping my fingers into her hair. I want to lose myself in her, in the soft mouth and intoxicating sighs and gentle touches. I would have forgotten we were in public if a glass didn't shatter across the room, jarring us apart from each other.

"Good husband," Gwen says softly, dragging her thumb across my bottom lip to wipe away her lipstick.

Our table laughs and claps softly, turning to each other to talk about first loves and weddings, but I once again can't hear what's going on around me. Because the words *good husband* are now forever intertwined with the feeling of that kiss. My pulse won't slow, and I can't hide the effect Gwen is having on me. She must see it, must feel it, because it's reflected in her eyes, slightly hooded and filled with desire.

But in a single second, Gwen shifts. The lust clears from her expression, and she removes her hand from my leg, twining hers together in her lap. She leans into the conversation next to us, asking about the couple's eldest daughter who's pregnant with their first grandchild.

The change is so sudden that I'm left stunned into silence. Throughout the rest of the night, she's charming and gorgeous and engaging, but she doesn't make another move to touch me more than is absolutely necessary. There's a coldness that settles over me without her touch that's intolerable. And I'll do anything to fix it.

# Chapter 19
## *Gwen*

Every moment since I got home this afternoon has been so tense, I feel like I'm being torn at the seams. We spend the entire drive back in absolute silence, Charlie's grip on the wheel so tight that his knuckles are white under the ink. The car inches slowly through evening traffic out of the city.

For the last few months, I could convince myself I'd been imagining the feeling of his eyes on me when I'm turned away, the unending current of electricity between us. But not tonight. Every touch was a second too long and an eternity too short. I feel out of my mind with need and frustration, each emotion feeding the other until I'm clenching my teeth to resist acting on them.

And that fucking *kiss*. It's ridiculous and cliche and reminiscent of an early 2000s rock ballad, but I feel like I've been waiting my whole life to be kissed like that. And Charlie's reaction—like it wasn't just a requirement of our agreement, like he wanted me to kiss him. Like he wanted me to *want* to kiss him.

*This isn't fucking fair*, I think as we pull into the driveway. It's not fair that his actions are so at odds with his words, or that

I'm so attracted to him I interpret every lingering glance as lust. It's not fair that I've convinced myself he wants me, too.

I don't wait for Charlie to open my door as we pull up to the house. I feel childish, nearly stomping as I make my way to the front porch. I put the code in wrong twice before I can press my thumb against the reader, Charlie too close behind me, the warmth of his body only fueling my angry-horny fugue state.

As soon as I'm inside, I march straight to the kitchen and throw my coat on the counter, pouring myself a glass of water from the tap and trying to calm myself down. I've never been particularly good at calm, though. I'm especially bad at it when I can hear the object of my frustration calmly hanging up his jacket, taking off his shoes, even collecting my coat from the counter and putting it away properly. It's maddening.

I know he's standing there. Probably leaning against the peninsula, his eyes searching the tension in my shoulders and the way I roll my neck for the answer to how to navigate this.

"Gwen...." he starts, his voice so soft and kind.

I drop my glass in the sink and whip around.

"Don't."

Even though I'm desperate for answers, I can't face them right now. I'm too angry at him, too afraid I'm about to be embarrassed, too worked up. My blood is boiling under my skin, and I know I'm reacting irrationally, but I can't stop.

"Please, I want to talk, to explain—"

"Explain what?" I cut him off, checking his shoulder as I walk past him, moving around the kitchen table, trying to put space and heavy furniture and *anything* between us. "You're going to explain what happened at that dinner? How that *kiss* was part of our business arrangement? We're a means to an end for each other, right?" I laugh and tilt my head to the ceiling, the sound slicing my throat like shards of ice, hot tears welling behind my eyes. Fuck being an angry crier.

Charlie is quiet for so long that the rushing in my ears finally ebbs, my pulse slowing just enough to let reason slip in and force me to wipe my eyes. When I lower my head, he won't look at me, and the pit in my stomach grows until I feel like it's swallowing me whole. Embarrassment slams into me, hard and fast and cruel, replacing anger so quickly it makes me nauseous. I read too much into all these insignificant moments—his hand over mine at the pig farm, and the glances across the table, and his fingertips on my spine. I can't believe I was so fucking stupid. He told me what he wanted that first night. I'm the idiot who couldn't keep my shit together.

He's gripping the counter's edge so tight, so still he has to be holding his breath. His head is bent, and his hair hiding his eyes, and I suddenly miss the tiny apartment Ana and I were holed up in before all of this. At least there, I could disappear. At least there, I knew who I was to everyone around me.

Charlie still hasn't said anything, and now I think he doesn't know what to say. How do you respond to your rent-a-wife when she's just overstepped your boundaries by one hundred fold? I'm getting whiplash from how quickly my emotions are changing, but I can't force him to apologize for not wanting me the way I want him.

"Charlie, look, I'm sorry, okay?" My voice is high and pleading and honestly, I wouldn't be surprised if he wants to end our arrangement now. *Fuck, fuck, fuck.* Sure, Ana's done with treatment, and her bills are paid, but the last few months have done a number on me, and I don't want to lose him. "I misunderstood some things that happened between us and it was so inappropriate to get upse—"

"Stop." His voice is weak and begging, but he still hasn't lifted his eyes. I'm rooted to the floor, unable to move. "Of course...." His hands squeeze the counter even tighter as he forces a breath out. "Of course I want you, Gwen."

When he finally looks at me, all I can see is desperation. A deep well of something he's hidden deep for so long, it's nearly iced over. Physical pain couldn't put this look into his eyes.

"Every single touch from you is torture I beg for. I've wanted you since the second I saw you, and instead of acting on that, I opened my fucking mouth and offered you money and support in exchange for your friendship." I want to say something, anything, to quiet the guilt clearly gnawing at him, but he pushes off the island and stalks toward me like he's afraid I'm about to run. Like he needs to hold me still with his own hands. "I made it impossible, because no matter how much I wanted you, and no matter how much interest I thought you showed, I could never be sure I wasn't holding too much over you. And I was never certain that you would feel you could say no and everything would stay exactly the same. That you and Ana would still have all the support in the world, and we could still be partners and work together and be...be friends."

Every goddamn cell in my body wants to fold myself around him. I want to drag my fingernails against his scalp and soothe him. To make sure he knows I never thought he would use the money for Ana against me. To tell him to match his breaths to mine.

"I know, Charlie," I say on an exhale, closing the distance between us by a step. We're so close I could reach out and touch him. "I don't know how to convince you it's true, but I want you. I don't feel like I owe you this. I don't feel obligated. I know you would never ask this from me in exchange for everything you've done. You're not Ben. You're *my* Charlie."

He looks at me like he can't believe me. Like he doesn't know how. I reach out my hand and lace my fingers through his, squeezing.

"Please believe me. Please trust me," I whisper, desperation in my voice.

Because that's what I am. Desperate to touch him, to kiss him again, to feel his skin on mine, to break the tension that's been building for months. His fingers slip into my hair, cradling my head and tilting it so I can't help but look directly in his eyes.

"I want to be whatever you want, whatever you need," he murmurs, and my heart clenches.

"I just want you, Charlie," I say. I don't know how to explain that I don't need anything else.

He hesitates for just a moment, like he's waiting for me to balk or pull back. And then his lips are on mine again.

The fire he ignited at that table is rekindled a thousand times over as he kisses me. I pull my hands from his to grasp the back of his neck and force myself closer to him. My lips open on a gasp as he moves his hand to my thigh, slipping under the slit of my dress and yanking my leg up around his hip. Tongues and teeth and lips meet, both of our breaths heavy and heartbeats loud as he kisses down my jaw and lifts me, pushing me onto the dining table.

My legs fall open for him on instinct and he stands between them, kissing down my neck and chest until my back arches and I have to lean on my hands to support myself.

"So fucking beautiful," he whispers against my skin, teeth nipping the swell of my breasts and the slope of my shoulder. "Every goddamn day, but especially today. Beautiful and confident and charming and brilliant."

I can't form coherent sentences. *Yes,* and *Charlie,* and *please* slip out of me on moans and heavy breaths as one hand slips further up my leg and the other pulls down the strap of my dress. I can feel how wet I am already. My hips lift, seeking his touch, and he pulls away to stare down at me. His eyes are wild, hair mussed and cheeks flushed, and there's no denying he needs me as much as I need him. It's intoxicating in a way I've never felt, in a way that's addicting.

"I want to touch you," he whispers, his fingers tracing the slit in my dress, hiked up so high it's nearly exposing me. "Can I touch you, Gwen?"

I tilt my head back, reveling in his voice, the feeling of his fingers on my body.

"I need to hear you say it, mia filettatura," he says, drawing my eyes back to him. I nod frantically, and his hand grips my thigh harder.

"Yes, please touch me," I beg, my chest heaving.

His eyes trace my figure once more, disheveled and needy, before he leans down and grips my hips.

"Arms," he says, his voice gravelly, and I latch myself around him. My mouth is on him before he can say anything else, and he carries me to our room as our teeth and tongues clash, consuming each other.

He lowers me slowly onto the bed, crawling on top of me as his mouth seeks out mine, like it's impossible to separate. The desperation is mutual, our hands mapping every inch of skin, mine pulling at the button down shirt still tucked into his pants.

When he moves backward to stand at the foot of the bed, I think it's to catch his breath. He unbuttons his shirt, and when I sit up to help, he takes a step back.

"Take off your dress, Gwen."

There's something in his tone that's wrong. Off. The look in his eyes has changed. Still hungry, still dark and filled with lust. But there's something calculated in his expression, like he's thinking three steps ahead.

But I don't want controlled, commanding Charlie. I want him to let go under my touch. I want him out of his mind with pleasure, like I know I'll be.

I tilt my head at him, watching him unbuckle his belt before I reach out and stop him.

"What just happened?" I ask, pulling his hand away from his waistband.

A flicker of something vulnerable passes over his face before he reverts to *that* look. It reminds me of when we sat in the living room of the pig farm with Emily and strategized Kayden's torture. Or of how he looks when he's teaching me how to aim a gun.

"I want to see you, to touch you," he says, and even though I know that's true, it feels like that's not the *whole* truth. I shift up onto my knees, pulling the strap of my dress back over my shoulder.

"You're lying," I say, tugging at his hand and searching his gaze. "I mean, there's something else. Something changed."

He's frozen solid, his expression a mask. My whole body is on edge, but there's a feeling in my chest I have to listen to.

"Nothing..." he stumbles a little, taking a step back. "Nothing changed. I want you. You said you want me. If you've changed your mind, we can stop."

His voice sounds almost robotic, and my chest clenches.

"It feels like *you've* changed your mind," I say, trying to keep the accusation out of my tone. Charlie opens his mouth to argue, but I stop him. "Your whole demeanor shifted as soon as you stood up. Like you started planning out how you were going to touch me."

His brow furrows, and he opens and closes his mouth a few times before he can find an answer.

"I guess I was doing that. But I want to be what you need."

I shift so I'm sitting cross-legged, aware that my neckline is pulled low and my hair is disheveled, but I can't keep touching him without understanding.

"I don't know what you mean by that," I say, patting the space next to me on the bed.

He looks a little bewildered for a second, but finally sits down next to me.

"When we're together, I..." he stutters, dragging a hand down his face. "I'm in control. That's the person you know me as. Decisive, vindictive, exacting. I want to be the man you want."

The feeling in my chest gets tighter as his eyes meet mine, filled with confusion. It's rare for Charlie's emotions to be clear on his face, but this is a moment of true vulnerability.

"You are not *just* those things." I press my fingers into his palm and slide them so we're interlocked. "There's so much more to you than that. You can be cruel and kind and everything in between. You go into the world and willingly bloody your hands for what you know is right, and then you come home and cook for me and quiz Ana on SAT questions. This wouldn't be the first time you've been soft with me, Charlie."

He squeezes my hand, his eyes dropping to where they're interlocked.

"It's not just wanting to be soft, Gwen." He takes a deep breath, like he's fortifying himself for something. He's afraid, I realize. I don't know if I've ever seen Charlie afraid before. "I want to give everything to you. I want to hear your voice telling me how to move, how to touch." A silence, just two beats too long. "I want to submit. To you. Here."

He's shaking under my fingers and I can feel his pulse ripping through him like a tide.

"Is there something wrong with wanting that?" I ask, cradling his cheek with the hand not grasped in his.

His Adam's apple bobs with a hard swallow.

"Submission is weakness." He nuzzles his chin into my palm like his body's natural reaction opposes his words. "I force submission from people all the time. I bring them pain and terror, and when they finally break for me, they have *lost*. And if I give that to you, you'll control all of me, and I don't know who I'll be anymore."

My heart feels like it's in a vice, his words pained and vulnerable. I think about the way he touched me tonight, every kiss and breath. And the moment that stands out more than any other is the way the word *please* sounded, him begging me to let him touch me.

It's never been something I've consciously thought about before. No former partner has ever asked me to submit or to take control. Sure, I feel more comfortable making choices for my everyday life, but it was never something that bled into my bedroom, or my partner's, or the walk in at work. But when I think about Charlie begging for me, heat fills my chest like a bonfire.

"I think I would like it," I say as I drag my fingernails down his neck, shoulder, arm. "My life has been nothing but chaos until I met you. Controlling what I can has always felt good, natural. I don't want the demanding, decisive version of you. I want you, whatever version is the most honest. Whatever version brings us the most pleasure."

He shakes his head like it's not possible to believe.

"Even if that was true, I couldn't put that on you. I promised to take care of you."

A familiar heaviness tugs at my chest at how much he's thought about this, how careful he is that he never adds to my burden. Since the moment I met him, Charlie has been softening every blow that comes toward me, making the parts of my life he can influence as easy as possible. And I think I've done that for him too—given him a soft place to land in a world that's purposefully, necessarily hard. Taken care of him in the ways I'm able to. Met his viciousness. But maybe this is another thing that I can give him that feeds me, too.

"But Charlie," I whisper, leaning my body into his, "you looked so pretty on your knees for me."

He takes a moment, but eventually he meets my eyes. Fear and desire battle in equal spades in his expression, and I wish there was some way to convince him of how I feel.

"Are you sure?" His voice shakes as he asks, and I squeeze his hand.

"We'll take it slow. Just be together in whatever way feels natural," I murmur, sliding closer to him on the bed and resting my head on his shoulder. "There are no expectations here. We can figure this out together."

The tension in his body loosens, and he sighs as he wraps his arm around my hip and pulls me close. It feels good to be wrapped around each other like this. Right. When it seems he's finally relaxed, I shift and rest my forehead against his.

"Can I touch you, Charlie?" I ask, placing a featherlight kiss against his lips. He chases my mouth as I pull away, nodding. "I need to hear you say it."

He opens his eyes and looks at me like he can't believe what's happening is real.

"Please, Gwen."

Even though my body is pleading for me to go fast, I do my best to honor my word.

With my hands cradling his face, I press my lips to his. The kiss is slow and gentle, sweet and perfect. Charlie plants his hands on the bed, gripping the comforter like he's afraid to move. I kiss his lips, his jaw, the column of his throat, every leaf of the olive branches inked on his neck. His breathing is heavy, and his shoulders shake a bit, and I wonder if it's fear or restraint. I fiddle with a button on his shirt, enjoying the way his breath sharpens when my fingernails brush his chest.

"Can I do this?" I ask, releasing the first button. He grips the bed tighter.

"Please," he whimpers, and I acquiesce.

Pushing the shirt off his shoulders, I trail kisses down his arm and back, up his neck, until I'm back at his mouth.

Each time we move to a new item of clothing—his belt, his undershirt, his pants—we go through the same process. I ask, he begs, I press my mouth to every inch of skin I can find. If I thought moving slowly would relieve the tension, I couldn't have been more wrong. Every touch from me makes his voice more desperate the next time I ask for permission. Every inch of control he gives up to me fills me with a sense of euphoria I can't explain. Like his trust is an aphrodisiac. When Charlie's in nothing but his boxers, I slip off the bed and stand in front of him, a near perfect inverse of our positions on the kitchen table.

"Do you want to touch me, Charlie?" I ask, and when he nods, I reach forward, pull his hand, and place it on my hip. "Go ahead."

With reverence, he runs his hand up my hip to my ribs, the soft silk of the dress slipping under his touch. My eyes are closed, soaking in the feeling, when I feel his lips on my shoulder, the inside of my elbow, my fingertips.

"Can I do this?" he asks, finding the zipper on the dress in the middle of my back.

"Yes."

His eyes don't leave mine as the dress falls off my shoulders, skimming my hips and pooling on the floor at my feet. He leans forward and takes my face in his hands, kissing me again and again.

"Perfect," he whispers against the skin of my neck.

I stand there in front of him, in only my underwear and these ridiculous heels, and let him touch me. He kisses and bites, grabs and brushes, everything eager and soft, slowly ratcheting me higher and higher. I can't help but latch my fingers into his hair as he pulls my nipple into his mouth, the slightest tinge of pain heightening my already-overwhelming pleasure.

He kisses down my sternum, bracing my ribs with his hands so that when I arch back under his touch, he's supporting me. He keeps moving down, tongue and lips and teeth, until he's nipping at the top of my underwear.

"I'm going to touch you now." He says it like a question, looking up at me, nearly all the fear gone from his expression.

"Yes, now, please."

I feel like I'm going to come apart the second he does, my body humming with pleasure. But he doesn't touch me, not where I need him. He just rests his hands on my hip and shifts me toward the bed so we've switched places yet again. And drops to his knees.

He lifts my foot and places it on his chest, undoing the strap and removing the shoe before kneading his thumbs into my arch. It feels so unspeakably good, I can forgive the fact that it relieves some of the tension in other parts of my body. He repeats the process with my other shoe, placing kisses on the inside of my calf.

"I thought about this earlier," he says under his breath, teeth skimming the inside of my thigh. "About what you would do if I touched you like this."

I don't know if I say *me too* out loud, but he grips my legs a little tighter and shifts me so my ass is perched at the end of the bed.

"Please let me make you come," he begs, and the sound of his voice alone has my back arching. He kisses the inside of my knee. "Please."

"Yes," I pant, letting my legs fall further open. "Make me come, Charlie."

He doesn't waste a second. Almost before I realize what's happening, he slips my underwear down my legs, baring me to him. I would be self conscious being exposed around anyone else, but I can't when he's looking at me like that. Eyes wild, shoulders tense, vibrating with his own need.

I was right, all those weeks ago. His inked hands do look good against my skin.

"Fuck, so fucking perfect," he says before spreading me open with his hands and licking me from pussy to clit.

We groan together, the pleasure at finally being touched where I need him overwhelming, making me delirious. He takes his time, finding the rhythm and motions that have my hips lifting off the bed. My legs are slung over his shoulders, his head trapped between my thighs as he sucks on my clit.

I know I'm saying something, moaning his name or maybe nonsense, and I fall back against the bed, which only allows him to bury himself closer. My body feels strung like a bow, toes curled against his shoulder blades, stomach muscles coiled, fingers clamped in the sheet above my head. I'm hovering around the edge of the orgasm of a lifetime, but can't seem to fall over the ledge.

Just when I think I'm going to lose all the momentum we've built, Charlie presses a finger inside of me, pumping along with the rhythm of his mouth. My back arches, my breath catching in my throat as he adds a second finger, groaning as I squeeze my thighs around his head.

He moans, and it's the vibration against my clit that sends me over the edge. My stomach clenches and heat unfurls through my whole body as my orgasm rips through me. I can feel my pulse in every inch of my skin as pleasure sinks into my bones, blacking out my vision momentarily.

Charlie slows his movements, working me through every wave of pleasure, extending my climax until I'm shaking, my muscles exhausted. I slowly relax, feeling Charlie's lips on my thighs, murmuring words I can't hear over the rushing in my ears. When I can muster the energy, I sit up and run my fingers through his hair, scratching at his scalp until he lifts his face toward me.

"Come here," I ask, my voice rough and low.

He peppers kisses over my entire body as he stands, finally taking my mouth with his. I can taste myself on his lips and open further to deepen the kiss.

I scoot further back on the bed and he chases my mouth, crawling over me and settling on top of me as I lay down. I can feel his cock, hard and trapped in his boxers, as I wrap my legs around his waist.

"Gwen, please, I can't—" Charlie starts, but cuts himself off on a groan as I pull him closer, grinding my center against him. He drops to his elbows, drawing my bottom lip between his teeth as he grinds against me. He's already working me back up, the exhaustion from moments ago forgotten under his body.

"I want you, Charlie," I pant into his shoulder as he kisses my neck, likely leaving a mark. "I want this, us, together."

He pulls back to hover over me, and I brush his hair out of his face.

"How do you..." he hesitates, glancing down at my bare body and then up at the ceiling, cursing something in Italian that I don't understand but makes me smile. "Can you tell me how you want to fuck me?"

A spark lights up under my skin at the thought of asking for exactly what I want, of knowing he'll give it to me. A thousand scenarios flash through my mind, each one hotter than the last.

But something stops me from asking for them. Because even if I don't get all those fantasies, if we decide tomorrow this was a bad idea, I want this intimacy with him more than anything else.

"Maybe for tonight we just feel out what seems natural," I say, tracing the tattoo of Hermes on his ribs, face agonized and turned toward the heavens. Charlie shudders under my touch. "If that's okay with you?"

He presses a kiss into the crown of my hair, and I feel my heart skip a beat.

"Yes, that's okay with me," he mutters into my hair. "We have lots of nights ahead of us."

I flush, my heart now pounding loudly in my chest. I refuse to read further into his words, to let the oxytocin fool me into taking them at more than face value. Partners, friends, and fucking. Mutual gratification.

My stomach dips, but I chase the feeling away by pressing my lips to Charlie's and trailing my hand down his chest, to his stomach. I brush my hand over his cock, desperate to feel him, and he curses into my mouth.

"Please, mio filo, you're torturing me," he moans, his hips jerking, forcing his cock into my hand.

"Ironic," I laugh, reveling in the blissfully pained look on his face. "I am getting addicted to the sound of you begging, though."

"I have no issue begging for you, Gwen," he says, and my name sounds a bit like a prayer on his tongue. "All I've wanted to do for months is beg for you to touch me, to let me touch you. And I'll keep begging for you until you tell me to stop."

His words thrum through my body. I'm painfully turned on, my pussy clenching around nothing, desperate for him again.

"You have condoms?" I ask, slipping my hand against his cock again.

He nods repeatedly, seemingly unable to react coherently to my question until I release him. He shakes himself, kisses me once, and then hops off the bed. When he returns from the bathroom, he tosses a handful of silver wrappers on the nightstand, keeping one tucked between his fingers.

"Optimistic," I taunt, but my teasing tone disappears as soon as lowers his head between my legs again, working me with his mouth until I'm soaked, pleasure warming my skin.

"I should have said something before we started, but I've been tested since my last partner and everything came back negative," he says as kisses up my stomach, resting his head on my sternum and looking up at me.

"It's been years, but same here," I reply, running my fingers through his hair again. His chest rumbles, and I can't help but laugh at how much he looks like a pleased cat. "I'm not on birth control, though."

"That's okay," he says, pressing a kiss to the space between my breasts. "You're sure you want this?"

I slip my fingers beneath the waistband of his boxers, tugging them slightly.

"Just as much as you do," I say, leaning up to kiss the hollow of his throat as I work his boxers down his hips.

"I promise you, that's not possible," he breathes, but before I can argue, he captures my lips with his own, helping me remove the last of his clothes.

I barely register the floral tattoo wrapping up his left thigh as he sits back. I'm mesmerized by him. The muscle and scars and ink, all making Charlie who he is. A vicious man with a soft soul. Someone who believes in fate.

He hands me the foil packet and I carefully tear it open. The wrapper disappears onto the floor with our clothes, and I carefully roll the condom on to his cock, stroking him as I do. He hisses at my touch, his breathing turning labored, and when I finish, he grabs my hand and laces our fingers together.

I watch his face as he positions himself at my entrance and slides into me, slow and deliberate. The feeling of him inside of me is so good, so full, words escape me. He keeps his eyes on where we're joined until he's fully seated. We both take a few deep breaths, adjusting to the feeling of being this close.

"You okay?" I ask when he doesn't move for a few minutes.

He looks at the ceiling again and then back to me, a pained smile on his face.

"I have possibly never been better in my life. Just need a moment."

Something about him nearly losing it so quickly fills me with a sense of pride that's probably toxic. I lift my hips off the bed, rocking myself on his cock. Pleasure and laughter rip through me in equal spades as Charlie grips my hips to still me.

"Gwen, I need to feel you come around my cock, and I can't do that if you keep doing *that*," he groans, and I think about ignoring him. About seeing how quickly I can make him come. Of overwhelming him with pleasure again and again, until he doesn't know if he's begging for more or for me to stop. But I resist the temptation and relax my hips back onto the bed.

After a minute more, he moves to brace himself over me, lifting one of my legs high around his hip along the way. Slowly, he withdraws himself to the tip, holding himself there as he kisses the juncture of my neck.

"You are incredible." I feel his words more than I hear them as he slides back into me, forcing my back to arch as he fills me. "Beautiful." Another thrust. I clench the hand wrapped in his, and he moves them both near my head, not holding me down, just pressing our bodies closer. "Fucking Christ, Gwen, you feel better than I imagined."

His mouth is on my shoulders, my neck, my breasts, urging me closer and closer to another peak. I moan his name into his shoulder, leaving marks with my teeth, unable to stop myself from clawing closer to him.

He doesn't stop. Words and bites and kisses. Every time he

thrusts into me, our bodies pressed tightly together. I hear my name over and over, whispered and moaned against my lips, and with his teeth wrapped around my nipple, and into the place where my shoulder meets my neck. It's too much, too good, too close.

My orgasm hits me without warning, stronger than the last one, pulling me under like a riptide. I feel myself clench around Charlie, fingernails digging into his back, chanting his name into his neck.

His lips find mine, and he murmurs something that sounds like *yours* until he stills, breath caught and muscles tight, forehead pressed to mine.

After a moment, he lets out a breath, and we're panting against each other, skin sticky with sweat. Charlie kisses my lips, my cheeks, my forehead, any skin he can reach without shifting his position. When I finally collect myself, the last waves of my orgasm receding into a tingling sensation in my limbs, I can't help but laugh.

I feel his smile even as I keep my eyes closed, his own laugh huffing against me where his lips meet my skin. He shifts gently, slipping his cock from inside me, prompting me to moan involuntarily. He rolls over next to me and immediately tugs me on top of him, cradling me against his chest and pressing his lips to the top of my head.

"We should clean you up," he says, his words muffled by my hair.

"In a few minutes," I mumble against his chest, my pounding heart soothed by the slow rise and fall of his chest.

"Okay, just a few minutes."

I must drift off, the adrenaline drop and comfort of Charlie's arms lulling me to sleep, because I wake a little while later to him lifting me from the bed, an arm under my legs and around my waist.

"I can walk," I yawn, trying to blink the haze from my eyes.

"And I can carry you." he says simply, propping me on the edge of the tub and starting the shower.

We rinse off together, silent and sleepy, a few lazy kisses exchanged here and there.

He does the same thing three more times that night, after every time we wake up tangled together, desperate for each other's touch.

# Chapter 20
## *Charlie*

The sun peeking through the curtains is warm on my skin when I wake up. It has to be nearly noon, but I don't move a muscle, because Gwen is tucked into my side, breathing steadily. She's wrapped her body around me, her leg curled over my hip and her fingers twitching on my chest. Copper hair floats around her like a tangled halo.

I never want to leave. I'm content to the point of pain, each of her heartbeats increasing this strange and pleasant pressure in my chest.

The most poignant emotion I can identify is *gratefulness*. When I'd laid her on our bed, my first instinct was to lock down my desire, to suppress what I wanted and execute the carefully thought out steps I'd performed with every previous partner. She'd noticed the change, and I don't know if I'll ever be able to express how thankful I am that she did. That she pushed me to be honest, that she wants me for who I am.

I watch her sleep for a while longer, feeling relaxed in a way I haven't in a long time. Eventually she rolls over, stretching her arms above her head and slowly blinking awake. I take my time soaking in her body, the way she forces her back to arch, lifting her breasts. The sheet twists around her waist, and I want to unwrap her again, to witness her naked and moaning in our bed.

Gwen's surprised expression when she notices me stops that thought process in its tracks. It passes in a moment, her cheeks heating before she pulls the sheet up over her chest.

"Morning," I say, suppressing the desire to touch her.

"Sorry, I kind of thought all that was a really vivid dream," she mutters, covering her face with her hands.

My stomach drops a bit, but I try to temper my reaction, reaching over to pull her hand away from her face.

"Are you okay? With what happened?" I ask, running my thumb over her fingers.

I thought I would hate having my emotions be so out of control, but the need to comfort her, to ensure we didn't cross any sort of line, outweighs any demand for restraint.

She rolls back toward me, giving me an apologetic smile.

"I'm sorry. I'm not doing this super well." She presses a kiss into my chest that deflates some of the anxiety building there. "Yes, I'm very okay with what happened. Thrilled even. Thank you for trusting me."

I can't see her expression, because she's nestled herself into my side, but I pull her even closer, pressing my lips into the top of her hair.

"Thank you, too," I whisper.

We lay there for a moment, listening to the sound of each other's breathing.

After some time, I feel her shift underneath me. When I lift my arm, she rolls out of bed, dragging the sheet along with her, wrapping it around her.

"I'm going to go, you know," she waves at her body, and something in her expression is a little guarded.

"We showered like five times last night," I joke, leaning over to grab the end of the sheet and tug her back toward the bed.

She smiles, but she can't quite seem to meet my eyes. Is it really embarrassment, or self consciousness? I told her I would beg for her, and I meant it. She can't honestly believe I'm not overwhelmingly obsessed with everything about her.

"Still need to brush my teeth. Get ready for the day," she mutters. "I've got to pick up Ana soon."

There's a pinprick of doubt popping the bubble of elation in my chest as I observe her. She's uncomfortable, and not just being naked around me. She shifts her weight from foot to food, fiddling with the hem of the sheet, and my stomach sinks.

"Gwen..." I start, but I don't know what to say. She said she was thrilled. I need to believe her.

"I just need a few minutes, I promise," she says, her eyes apologetic and her smile almost a grimace.

If she needs space, I'll give it to her, even if my natural inclination is to wrap my body around her. I let go of the sheet, and she disappears into the bathroom.

As I listen to the water run, to the sound of Gwen's soft humming over the shower, I try to temper my anxiety. I scrub my hands down my face, counting my breaths and centering myself. Last night I said I would do anything for Gwen, and I meant it. What she's given me, the trust, vulnerability, and patience she's offered, can't be quantified. There's no way I can return something that I can barely explain.

So whatever she wants. If she comes back in this room and says this was a mistake, that she wants to go back to partners and friends, I'll do it, even if it tears me apart. If she wants the world burned down or gilded, I'll give it to her happily. Anything for Gwen.

She takes her time getting ready, and every second just makes me more certain.

When she finally returns her hair is damp and she's wrapped in an oversized towel. The sheet is folded and tucked under her arm, which I can't help but smile at.

"Okay, sorry about that, just needed a minute to collect myself," she rushes out, nearly tripping over herself as she places the sheet gently at the foot of the bed.

I smile at her, arms crossed over my chest, leaning up against the headboard.

"Nothing to apologize for," I say, wishing she would come closer, but keeping my hands to myself.

She grips the top of the towel like she's afraid it's going to fall.

"That was kind of inevitable, don't you think?" she blurts out, her words too loud and too anxious.

I tilt my head at her.

"Inevitable?"

"I mean," she hesitates, biting the inside of her cheek. "It was bound to happen. We spend all our time together. We sleep in the same bed. I mean, you're going to be my husband." Flush crawls up her chest and neck from under her towel, and my body reacts instinctually to that word on her tongue.

"Do you want this to happen again?" I ask, trying to keep my tone neutral. She can say no. I need to know that *she* knows nothing will change if she does.

She's still blushing as she nods, meeting my gaze intentionally for the first time this morning.

"If you do, yes. We can update the contract if you want. Partners, friends, benefits?" Her voice cracks on the last word, her nose wrinkling at the word.

It's more than I could have hoped for that first night in my kitchen. More than I probably deserve. My father used to tell me not to ignore the small kindness of fate, and I won't now.

"I'll add an addendum, if you want," I say, leaning forward and taking her hand. "Whatever you need, Gwen."

She looks almost like she wants to argue, though I don't know if it's with me or herself. But after a moment, the expression clears, and she takes my face in her free hand and kisses me. It's soft, and easy, and the kind of kiss you give someone when you know there will be a next one.

"Looking forward to our expanded partnership," she whispers through a laugh, and I pull her down on top of me.

# Chapter 21
## *Charlie*

Gwen and I have parked outside of the high school, anxiously watching the clock. Kids stumble out, one by one, their eyes glazed over, pencils clutched in their hands. Gwen's fingernails are cutting into the skin over her arm, creating those deep crescent moon indents. I reach out and brush her hand away.

"She's going to do great," I say, soothing over the irritated skin with my thumb.

"I know, I just worry about her," she murmurs, her eyes flickering between the clock on the dash and the exit of the school. "She's had a long week."

I hum in agreement, watching Gwen try to push down her anxiety. Ana was back at the hospital on Thursday for new scans and a biopsy to check if the radiation treatment worked. The oncologist said it would be a week or so before we got results back, and Gwen's been understandably on edge ever since.

That edge has been soothed by the new routine we've found together. Taking Ana to school in the mornings, training some new skill or staying in the city to work with the Costa

Family Foundation. Making dinner with Ana while I quiz her on algebraic equations. Forgoing sleep to make up for all the lost time.

The exhaustion barely affects me. Touching Gwen, learning how to make her fall apart under my hands, trusting her more and more every day, is better than any rest I've ever gotten.

As unfair as it is, the more she gives me, the more I want from her. It's a vicious cycle that I'm a willing victim to.

"There she is," Gwen whispers, unbuckling her seatbelt and breaking me out of my daydreaming.

Ana appears in the main archway of the school. Her hair is knotted in a loose, messy bun on top of her head, and her sweatshirt is tied around her waist. She looks tired, like the rest of the kids, but she's not openly sobbing like the kid sitting on the brick planter.

I don't remember the SAT being this traumatic.

Gwen pops open the door and waves at her sister, whose face lights up when she sees us. I get out too and watch her make her way toward us.

"She doesn't look devastated," Gwen whispers through a smile.

"Told you she'd be fine," I reply.

Ana walks straight to Gwen and slumps into her arms, squeezing tightly.

"You did it, kid," Gwen whispers into her hair.

"I'm just glad it's fucking over," Ana groans, and Gwen swats her on the head.

"Dont' say *fucking*," she chastises, but her smile is wide and her words have no bite.

To my surprise, Ana makes her way around the front of the car and wraps her arms around my waist.

"Thanks for making sure I didn't completely fail," she says.

After a moment of motionless shock, I put my arm around her shoulder. I swallow past the lump in my throat, which only gets worse when I see Gwen's expression over the top of the car.

"You did that. I just made some flashcards," I say, unable to look away from Gwen.

She's always been so easy for me to read. Not just because of who I am, but because she's got such a short leash on her emotions, they pour out of her without restraint. And I know what look I see in her eyes.

"But they were fantastic flashcards," Ana says, releasing me from the hug and breaking my eye contact with Gwen.

I open Ana's door, asking her about the test, trying to rein in the feeling in my chest.

We take Ana out to lunch, and she fills the conversation like she always does, talking about the hardest questions on the exam and making jokes about how bad a score she can get and still get into Carnegie.

The live wire between Gwen and I feels different. Hyper-sensitive. She's sitting next to me in the booth, her attention rapt on Ana, but I can almost *feel* her thinking about me. She's on my right, and every time her hand bumps into mine while we eat, I almost jump out of my skin.

It's a relief when my phone rings, giving me the chance to focus on anything else but the way Gwen scrunches her nose when she laughs with Ana.

*Aurelio Costa* flashes across my phone screen, and my blood immediately turns to ice. My father rarely calls me directly. Mama has always been the talker, calling just to check in. The last time my father called me was the day of mama's attack.

I excuse myself from the table abruptly, cutting off Ana mid-sentence. Gwen grabs my arm before I can leave, her brows raised and her eyes filled with worry. I try to smile, but it comes out as more of a grimace, because the only thing running through my head is *she's gone, she's gone, something happened and she's gone.*

I step out into the hot summer afternoon, trying to find a relatively secluded area before picking up the call.

"Pa," I answer, trying to keep my voice level.

"She's coming home." His voice is shaking, filled with raw relief. All the dread I was feeling disappears in an instant. "The physicians say she can come home. She's healed enough, and she's even started talking. She can come home."

I slump against the window of the flower shop I'm in front of, scrubbing my eyes. *She's okay. She's alive. She can come home.*

"She's coming home," I repeat, though I don't know if it's the first time I've said it out loud. "You called Clara?"

"Yes, and Gia and Alessia," he replies on a sob.

It takes him a moment to collect himself, and I'm thankful for it, because the relief I feel is overwhelming. The guilt, too, though I try to swallow that down.

"Okay, yes. My god, she's okay." I clear my throat, near tears for the second time today.

A bell rings softly, and when I look up, Gwen appears in the doorway to the cafe. She whips her head around, and when she spots me, she looks scared.

I genuinely smile at her this time, the tears I've been holding back finally falling. She moves through the crowd of afternoon shoppers, pushing her way through until I'm able to grab her around the waist and pull her to my side.

"She wants you here, Carlo," my father says on the other end of the line, his voice cracking. "She's asking for all of you— the entire council."

I think Gwen can hear him through the receiver, but she

doesn't ask questions, just wraps herself tighter around me. And I realize I want her here, that her presence makes the relief sweeter.

"Tell me when, and I'll be there," I say, leaning my head back against the window and staring at the sky.

"You should bring her." He says it quietly, not a command but a request, an offer. "Guinevere. If she is really going to be your wife. She should come, too."

I look down at Gwen, still clearly concerned for me, but no longer afraid. She nods. She doesn't even completely know what's being asked of her, but I can see the trust in her eyes.

"When?" I ask, pressing my lips to Gwen's forehead.

"Be here by next Saturday."

# Chapter 22
## *Gwen*

Dusk is settling in the sky, muted pinks and oranges fading quickly into blues and purples, color dancing along across the dashboard as we inch down the highway toward Dullas. I lean against the window, tilting my face into the fading warmth.

Charlie's quiet as he drives, his fingers tapping an uneven rhythm on the steering wheel. The past week has been a strange combination of stress and elation. We've spent most nights with his head in my lap on the couch, where he tells me about his mom—about her attack, but also just about *her*. Stories of her when he was young and learning, picking up on her mannerisms and watching her analyze everything around her. Of how she commanded respect, how everyone trusted and feared her in equal spades.

I've felt nauseous with nerves all week, and even though I've tried not to be obvious about it, I think he knows. It means something that I'm coming with him, meeting the rest of his family, the council. Emily texted me a few times, giving me insight into the cousins and aunts, reminding me to listen more than I speak, which shouldn't be a problem, because I have no idea what I would say.

Honestly, I'm anxious about the flight itself. I've never been overseas, and the idea of getting on a plane that's crossing an ocean is mildly horrifying. I would be more worried about being so far separated from Ana, but she's absolutely thrilled to be spending the first weekend of summer vacation at her best friend's.

"Are you thinking about the flight?" Charlie asks, clearly trying to rein in a laugh.

I shoot a glare at him.

"How could you tell?"

"You're clawing at your arms again," he says, and I realize he's right. Such a shitty nervous habit.

"I don't love flying, but I especially don't love the idea of falling out of the sky only to crash and drown and for our bodies to never be discovered," I say, slightly incredulous that he's so comfortable with the concept. I suppose if you've flown hundreds of times in your life, you get used to it.

"You didn't take many flights as a kid?" he asks, taking my hand in his.

"We took trains mostly. Or drove," I admit, feeling a little splinter in my chest, a bittersweet memory finding its way to the surface of my mind. "I love road trips."

"When's the last time you went on one?" he asks, and I shut my eyes. He's shared so much with me. I can find that strength.

"Before Ana was born. I think I was around nine. Isabelle wasn't so bad when I was really young. Still desperate for attention from some guy, I'm sure, but she had time for me. I'd watched this movie, I don't even remember which one it was, but it was set at Coney Island, and I couldn't shut the hell up about it." I let my eyes flutter open, watching the trees in the fading light as they whip past us. "She rented a car, and we drove almost five hours straight. Sat on the beach, rode roller coasters on the boardwalk, ate hotdogs and ice cream, the whole bit."

Charlie's silent, his thumb rubbing soothing circles on the top of my hand. There's a lump in my throat that's hard to swallow past.

"It's complicated, you know?" It's not really a question, but he nods anyway. "She's not all bad. And I have a lot of good memories of her from when I was young. But my love was never really enough for her, and neither was Ana's. And as I got older, she saw me more as a second parent to Ana than a kid of her own."

"I know," he whispers.

I imagine he does, with all the research he did when we first met. For the first time, I feel a little empathy for the single mom who probably thought she was doing everything she could to find a safe life for me.

"Sorry, this is a bummer topic," I shake myself, but he squeezes my hand and lifts it to his lips, kissing my knuckles.

"I want to know everything about you."

He's being sincere, that much is obvious. It fills my chest with that same strange, painful, beautiful feeling I had watching Ana hug him outside of the school. I break his gaze, cheeks heating, hoping that he can't read me the way he reads everyone else.

Half an hour later, we pull up to a private hangar where security agents check our passports and direct us down a paved road running parallel to a runway. Attendants meet us and unload our luggage, ushering us into an empty lobby with low, comfortable lighting and damn near a whole buffet of food laid out.

"I thought you said you fly commercial unless you're working," I whisper, hugging my arms around myself and trying not to touch anything.

"I do, and we are, but there are perks that come with being a Costa."

Perks, apparently, include private security screening, someone handling our bags for us, customs clearance before we even leave the lobby, and a private ride directly onto the tarmac after the rest of the plane has boarded. We're ushered to first class with a few other passengers who look vaguely familiar and probably famous, and there's a glass of champagne in my hand before I'm even fully seated.

I know I should soak up this experience. I haven't been on an airplane since I was a pre-teen, when one of Isabelle's ex's invited us to his family home in Maine. We'd flown coach, and there was so much turbulence I'd ended up crying in her arms the entire flight. But I'm distracted.

Charlie is careful to hold my hand when we step onto the plane, and point out the emergency exits and safety equipment, and talk me through our flight path while keeping his palm on my lower back, like he's steadying me. And everything about him, and the way he's caring for me, and the way my body is reacting, is overwhelming. I feel like I'm on the edge of screaming, but I don't know what will come out of my mouth when I do. At this point, I'd prefer the flight phobia.

It's hard to be anxious, though, with the sheer luxury of this experience. Each pair of seats can be modified into lie-flat beds, and a private mini bar is stocked with snacks and drinks. It's like we're in a tiny capsule, the sliding door by the aisle seat able to shut us off from the plane.

"I doubt I'm going to be able to sleep," I mumble after the incredibly gorgeous flight attendant notes when we'd like our beds set.

Charlie rests his arm around my shoulder, pulling me tight against him.

"Try, mia filettatura," he insists, kissing my temple in a way that makes my stomach clench. "We'll be there so much sooner if you do."

It's probably a function of the luxury of the experience, but once we've taken off, I'm a lot less afraid than I thought I would be. The attendants serve us a light dinner that tastes better than most things I can cook, and the night sky makes it impossible for me to see the terrifying ocean beneath us.

Once our seats are transformed into beds and I've changed into sweats and one of Charlie's t-shirts, Charlie tucks me into his side again, and I wrap my body around his. I drift off to the hum of the plane's engine and Charlie's whispered stories of sparkling seas and white-washed stone.

## Chapter 23
## *Charlie*

Gwen sleeps nearly the entire eight-hour flight to Rome. I probably should have too, but I couldn't stop staring, or muttering stories about my childhood to her, or running my fingers through her hair.

I want to drown in her.

I can't explain it any other way. It's a desperation I didn't know I could feel, a joy bordering on pain. It's unfathomable that I once believed I could live my entire life with her and not beg to be her entire world. That I once thought fate brought us together to solve mutual problems.

I was wrong. Fate didn't bring us together. *She* is my fate.

I wake her when we start our descent into Rome, and the first thing she does when she blinks awake is smile at me. It warms me from the inside out.

We deplane, and another conspicuously dressed security agent meets us at the end of the jet bridge. Gwen's a little jet lagged, rubbing her eyes as the agent ushers us toward a private lounge.

We have enough time between flights for a quick breakfast. Gwen seems more quiet than usual, but I don't push her. This weekend must be overwhelming, not only meeting my family, but being so far from Ana. Especially while we're still waiting for her results to come back.

It feels like everything is happening at once. It's an effort to bite my tongue, to stop myself from adding one more thing to her plate. I have to remind myself that we have all the time in the world.

The flight from Rome to Bari is mercifully short and almost completely over land, which means Gwen spends most of the time staring out the window, grinning from ear to ear at the sight of the horizon and the bright blue waters of the Tyrrhenian and Adriatic.

We land in Bari, and it's drier than I remember. The smell of the sea is sharp and soothing, and the afternoon sun feels familiar against my skin.

Once the airport car service takes us to the private lounge, we have a few minutes to spare before our luggage arrives. Gwen disappears into the bathroom with her carry-on.

We won't see my family until tomorrow, but this afternoon still feels important. I want Gwen to enjoy herself. To feel welcome here, like this is a place she can see herself coming back to, maybe calling a second home. I try to put myself together a bit in the restroom, brushing my teeth and splashing cold water on my face, shaking off the lack of sleep as I step back into the lounge.

One of my mother's drivers arrives, and we discuss my plans for the day until I hear the bathroom door swing open behind me.

I can't help the way my jaw drops. She's changed, no longer in comfortable clothes suited for a long flight, but into a white sundress covered in small, bright red flowers. They're embroidered, not printed, making the fabric seem like it's rippling with the petals. Her hair is tied up, exposing her neck and shoulders, soft tendrils loose and curling around her face. The dress ends mid-thigh, the long legs I've knelt in front of, kissed and bit and begged to open, on display.

She clutches her bag in front of her, rocking back and forth on her toes. After a few moments where I struggle to form cohesive thoughts, she blushes. Every inch of exposed skin, from her shoulders to her temples, burns brightly, and I want to follow the path of her flush with my tongue.

"It's nice out." She shrugs, still avoiding my gaze. "Is this okay? I brought something more formal for tomorrow, obviously, but I thought since it's warm and..."

I don't let her finish the thought. I'm across the room in an instant, pulling her body flush against mine and kissing her like she'll give me the oxygen I need to function again.

Her lips part so easily for me, letting me in, demanding as much from me as I am from her. Her hands find the back of my neck, fingernails scratching into my scalp as she pulls herself up closer to me, standing on her toes. I can't stop kissing her. Can't stop gripping the fabric at her hip, or running my fingertips over the exposed skin of her back and neck. I'd spend the rest of my life in this airport lounge if it meant kissing her like this, warm and sun-soaked and beautiful.

She's the one to pull away, her hands still wrapped around my neck possessively, making my blood hum.

"You like the dress?" she asks, her voice teasing.

I press my lips to hers again.

"I'm buying you a hundred of them," I say, kissing up the column of her throat while she laughs. "In every color you can find."

I don't let Gwen unwrap herself from me as the driver returns from wherever she disappeared to and informs us that the car is ready. I only release her so she can slip into the back of the car, but my hand is on her thigh as soon as possible.

"I thought the airport was close to the city center?" she asks as we get onto the highway, headed north.

"My parents raised us in Bari, but our family home is in Trani," I say, warmth and contentment spreading through me as I watch her take in the olive trees and grapevines. Her eyes light up, darting around like everything's moving too fast for her to soak up. *We'll come back*, I want to tell her. *So you can see everything.* "Only about thirty minutes away."

There isn't much of a view of the sea on the drive, so when we get to Trani, I have the driver drop us near the port, telling Gwen to leave her bags.

Hand in hand, we walk along the docks, the blue and white boats knocking against their slips, soft waves lapping against the rocky shore. She asks about my family, and growing up somewhere so beautiful, and where else I've traveled. I tell her everything, because I can't help myself. I want her to know every part of me. To know I trust her.

We find a trattoria and sit at one of the little outdoor tables, tucked under an awning so her shoulders don't burn in the sun. Over fresh seafood and sweet wine, we never stop sharing and touching, our lips and hands and her foot against my leg under the table. All this time we've been together, and I've never found myself without something to say to her, without a reason to touch her.

We keep eating until we're full, the wait staff kind and familiar, asking when I got back home and when they'll see the other Costa troublemakers. The town is small enough that, even in the tourist-heavy summer months, the locals remember each other.

No one asks about my mother. I don't know if that means we've kept our secret well or haven't at all. I'm not sure it matters here.

The walk to the resort I booked for us is short and pleasant, the cool breeze picking up the strands of hair that have fallen out of their tie. She's clearly exhausted, but there's a relaxed smile on her face that feels brand new. I've never seen her so at ease.

The stone facade of the building radiates the warmth of the day as the sun sinks behind it. I take Gwen's hand and press her fingers to my lips, trying to impress even a drop of what I feel for her into the motion. If it takes decades, I don't mind. I'll prove to her what we are.

I slip the room key from my pocket and lead Gwen to the central staircase. There are elevators here, but the beauty of the architecture of these buildings cannot be understated, and I'm desperate to admire her against the backdrop of my home.

When we reach our door on the top level, I greet the security guard that my father likely stationed. Trani is safe, but we'd be fools to believe our enemies didn't know this is our home.

The penthouse is quiet, and despite the measures taken, I feel the need to sweep the suite, ensuring she's safe while we're here. When I'm reassured, I turn to find Gwen, but she's not trailing behind me. The small kitchen and living room are empty, so I slip back into the bedroom. Through the bathroom's open doors, I see her sitting on the edge of the clawfoot tub big enough to fit both of us with room to spare. Gauzy drapes framing the open window float in the warm breeze. The view is breathtaking; the sky bursts in oranges, pinks, and purples that are reflected in the still sea. Her hair is down, moving gently in the wind, exposing her shoulders to the wash of sunset.

I will prove to her that this is more than an advantageous agreement. Partners, friends, *benefits*, soulmates. Because I am too selfish to have less than all of her, to allow her to think she owns anything less than my soul.

I could stand here for a lifetime and watch this private painting in front of me, but I cross the room and trail my hand down her back, her smooth skin lighting me on fire from the inside out.

"Your home is beautiful," she says softly, not taking her eyes off the sea.

She is my home. She is beautiful.

"I'm glad you like it," I say instead, combing my fingers through her hair slowly.

She turns her face up at me and her smile is so pure and undiluted it's like drinking straight from the bottle.

"Thank you for bringing me here, trusting me with this," she says, leaning into my body so her head is resting on my chest. "I hope I don't screw this up."

"You're going to be perfect," I say, dragging my nails against her scalp like she does for me. She seems to enjoy it, almost burrowing into my body. "You were meant for this."

She peers up at me, and I beg her with my eyes to hear the words I can't say yet. *You were meant for me.*

I cup her face with my hands and press my lips to hers. Softly, like I'm asking her permission, which I am. With deft fingers she untucks my shirt from my pants, trailing her fingers over my stomach, leaving goosebumps across my skin. I lift her against me, my hands under her thighs, her legs wrapped around me. I grip her ass, unable to contain my groan as she slips her tongue in my mouth and her fingers into my hair. Her ankles hook behind my back, digging into my spine as she grinds herself closer to me.

I walk her backward to the bed, unable to separate myself from her, trailing my lips down her throat, over her collarbones, to the neckline of her dress. Her chest heaves, pressing her perfect tits into the hem.

"Can I touch you, Gwen?" I ask against her skin, my fingers brushing over the bodice of her dress, pulling a loose thread from one of the embroidered flowers. I tuck it into my pocket. "Please?"

She grips the comforter above her head, shaking her head no. I pull my hands back, but leave my lips against the swell of her breast, nipping at the edge of her dress.

"Okay, mio filo," I breathe, grasping my hands behind my back.

She shakes her head again, her eyes pinched shut in determination. I try not to smile, but she must feel the tilt of my lips against her, because she's suddenly sliding away from me.

"I want to touch *you*," she pants, propping herself up on her elbows. Her pretty dress is barely covering her, rucked up around her waist.

My hands strain against my own grip.

"Anything for you," I swear.

She gets that look in her eyes like it's a challenge, like I'm daring her to test my resolve. Maybe I am.

She shifts so she's on her knees, ass against her heels, before reaching for my shirt again. Movements slow and sensual, she rocks her hips back and forth, almost like she's dancing to the rhythm of the waves on the shore outside. Once my shirt's completely open, she pushes it over my shoulders, her hands lingering on my collarbones.

"Don't let go of your hands," she whispers in my ear as she tugs the shirt all the way down my arms. It bunches on my wrists, and even though I could easily release my grip and free myself, it still feels like a restraint.

My blood is thundering in my veins, my heart pounding so hard I can barely think past it.

"If you want me to stop, just say so, and I will, okay?" she asks, eyes clear and skin flushed.

My whole body is filled with a low, pleasant buzzing

feeling as she leans forward and traces the olive branches tattooed on my neck with her tongue.

Her mouth drives me to the edge of sanity. Every lick and kiss and bite across my chest, my throat, my arms, my stomach has my muscles tightening. She's slow and careful compared to the frantic rise and fall of my chest, leaving teeth marks in her wake. Her fingertips softly run down my back when her teeth skim my bicep. Featherlight kisses torture me as she places them along my hipbones. My cock is painfully hard, demanding to be inside her. I can't suppress a whimper as she drifts her knuckles over its impression against my zipper.

"Please," I pant, head thrown toward the ceiling, grip on my own hands white-knuckled. "Don't stop, please."

But immediately the heat of her body disappears. When I snap my head down, her lips are puffy and full, but the lust that had filled her eyes has been replaced by something close to fear. She shakes her head a bit.

"Sorry, you said *don't* stop," she says, almost to herself. She closes her eyes and takes a deep breath, seeming to resettle herself. "I reacted to *stop*. I didn't know if it was too much."

My heart is in my throat, making it nearly impossible to speak.

I was never under the impression that the support Gwen and I exchanged had comparative value. What I gave her was never worth more than what she gave me. But it wasn't until this moment that I realized she might care about me as much as I care about her.

"I'm okay," I breathe, trying to calm her anxiety. "I didn't think, mio filo, I'm sorry. I wasn't trying to scare you."

"You don't have to be sorry," she says, her shoulders finally relaxing. "Maybe we should pick another word, though."

"Lemon." The word slips from my lips without conscious

thought. Gwen raises her eyebrows at me, a smile pulling at the corner of her lips. "They make me think of French 75s."

"Okay," she whispers, trailing a single finger from the hollow of my throat to the waistband of my pants. "Lemon."

I tell myself I can be good for her. Keep my hands to myself. Even when she loosens the buckle of my belt. Even when she undoes the button and slips her hand into my boxers, making me pant her name over and over.

She touches everywhere she wants, her breaths growing heavier as she works herself up. Her hand disappears under her dress as she takes my cock down her throat, and I can't help it anymore.

"Please, Gwen," I beg, my voice breaking on her name. "Please let me make you come. I need you."

For a moment, I think she's going to ignore my pleas, but she meets my eyes, her mouth still wrapped around me, and pumps me down her throat a few more strokes before letting go.

"Okay, Charlie," she says, her voice breathy and eyes glazed.

The blankets rumple around her as she lets herself fall backward, propping her head up on the pillows. My heart tumbles over itself, losing all sense of rhythm as she runs her thumb along her bottom lip, collecting her own saliva and my precum, sucking it off her own finger as her legs fall open.

"Make me come however you want."

It's an invitation I would walk through fire to meet. I shuck off my pants and boxers and crawl between her knees.

"Thank you."

Running my hands down her thighs, I spread her further. Her panties are pale pink lace, complementing the petals on her dress, and she's going to be the death of me.

She arches the small of her back when my mouth meets her clit over the lace, nearly soaked through already. I grip her thighs so tightly I'd worry I was hurting her if her soft moans of pleasure weren't filling the entire room. I hook one finger under the fabric and pull her panties to the side.

"So fucking perfect," I groan, unable to rip my eyes away as I watch two of my fingers disappear into her pussy, hard and fast.

Her gasping breaths chip away at my control as I pump into her, feeling her clench around me as I curl my fingers. Despite how hard I am, the thought of stopping and filling her with my cock barely crosses my mind. I press my hand harder against her thigh so I can see her. She's moaning my name, cursing and crying out for more, and I can't deny her anything.

"Charlie, fuck, so good, you're doing so..." she cuts herself off with a cry, her hand moving to pinch her nipple. "Fuck, it feels like..."

"I know, mio filo," I soothe, keeping my pace and watching her eyes roll back in her head. "You said to make you come however I want. I want this, if you like how it feels."

"Yes, yes, yes," she chants, her hips lifting to meet my thrusts. "Feels so good, Charlie."

My body's on fire, sweat dripping down my temples as her whole body shakes and finally breaks. She soaks my hand as she comes, her pussy clenching my fingers as I work her through her orgasm. I don't stop pumping my fingers into her, even as I take her clit into my mouth. The feeling of her hands in my hair, pulling and pushing, grinding her pussy against my face, causes any lingering control I had to slip. I lick and suck her clit, savoring the taste of her orgasm on my tongue. A state of euphoria takes over as I bury my mouth against her, barely stopping to breathe until she comes on my fingers and mouth again.

As the waves of her orgasm recede, I slow my movements, bringing myself back down to earth with her. She's breathing hard, her chest and stomach rising and falling, glistening with a sheen of sweat. Even though my body realizes I haven't come—my dick is painfully hard, pressed against the sheets—the satisfaction of bringing her so much pleasure is a release in itself. All the while, she runs her fingernails through my hair, soothing the places where she pulled. I feel like I've been skydiving, the adrenaline of the fall a contrast to the jarring landing back on earth.

"Come here," she pants, gently pulling at my hair.

I crawl up her body, meeting her lips with mine. A hand travels between us down my chest until she's teasing my cock with her fingertips. But I tug her hand away, wrapping it around my neck. As much as my body suggests otherwise, I need this more. Her body wrapped around mine, her slow and steady breath against my skin. She breaks the kiss, leaning back with her eyebrows raised, and I'm relieved not to see any hurt or rejection in her eyes.

"How are you feeling?" she asks as I lay my head against her sternum, listening to the beat of her heart.

I laugh, kissing her ribs and the underside of her breast, anywhere I can reach without moving.

"I think I should be asking you that," I reply, my body shaking slightly as I breathe deeply.

"That's not how this works," she says, trailing her fingers over my shoulder, her voice a bit chastising. When I look at her, she still has her eyebrows raised, and she pats her chest.

I take it as an invitation and move so I'm holding her, my head tucked under her chin like hers has been under mine so many times. She makes soothing circles on my back and I time my breathing with hers, feeling less and less unmoored with each exhale.

"How *are* you feeling?" I ask, pressing my lips into the hollow of her throat.

"Incredible," she says, almost laughing. "A little surprised, too. And my skin feels all tingly. A little selfish, if I'm being honest." I drag my hand down her side and feel the tiny hairs on her skin stand up under my touch. "Now it's your turn."

I consider lying, or only telling her about the euphoria of watching her fall apart for me, of knowing I can make her feel like that. But this weekend is about trust, in all things.

"I don't feel like you were being selfish," I promise, nipping at her neck and tasting the salt of her skin. It soothes me a little more. "I am a little shaky. I felt a little like I was having an out-of-body experience. Coming out of it was a little jarring," I admit.

She doesn't react at first, just keeps up her soft touches against my skin. After a minute, she exhales.

"It's felt like that for me before," she admits, and I roll off her chest so I can look in her eyes. She's chewing on her bottom lip, avoiding my gaze. But I put my hand on her cheek and find her eyes.

"Why didn't you say anything?" I ask, my chest tightening with guilt that I didn't notice. She always seemed so elated, like she was floating on a cloud.

"I didn't really know how to explain it. It wasn't a bad feeling, just kind of surreal." She traces the olive branches again, this time with her fingertips. "I looked it up. It's pretty common."

I'm not new to this world, but refusing to engage in dominance and submission for over a decade has protected me from the realities of dropping, even if I've witnessed it happen.

"Yeah, it is," I say, swallowing hard. She smiles softly and kisses my forehead, and my muscles uncoil a fraction more. "This helps, though."

"This?" she asks, kissing my jaw and neck.

I pull her against me, her skin against mine like an anchor in a storm.

"Just holding you. Listening to you."

She wraps her arms around me and hums, her legs tangling with mine.

"We can do that. It helps me too," she says, her smile pressed against my chest. The last bits of light through the window look like silver starlight in her hair. "For as long as you want."

*Forever*, I think as the sun dips below the horizon. *Forever is how long I want.*

## Chapter 24
### *Gwen*

Iɪt's a good thing we didn't have to be at the Costa home until evening, because it took us all afternoon to recover from the jetlag and our sleepless night. Even now, I can feel Charlie's lips against my neck, his teeth on my inner thigh. If I wasn't half-terrified of what I was about to face, I'd drag him back to that gorgeous hotel and refuse to let him leave the bed until we had to get on our flight.

Emily sent a few more last-minute warning texts about the way the family interacts with each other and how Lucia, Charlie's mother, is fairing.

On the drive over to the house, Charlie is anxious. He shares more stories about his family, but his leg bounces and his grip on my knee is tight. I try to smooth the sky blue silk gown I'm wearing—apparently family dinners are a formal affair—but my palms are sweating and I'm afraid to stain the fabric.

The same driver from yesterday pulls through a massive wrought-iron gate and up a dirt path lined with oleander. At the end of the drive, standing like a fortress, is the Costa family home. The stone is bleached near-white from the sun, and towers topped with terracotta shingles are evenly spaced across the facade. I have to crane my neck to see the top as we pull up, and the reality of what I'm walking into suddenly hits me.

These are some of the most powerful people in the world. Not by political sway or money, though they clearly have both, but mostly by the fear and respect they instill in the world. They are a small family, and yet they're an empire. A dynasty I've somehow found my way to the center of.

I try to keep my heart rate down, remembering that Charlie wants me here. That, as intimidating as their family is, he wouldn't have brought me here if he didn't believe I could handle it. And as terrifying as walking through those doors will be, I *want* it. I've never felt more sure of my future than when I imagine it beside Charlie, finding justice for those who need it, making the world just a little safer. I want to learn and prove myself to them, to be a Costa.

Charlie opens my door and holds his hand out to me, and when he helps me from the car, I don't see any hesitation in his eyes. Nerves, sure. But not doubt.

"We can do this," I say, but it comes out as more of a question than a declaration.

"Together," he replies, bringing my hand to his lips and kissing my knuckles. "Fate hasn't steered us wrong yet."

The foyer is unsurprisingly grand, bigger than mine and Ana's old apartment, and a million times more opulent. A member of the house staff greets us and ushers us down a long hall, our steps echoing loudly against the high ceilings and plaster walls. Charlie seems to loosen with the familiarity of his surroundings, pointing out family portraits from generations past and art that his grandmother, Sofia, collected.

Chatter and laughter grow louder as we near an arch at the end of the hall. Charlie stops just before we enter and tips my chin up to look at him.

"They're different from most families, but they are still the people I love most. And they will love you because..." he cuts himself off, and I feel my face flame involuntarily. I have to break his gaze, afraid of what he'll say, or what I will. "Because you're going to be my wife."

I nod, staring at one of his cufflinks, trying to force my blush to crawl backwards. He gives me a moment to collect myself, clearing his throat and adjusting his tie. And then we walk through the archway.

The first thing that I notice is all the color. The walls are covered in bright art, and credenzas lining the walls host family photos, blown glass vases, and other trinkets. But it's not just the decor that's bright.

The five people seated at the table are also dressed in brilliant colors, mostly pastels, but also beautiful jewel tones. I catch Emily's eye immediately, surprised to find her in a pastel purple floor-length gown. She's changed her hair since I last saw her, the severe cut accentuating the strong set of her shoulders. She looks gorgeous as she winks at me.

It takes me a moment to realize the room is silent, everyone's eyes squarely on us. Charlie guides me gently toward the head of the table.

Emily and Charlie both warned me, but it doesn't stop the tug of pity from pulling at my heart when we greet Lucia. She's in a wheelchair, her lower half covered in multiple blankets. She wears a thick, high-necked sweater, but burn scars still crawl up her throat and one side of her face. Her hair is short but full with dark, tight curls, highlighting her high cheeks and soft green eyes. Charlie's father, Aurelio, clutches her unscarred hand in his like he's afraid she'll disappear if he's not holding her.

"Ma," Charlie says, dipping down and kissing his mother's unscarred cheek. "You look more beautiful than ever."

Lucia laughs at him, the sound cracked and rough. She shakes off her husband's grip to pat her son on the cheek.

"Always such a terrible liar, Charlie. Leave that to the women of this family," she chastises, and I see his eyes brim with tears. The relief he must feel at seeing her here, making jokes and joining them for a meal, is incomprehensible.

"Your strength is your beauty, Mama. It always has been," he argues, placing a kiss against her palm.

"Speaking of beauty," she says, pushing his face out of the way and leaning forward a bit, wincing with the effort. "I'm incapacitated for four months and you find yourself a siren?"

Charlie laughs, and I reach my hand out to her.

"Twice as beautiful and tenfold as deadly," he says, winking down at me, doing nothing to help me suppress the blush finding its way back to my cheeks. "Mama, this is Guinevere Byrne. Gwen, my mother."

"It's wonderful to meet you, Signora Costa," I say, and she pulls me in with a surprisingly firm grip, placing a kiss on my cheek. "Charlie's told me so many stories about you and your family."

"Good to know he hasn't tricked you into being here. I know how demanding he can be." She raises her eyebrows at Charlie, and I see the tips of his ears redden.

"Gwen's more the demanding one, if you'll believe it," he says, and I fight the urge to punch him in the side. "But I promise, she's well-informed."

Something unreadable passes over his mother's expression, but she quickly turns to Aurelio. He's tall and lean, almost willowy, with his sunken cheeks and hollow eyes. I wonder what he looked like before Lucia's attack. If his skin was less sallow, his dark eyes bright like Charlie's often are.

"Look, Charlie's found himself Circe for a wife," she says, gripping his hand again.

But Aurelio doesn't get an opportunity to respond, because from the archway, a sweet, slicing voice breaks in.

"Not his wife yet, mama."

We all turn, and I'm stunned by the woman standing in the doorway. Her dark curls sit atop her head in a bun that is somehow both messy and elegant, a feat I've never been able to achieve. She's tall, nearly as tall as I am, her body lithe and strong under her bright red dress. There's something terrifying about her smile, the way it lures you in and puts you on edge all at once. If anyone is a siren, it's her, elegance so severe it's a warning.

"Clara," Charlie says simply, moving us a step backward so Clara can approach their mother.

"Carlo," she says, her voice monotone. Her eyes flicker to me, but she says nothing, and I do my best not to bristle. Her posture softens immediately as she turns to her mother and takes both of her hands.

"Mama," she whispers, pressing her lips softly to her cheek and wiping away the bit of lipstick she leaves behind. "I had every confidence you'd be at the head of this table again."

I feel more than I see Charlie wince, and Aurelio's eyes flash to his son and then to me, almost apologetic.

"Clara, mia rosa, mia spina," Lucia says quietly, assessing her daughter in a way that feels wholly different from how she looked at Charlie. "Did you have faith in me, or lack it in yourself?"

If the room was silent before, it's nothing compared to now. No one moves or even breathes as Lucia waits for Clara's response. Her calm expression doesn't slip, though, just hardens as she looks down at her matriarch.

"Faith in one Costa is faith in us all," she finally says, and after a moment, her mother's face breaks out in a smile so vicious it's obvious where Clara learned hers.

"Always the politician." Lucia says it like a compliment, fixing her daughter's lipstick with her thumb. "But don't be mean to Gwen; she's going to be family."

Clara turns around, that smile raising the hairs on the back of my neck. Charlie squeezes my hip, and Clara tracks the movement.

"Of course," she nearly purrs, holding her hand out to me. "It's so nice to meet my future sister."

"I could say the same," I reply, surprising myself with how calm my voice sounds. We shake hands briefly, and Clara looks me up and down once more before turning back to the table.

"Papa, I've missed you," she says, crossing behind her mother and kissing Aurelio's cheek.

Charlie ushers us toward the other end of the table and introduces me to Alessia and Mauricio, Emily's parents. As soon as pleasantries are over, Emily snags me by the elbow and drags me to a seat.

"It took like two hours to figure out the seating arrangement with you here, and I'm not letting Clara fuck it up, so make Charlie pull out your seat before she notices what's going on," she hisses in my ear, her words running together in a single breath.

Charlie seems to catch on quicker than I do, because he pulls out Emily's chair next to Aurelio's and then mine next to hers. Clara's eyes flare when she sees him slipping into his own seat.

There's a commotion in the hallway as the last of the guests arrive. A woman close to Alessia's age is dressed in a shimmering gold dress, standing out from the rest of the family. She's short, and her frame is thin and lithe. Her smile is pleasant, but the look in her eyes is almost angry. Charlie whispers *Gia and Beatrice* in my ear.

I didn't even notice the second person at first, but trailing in

Gia's shadow is Beatrice. Her face is blank, and if I had to assign an emotion to her, it would be *bored*. That is, if it wasn't for the way she seemed to find the blind spot in her mother's every movement, shifting so that when Gia turns to greet someone, Bea is carefully behind her.

"My sister," Gia says, her bright voice nearly bird-like. She approaches Lucia delicately, waiting for her to reach out her hand.

"Gia, it's so good to see you," Lucia says, placing her hand in her sister's and letting her squeeze her fingers.

"Me? It's a miracle to see you alive," Gia replies, looking down at her sister with something like disbelief in her eyes.

"Bea came with her," Emily mutters, and Charlie's eyes meet hers before looking back to the pair hovering near his mother.

"I know." Charlie almost sounds disappointed, but I have more sense than to ask why.

Bea greets Lucia quietly after her mother finds her chair. I watch as Lucia beckons Bea forward and whispers something in her ear that makes her lips tilt in a smile, before pressing a kiss to her cheek.

"Zia Gia," Charlie says, clearing his throat. "I'd like to introduce you to my partner, Guinevere."

Gia shimmies into the seat across from me, reaching her hand out and smiling pleasantly.

"Guinevere—what a lovely name," she compliments, grasping my hand lightly before turning to Charlie. "It's good to see at least one child in this family is taking their responsibilities seriously."

Emily catches her parents' eyes across the table and grimaces, which they seem to find funny. But both Bea and Clara seem less entertained. Clara sneers as she takes the seat opposite her mother at the head of the table. Bea sits between

Clara and her mother, finding her way into the shadows again.

"Ah, give the kids a break. They're doing well for themselves," Alessia chides, tossing a wink to her daughter; Emily struggles to contain her laughter.

"I don't think it's so funny, Emily," Gia snaps, eyes narrowing on her niece. "By the time we were your age, we were all married and raising you lot. I had already lost Enzo. You live too comfortably."

Lucia clears her throat, and everyone turns toward her immediately.

"Perhaps we can save the criticisms of our progeny until the dessert course, yes?" she asks lightly, tilting her head at Aurelio, who taps his glass with his fork.

I try to process everything that's happened so far as house staff serve the first course, but I barely know where to start. The Costas maintain some strange balance between obvious love for one another and threatening tension. I feel like a guppy invited to a dinner party with sharks, but I try to keep a pleasant smile on my face as conversations break out across the table and everyone begins to eat.

Charlie introduces me to Bea, whose expression doesn't change a bit as she makes small talk. Her eyes keep flicking to her mother, who seems to be absorbed in a conversation about recent developments in Central America with Mauricio and Alessia. Emily asks me about Ana, suggesting she could do some *light investigation* to see if the SAT prep questions she helped Charlie create were effective.

I keep waiting to hear from Clara, but she's silent. When I glance at her, inconspicuously as I can, she's watching her father help her mother eat, her aunts trade jabs and jokes over Mauricio's plate. Charlie puts his arm over my shoulder, but she says nothing.

As second and third courses are served, I can almost delude myself into believing this is a normal family dinner, despite the formal gowns and the fact that everyone but me is packing. Sparkling water is poured into champagne flutes–no alcohol is allowed at Costa family dinners, apparently. Emily's parents ask about the research she's doing into some spider in Madagascar, and she goes into vivid detail about skin necrosis—to the delight of her father. Bea asks about the foundation, and Charlie provides updates on a few of the families they've helped resettle in rural China. Everyone is polite, other than Clara and her disinterest.

"Gwen," Lucia calls out, interrupting Charlie and Bea's conversation about her trip to Japan. "Have you decided if you'd like a wedding in the States? Our home is open to you, of course, if you'd prefer something more Mediterranean."

I don't even have time to stammer out an answer, because Clara's silverware cracks heavily against her plate. Charlie's hand grips my shoulder, but I don't pull my eyes away from his sister.

"That's a little presumptuous, don't you think, Mama?" Clara asks, and I hear Emily choke on her food next to me.

I have a feeling Lucia is rarely questioned like this, even by her successor.

"Why would it be presumptuous, mia rosa?" Lucia rebuts, a challenge in her eyes and a smile pulling at one corner of her mouth.

Clara doesn't buckle, but it's clear it's an effort.

"The council has not approved her."

*Approved?* I fight the urge to turn to Charlie, knowing it will give away my lack of knowledge, even as his thumb rubs circles on my shoulder.

"We barely know her."

Aurelio clears his throat and looks to his wife, who nods.

"Clara, Gwen has proven herself over the past months. She's kept our secrets, learned our ways, even worked on a target with Charlie," he says, sending me a small smile that I can't seem to return. "You've received the reports, the same as your mother. Even her sister doesn't know much, and she lives with them. There's no reason for the council to vote against her."

Some part of me realizes Aurelio is on my side here, but my mind sticks on the word *reports*. Has Charlie been...reporting on me? Without my knowledge? It's now an effort not to shrug Charlie's grip off my shoulder. I can feel the anger building under my skin, my short fuse already burning.

"While I appreciate Guinevere's ability to keep her mouth shut, I'll reiterate that we don't *know* her," Clara emphasizes, barely sparing me a glance as she sets her gaze on her father. "Carlo may not be the next leader of this family, but his position is critical. Trusting some broke waitress because Charlie is easily swayed by a pair of good legs is irresponsible."

Emily mutters *Jesucristo* under her breath, but I barely hear it over Charlie's near growl.

"You don't speak about her like that," Charlie says, his voice low and cutting. Clara glares at him, her expression a mix of fury and disbelief. "She *will* be my wife, and I swear to God, Clara—"

"What? You'll challenge me?" Clara cuts him off with a laugh, and the sound is laced with pain and betrayal so visceral it reverberates through the room. "You think a single member of The Syndicate, much less the council, would follow you after what you've done? Our mother is attacked, and what do you do? You don't sit by her bedside, think about our family, or put hardly effort into hunting down her attackers." She points at me without looking at me, and I'm half tempted to snatch her fingers out of the air and break them. "You decide our mother is obsolete. Unable to lead. In all but her heartbeat, *dead*. And you find the first thing desperate enough to open its legs for you and decide you're ready to lead us."

Charlie's out of his seat in an instant, Aurelio reaching out and grabbing his son by the arm to hold him back. My mouth is dry, and despite my instinct to reach for Charlie, I'm locked in my seat.

"Enough." Lucia's voice is clear and final, silencing the protests and arguments across the table. "Sit, Carlo. You as well, Clara."

She's only half out of her seat, her fingers gripping the edge of the table, but Clara sinks back down. Charlie sits as well and tries to grab my hand, but I shake it off, my pulse still pounding through my veins.

"Your love for me is fierce, daughter," Lucia says with a soft smile, the most unguarded I've seen her all night. Clara's shoulders loosen a bit at her mother's words, and she sits more comfortably in her seat. "You have kept The Syndicate strong in my absence and proven your ability to lead us. All while sitting at my bedside, keeping me informed, briefing me even when I couldn't speak and tell you I understood. Your faith in me is admirable."

Clara's expression is equally touched and smug as she glances at Charlie. His face is stone, the same look I remember from the pig farm. Compartmentalized. My heart is pounding in my throat, and I'm certain they can all hear it.

"But Charlie made the right choice."

Clara's mouth drops open, and everyone else at the table gapes at Lucia except Aurelio, who just holds his wife's hand and watches her speak with admiration filling his gaze.

"I will never be the leader I was before my attack. It will be months, maybe years, before I can stand again. Being in this chair alone is a miracle. *Healing* was a miracle." She looks at her husband, and he pulls her fingers to his lips and kisses them like Charlie has done to me so many times. "It is time for the next generation of Costas to govern The Syndicate."

"Mama—" Clara starts, but Lucia glares at her, effectively cutting her off.

"This is my final decision, Clara, and you will abide by it," she says, and Clara's shoulders drop as her expression shutters. "There will be a year of transition, but by next summer, The Syndicate of Fate will fall to the next generation." Lucia turns to Charlie, her expression much softer. "Despite your sister's insistence, I was never under the impression you had lost faith in my recovery, my son. You put The Syndicate first, as is demanded of all of us. The mark of a true leader."

Even I hear the threat laced through those words. The room is once again silent, Clara's deep breath the only perceptible noise.

"I am the heir," she says, but her voice breaks at the end, and it comes out as more of a question than a declaration.

"You have been raised as such, yes," Lucia allows, seemingly unbothered by the pain in her daughter's voice. "But there have never been first born twins in the Costa line. There is no precedent. If Charlie is more capable of prioritizing our work, perhaps he is better suited for the role."

Charlie stiffens in his seat next to me, likely sweltering under the glare Clara is sending his way.

"Mama, I did not intend to—" he begins, but again Lucia cuts her child off.

"I care little what your intentions were. What I *do* care about is the future of our work. The children who we have pulled from the arms of traffickers. The evil we have eradicated, and the poison we've burned from this earth. Even as small as our impact is, it is necessary. And if my daughter is unable to correctly set her priorities, I will choose an heir who can."

Charlie doesn't say a word, doesn't reach for me or react. Everyone is holding their breath, waiting for someone to break the silence. It should be unsurprising that it is again Lucia.

"Guinevere, my dear," she coos, the maternal tone jarring compared with the way she's spoken to her children. "I do apologize for my daughter's spiteful words. Regardless of the way you and my son found each other, your affection is clear. And everything Charlie has told us gives us nothing but confidence that you will be an excellent partner for him, whatever role he must take." She lifts her scarred hand and places it against her chest, giving me a look laden with empathy. "And I hope Ana's scans come back clear. She seems like the sweetest young lady."

There's no threat there, nothing but care and compassion in her voice. In any other situation, this would simply be my future mother-in-law passing on her sympathies.

But all it tells me is that Charlie included Ana in his reports.

Not just her illness, but *her*. Her personality, her resilience.

Maybe Charlie was right. Maybe I am made for this. Maybe I've learned to control myself under his tutelage. Because I shove all my anger and fear down to some place in the recesses of my heart and return Lucia's smile.

"Thank you–for your confidence and your well wishes."

Lucia looks around the room, completely unphased by the way her sisters, brother-in-law, and nieces seem unable to look at her. She pushes her plate away from her and turns to pat her husband's cheek.

"Well, it's been a delight having the family together again, but I'm exhausted. My love, help me back to our room, will you?"

Aurelio stands and navigates Lucia's wheelchair back

toward the hall, turning over his shoulder to look at his children.

"We love you both." He says it like an apology.

Like Lucia's departure was a signal, everyone else gathers themselves. Clara glares at Charlie, Emily, and Bea–a clear order to stay seated. Alessia and Mauricio exchange worried glances with each other, but Gia just rolls her eyes.

"Don't kill each other," she mumbles, brushing her hand down her shimmering dress. "Who knows which one of you she'll put at the helm next?"

When it's just the cousins and I left in the dining room, and the final snap of the door closing can be heard down the foyer, Clara turns to Charlie.

"What the fuck was that?" she nearly screams, on her feet in an instant.

Charlie just slumps back in his chair, running his hands through his hair and looking bewildered.

"You think I planned that? The last thing on the fucking planet I want is to lead The Syndicate and you know that," he argues, crossing his arms over his chest and glaring at the ceiling.

"It doesn't matter if you planned it!" Clara yells, slamming her hands on the table, making the plates clatter. "You and Gwen started this doomsday clock. I'll never forgive you."

"Oh please, dial it down a few notches," Emily sighs, dropping her arms on the table and laying her head on them. "It's not like they were going to live forever, Clara. You were going to have to get married eventually."

Clara's still pissed, but she seems more defeated than anything now, dropping ungracefully back into her chair with an *oomph*. The change in tone without the older generation in the room is stark. Fewer accusations. Less formal hierarchy. More bitching. I have whiplash from Clara's quickly shifting mood, but even that isn't enough to distract me from my simmering anger toward Charlie. My skin prickles unpleasantly when I feel him reach for me. As if I would want his touch, his comfort. As if he wasn't the one who ripped that from me.

"You want to apologize to Gwen for basically calling her a gold digging whore in front of her future in-laws?" Bea asks, her eyebrows raised at her cousin.

Clara turns toward me, a grimace that seems genuinely remorseful plastered on her face.

"Oh shit, yes, sorry," she says, reaching over Charlie to grab my hand. "That wasn't fair. I have a habit of being inconsiderate of others' feelings when I'm trying to make a point, but I try not to do it with family." She smiles at me like she wants me to trust her, and I really don't know if I should. "I know your agreement wasn't like that, and honestly, even if it was, that isn't my business. I'd dance naked in Times Square if it meant saving my brother."

"You're not pissed at him?" I ask, finally letting my confusion break through my carefully constructed wall. I wish it didn't feel like a weakness.

"Oh, I'm definitely pissed at him. If he wouldn't have met you, I could probably have put off getting married for like five more years," she sighs, picking up her fork and pushing her food around her plate. "Where the hell is dessert? If they're not going to let us drink at family dinner, we should at least get sweets."

She clinks her fork against her glass, and a few moments later, there are little dishes of panna cotta topped with bright red raspberries in front of us.

"Lucia's not going to give The Syndicate to Charlie. Clara's earned it," Emily says, and I can tell it's for my benefit. She doesn't lift her head from her arms, her eyes closed like she's fighting a headache. "She just doesn't want to share her throne."

"Shut up," Clara sneers through a mouthful of dessert. "I just think it's fucking medieval that I have to get married to take my position."

"It's not about the wedding, it's about—"

"*Expanding the network of The Syndicate*, yeah Charlie, I took the same lessons you did as a kid," Clara interrupts her brother, scooping another large spoonful of raspberries and cream out of the glass. "We're barely on the other side of thirty and I've made dozens of agreements with organizations and families. I've personally cut the heads off enemies." Charlie glares at her and she rolls her eyes. "Okay, fine, I made you do it, but it was my call. The *one* partnership I make through marriage should not count more than everything else I've done."

I feel for Clara, even though the whole *first thing desperate enough to open its legs* line still stings.

"Can't you do what Charlie did and find a rent-a-spouse?" I ask, and Charlie turns to me with his eyes wide while Clara cackles.

"Did he tell you I called you that? Oh my God, I'm so sorry, but that's so funny," Clara laughs, and Bea and Emily join with soft chuckles under their breath.

The only ones not laughing are me and Charlie.

"You know that's not—" he starts, but I refuse to be the first person to let Charlie get a word in, especially with anger heating my blood.

"Oh, don't think you can calm me down right now. Reports? Approval? Did you not think it would be appropriate to inform me I could have spent all this time with you, and your family might have rejected me?"

All three of the Costa women are staring at Charlie open-mouthed as he blinks at me, seemingly unable to come up with a response.

"You didn't tell her?" Emily asks, her voice cold and cutting. Bea's looking at Charlie like a disappointed parent, but Emily and Clara are just as angry as I am.

"He did not tell me. Not that he was writing reports about how *well I was doing*, or that he was including details about Ana in those reports. He also failed to explain that you all could decide I wasn't up to the task." The guilt is clear in his eyes, but it doesn't assuage me at all. In fact, it only makes it worse. "What would happen if they said no, Charlie? Ana and I would be out on our own again? You'd be fine just dropping us back at our old apartment?"

As I say the words, something cracks in my chest, and I realize I'm not angry. I'm heartbroken. For a person who spent her whole life saying she didn't need anyone but herself and her sister, I sure as fuck gave him enough of my heart that he could break it.

"I'd never abandon you two," he says, his voice pleading. "You have to know I would financially support you two for the rest of your lives."

Clara, Bea, and Emily simultaneously curse under their breath as my chest tightens, pulling those little fragments of my heart further apart.

"That's not what she's talking about, asino," Clara reaches over and smacks him on the back of the head before she turns to me. "He doesn't mean it like that."

"I wouldn't let them say no, Gwen. It wouldn't happen." Charlie seems to have realized his words, nearly panicked in his effort to clarify.

"He doesn't have that power, though, does he?" I ask Clara, and she glances at Charlie empathetically before shaking her head at me. "You should have told me. You should have let me know there was a possibility this would all end, before...before everything changed between us. If they rejected me, you eventually would have had to marry someone else. And I don't know if I could have watched that."

"If it helps, I was just being a colossal bitch because I was angry," Clara says, coming to bat for her brother. "My mother was right; you'll make an excellent Costa. There's no reason for anyone to vote against you, even me."

Charlie reaches for me, but I keep my hands firmly in my lap.

"Thank you, Clara," I say, clearing my throat and trying to repress the tears welling in my eyes. "But he should have told me. And I know I'm committed to this, and I have no intention of backing out, but I think I have a right to be pissed."

"Oh yeah, definitely be pissed," Emily says, finally lifting her head from the table. She grabs my arm and pulls me to stand with her. Charlie follows immediately, his shoulders tense and expression anguished. "Gwen's going to come stay with me tonight, and I'll get her back to D.C. tomorrow. You figure out how you're going to fix this little shit show you've created."

"Oh, can I come? I'm also mad at Charlie, mostly in solidarity, but also because I had no idea Gwen existed until tonight, so I feel lied to as well." Bea stands up, smiling at me for the first time this evening.

She misses the glance that Charlie and Clara share, and I suddenly remember that there are more things at play than just my relationship.

"I'll come, too," Clara announces, standing and snagging Charlie's dessert as he stares at us. Emily leads me around the table, and we all link arms like girls on the playground. "We can all be mad at Charlie together."

And I am pissed. But my anger is mollified a little by the

women around me, which I think is their goal. Bea whispers in my ear that she loves the color of my dress as we start down the hallway.

"Gwen," Charlie calls out, and we all stop and turn over our shoulders like it was something we practiced. It would be funny if I wasn't still ready to stab him with a fork again.

"I truly am sorry, mia filettatura."

And I know he is. I'm certain that, deep down, Charlie doesn't want to hurt me. But everything I start to say turns to ash on my tongue. I can't respond because I know I'll crumble, and the fact that I can forgive him so easily is terrifying. But I know better than most that the easiest hearts to break are the ones handed to us willingly.

## Chapter 25
### *Gwen*

"So the trip did not go well?" Kenzie asks, swinging our joined hands as we walk up New Jersey Avenue.

Ana's at summer softball league training, trying to recondition her body after a season off. So I'm dragging Kenzie to Catalina's for a drink, listening to her lament about spending her day off at another bar. I sigh, wishing I could tell her everything.

"It's complicated. But yeah, we had a fight, I guess."

"Yes, it seems like you've had quite the tussle," she taunts, poking my side where my shirt rides up with her fingernail. "Could this possibly be a hickey? On your ribs? I wonder who possibly could have caused this scandalous little thing?"

I drop her hand immediately, embarrassment heating my skin. When I twist and lift my shirt, I see what she's referring to —an undeniable hickey, a few inches under my bra band.

"Oh, shut up," I shush her, swatting at her side and dragging down my top. I thought I'd be safe wearing something oversized, but obviously I was wrong.

"I will absolutely not shut up," she squeals, trying to lift my shirt back up.

"McKenzie Willard, we are in public," I say, dancing away from her and nearly tripping over a bunch of parked e-scooters. I glare at her, but she's fully cackling now, holding her belly because she's laughing so hard.

"You weren't going to tell me about this little update?" she asks, her voice still teasing.

I raise my eyebrows at her, incredulous.

"I don't know what you're talking about," I reply, trying to organize my thoughts.

There's no way she can know that this is a relatively recent development. Charlie and I live together. She had to assume we were sleeping together.

"Look, I've been very respectful and understanding of whatever arrangement you've got going on, but now that you're getting laid, I'm exercising my rights as your best friend to be privy to all details, thank you," she demands, looping her arm through mine and dragging me toward the bar.

"I don't understand," I admit, half a step behind her.

She yanks me forward and I have to jog to avoid falling.

"You think I don't know when my best friend is or is not getting it?" she scoffs, obviously offended. "When you and Natalie were hooking up in the walk-in, you used to send me actual paragraphs describing your orgasms. There's no way you wouldn't have given me bare minimum details if you and Charlie were sleeping together. Plus, the only times I've seen you together, you avoided touching like you were allergic to each other."

I yank her to a stop in the middle of the sidewalk, gawking at her.

"You knew I wasn't sleeping with Charlie and you didn't say anything? Didn't you think that was odd?" I should deny it, telling her Charlie and I have been head over heels for each other from the start. But the pressure of keeping this to myself has been overwhelming, and denial seems impossible anyway.

"I assumed you had your reasons." She shrugs, acting like this truly is no big deal. "Not every relationship is about love or lust or whatever."

I bristle at her words, immediately shrugging out of her grasp and crossing my arms.

"It's not like that," I start, but Kenzie interjects before I can get worked up.

"Look, I know you've got a complex about your mom and her endless parade of shitty, rich boyfriends. But I think you're letting the pain she caused turn you into kind of a judgmental bitch about this, if I'm being honest," she huffs, glaring at me in a way I've never seen from her before. "The reasons people choose their partners are none of our business. If someone wants to be with someone for their money, or sex, or because they're soulmates written in the stars, that's completely up to them. There's nothing *wrong* with that, as long as no one is hurting each other. And yeah, your mom sucked because she let her choices affect you and Ana, and prioritized her partners over her children, but the choices themselves are not the problem here. And you're doing this gross thing where lying to yourself and to me just so you don't have to admit that maybe there *are* good reasons to make these kinds of decisions. So, you know, you should stop doing that."

Kenzie is out of breath, the anger fading from her expression, replaced by a slightly embarrassed grimace. We're both quiet for a bit, standing on opposite ends of the sidewalk, avoiding each other's gaze.

"You've been wanting to say that for a while now," I guess. My chest is tight with shame.

"Not to dig in, but it's been bordering on slut shaming. And

I know Isabelle's a massive bitch, but it feels like you're using this mentality to punish yourself, too."

I wrap my arms tighter around myself, trying to fight the nausea settling in my stomach. Maybe Kenzie's right. Maybe I was so mad at Isabelle for abandoning us, I villainized everything about her, even parts that probably didn't deserve it.

When I was young, before Ana was born, she used to help me get dressed for school and talk about how, one day, I'd have a million outfits to pick from. That I could have a dress in every color if I wanted it. That we'd drive to the seaside and shop at the stores with pretty pastel colors in the windows whenever we wanted. She had dreams, and at some point, they included me.

Maybe there was a time when she wanted support, too. Things changed, of course. Boyfriends and fiances and husbands with money came and went, and there were never dresses or school supplies or trips for me and Ana. But maybe I took my anger too far.

"Charlie and I had an agreement," I say under my breath, trying to swallow down this misplaced pride. "I can't really say a lot about it, but I needed help with Ana's bills. And he needed someone willing to marry him."

Kenzie moves to stand directly in front of me and wraps her arms around my shoulders, hugging me tight.

"I would have said yes, too," she whispers, squeezing me as I slip my arms around her waist. "And not just because he looks like that."

I burst out a laugh, tears falling involuntarily down my face.

"It *does* help that he looks like that," I chuckle into her shoulder, blinking back more tears. She unwinds herself from me and pulls me up the street again.

"I'm sure it was less fun when you weren't fucking his brains out."

I smack her on the shoulder, looking around to make sure no one heard her.

"Jesus, Kenz," I say, trying to find the good vibes of our earlier conversation again.

"He left a hickey on your ribs, dude. That's not even a hickey-friendly zone. You guys are having crazy sex, I can tell," she laughs as we finally spot Catalina's on the upcoming corner. "You can't be all that mad at him."

I don't answer, mulling over how to approach this as we push the saloon doors open. Catalina's is nearly empty, which is unsurprising for an early Wednesday afternoon. Some classic rock station plays softly over the speakers, and the decor looks even more odd in the daylight than it did all those months ago. Catalina herself is behind the bar this time, and Kenzie and I belly up right in front of her.

"Gwen, my favorite ginger," Catalina sings, leaning over the bar to pinch my cheeks. "You've brought an angel into my bar with you. Did you know that?"

I warned Kenzie about Sammy and Cat's energy, so she just smiles and holds her hand out.

"Nice to meet you, Catalina. I'm Kenzie." Her voice is higher than usual, a faint blush creeping over her tanned cheeks.

I elbow her in the side as she and Cat exchange greetings, but she ignores me.

"Where's our gloomy, mysterious asshole?" Cat asks, opening the dishwasher below her and drying glasses. I roll my eyes, and Kenzie laughs.

"He's in a little bit of trouble," Kenzie says, and I throw her a look.

"He's not in *trouble*. I'm not his mother or his teacher," I grumble, picking at the coaster in front of me. "I'm upset because he kept some important things from me, and I'm giving him space to figure out how to fix it."

"Oh, how very mature of you," Cat teases, stacking glasses on a tall shelf.

While her back is turned, Kenzie raises her eyebrows at me and mouths *oh my god* before swiveling back to stare at Cat. I can't exactly blame her.

"I'm pissed, but not *leave him* pissed," I say.

I don't tell them I don't even know if leaving him is an option at this point. Even if I wanted to, I'd be followed by The Syndicate for the rest of my life. More troubling, I'd be haunted by the memory of Charlie—his soft touches and gentle support, the way he kisses me like it's a gift and fucks me like it's his job. There's no point in pretending I'd be willing to give him up for something he can fix.

"You two want a drink?" Cat asks, and we both order light ciders since it's admittedly barely after breakfast on a weekday. "Has he appropriately groveled yet?"

"Oh, yes," Kenzie cries, smacking her hand on the bartop and jolting a few of the other patrons. "Groveling is key."

"I don't want him to *grovel*," I say, gulping down half my drink. That statement is half true. I don't want him to grovel in this specific situation. Although, I can think of a few situations where some significant begging would be acceptable. "I want him to explain himself, and then tell me exactly what changes he's going to make to ensure I'm not caught off guard like this again."

"Boring," Kenzie grumbles, and Cat laughs, making Kenzie's face light up.

"The center of my universe, here behind this bar," Sammy's voice calls out as appears from the back office. He sweeps Cat up and peppers kisses up and down her jaw while she giggles.

I see Kenzie visibly deflate next to me, but as soon as he

releases Cat, Sammy immediately turns to us, dropping his elbows on the bartop and his chin into his hands right in front of my best friend.

"My god, you're an absolute showstopper," Sammy says, smiling at Kenzie. Her eyes flash to Cat, who's already pouring Kenzie another drink—bless her. "Catalina, my love, tell me you've already offered her my hand in marriage."

Kenzie blinks rapidly, and Cat grabs Sammy by the arm, chastising him for shocking *the pretty angel* into speechlessness.

"I told you. They're *open*," I whisper to my friend while Sammy's distracted by Catalina.

"I thought you meant they liked to talk or something," Kenzie replies, her eyes wide with interest.

"Sorry, should have been more clear," I mumble as Cat winks at Kenzie. She doesn't seem to mind the misunderstanding, though, especially with Cat looking at her like that.

"My muse tells me we're upset with Carlo," Sammy breaks in, passing me and Kenzie our refills, even though Kenzie's glass is still nearly full.

"We're upset with a decision Carlo made, not with the man himself," I say.

"That's a very responsible way to think about fighting with someone you love," Sammy replies.

I haven't said it out loud. But even hearing it in Sammy's voice isn't shocking or scary. It feels like I've thought it a thousand times before.

"Oh my god, does she love him?" Kenzie asks, dropping her drink on the counter and staring at Sammy like he knows better than I do.

Cat scoffs, still drying and stacking glasses.

"Of course she loves him. And before you ask, he loves her too. He loved her all the way back in February," she declares, like she's some sort of expert on the inner workings of both of our hearts.

"Gwen deserves that whole *love at first sight* thing," Kenzie says, mostly to Cat. But Sammy's eyes are on me, probably wondering if I'm about to deny it.

I can't, though.

"Charlie believes the universe brings him where he needs to be, with who he needs to be with. And even back then, I could see he needed you."

# Chapter 26
## *Charlie*

"So, why's she pissed at you?"

If I wasn't the only other person in the room, I wouldn't know Ana was talking to me. She has one earbud still in, and her eyes are glued to her laptop screen, refreshing her browser again and again. SAT results are supposed to come in tonight.

"Who's pissed at me?" I ask, trying to remain casual.

Gwen and I have been painfully business-like in private since Italy—partners, *not* friends, *no* benefits—but I thought we'd done a pretty good job keeping up appearances in front of Ana. Judging by the way she's raising her eyebrows at me over her computer, I guess not.

"I'm not oblivious," she mutters.

I rinse the dish in my hands and watch Gwen out the kitchen window, pacing back and forth on the back patio while talking on the phone. If she feels my eyes on her, she doesn't react.

It's not my place to tell Ana if Gwen hasn't said anything to her. Still, I won't outright lie to the kid.

"I handled a situation poorly in Italy," I say, abandoning the sink and joining Ana at the table.

She barely looks at me, just keeps clicking her trackpad on a regular rhythm.

"With your family?"

We'd told her as much as we reasonably could before we left—my mom had been sick, she was getting better, and I wanted to introduce Gwen to them.

"Yeah, with my family."

Although that's not really true. Aside from Clara's absolutely repellant behavior, which she and Gwen seem to have overcome, there were no sticking points with anyone but *me*.

"If it helps, I'm pretty sure Gwen would handle the situation pretty poorly if you met our mom, too," she says, a smile pulling at the corner of her lips. "Actually, that image is pretty funny."

I can't imagine Gwen interacting with Isabelle. There's so much pain between the two of them.

"True, but this one was all on me, not my family. She deserves to be pissed."

I didn't hide the council vote from her out of malice, but I still should have told her. Even with Clara's threat, I couldn't imagine a scenario where Gwen didn't become my wife. But she proved to me every day that I could trust her with everything, and I didn't meet my end of the bargain.

Ana clicks the refresh button repeatedly, breathing through her nose deeply like it's calming her. Which it clearly isn't.

"Did you lie to her?" she asks. She's still not looking at me, but I can feel the accusation in her tone all the same.

"Not exactly, but I kind of blindsided her with some information."

"Same thing," Ana mutters, and I involuntarily scoff, which

definitely gets her attention. "Look, Gwen assumes the worst in everyone, except for maybe me and Kenzie. She especially assumes people won't keep their word. She's an *actions speak louder* girl."

"So you recommend a grand gesture?"

I had been considering it, but was unsure of the execution. How do you show someone they are your entire world? How do you convince them there's nothing that could stand between the two of you?

"Less grand gesture, more put your money where your mouth is," she replies, typing on her phone at lightning speed and turning back to her computer. "Not actual money. It's an idiom or whatever."

"An idiom or *whatever*? Please tell me that's not how you responded on the SAT," I tease.

Ana just rolls her eyes. It's becoming a habit.

"That's a joke only an old person would make, you know that?" Before I even have a chance to argue, she shoots up from her chair. "Oh my god, they're here."

"Your scores are in?" I ask, but she's not listening to me.

"What the hell? I need a password to access my scores? I have a *password*?" She starts frantically scrolling through her phone, and I stand up from the table.

"I'll get Gwen," I say, patting her on the shoulder as I pass.

"Okay, yeah, ask if she knows what my password is," she mumbles, moving back and forth between her screens like the scores are going to disappear if she doesn't find her password quick enough.

I open the door and lean against the frame, watching Gwen stare at her dark phone. It's dark, and the light from the windows is the only thing illuminating her. She reminds me of how she looked in that alley, almost a year ago now.

*Put my money where my mouth is.* Maybe that's not such a bad idea.

"Hey, Ana's scores are in," I say. I wish I could touch her. Pull her into my arms and kiss the space under the corner of her jaw, where I can feel her pulse against my lips.

"Okay," she whispers, her arms still tight around her. "That was Ana's oncologist. She wants us to come in next week to discuss the results."

"Is she okay?" I ask as I step out into the night with her and shut the door, glancing behind me to make sure Ana's still distracted by finding her password. It feels like time has stopped. Ana's got an entire future ahead of her, and it rests on this moment in the darkness.

When Gwen turns to me, tears are cutting paths down her cheeks, but the relief is so clear in her features that the clock starts moving again.

"She said it's good news. She said not to worry."

I don't even think before I step forward and wrap my arms around her. She doesn't hold me, but she doesn't push me away either. She just lets herself cry, the falling tears seeming to ease the tension in her body until she's leaning into me, letting me hold her together.

"It's over, Gwen," I say into her hair, trying to give her everything without demanding a thing in return. My support, my heart. "You did it. *She* did it."

She nods against me, dragging in harsh breaths like the relief is pulling her underwater.

"I know," she chokes out, her voice cracking and tight. "I'm just..."

She can't seem to finish, and I don't need her to explain. Ana's not my sister or my kid, but even I'm overwhelmed. I rub my palm in circles on her back, listening to her calm her breathing. I feel her wipe away her tears with her sleeve before she pushes against my chest.

It's excruciating, letting her go, knowing she wants me to.

But I broke her trust, and now I know how to earn it back. To show her I meant every word in Trani.

"Her scores are in?" Gwen asks, hiccuping on the last word.

She wipes the tears from her cheeks and the mascara from under her eyes. My whole body itches to help, to comfort her, but I slip my hands into my pockets instead.

"She can't find her password to the website, but she got the email," I say, and Gwen laughs and she rolls her eyes.

"That's because she had them email me the password so she wouldn't lose it," she mutters, swiping up on her phone and searching through her email.

When she looks back up at me, she's built that beautiful, strong wall around herself again, and I don't think Ana will even know she's been crying.

"Thank you," she says as she walks past me toward the house. "For being there for both of us."

It takes me a few moments, listening to Gwen read the email to her sister, before I can steady myself the way she did and walk back into our home.

# Chapter 27
## *Gwen*

"All right, that's enough."

Ana's voice is a shock to my system. I've been sitting in silence organizing the closet for what must be hours. All socks have been turned right side out and paired. Charlie's shirts are organized by sleeve length and color. All of my pants have been put on those fancy pants-specific hangers with the clips. It's been a productive day.

"What are you talking about?" I ask, glancing over my shoulder as I pull all my t-shirts out of a drawer and start refolding them.

I saw a video where someone stacked them on their side in the dresser so they could see all their options. Hence, the inspiration for today's reorganization.

"You're soothing your anxiety by cleaning and organizing. It's your M.O.," she replies in her teenage attitude voice.

I wish she was wrong.

I don't even really know why I'm tense. It's not like I have some sort of decision to make. As much as I'm pissed at Charlie about not telling me about the council vote, I'm not going back on my word. We're in this together, and we'll get through this.

Maybe it's because I haven't seen Charlie make any effort toward resolving things between us. It's not like I want him to put on a show, but some sign that he realizes he hurt me and will attempt to change would be nice.

There's been this pit growing in my stomach every day since we got back from Italy. Because what if he doesn't address it? What if he's fine acting like this forever—just two objects floating around each other? What if he loves me, and he's fine with loving like this?

After everything that's happened, it seems impossible. But I've only known him for six months. People aren't always what they seem, no matter how much I wish differently.

"I'm not anxious about your appointment, you know that, right?" I ask, trying to stack the shirts like the video said and watching them fall over and crumple in the drawer.

"Oh, I know," she responds, grabbing a pile of sports bras from the ground and tossing them in a drawer. "You're mad at Charlie and it's making you all Martha Stewart."

I really didn't think I was fooling Ana. She knows me too well to miss when I'm avoiding the only other person we live with.

"You don't need to worry about that," I say, shoving the shirts in a drawer and giving up.

Whatever, they're at least all folded now. An improvement.

"I'm not worried." Her smile is almost triumphant. "I'm part of the solution."

I raise my eyebrows at her, but all she does is smile that big, ridiculous smile at me.

"You're not responsible for my and Charlie's relationship," I start to argue, but she just shakes her head and plops her hands on my shoulders, maintaining that grin.

"I am merely a supporting role in today's activities. Now

please go shower and shave your legs," she directs, dragging me out of the closet and toward the bathroom. While I stand in the middle of the room, she turns the water on and hunts for my curling iron.

"Why do I need to shave my legs?" I ask, leaning against the counter. There's a little bubble of hope in my chest that I'm trying to squash in the name of self preservation.

"I mean you don't *need* to, but I think you'd be happier if you did," she says, yanking my makeup bag from under the sink and pawing through it.

"You're not going to tell me what's going on?" I hate surprises, I really do.

"You're going to figure it out in like an hour, so just chill. Also, tell me where your dry shampoo is."

A half hour later, my legs *are* in fact shaved, and Ana's wrangled my slightly oily hair into pretty waves. While I was in the shower, she seemed to get herself together as well. I've never seen the dress she's wearing—it's pale gold and covered in a pretty floral pattern. It looks lovely on her.

The pit in my stomach has turned into a black hole of nausea. I feel my nails dig into the skin of my arms as Ana finishes my makeup.

"Ana..." I start as she lets me look in the mirror. This can't be happening. I didn't ask for this. I didn't need this much.

"Just take a deep breath and accept it, okay?" Ana murmurs, like she's comforting me. That's not her job.

But maybe, just this once, I'll let her.

Ana hands me a garment bag that I'm terrified to open. I breathe out a sigh of relief when crimson red, not white, fabric spills out as I open the zipper. It's simple, sleek satin and tea-length. When she helps me slip it over my head, Ana murmurs, *knew it.*

My heart is beating so hard I don't have the capacity to ask questions. Ana seems to have everything completely under control, though. She hands me shoes, makes sure I have my phone, says my purse is already in the car. It's like I'm floating through space, unable to think further than the next step in front of me.

When we walk out the front door, Zane and Kenzie are waiting by the sedan.

"Oh fuck," I finally whisper, and Ana laughs behind me.

"Yeah, I thought that might be your reaction," Kenzie says as Zane opens the back door. She slides in and holds her hand out to me. "I've got shooters, don't worry."

The entire drive to wherever the hell we're going, I can't speak. I'm worried about what will come out if I do. *Where are we going? Take me home. Is this real? Do I want this? God, I hope I'm wrong. Please, please, please let me be right.*

When we pull up to the county courthouse, I *know* I'm right. There's a buzzing under my skin and I feel lightheaded. Kenzie and Ana are gripping one of my hands each, and I can feel my palms slick against theirs.

"Zane, don't move," Kenzie orders, and he holds his hands in the air before activating the divider between the front seats and us.

Kenzie turns to me, fucking gorgeous in her champagne silk dress and bright red lipstick, so serious as she stares in my eyes.

"If you don't want to be here, just say the word, and we'll force Zane at gunpoint to drive us off into the sunset." She doesn't seem like she's exaggerating. She'd do it for me.

"Charlie said to tell you he said *fuck the vote*, whatever that means," Ana says, leaning her head against my shoulder.

*Fuck the vote.* We're at this courthouse, and he doesn't care about the vote. My hands are shaking, my pulse so quick it's making my breathing shallow.

He told me he wouldn't let them say no. And I have no idea how much a certificate means to The Syndicate, but he's making one thing clear. He won't be separated from me easily.

"This is nuts," I whisper, and Kenzie pops a brief kiss on my forehead.

"Yeah, but crazy things happen when you love someone."

Ana taps on the divider, and it's only a few moments before Zane's opening our doors. Ana and Kenzie slide out, and I take a deep breath. It doesn't slow my heart.

Peripherally, I take in everything around me when I step out of the car. The pretty Greek columns framing the stairs to the courthouse. Sammy and Catalina, also dressed in shades of white and gold, smiling at me from the stairs. The bustle of people just going about their day, doing their jobs. But I can't help but stare at Charlie.

It's not what he's wearing—though I could ogle at him for the rest of my life, with those tattoos peaking over his all-black suit. It's the way he's looking at me. He's letting me see everything. All his guilt, and his joy, and not one single drop of hesitation.

Ana and Kenzie join Sam and Catalina, and I guess I've made it clear I'm rooted to the spot I'm standing, because Charlie comes to me.

"I may have gone a little extreme on the *show you* part." He says the words against my skin as he presses his lips to my cheek. It's the first time he's touched me like that since Italy, and it burns in my veins.

"Just a little," I whisper, not trusting my voice.

He smiles at me, and he doesn't put his wall back up. I see it when the nerves filter through his expression.

"I told Kenzie to give you an out, but I'm going to say it again," he starts, clearing his throat and lacing my fingers through his. "If you don't want to do this, I will never hold it against you. We can go home and talk this out like rational adults."

He seems to steady himself, holding on to me like a life raft in a storm. My heart is in my throat, and I'm trying really hard not to ruin the makeup Ana so patiently did for me.

"I love you, Guinevere." The words soothe something in me, settling like a chord falling into harmony, like a piano being tuned. My pulse slows into an even rhythm, but I can still feel my heartbeat in my fingertips. "And even though I meant it when I said I'd never let the council refuse us, and I know you'll thrive in my family, I wanted to give you proof. That I'd choose you over my The Syndicate. That you are my fate, mia filettatura, my thread. Ever since I saw you in that alley, I knew I was tied to you. And I'd like to remain that way, in every form possible."

There's so much joy in his eyes. So much vulnerability. He's looking at me like I really *am* his fate, like he can't imagine his life without me. I pull my hands from his and place them around the back of his neck, feeling the soft, steady rhythm of his heartbeat, and I know it's the same for me. That I want us to be wrapped around each other, hands and hearts and futures, for as long as humanly possible. He swallows hard against my palms.

"Carlo Costa, did you bring me here to marry you?" I ask, pressing up on my toes and ghosting a kiss over his lips. He closes his eyes, chasing me as a pull away.

"I did," he says, settling for a kiss on my forehead. "But I have to warn you, I'm fairly certain my sister and father will put me in an early grave if we don't do a big wedding in Trani as well."

And as lovely as that sounds—the big wedding surrounded by the people we love in a beautiful place—this is even better.

Because this is for us. Not The Syndicate. Not the contract. Not to fulfill an agreement.

But for two people with their souls tied together.

"You can talk me into that later," I mutter, finally pulling him down to press my lips to his.

I've missed the feeling of his hands against my hips, the soft hum he makes when I open my mouth for him, the warmth and comfort and stability of Charlie holding me, knowing he's never once thought about letting me go.

"I could kiss you in front of this county municipal building forever, but we do have an appointment to make," he says, still placing small kisses on my lips like he can't quite seem to separate himself.

"Okay," I whisper, wrapping my arms around his middle and burying my head against chest. "Let's go get married."

He unwinds my arms from around him and pulls me by the hand toward the stairs and columns. He's thrilled. To *marry me*.

"Charlie," I say, planting my feet and tugging on him to stop. When he turns around, his grin is so wide it's got to hurt. I've never felt less like a means to an end in my entire life. "I love you, too."

We sign a shocking amount of paperwork, pay our fees, and wait in line with the people we love, laughing and talking. There's not a moment where Charlie lets go of my hand.

When it's our turn, we file into a dimly lit room, Ana standing next to me and Zane next to Charlie. We repeat the vows the judge dictates. Charlie reaches into his pocket and pulls out a long, red thread, tying one end around the ring finger of my right hand.

"From your dress in Trani," he whispers so only I, and maybe the judge, can hear. "Ana insisted you'd want to pick out your own ring, anyway."

I can't respond, because if I do, I know I'll cry again. So when the judge tells me to, I tie the other end of the thread around Charlie's ring finger.

And right before he kisses me, for the first time as my husband, he whispers *my thread* against my lips.

# Chapter 28
## *Gwen*

I thought my heart would be racing, but it's not. It's just loud. *So* loud. He has to hear it from across the room, leaning against the door, staring at the box in his hands. Or maybe his heart's beating just as hard, and he can't hear mine over his own.

I'm sitting cross-legged on our bed in an oversized shirt and bike shorts. I thought about dressing up for this, about digging through the drawer of lingerie, half of which still has the tags, and finding something that screamed control and dominance. But it didn't feel right. As much as we've talked and planned, laying in bed tucked against each other, this moment seems too vulnerable to be fully orchestrated.

I think there's a lot of things people get wrong about control, and about giving it up. Based on the things I've seen and read, I should take control of this moment. Tell Charlie to come to me, direct him to take off his clothes, or take mine off. Dictate his choices to relieve him of the burden of them. And fuck if that hasn't worked for us before.

But for us, domination is about compassion. It's a walk on a tightrope, balancing desire and comfort, vulnerability and abandon.

And right now, that balance requires patience. Every moment between us feels big and momentous, like we're excavating our true selves from underneath layers of pain and expectation. There's no one else I could do this with.

"I didn't know I could trust someone this much." He's still looking at the box when he says it, and his voice is tight with emotion.

Ever since the courthouse, he doesn't hide anything from me. Not when we're alone, or with our friends and family, not when he's teaching me to kill, not ever. It means more than the thread I can't remove from my hand, even though we had to separate the sides.

"I think you didn't know you could trust *yourself* this much," I reply, trying to ease the tension coiling in his muscles. And it works, because he looks up at me, and his smile is so soft and genuine I could cry.

He walks toward me slowly and sinks to his knees at the edge of the bed, placing the box next to me and crossing his arms to lean his head against them. I shift forward and run my fingers through his hair at the crown, watching his eyes drift shut and his shoulders relax. This feeling, like I've brought him even one moment of calm and reassurance, will never get old. I'll never get tired of feeling like this with him.

"Open your present, mia filettatura," he says, keeping his eyes closed.

I know what's in the box—we've sent links back and forth for days—but I humor him.

I slide my finger under the hinge and lift the lid, revealing an assortment of toys laying on top of a bed of silk. A midnight-black dildo, smooth and soft under my fingertips. Next to it, a small black bumper with a round, open base. Folded neatly underneath is a black harness made of vegan leather, the straps connected with a shiny silver ring. A small bottle of lube is tucked in the corner.

When I look back at him, his eyes are open, his stare imploring.

"Thank you for my gift," I whisper, leaning over and kissing his forehead.

"Anything for my wife," he says, reaching toward me.

I raise my hands as he pulls my shirt over my head by its hem. He tosses it to the ground, and I'm naked from the waist up, heat spreading over my skin with the way he looks at me. He practically crawls onto the bed to kiss my stomach, my ribs, my collarbones, the valley between my breasts.

The sound of his breath against my skin, the gentle way he traces the lines of my body with his hands, the murmured words spoken so softly, I know this is worship. This is *being worshiped*. Being touched by him like this is a religious experience. There's nothing I want more than to free fall into this reckless, overzealous love.

He makes me want to believe in soulmates.

He finally crawls fully onto the bed until he's pressing me backwards, and he only takes his mouth off my body to help me pull his shirt off. The feeling of his chest against mine, warm and drumming with the beat of his heart, is both comforting and carnal, and I arch my back to press as much of my body against his as possible. We could do this for hours, teeth and lips and hands and skin, half dressed and panting against each other. But I want what comes next, and I know he does, too.

I reach for his waistband, unlacing the neat little bow at the tie, and I can't help but grin at the endearing image of Charlie untying and retying the laces of his joggers, nervously adjusting his clothing.

I love him. I love him in this, and I love him trying to hide his nerves, and I love him joking with Ana, and I love him teaching me to angle a knife against an artery, and I love him on his knees for me.

He pulls my thighs around his hips and rolls us so he's underneath me. I feel his cock hard and pressed against my ass, so I rock back against him. The olive branches inked onto this throat stretch in front of me as he arches his head back and squeezes my thighs.

"Fuck, Gwen," he pants, and it's the most intoxicating thing I've ever heard.

I want to do it again, to drive him to the edge of pain, to hear his voice break for me. But we have plans, and I can't get carried away.

I lean forward and lick up the column of his throat, savoring the salt of his skin on my tongue, the subtle sweetness of his cologne in my nose.

"You sure you want this?" I ask against his shoulder, his neck, kissing between words. His fingers slip into my hair until his hands are cradling my head, and he pulls me back to look into my eyes.

"I'm sure." No hesitation in his eyes. No worry, no shame, no fear. Just eagerness and anticipation as he pulls me down close to kiss me. "Please, mio filo, fuck me."

The words break me and stitch me back together all in the same moment. Charlie's trust, his vulnerability, is the thread that binds this new version of myself, loved and unafraid.

I unwrap my body from his and clamber off him, trying to hide my apprehension, but I'm bouncing on my toes as I stand to the side of the bed. He gives me an endeared smile, a shaky laugh slipping from him as he sits so I can stand between his legs.

He peppers soft kisses on my shoulders and chest as he hooks his thumbs into my shorts and pulls them down my legs.

When I kick them off, he reaches for the box at the end of the bed and starts pulling out the contents.

We've watched about a dozen videos, both of the erotic and educational variety, so it doesn't surprise me when Charlie takes the lead, sliding the bumper over the base of the slim silicone cock and fitting it into the silver ring. The person I was before Charlie would have thought research before sex would be a mood killer, but few things have been hotter than laying in bed, watching porn, discussing what looks intriguing and what doesn't. Pressing my lubed fingers and toys into his ass while I have him talk through his fantasies. What he wants me to do to him, for him, with him.

The devotion in his gaze is overpowering as he wraps the harness around my waist, pulling the strap until it's snug, but not tight. He runs a finger under the leather, ensuring it won't bite at my skin, and I can see the hairs on his arm standing straight. He wraps each hanging strap around my thighs, one at a time, pressing his lips against my stomach. When the harness is secure, he leans back, his eyes dark and hazy with lust.

It's a little odd, the way I have to shift my hips and redistribute my weight, but it feels nice. I take the dildo and adjust it so the bumper sits comfortably against my clit. I'm already soaked, and the silicone slips pleasurably against me as I stroke the toy again.

Charlie's cough has me looking up from where my hand meets silicone. He's so gorgeous like this—pupils blown out, hair out of place from my hands, chest rising and falling hard as he grips the edge of the mattress. His eyes can't seem to settle on any part of me, tracing my breasts, climbing up my legs, watching me pump the toy between my legs in my fist.

"If you want me to stop?" I ask, rolling one of my nipples between my fingers.

"Lemon," he says, the whites of his knuckles the only sign that he's holding back.

"Good husband," I murmur, and I swear he whimpers when I twist my nipple harder and let out a cry. "Do you want to suck this for me?" I ask, pumping the dildo between my legs.

He nods quickly and then remembers his voice.

"Can I touch you while I do?" He's pleading like there's nothing he wants more.

It's intoxicating, and I nod.

He doesn't waste another second, flipping our positions so my ass is perched on the edge of the bed and he's standing in front of me. He trails his fingers down my jaw, over my peaked nipples, down my stomach, until he's gripping the toy.

"You're incredible," he murmurs, dropping to his knees and kissing the inside of my thighs. My body is on fire with the way he touches me. "My beautiful wife, my thread of fate."

He pulls my body further down the bed and wraps his hands around my ass as he lowers his mouth onto the dildo.

The image of Charlie on his knees for me, mouth wrapped around the toy, is fucking incredible. I knit my fingers into his hair and pull so I can see his eyes, glazed over with lust and begging for me. He shifts his hands further toward the inside of my thighs, so his fingertips can just barely press into my pussy.

The bumper grinds against my clit as he sucks, and the sounds he's making are driving me over the edge of sanity. He breathes heavily through his nose, never stopping, never taking his eyes off me.

"Need to be inside you," I pant, and I have no idea whose voice that is. She's desperate and demanding all at once. Charlie pumps his fingers into my pussy one last time before pulling back.

He tells me I'm beautiful all the time, but when he looks at me like that...

"You're beautiful," I whisper, unable to keep from saying it out loud. I press my palm to his cheek, rubbing my thumb over his swollen lips.

He closes his eyes and breathes deeply, turning to press a kiss into my palm. I've loved that, every time he's done it.

He stands up and cradles my face, and my entire body buzzes. Lightheaded and euphoric with the feeling of him so close to me, I sway into his body, trailing my teeth and tongue and lips over his collarbones.

"Lay on the bed, mio marito," I whisper against his skin, and I feel him laugh under my touch. I should learn more Italian, but I looked that one up as soon as we left the courthouse.

"Si, mia moglie."

It's inevitable that we end up with our bodies tangled again, me on top of him, the strap on caught between our stomachs as we kiss like it's the first time. We work together to remove his pants and boxers, and I'm out of breath by the time I'm standing at the edge of the bed with Charlie staring up at me.

"Thank you," I huff, trying to catch my breath as I coat my fingers in lube.

Charlie's pupils are blown wide, his chest rising and falling as he watches my movements.

"For what?" he asks, the last word breaking on a soft moan as I slip my fingers against his ass.

"For watching over me in that alley," I say, pressing into him gently. He throws his head back against the pillow, his shoulders taut. "Breathe for me, baby."

He nods and finds my eyes again, all of his muscles relaxing until I can pump my fingers in and out of him without resistance.

I'm not afraid of hurting him. I trust him to tell me if it's too much, or too fast. But there's an anxiety rooted somewhere deep in my chest, because I want him to let go. This is an extreme display of trust between us, and I feel like I've never wanted something more than his pleasure right now.

I pull my fingers out of him, and he watches as I coat the dildo and his ass with even more lube. When I position myself against him, he laces the fingers of my right hand through his.

"I love you, Gwen," he whispers. Electricity whips through my veins, sparking me from the inside out.

"I love you, Charlie," I say, and push into him.

It takes some breathing and relaxing—this is a step up from any of the toys we've used—but eventually I'm fully seated in him. His face is pinched in a pained bliss as he breathes through the new sensations. And even though I can't feel myself inside him, the new perspective is exhilarating.

Charlie spends so much of our time together begging to give me pleasure, to take care of me. There's something about giving him something new, focusing on him and his desires, that makes me feel like I've filled my chest with helium.

"Is this okay?" I ask, just barely pulling my hips back and sliding in. Charlie moans, and the sound is like a straight shot of liquor.

"So good, Gwen, please," he begs, still gripping my fingers tightly. I repeat the motion, and his legs widen a bit more, giving me more room.

"*You're* so good for me, Charlie," I say, finding a slow, gentle rhythm.

His cock is hard and laying against his stomach, leaking pre-cum that I wish I could lean over and lick. Instead, I settle for drifting my free hand over the underside. Charlie jerks and moans.

"*Fuckfuckfuckfuck*," he repeats, and I take his cock in my hand and pump it along with the motion of my hips.

The grinder continues to bump against my clit, still slick from my absolutely soaked pussy. The pressure isn't consistent enough to make me come, but it builds upon the feeling of euphoria I get from watching Charlie fall apart under me.

"Do you want to come like this?" I ask him, pulling out nearly to the tip and sliding back in, feeling his hips jerk into my hand.

"I think it's too much, for this time," he pants, finding my eyes.

There's a bit of guilt there, and I slow my movements, releasing his pulsing cock and trailing my fingers gently over his thigh. He shivers as I pump slowly back into him.

"Thank you for telling me," I reply, my breath thin from exertion. He looks almost relieved, and I hope the more we do things like this, the more he knows he could never disappoint me.

After a few more minutes, I slide out of him for a final time, and he's immediately leaning forward, grasping my hips and pressing kisses to my sternum.

"Can I take this off you?" he asks, rubbing the strap of the harness between his fingers.

I agree, and he carefully removes the entire contraption, setting it on the floor on one of the towels we brought out. He pulls me on top of him, sliding his tongue into my mouth and kissing me until we can breathe.

I can't help but grind on his cock, my clit throbbing with need. He groans into my mouth, reaching his hand out toward the nightstand.

"It's okay," I say, pulling back just a few inches to look into his eyes. "I went to the doctor. Got birth control. If you want, I mean." I'm missing a few words in my explanation, but my need is too potent to be eloquent.

"When did you have time to go to the doctor?" Charlie asks, and then seems to shake himself out of his shock. "Wrong question. You want to go without a condom?"

The thought of Charlie bare inside of me has my cunt clenching around nothing, and I grind against his cock again.

"I would like to, but only if you're okay with it," I reply.

His mouth is back against mine before I even finish the sentence, rolling my bottom lip between his teeth. He rolls us so I'm pinned beneath him, my hips still fighting to get as close to him as possible.

"Anything for you, my perfect wife," he says, pulling back and lining his cock up with my pussy.

He pushes into me slowly, and I was right. It's so much better. Feeling him inside me, being this close, it's a whole new level of fucking Charlie.

"I thought about this," he mutters, almost like he's saying it to himself as he reaches for a spare pillow and shoves it under my hips. The movement lifts my pelvis so his cock is hitting an angle inside of me that has my eyes rolling back in my head. "When you first looked over the contract, and you asked about kids. I thought about filling your sweet, perfect cunt up all the way back then. Did you know that, Gwen?"

I can't answer, because he's rocking into me, one hand on my hip and another on my abdomen, his thumb barely brushing my clit. The feeling is overwhelming, like fireworks bursting under my skin, and we've barely started.

"I asked you a question, mio filo," he says, his voice shaking a bit as he pumps into me faster. When I finally am able to catch his gaze, I smile at him.

"Someone feels like switching up the roles," I laugh, and he pulls completely out of me, rubbing the head of his cock against my clit.

"We promised to do whatever felt right that first night, and I'm acting on instinct," he says, a smile on his face as he pushes back into me swiftly, his cock so deep inside of me I can't help but cry out.

"Harder, Charlie, please," I say, and even though it feels like I'm begging, I know Charlie would do anything I asked right now. Change his pace, our position, fuck me however I told him to. There's something electric about the power exchange, the way we can read each other's bodies and minds.

He does exactly as I ask, pressing his thumb with more force against my clit and fucking me into the mattress, each thrust moving me further and further up it until I have to brace my hands against the headboard above me. Charlie's cock fills every inch of me, and I spread my legs as wide as I can so he can get closer, harder, faster.

"Anything you want, Gwen," he says, breathing hard and trickling sweat down his chest.

My orgasm rips through me without warning, the build and fall so sudden that I nearly black out with pleasure and shock. I hear Charlie cursing in Italian above me as I arch against him, wave after wave of pleasure ripping me apart at the seams. He doesn't relent, and his fingers on my clit and cock rocking against my g-spot drag out my climax until Charlie drops to his elbows above me. His tongue is against mine, both of us desperately riding our pleasure and each other's until he stills, every muscle in his body corded tight as he spills inside me.

I felt like I've run a marathon. My breath comes so heavy that my chest touches Charlie's as I try to come back down to earth. After a few beats, Charlie pulls out of me and drops to my side, immediately wrapping me in his arms and burying his nose in my hair.

Eventually, we'll clean up each other and the room, but for now, we lay in each other's arms, murmuring declarations of love and affection while we trace the red string tied around each other's fingers.

# Chapter 29
## *Gwen*

"Isn't this kind of silly?" I ask, leaning over the glass case and staring into the sea of gems and gold, diamonds and silver. "We're married. I don't need an engagement ring."

Charlie puts his arm around my waist and slides his hand over mine to fiddle with the red string still tied around my finger.

"You don't have to get one if you don't want one," he says quietly, surveying the options at the third store we've visited this morning. "But my family threatened me with a prolonged torture if I didn't give you a proper engagement and wedding."

I move past the diamonds, gorgeous and lab-grown, but somehow not calling to me.

"Your mother sent us an entire garden of flowers as congratulations," I argue, eyes running over the blue gems, topaz and aquamarine and sapphire, all shimmering like pools of pure ocean.

"Yes, and my sister called to make sure I recognized the congratulations came with stipulations," he sighs.

I wasn't naïve enough to think Charlie's grand gesture

meant anything to The Syndicate. And although he's ruffled a few feathers—namely Clara and Lucia's—Emily assured me that no one intends on voting against us. As long as we play nice and have a big Costa wedding.

"All right," I agree, wandering further down the display. "We've got to find something today, though. Ana's appointment is in the morning, and I want her to know I'm focused on her."

His lips find my temple as I scan the last case in the row. They're all so gorgeous and bright, and I'm fighting a little smile as I lean in closer.

"We really do have a theme," Charlie chuckles, scanning the row of rubies, garnets, and rose quartz set in shades of gold.

"Seems fitting to replace the thread," I say, catching the eye of the jeweler who is giving us some privacy.

I ask him to show us the lab-grown options, and he shuffles through the gems, picking through options and holding them out to us to examine.

Finally, my eye catches on a pear-shaped ruby surrounded by little clusters of diamonds.

"It looks like you," Charlie mutters as the jeweler hands it to me. The shining gold nearly twinkles in my palm as I hold it. Charlie asks him more questions, but I can't help but slip it on my finger to see how it looks.

"Okay, I changed my mind," I say, twisting my hand and watching the light reflect in the little angles of the stones. "I love engagement rings."

"You're sure?"

"Totally sure."

Ana doesn't really look like she believes Dr. Mya. Or she's afraid to. But Dr. Mya is undeterred.

"Your biopsy came back negative for all evidence of cancer." They grab my sister by her shoulders and squeeze, looking her directly in the eyes. "But yes, Banana. You are cancer free."

The relief I feel is indescribable. I don't want to cry, but I feel like every bit of guilt and fear that has been holding me up for the last six months has been released. I'd give anything for her to never have gone through this, but it's *over*. My muscles feel unraveled, and if Charlie didn't have his arm around me, holding me up, I'm not sure if I'd still be standing.

The more Dr. Mya talks, the more Ana seems to realize that this is real. Her hard expression melts inch by inch, her careful, neutral frown slowly morphing into a smile. She'd walked into this office like she was ready for her doctor to have lied, prepared to hear that the radiation therapy didn't work, that she was one of the miniscule number of people who had worse outcomes. She had held her head high, not holding my hand. Wanting to face this on her own.

But maybe without thinking, she reaches backwards as she listens to Dr. Mya. Charlie keeps his arm around my waist as I reach forward and cling to Ana's hand.

When Dr. Mya leads us out of their office, Ana's still holding back a little. Her smile's still dimmed, her shoulders tense, arms wrapped around herself a little too tight. But as soon as the door closes, she turns to me and Charlie, tears welling in her eyes.

"Permission to say fuck?" she asks, her voice wobbling.

I choke out a laugh, feeling like I'm breathing for the first time since we walked into the hospital. Maybe since we came here for the first time, months and months ago.

"Permission granted."

Her tears fall as she throws her arms around me. It's not the first time I've felt like Ana was the thing holding me together.

"Thank fucking god, right?"

"Couldn't have said it better myself, kid," I say.

It really is over. There's a tiny pit of fear in the bottom of my stomach that it's too good to be true, that we can't trust this news, but I try to battle it down. Ana is safe. Healthy and happy and safe.

"Perfect score on your SATs and a perfect score on your scans. What are we going to do with you?" Charlie asks, ruffling her hair.

She shakes him off, but wraps one arm around his middle and hugs him, too.

"I did not get a perfect SAT score," she grumbles, latching on to my hand as we make our way to the elevator bank.

"A 1520 is nothing to downplay," Charlie argues as we all ignore the creepy kid's voice. "Carnegie's going to be begging for you to accept their offer."

Her cheeks turn red as she tells us about Gray's scores and application requirements and deadlines, and I'm so fucking happy. She deserves this. She deserves good SAT scores, and summer college visits, and a distinct absence of cancer. She deserves all the good things coming to her. We both do.

Should have known it couldn't last forever.

Because as we exit the elevator on the ground floor, a vaguely familiar voice rises from the front desk. My stomach's already tying itself in a knot when I look toward the commotion. Where a redheaded woman in a sundress and an oversized hat is arguing with the security staff.

"Is that..." Ana asks, and I grip her hand and push her behind me.

Charlie's already at my side, telling Ana we'll handle it.

"She's my *daughter*, and I have a right to see her if she's *dying,*" Isabelle's sharp voice rises over the muttering of the rest of the patients and visitors as we get closer.

I steel myself, ready for whatever nightmare my mother always brings.

"What are you doing here, mom?" I ask, keeping Ana squarely behind me. She must not want to see her, either, because she's not making her presence known.

"Guinevere, thank goodness. Tell these people I'm Morgana's mother," she sighs, dragging her manicured nails through her hair.

I hate that I picked that habit up from her. Pressing my nails into my skin, too.

"We were just leaving. We'll take Ms. Byrne with us," Charlie says, laying the accent on thick as he placates the check-in staff.

I don't know how she missed him before, but Isabelle's suddenly assessing him like he's a target, a prize.

"Jesus Christ, mother, come on," I say, shooing her toward the exit.

Ana must peek her head around, because our mother lets out an exaggerated gasp.

"Oh, my baby Morgana," she cries, pushing past me to wrap Ana in her arms.

I'm so shocked I barely have time to react, but before I can pull Isabelle off of her, Ana shakes her head, grimacing at me. Her hand is still in mine.

She's telling me to leave it. Brave of her.

"Hi, mom," she says quietly, and it pinches my heart a little.

Isabelle barely knows her. Doesn't know that she doesn't like being called Morgana. Doesn't know about her surgeries and scars.

"Mom, she's got some skin irritation. Please be careful," I

chide, and she whips around to look at me, dropping her daughter.

"Well, how would I even know that? I have no information! I had to hear from someone *other than you* that my baby girl was sick," Isabelle scoffs.

"I haven't had a working phone number for you for years," I shoot back, trying to keep my tone neutral. "How exactly would you have expected me to contact you?"

"You didn't even try," my mother accuses

"Why don't we take this outside so we don't bother the other patients, yes?" Charlie suggests, and I look around to see plenty of eyes on us.

Isabelle agrees easily, putting her arm around Ana, cooing things like *poor baby* and *my daughter*.

When we get outside, the sticky heat nearly unbearable, Ana shrugs off Isabelle's arm and finds her way to Charlie's side. Through the anger rising under my skin, there's some little part of me that's so fucking happy I picked someone she could trust.

"I apologize that I didn't make more of an effort to contact you, but you really didn't provide a lot of options. I've had the same phone number since I was thirteen. You could have called any time."

Out of the corner of my eye, I see Ana grab on to Charlie's arm. Fuck, this was supposed to be a great day for her.

"Maybe we should let your sister and mom talk," Charlie offers, and I know he's already halfway to calling Zane to whisk Ana away. But Isabelle cuts in before any of us can move.

"I'm not letting you leave with my baby," Isabelle cries, accusation lacing her tone.

"She's sixteen, mom. And Charlie is my husband. She's safe with him." I'm trying to keep myself controlled and careful, but I can already feel the range slipping in.

"Oh yes, I've heard about your *husband*," she sneers, glancing at my brand new ring and turning to look at Ana. "See, she tells you I'm a terrible mom, but look at her."

My heart stills in my chest, my rage bordering on wrath now.

"What exactly is that supposed to mean?" I demand from Isabelle. I can feel Charlie's presence right behind me.

"You're a hypocrite," she accuses, honest to god tears welling in her eyes. "You judge me for dating a few guys, trying to build a life for you two, when you've done so much worse."

She knows. I have no idea *how* she knows, but she does. My anger is laced with panic now, because I can see this crash ahead of us, and I have no way to stop it.

"What's she talking about, Ginny?" Ana asks, her voice small and almost afraid.

"We can talk about it later," Charlie mutters at her, but Isabelle's not having it.

I have no idea what she gets out of this, ruining this for Ana and me, but she's sure committed to the bit.

"When did your sister tell you she was seeing Charlie?" she asks, her eyes glaring at her youngest daughter.

"Mother, enough." I demand, but Ana's looking at me with her brow furrowed, and I can feel my heart breaking in my chest. She's going to hate me.

"February. After my surgery." I close my eyes, trying to collect myself.

"And how long did she say they had been together?" If that's fucking glee I can detect in Isabelle's voice, Charlie's going to have to do a stellar job of convincing me not to kill her.

"Ana, you don't have to listen to this," Charlie offers, and when she turns to him, I can already see the pain replacing trust.

"Six months." Her voice is small, timid, nothing like the Ana I know.

"Strange, then, that your father called to tell me that Guinevere offered to crawl into his bed over dinner in February. An odd thing to do, for a woman in love."

Isabelle's words hit their mark, even if they're half a lie. I don't know who's embellishing—Ben or Isabelle—but there will be consequences. I have no reservations about ripping Ben limb from limb.

"I don't understand," Ana says, waiting for me to meet her gaze before she continues. "Why were you at dinner with Ben?"

"It's not what she's say—" I start, but my mother speaks right over me, and I can see Charlie restraining himself from lashing out at her.

"For money, of course," she laughs, like it's something funny. Like destroying her daughters in front of her is a game. "She's told you how awful I am for dating men with money, and she goes to your own father, offering herself up for some cash."

Ana and I can only stare at each other. I watch her put together the pieces, retrace the timeline in her mind.

"You promised me." But she's not talking to me. She turns to Charlie, shaking his hand off her shoulder. "You promised me you weren't here because you pitied the cancer kid."

"Ana..." I start, but tears start flowing as Ana whips around.

"You promised me, too, that you weren't changing your life for me." She crosses her arms over her chest, her glare so familiar I know it's a twin to mine. "You lied to me. We don't lie to each other."

"It's complicated, Ana," I start again, my own tears welling in my eyes. But she just shakes her head, unwilling to accept that.

"I'm done being fucking lied to." She turns to Charlie, and I know he won't be able to keep the truth from her. "Did you give my sister money for my treatment?"

He looks at me, and I can see him asking for forgiveness. But it's not needed. Ana's right, she deserves the truth, or as much of it as we can give her.

"Yes," he admits, and pain flashes through her eyes. She twists back to face me.

"Did he force you to sleep with him in exchange for the money?"

My eyes pop open, panic taking over and constricting my chest. I try to reach out for her, but she pulls away.

"No." I leave no room for second guessing. "Charlie and I came to an arrangement. He helped with the cost of treatment, and I agreed to eventually marry him. But I promise," I emphasize, my voice cracking, "I promise you I really do love him. This started out as something else, and I'm sorry I lied to you, but I'm telling you the truth now."

Ana shakes her head, and I don't know if it's in disbelief or because she's overwhelmed.

"Oh, please," Isabelle cuts in. "You can't exactly trust her."

Charlie glares at Isabelle, the promise of a long, painful death obvious in his eyes. But it's Ana who speaks up.

"And I can trust you?" she demands, and Isabelle looks shocked. "I haven't seen you in years, and the first thing you tell me is that my sister is a liar and a hypocrite. You don't ask about me, or my treatment. You don't know anything about me. I don't know why you're here, but I don't *want* you here." She points to me, still sobbing, and I feel like my heart's been ripped to shreds and shoved back in my chest. "She raised me. This is totally fucked, and I'm going to be mad about it for a long time, but I know she loves me."

Ana steps back from all of us, grabbing the hem of her t-shirt and wiping her eyes.

"I need some space, and I need her gone," Ana declares, waving off Isabelle.

*Would be my fucking pleasure.*

"Do you want me to call the McCallums?" I ask, my voice tight and wobbling with the effort not to cry.

"I can take the damn bus. Or I'm sure you can just call the lady who follows me around at school all the time?" She huffs at our bewildered looks, throwing her bag over her shoulder. "I'm not an idiot, guys. I assumed she was there because of Charlie's work with the Foundation, but that's probably a lie, too."

Guilt slices at my chest, but I try to keep my face neutral.

"Please tell us next time you suspect someone's following you," Charlie asks, and she glares at him.

"Please tell me next time you decide to get in some weird arranged marriage with my sister so she can afford my cancer treatments, how about that?" she yells, throwing her hands up in the air. "Do you realize how ridiculous this all sounds? I'm going to Gray's and I'm only communicating with you two via his mom until further notice."

Ana makes her way to the bus stop, and I double check her location is still on while Charlie calls Lily and gives her instructions.

"What exactly was your goal here, mom?" I ask, exhaustion taking over my body as I turn to Isabelle.

The urge to kill her for hurting Ana fades as I see the pain in her eyes. She's hurt that Ana walked away. Charlie slides closer to me, and I feel just a little more calm.

"I was worried about my daughters!" my mother exclaims, just a little too over the top to be honest. "Ben got a hold of me in Marseille and told me about your little stunt."

"Jesus Christ, you don't actually believe him, do you?" I implore, begging her to see. But Isabelle just raises her eyebrows impatiently. "When Ana got sick, I came to Ben and asked for the money to help his daughter. Because he's her father, and that's what he should do. And he said he'd give me the money if I was his mistress. Said something about wanting to test out the newest model."

The words hit Isabelle like a slap across the face. She only allows herself to be stunned for a moment, pushing her hair out of her face and rearranging her features into something like disdain.

"You're lying. You're covering so your new meal ticket won't turn on you." She sounds like she truly believes it, too.

I turn my head up and catch Charlie's gaze, and it's a balm to the ache in my chest that there's no distrust or fear in his eyes. He knows Isabelle, or Ben, is lying.

"Is Ben still married? Because he was four months ago." Isabelle flinches again, and I soften my tone a bit. "I know there was a time when all you wanted was for us to have everything. That you were trying to provide for us. And I'm sorry for being angry at you for that. I understand better now the lengths you'll go for someone you love." I take a deep breath and reach for my mom's hand. "But at some point, your priorities changed. And I'll never apologize for getting Ana out of that environment."

Isabelle only huffs more, snapping her hand to her chest. And I'm not angry, not for her inability to understand. Just for the way she hurt us in the process.

"I'm going to call Linda and let her know what's headed her way," I say to Charlie before tugging him down so I can whisper in his ear. "Please don't kill her. I have a plan."

He kisses me softly, and even though my heart is in shreds, I know he'll figure out how to piece it back together.

# Chapter 30
## *Charlie*

Ana's standing at the top of the McCallums' staircase, arms crossed over her chest and hip leaning against the banister. Gray's right behind her, his face equally annoyed. I'm pretending I'm not hiding in the kitchen with Linda and Paul, Maddie sitting on the edge of the island clinging to her dad's arm.

"I'm still pissed," Ana calls down to her sister, who's standing at the bottom of the stairs.

We let her cool off over the weekend, take some needed space, but she can't live at the McCallum's forever, however much she might want to right now.

"Swear jar!" Maddie yells, kicking her feet happily.

Paul shushes her, trying to avoid pulling Ana's attention to us. Or really, to me. Gray's parents are still in Ana's good graces.

"You're allowed to be pissed," Gwen sighs. "Just be pissed off at home."

Gray wraps his arm around Ana's shoulder, protective like a brother.

"Ana's welcome to stay here as long as she wants, right mom?" he declares.

Linda cringes.

"I'm not getting involved," she calls, and Gray scoffs, whispering in Ana's ear.

"Look, absolutely nothing is changing. Charlie and I are still married; we're staying in the same home. You deserve an explanation, but you have to trust us that nothing has changed."

Ana glares at Gwen for a few moments before turning on her heel and marching into Gray's room, the sound of packing echoing down the hall. Linda and Paul both breathe out a sigh of relief.

"Sorry about this," Gwen mutters, joining us in the kitchen and moving directly in front of Maddie.

The present is messy enough that I shouldn't think of the future. But watching her pick up the toddler and balance her on her hip, making faces that cause Maddie to erupt in giggles, I can't help it.

"Don't worry, you handled the black hair dye incident of freshman year. We owed you one." Linda and Gwen share a look before Ana comes stomping down the stairs, her bag under her arm.

"This does not mean I forgive you."

Gwen and Ana are in the back seat together, as usual, but Ana will barely look at her sister.

"I promise, we'll give you as much of an explanation as we can," I say, watching her in the rearview mirror.

She huffs and rolls her eyes.

"Oh yeah, I'm totally looking forward to the story of how you blackmailed my sister into marrying you."

I think about that first night at Catalina's, when Gwen thought I was doing just that. Her grandmother's watch still sits on her shelf in our office, surrounded by new books and old photos, all our memories.

"We already addressed that," Gwen argues, her mom-voice in full force. "There was no blackmail involved."

"Oh, and I'm just supposed to believe that? What if you have Stockholm Syndrome? What if he's still threatening you?" Her voice climbs higher and higher, and I can't tell if she's actually afraid Gwen's in trouble, or she's just validating her own anger.

"Zane, pull over," I order. Ana's eyes catch mine in the rearview as Zane smoothly glides against the curb and puts the car in park. "Get out of the car."

He and I both do, stepping out onto the suburban street. Both Gwen and Ana roll down their windows.

"What's this?" I hear Ana ask, but she's on the driver's side of the car. Gwen's suppressing a laugh while she stares at me.

"Gwen, you are free to go. The keys are in the ignition. If you are afraid, or I've blackmailed you, or whatever, please feel free to take the car and make your getaway." I try to keep my tone serious, but the look on Gwen's face is making it difficult. I glance over the roof of the car to see Zane with his arms crossed, staring at Ana like she's being ridiculous.

"Fine! Gwen's not a victim of extortion, I understand. Please get back in the car and turn on the AC," she whines, and I lean through the window to kiss Gwen before getting back in the car.

As Zane starts back down the road toward the highway, I continue." As we said at the hospital, your sister and I had a mutual understanding."

Gwen's staring at Ana, who refuses to look at her.

"And this understanding included paying for my treatment?"

"Yes," Gwen says, all the humor gone from her eyes. "I'm sorry, Ana, but our insurance didn't cover the cost, and I didn't know what else to do. Charlie's offer was a miracle."

Ana's biting the inside of her cheek, staring at her feet. She looks so young. Too young to think about medical bills.

"I know you didn't want Gwen to change her life for you, but that comes with the territory of being a parent," I say, which has her head snapping up to meet my gaze.

"She's not my mom," Ana barks. Gwen's face blanches, and for the first time, Ana looks guilty. She turns to her sister, tucking her bare feet under herself. "It's not fair to you, having to do all this for me when I'm not even your kid."

"You think I care?" Gwen replies, her voice on the edge of cracking. "You're the most important person in the world to me. I'd do anything, and I mean *anything*, for you. I wouldn't trade our relationship for anything."

Ana purses her lips, taking deep breaths through her nose like she's fighting tears.

"So he gave you the money, and you agreed to marry him?"

"Yes," she replies simply, and I fear what question is coming next.

"Why?"

"We can't tell you," I say, watching the small amount of trust we just built with her leave her eyes. "I'm sorry, but there really are some things I can't tell you until you're an adult. But I swear that once you're eighteen, if you want to know, Gwen and I will tell you."

Ana looks down at her hands again. I know this is going to be hard for her. I wish I could make this easier. Life's given her enough difficulty on its own. She shouldn't have to be so strong.

"I'm assuming that's also going to be the answer to *why do I have a bodyguard*?" she mumbles.

"Unfortunately, yes," I admit, grimacing.

I know this is necessary, that she's too young right now to fully understand the scope of the secrets she'll have to keep if she knows. But I also know it hurts Gwen to keep these things from her.

"This is all my fault," she mutters, tears dropping onto her lap.

"It's not," Gwen says, and I nod along with her. So does Zane. "It's not your fault that you got cancer, and it's not your fault that it costs money to treat it, and it's not your fault I needed help to pay for it. The world isn't always fair, but that doesn't mean it's your fault."

"You already do so much for me," Ana whispers, wiping the tears from her eyes with her sleeve. "And I thought this was finally for you, you know? I hate it was for me."

They're so alike, Gwen and Ana. So desperate to prove that they can do everything on their own, that no one needs to inconvenience themselves to support them. Gwen reaches out for her sister's hand, and Ana lets her take it.

"I'm sorry we lied to you," I say, and I mean it. Even though there was no logical way for us to tell Ana from the start, I'm still sorry. "And I'm sorry we can't tell you everything now. But I promise moving forward, we'll be as honest with you as we can."

She collects herself for a minute, her eyes red-lined but dry as they meet mine.

"You really love her?" she demands, her voice wobbling a little. "You swear that you guys aren't lying about that?"

"I've never lied to you about that," I promise. "I loved your sister from the moment I saw her. I swear, Ana."

Months ago, as we sat in a cafe, Ana gave me one of these looks. Like she was trying to find the lie she knew was there in my eyes. It had been easy to put on a facade, knowing it was necessary to make Gwen and I work.

But now, I give her the same grace I do Gwen. I don't put up any walls or shows, I just let her see that I'm being honest. That I love Gwen, and I love Ana because Gwen loves her.

"Okay," she whispers. And we drive home.

## Chapter 31
### Gwen

I press the tip of the blade under Ben's chin, watching his pupils dilate in fear. He tries to force muffled screams from behind the gag, but it seems he's too afraid to thrash his head back and forth anymore. Probably for the best.

Charlie's fingers trail up my arm as he presses his lip to the corner of my jaw. My head swims pleasantly, and I let my eyes flutter shut just for a moment as I lean into the sensation.

"Playing with your food, mia filettatura?" Charlie whispers into my skin, and the smile that spreads across my lips is impossible to suppress.

"He deserves it," I say, feeling a small trickle of blood flow down my fingers. The boat rocks again, and I lean against Charlie for support.

We've been out here for a few hours with Ben. His body is littered with slices and bruises, evidence of our time together. Charlie has praised me multiple times for how much I've learned, based on the fact that Ben is still alive.

Charlie unties Ben's gag, and he immediately starts screaming for help, which is useless. There's no one around us for miles. The little yacht we're on is nice—it's a shame it'll be at the bottom of the ocean soon.

"You're certain I can't have your mother join us?" Charlie asks, close to my ear so I can hear him over Ben.

I had thought about whether my mother deserved this. If she had hurt me and Ana enough that I could put a knife or bullet through her heart. Or at least ask Charlie to do it.

But after significant consideration, I decided I couldn't. Even after everything that had happened between us, I know she once loved me. Maybe she still does, in her own way.

"Thank you, my love, but no," I reply, palming the handle of the knife while the boat settles. "I'm getting exactly what I want."

Ben's cries turn to whimpers as my husband wraps his arms around my middle from behind, pulling me against him. I can feel him, hard and straining against the zipper of his pants, and I arch my ass against him with a smile. It never gets old, this feeling when we kill together.

Charlie huffs a laugh into my neck and separates our bodies, busying himself with a wide variety of blades and tools. Ben's eyes grow wide in fear, and he yanks against his restraints again. Desperate to save a life worth nothing.

"You're going to get caught," he pants, his voice desperate and cracking under the weight of his screams. Charlie takes a seat at the table on the other side of the room. "I'm your sister's father. Someone's going to make the connection."

"Honestly, thank you for the opportunity to talk about this, because I'm *so* proud of how we got around that," I say, stabbing the knife directly into his thigh. I can hear Charlie's laugh over the sound of Ben destroying his own vocal chords. I might be enjoying this a little too much.

"It took some patience, which is *not* my virtue," I sigh, slipping into Charlie's lap. His hands wrap around my thighs as I sink into him. One hand settles on my hip before dragging up the side of my shirt and drawing indiscernible shapes on my ribs. "But we have a friend who was extremely helpful in setting up as much distance between us as possible. And setting *you* up for a very tragic downfall."

Ben struggles for a moment, but the pain must be overwhelming, because he lets out a cry that fills me with vindictive glee. Emily really has been a godsend with all of this. It's taken months, but we've laid all the evidence we needed to. Manipulated Ben's accounts to make it seem like he's withdrawn sizeable sums of cash at regular intervals. Planted rumors with his staff and neighbors that he's getting involved in even less credible businesses than before.

Maybe I'm cocky, but it feels surprisingly easy to convince the world that Ben would be involved in an unfortunate incident of drug trafficking gone terribly bad.

"Please," he begs, and I'm relieved we've gotten to the bargaining stage. As much as I'm enjoying my vengeance, I'm starving. "Please, I'm sorry about the whole money thing. How about I pay you back for the treatment, huh?"

"You can't honestly believe that money is the issue here," Charlie scoffs, and I scratch my nails against his thigh. "I bought this boat just to kill you on. Well, technically, *you* bought this boat, Ben. But we both know how fickle finances can be."

I'm lucky enough not to know yet how it feels to face death. I'm sure that I'll be surprised by my reaction when I do. But I certainly didn't expect Ben to start bawling. He's incomprehensible, begging and screaming for his life, with spit and snot mingling with his tears as he chokes on his own saliva. It's pathetic.

I turn in Charlie's lap and throw my arms around his shoulders, touching my nose to his. He's so beautiful. I don't say it enough, but he really is. Hair messy, smile kind, that devoted and lovesick look in his eyes. The feeling in my chest, like I could turn and find him in a crowd no matter how many people surrounded us, is always there. Pulsing like a living thing between us.

"Take me home, Charlie," I whisper, brushing my lips against his. He presses my body against his, and the sounds of everything around us slip away as he kisses me.

"Anything for you, mio filo," he says.

An hour later we're walking along the shore, Emily having dropped us off at a private dock before taking off up the shoreline. On the horizon, there are no emergency boats. No investigation. Not even a ripple where the yacht sunk under the night sky.

Even if there is an inquiry into Ben's disappearance, there's nearly one hundred thousand dollars' worth of cocaine in the hull of that ship, safe in watertight containers. Emily's permanent career should be alibis and cover stories.

There are never a ton of stars in the D.C. night sky, but as we walk toward where Zane is supposed to meet us, I feel like I see more of them than usual. Bright and winking, they follow us on our path as we walk hand in hand, husband and wife, into the night.

# Epilogue One
## Gwen

*Eight Months Later*

**M**y hands are shaking as I clasp them in my lap, trying to hold still so Ana can finish painting my lips a red that matches the stone on my finger. My eyes are closed, but I can hear Kenzie and Clara making polite conversation behind me. Well, *Kenzie's* putting in an effort. Even without looking, I can tell Clara is still fuming.

"Okay, all done," Ana announces, swiping her thumb under my lip once more.

When I open my eyes, I have to blink back tears. Not just because Ana did a wonderful job—she did all of our makeup perfectly—but because of how happy she looks. My beautiful, brilliant, cancer-free sister, caring about the things she should care about, like her application to Carnegie and softball championships.

"Thanks, kid," I whisper, reaching back to pat her face. She smiles and scrunches her nose at me before brushing my hand away.

"No crying, and no touching faces," she orders, turning to Clara and Kenzie. "That applies to you, too."

Clara's only met Ana once, when she and Emily came for a visit to D.C. last winter. Ostensibly, it was a family Christmas celebration. In reality, we were strategizing about the threat lurking in Gia's team. The girls had stayed for dinner, and as soon as Ana went to bed, Clara had asked what position we'd like to train her for in The Syndicate.

I was less surprised by the question, and more by Charlie's reaction. He nearly bit Clara's head off, vehemently opposed to the idea of Ana ever joining The Syndicate.

"She's been through enough," he said, his arm wrapped protectively around my shoulder. "And she's under no obligation to take any sort of role with us."

But Clara had just kept her eyes on me, nearly bored with her brother's outburst.

"She can decide when she's of age, obviously," Clara said, sipping her glass of wine. "But you can guide her. She'd be good."

I have just over a year to decide. And I'm going to take every last moment until her eighteenth birthday to make that choice.

So I recognize that look in Clara's eyes. For the first time since we started getting ready this morning, she's not pissed out of her mind. She's assessing. Watching my little sister as she meticulously cleans her brushes and packs her bag. I catch Clara's eyes in the mirror I'm sitting in front of and shake my head, but she only smiles. Never a good sign.

"Ana, can you go downstairs and grab my shoes? I left them in our room."

Despite the fact that we are already legally married, Charlie's father had insisted we sleep in separate rooms the night before the wedding, in the name of tradition. So Ana and I spent last night watching movies and doing face masks. And I left a few things there, just in case I needed to get her out of the bridal suite at any point.

"Yeah, no problem," she shrugs, lifting the skirt of her midnight blue dress and padding out of the sunroom-turned-bridal-suite, her feet bare.

As soon as the door shuts behind her, I glare at Clara.

"None of that, she's not even seventeen," I say, standing from the vanity and walking to grab myself a water from the little dry bar Aurelio set up. Clara's eyes flicker to Kenzie, who's staring at her phone studiously. "Kenzie's become used to ignoring things she can't ask questions about, don't worry."

"I am checked out until invited back in," Kenzie mumbles, popping her headphones in and burrowing into the corner of the sofa.

"Your sister's smart," Clara says, that little calculating look in her eyes. "And she's got the disposition to do well in The Syndicate. She gets it from you."

It's still strange, having Clara's approval. At the council meeting in October, she was the most vehement vote in favor of our marriage. She made her argument to a crowd that didn't need convincing about how I'd proved my dedication to their family and mission through blood and gore. It was touching, if not slightly graphic.

"While it warms my heart to hear you say that, I'm not convincing her into anything," I say, forcing myself not to down a second bottle of water. There is no one in this building I want holding my dress up while I pee tonight. "She could decide she doesn't want to know anything else when she turns eighteen, and that's completely fine with me and Charlie."

We actually haven't discussed it much, but Clara doesn't

need to know that. Charlie takes my lead most of the time anyway.

She slumps into the vanity chair, dropping her head back and letting out a whine.

"Please, just let me train her? I'll adopt her or whatever, and she can become the next Costa matriarch after me. She's clever and has a good wit. She'll do fine."

My jaw drops a bit before I can recover, but it doesn't seem to matter, because Clara's not looking at me. Her eyes are clenched shut, and she's rubbing the bridge of her nose like she has a migraine.

"Going to have to pass on that one," I say, watching her crack her neck. One of their parents must do it, seeing how she and Charlie both have the habit. "Ana's been forced into enough. She'll choose this if she wants it."

"And she'll be over the age where I can adopt her once she does. Yeah, I know. Worth a shot," Clara mumbles, straightening in her chair and smoothing over her foundation where she rubbed it off.

"Deniz seems...nice?" I can't even convincingly finish the sentence.

Clara's date—and probable future husband—has barely said a word to me since we met yesterday. He hovers around Clara like she's the center of his gravity, and she generally looks like she's contemplating the most painful ways to remove his internal organs. Clara scowls at me, the steam back to rising out of her ears.

"Well, he at least looks fertile. You'll get an heir out of him."

"I would rather self-replicate than let that man impregnate me," she growls, adjusting the straps of her dress nervously.

"I've seen the way he looks at you. There's no way you're not fucking," I scoff, heading over to the garment bag hanging on the door.

"I didn't say that," she says, almost to herself, before catching my eyes in the mirror. "Also, since when is that your fucking business?"

I abandon my dress and cross back to Clara, yanking her hand off the back of the chair and cradling it in mine.

"Isn't that what sisters are for?"

For a split second, I think she's going to slap me across the face, wedding makeup or not. But then she gives me her vicious grin, pulling me down to throw her arms around my shoulders.

Ana returns, my shoes and a bottle of champagne in her hands. Kenzie takes her presence as a sign she's welcome back in the conversation and tosses her phone on the coffee table.

"I saw Charlie in the hallway and he gave me this," she says, waving the bottle. "Told me to share."

"Give me that, no champagne for you," I say, bopping her on the nose and snagging the ice-cold bottle from her. Clara procures champagne glasses out of god-knows-where.

"Oh, come on. In Italy, minors can drink with their guardians," Ana whines, cuddling up next to Kenzie. "Plus, I'm almost seventeen."

"How do you know Italian liquor laws?" I ask, popping the bottle to the sound of Kenzie's polite clapping. A little bit of foam drips out of the top, and I lick it off.

"Google," Ana and Kenzie say in unison, and I roll my eyes.

We toast to a future filled with whatever we can dream of, and Clara whispers *per cent'anni* after the glasses are empty.

# Charlie

The breeze off the ocean is cool, but the sun warms my skin under my suit as I stand in my family's backyard. The gathering is small—just my family, Kenzie, Sammy, Catalina, and a few close friends of The Syndicate. Only Ana will walk Gwen down the aisle.

Gwen had thought this unnecessary, but even if my father and sister hadn't insisted, I would have asked her to do this for me. Marry me in front of a crowd of the people we care for. Tell me she loves me in this beautiful place.

I can hear the sea rocking the boats against the docks, and the cries of gulls as they dive for their meals. All familiar sounds of my childhood. But I don't feel at home until I see her.

Ana's on her arm, and despite how lovely she looks, I barely see her. Because Gwen is, as always, a vision.

Long hair tied up, soft curls framing her face. Shoulders freckled and bared to the sun, the sleeves draped on her upper arms delicately. It's like she's floating above the terracotta tiles, the satin of her dress flowing like the waves of the ocean beside us.

Perfect. So, so perfect.

When they reach me and the officiant, Ana kisses her sister's cheek and takes the small bouquet from her hands before finding her seat next to Clara.

The words are a formality. Because I will show her every day how sincere I am about my commitment to her. We listen to the officiant tell us about duty, about sickness and health, about good times and bad, and all I can think is that the worst times with her will be better than the best with anyone else. When I slip the wedding band on her finger, over the red thread tattooed there, I wonder again what I did to deserve someone so fierce and loving and kind.

When I kiss her, I decide it doesn't matter. She is my fate, and I will follow her wherever she leads.

# Epilogue Two
## Charlie

"**A**bsolutely not." My voice sounds firm to my own ears, but I already know I'm going to break. *Anything for Gwen, right?*

"Give me one good reason," she retorts, not turning to me at all, keeping her eyes on the shiny motorcycle in front of her.

I should not have let her in here while I was changing the oil. I should not have craved her attention and presence so much that I practically salivated when she perched her round ass on my workbench and propped her feet on the back of the barstool I keep tucked underneath.

"First, motorcycles are death traps." That gets a glare over her shoulder.

"Riding a motorcycle cannot be statistically more dangerous than being married to you, or than half of the other shit you've taught me to do." She smiles and turns back to run her fingertip over the handlebars.

Internally, I try to get my dick under control. God, I love it when she torments me.

It's been a journey, learning that. Unearthing the desires I've kept buried without ever truly recognizing they existed.

Every time we fuck, or talk about fucking, or even just touch each other, I learn something new about myself. I can see it happening for her, too. She's bolder. Demanding but always caring. Soft and controlled. Perfect.

"Second, this bike is way too big for you, and before you make some god-awful joke about the size of things you already ride..." Her head tips back in a laugh and warmth like sunshine fills me at the sound of her approval. "You choose a bike based on a bunch of factors, like height and inseam. Learning to ride on a motorcycle you can't control can be deadly."

Her fingers drift over the controls a little longer before she turns on her toes and leans back against the seat.

"Okay, if you say so." Her smile is small, delicate, and dangerous, and it doesn't fool me for a second.

"There's no way that convinced you."

"You convinced me I need to learn safely, using the correct equipment," she replies coyly, just a hair too much innocence laced in her tone. I narrow my eyes, waiting for whatever is coming next. "So I'll go take lessons."

Her little shrug sets a fire in my blood, and I'm honest to god starting to think I enjoy burning for her.

"And where, exactly, do you think you're going to find these lessons?" I've already got an image of Gwen in tight pants, high boots, and leather that's going to be imprinted on the inside of my eyelids for the rest of my life. I am not sharing that with a single soul.

"Diego runs fleet, right?" she asks, referring to the twenty-two-year-old hellion that she met when she asked to learn more about Syndicate operations. "I'm pretty sure he can drive and pilot every vehicle on the planet. It wouldn't be too much trouble for him."

I think of Diego with his underdeveloped prefrontal cortex

salivating over my wife as he shows her how to position her legs, and I reconsider my rule against murdering staff.

"Or Lily?" she asks, dusting off her hands and pushing off my bike, making her way toward the door to the house.

I'm frozen in place thinking about Ana's defacto body-guard, a woman I've seen tape people's eyes open and slice into them with a scalpel, reaching around Gwen from behind and adjusting her grip on the accelerator. I briefly run through a list of Arctic-adjacent assignments I could stick Lily with for the foreseeable future.

I know Gwen is doing this to get a rise out of me, and she's hellishly good at it, but I feel this swirl of deep possessiveness and need to be the one to teach her this. To teach her everything, to learn from each other. It's probably incredibly toxic to believe that I can provide her with everything she's ever needed or wanted, that I can be the person to fulfill every desire, but I do. Because I don't just feel possessive over her—I am desperate for her to be possessive of me, too.

"No," I start toward her, and she smirks at me over her shoulder. "Please, Gwen, I'll teach you. I want to teach you."

When she faces me, her expression is filled with a little triumph and a lot of joy. And that's what I really wanted. To be the one to inspire that look.

"I really don't mind asking someone else, Charlie," she replies, sweet and sinful, and I want to tell her to ask me for the world. For heaven and hell and everything in between.

"I want to. Please," I say, reaching behind me to pick up a spare helmet and hold it out to her. "How about I take us on a ride and you can see how you feel on it?"

She grins so wide that it's got to hurt and pulls her hair into a low ponytail. When she's ready, I slip the helmet onto her, shifting it around to make sure it's snug and comfortable before tilting her head up to snap the clasp. She's already in jeans and tennis shoes, so I toss her my leather jacket to cover her bare arms in case something happens, but I already know this will be the safest ride of my life.

<br>

By the time we're cruising up to the park almost an hour later, her grip has loosened on my torso. At every stop, I squeeze her calf, and she runs her hand over my thigh. Riding has always been peaceful for me, but there's something almost Zen-like about having her experience this with me.

There's an overlook that Catalina and Sammy have hiked that is both secluded and motorcycle-friendly, as long as you're not caught by park police, so I search for the turnoff as we roll down the roadway. The dirt road is uneven, and her thighs tighten behind me, her body stiffening more as we follow the path. I take things slow, keeping an eye out for signs of hikers, but it's late morning on a weekday and there were no cars in the parking area, so I assume we're in the clear.

When we finally get to the overlook, I shut the engine off and pat Gwen's thigh to let her know she can move. Her legs are a little wobbly as she ungracefully slips off the bike, and I catch her hand before she tumbles over. The long arms of my jacket are shucked up around her wrists, but she has a hard time getting her helmet off on her own, so I tilt her head up and unclip it for her before removing mine.

"I fucking loved that," she says, nearly breathless as she smooths away the hair that's stuck to her forehead with sweat. She throws her arms around my torso, still holding her helmet, and hugs me so hard that the breath is knocked out of me for a second. "Thank you, Charlie."

Before I can respond, she unwraps herself from me, places her helmet on the seat of the bike, and walks to the edge of the lookout, pulling her hair out of the tie as she goes.

It's unseasonably cool today, and a constant breeze keeps the humidity from settling too much around us. Gwen teases her hair at the root, letting the wind pick it up and blow it over her shoulder. The sun is high and bright over our heads, warming my skin and reflecting off her like light on water. Against the backdrop of early summer, she looks peaceful, copper red and soft blush against endless green and blue.

My helmet still hangs loosely by my side as I walk up next to her, taking in the view of Shenandoah. I prefer it here in the fall, when the shades of orange and yellow blend with the sunset, but it's still gorgeous.

"Why'd you pick here to drive to?" she asks, bumping her shoulder against my arm.

"It's one of the few views I know of that's semi-private that you can get to by bike," I respond, shrugging against her touch.

"You could have driven me to a parking lot." I can hear the smile in her voice. "Or just around the neighborhood. But thank you for picking somewhere so lovely."

We sit in silence for a bit, the warmth of her body just barely touching mine, the creaking and rustling of the endless trees all we can hear. After a few minutes, she bumps my arm again.

"Why did you want to take me somewhere semi-private?"

The effect of her words in that tone is almost immediate. All the adrenaline from the ride, from her body wrapped around mine, comes roaring back through my veins. I want to think of something clever to say, but when I look at her, she's already got heat and trust in her eyes, and the look of her wanting me the way I want her erases all words from my mind. I finally shake myself.

"No nefarious intent, I promise, but I'm open to any shameless ideas you have."

The grin she gives me in response to that is electrifying, and she walks me backwards toward the bike like she already has something in mind.

"Hands on the seat," she directs, and like she controls my body more than I do, they follow her direction.

Her helmet rolls away somewhere and I don't pretend to care. The little smile and nod she gives me fills my chest with a sense of fulfillment, so small and yet so addicting, that I want to chase the feeling over and over and over. She moves closer until she's pressed up against me, her mouth against my jaw, so close as her lips whisper against my skin.

"You're going to keep your hands there until I tell you that you can move, okay?" She traces one hand over my shoulder and down my arm until she locks her fingers over mine. "Shift your weight now so you'll be comfortable and safe leaning against the bike."

I do as she asks, shifting my hips so I'm forcing the bike further into the kickstand. A pleased kiss against my jaw nearly has a groan slipping from me, but I hold back.

"You know, on the drive over here, all I could think was, *my husband would give me anything I asked for,*" she says calmly, shucking off my jacket and dropping it on the grass between us. "You'd teach me how to ride, and you'd protect me while we do it, and I wondered how I could possibly show you I'd also do anything for you."

My heart is beating out of my fucking chest as she sinks to her knees in front of me, her nails scoring my thighs through my jeans as she finds a comfortable position. Every time she touches me it feels like lightning under my skin, and my body is warring between holding still so she'll continue, and yanking her on top of this bike and wringing every last drop of pleasure from her.

"You know you do so much for me," I grit out, trying to hold on to my sanity. "More than I could have ever asked for."

She brushes her hand over my cock, and I jerk involuntarily. Given the look in her eyes, pupils blown so wide that the black of them nearly swallows her brown irises, that's what she wants. Me falling apart for her; me losing control for her; me listening to her direction in spite of it all. Fuck, I want that, maybe more than she does.

"I know. And I want to do this too." She takes a breath. "I'm going to suck your cock, Charlie, and I'm going to make myself come while I do it." Her voice is breathy but controlled as she reaches down and undoes the fly of her jeans, rolling them open until a sliver of black fabric becomes visible. This time I can't control the groan. "And if you're good and listen to what I say, if you don't move your hands, don't touch me, don't come," her voice skips as she slips her fingers over her underwear, "then I'll let you make me come, too."

Jesus fucking Christ. I'm nodding, even though I'm on fucking fire and have no clue if I can follow her instructions.

"Please, Gwen, anything," I beg, my grip on the seat tightening as she undoes my belt, the click of the buckle only ramping up my heart rate. Her movements are slow and teasing as she undoes the button and gently pulls my zipper down, the vibration of it nearly unbearable against my dick.

She yanks her hair back into the tie and I can't fucking stand how beautiful she is. Cheeks flushed and eyes shining, it's undeniable how much this turns her on, and it's impossible not to realize how lucky I am.

My jeans, with the belt still in the loops, are around my thighs in an instant, and all that separates me from the touch she's ghosting over my thighs, my cock, my ass, are tight black boxers being stretched to their limit. I could come from this feeling alone, from her touching and teasing, but I don't lean into the feeling, biting back the flood of adrenaline.

"Fuck, Charlie, you're so hard for me," she breathes, running her nails lightly down my pulsing cock, forcing a whimper out of me that has her smiling. Her fingers hook my waistband and my breathing is erratic as she slips my boxers down.

Her hands, her lips, her breath against me is going to drive me insane. Soft kisses on my thighs, the back of her knuckles on the underside of my shaft. I can hear her muttering curses and exclamations under her breath, and I can see the hand now slipped between her thighs is moving in slow circles.

I'm about to ask out loud, like an idiot, if it's truly possible for her to get this turned on by getting on her knees for me, when she carefully draws her hand from her jeans and sits back on her feet, holding her fingers out in front of her.

They're dripping wet, evidence of her arousal coating her fingers and her palm, and I have to bite the inside of my cheek not to reach for her.

"Fuck, Gwen," I choke out, because she leans forward and traces one slick finger on the underside of my cock, making me jolt. A soft laugh mingles with my groan in the cool summer air as she uses her arousal as lube, stroking me until my vision spots at the edges.

"So good for me, Charlie," she murmurs, licking the taste of her own pussy off my cock.

I'm going to fucking die.

She doesn't say anything else. She just keeps her eyes locked on mine as she slips her left hand back in between her thighs and wraps her mouth around the tip of my cock.

It's possible that nothing has felt this good in my entire life. I would think I was having an out-of-body experience, watching Gwen fuck herself with her fingers with my cock in her mouth, if it wasn't the waves of pleasure bordering on pain crashing over me. My nails are biting through the leather of the seat of the bike as I hold myself back from grasping her hair, touching her face.

She's not hesitant, but exploratory, watching my face for any reaction to what she's doing to me. The hand not fucking herself moves between grasping the base of my cock to cupping my balls to scratching my thigh, each change eliciting some unholy sound from me. She moves from licking to sucking, pumping me while her lips are tight at my crown to taking me deep into her throat.

I know I'm panting at her, begging for something that I can't explain. To let me come, for her to come, for her to stop, for this never to end. Flush creeps down her cheeks and chest and her movements become less coordinated, spit dripping down her chin as her fingers move quickly against her clit. She's moaning against my cock and I'm saying her name over and over again, drawing blood with how hard I'm biting the inside of my lip to keep myself from coming down her throat. It's nearly fucking impossible when she takes me as far as she can, her free hand pulling my hip as close to her as possible, her throat constricting around my cock as she rocks her hips against herself.

She breaks apart with me down her throat in an image that will be replayed every time I have to spend a night away from her. Tears leaking down her face, breathing hard from her nose, her cries muffled against my cock that she's still sucking. She lets the waves of her orgasm roll in and out as her movements become slower, more languid. And while I barely fucking staved off relief of my own, it feels like the edge has been taken off just a little watching her come.

She releases me from her mouth slowly, cleaning herself up

as she does. I'd do it for her—I *want* to do it for her—but she hasn't told me I can move yet. She stands as she pulls her fingers from herself, covered in the evidence of her orgasm.

"You did so fucking good for me, Charlie," she praises, holding her glistening fingers out to me. "Go ahead."

It's all the permission I need to lean forward and suck her fingers into my mouth, tasting her like the gift she is. When I'm done, she leans forward and places a soft kiss on my lips, my cock brushing painfully against her stomach.

"Would you like to make me come now?" She asks, her voice warm and satisfied, but still carrying a note of anticipation.

"Please, yes, please," I chant, the sweet pain of restraining myself from coming pulsing through me. I pull my boxers and jeans back up, leaving the belt undone, and she switches our positions so she's leaning against the bike now.

"You're going to make me come with your fingers," she says, slipping off her shoes and shimmying down her jeans. "*Just* your fingers, Charlie. Not your mouth. And when you do, I'll let you bend me over this bike and fuck me."

I'm on my knees in front of her before she even has to ask. Her ass, barely covered by her plain black underwear, slides up so she's leaning on the seat of the motorcycle. Her knees fall open, and I trace her calves, her thighs, her ankles, every inch of skin I can, with a featherlight touch.

She's already so wet, the fabric of her underwear damp as I ghost over her. Each little touch has her letting out a soft sigh, her legs twitching slightly when I touch the sensitive spot behind her knee.

I pick up one of her legs and drape it over my shoulder, opening her up for me further. I adjust, finding the right angle to continue teasing her. Without thinking, I press a kiss into her thigh as I put pressure on her clit.

Her hands are in my hair immediately, yanking me away from her.

"What did I say? Fingers only." Her voice is tight with desire, and I circle my thumb over her clit again. Her head tilts back on a moan.

"You said I could only make you come with my fingers. My mouth isn't anywhere near your perfect cunt," I say, getting as close to her as I can without actually licking her skin, which is what I desperately want to do.

"Every way you touch me gets me closer to coming, Charlie," she pants, and I'm nearly delirious with how incredible those words make me feel. "So, hands only."

I nod, pulling back and tracing her pussy over her underwear again and again. Soft moans fill the air around us, as I work closer to her clit on every circle.

Right before I reach where I know she wants me, I pull the fabric covering her to the side and slip two fingers inside her. She cries out my name, and I keep my other hand gripped on her knee to stop myself from stroking my cock while she screams for me.

She's so fucking gorgeous, the foot still on the floor to balance her lifted onto her toes, her back arched and her head tipped toward the sky. I desperately want her bare in front of me on this bike, freckled skin and perfect pink nipples on display for me as she rides my hand.

She's so wet, and it's easy to slip a third finger in, arching them against her g-spot with every thrust. She's so close, her pussy clamping around me, and I lean forward to suck her clit, desperate to see her come.

Again, she's yanking me backward, and this time, both of us let out a frustrated groan.

"I was so close, baby," she whines, her fingers pulling at the root of my hair so I have to look up at her. "You're not doing a great job at listening today."

She's not upset, despite being obviously frustrated. Actually, there's a pleased little gleam in her eyes. I know she loves seeing how I can't help myself around her. How I always need more—to touch her more, to taste her more, to fuck her more. She wants me unbound, and she always gets what she wants.

"I'm sorry, mio filo," I apologize, pumping the fingers still inside her in and out. Her breath catches, but she keeps her eyes on me.

"If you can't listen, I guess we'll have to make sure you follow directions," she says, her eyes glazed over. I don't know what she means, but I'll do whatever she says if she keeps looking at me like that. "Stop fucking me and put on your helmet."

I hesitate for just a moment, and she gives me the time to think it over. This is our routine now—one of us suggests something, based on porn we send back and forth or some idea she's read in a romance book—and we wait for the other one to consider it with no extra influence. There's no shame in a no.

I nod and carefully remove my fingers, keeping her balanced with the leg over my shoulder as I reach for my helmet on the ground. I slip it on, and she reaches down to slide the visor up.

"You tell me if you want to stop, okay?" she reminds me, and I nod again. "But now you can't put your mouth on me. And you'll be able to follow the rules."

I want to do what she wants. I'm desperate to make her come on my fingers. So I press the knee that's resting on my shoulder, opening her up for me again.

I'm slower this time, with more attention on her clit, following the pattern she uses on herself when she lets me watch her make herself come in our bed. When I slip two fingers back into her pussy, I press my thumb to her clit, keeping pressure as I do my best to stroke her g-spot on every thrust.

My name is on her lips between curses and prayers, *god* and *fuck* and *hell* and *Charlie* all slurring together. She's meeting me thrust for thrust, rocking her hips to fuck herself harder on my fingers. When she comes, she pulls back, but I keep up the intensity, using my grip on her thigh to keep rocking her through every wave of pleasure until she's near tears, her pussy soaking my hand.

Her body slowly relaxes, and she leans against her weight against me as she catches her breath. The inside of my helmet is humid, sweat dripping between the cushioning and my skin, but I couldn't care less. Every moment making Gwen come feels like the hottest moment of my life.

She smiles down at me, lazy and sated, hooking a finger into the opening of the helmet, shaking my head back and forth again.

"See, I knew you could follow directions," she murmurs, cracking her neck and rolling her shoulders out. "I think you've earned it."

I don't move as she slides her leg off my shoulder, turning around so her perfect ass is in front of my face. And then she bends over the bike.

"You can fuck me now, Charlie."

I'm never going to last, but I can't bring myself to care. I stand without bothering to take the helmet off, and when I scramble to find a condom, she holds one out to me, ass still high in the air.

"Where were you hiding that?" I ask, my voice muffled.

"Your jacket pocket," she laughs. I barely shove my jeans and boxers down far enough to free my cock, grabbing the condom from her and rolling it down my shaft as quickly as I can.

I position myself at the entrance to her pussy, reveling in the way she arches back, still eager after coming twice.

"Fuck, so perfect," I sigh, sliding into her wet cunt like it was made for me. She's whimpering, so oversensitized, and I try to be gentle as I pull out and thrust back in.

"You going easy on me, Charlie?" she asks on a moan as I slowly pump in and out of her, feeling the hot grip of her on my cock.

"Going easy on myself, too, mio filo," I say, grabbing her ass and spreading her apart so I can watch my dick disappear inside her. I can already feel my orgasm building at the base of my spine.

"I don't want easy," she argues, and her tone is more whimper than whine. "Please, Charlie, lose control for me."

I'm the one who begs, not her. So when she asks like that, I can't help but give her what she wants.

I wrap my hand around her ponytail and pull her up so her back is flush with my chest. She braces against the seat, and I let go of her hair so I can pinch one of her nipples between my fingers. The other finds its way between her and the bike, stroking her clit again, keeping gentle pressure as I thrust up into her.

"Anything for you, Gwen."

I fuck her harder and faster, letting her cries of pleasure fuel my stamina, desperate to feel her come on my cock. I don't know if she has another one in her, but I'll do anything to get her there.

"You feel so fucking incredible, Gwen," I pant, rolling her nipple between my fingers and smiling at the way she screams for me. "You own me. All I want is your pleasure. All I can think about is the way you look and feel when you come apart for me. Do you like that? Knowing how out of control you make me? How much I need you?"

"*YesfuckpleaseyesCharlie*," she pants, the words all rolling together in desperation. I press down slightly harder on her clit as I gently bite her neck, the salt of her sweat perfect on my tongue.

She comes hard, one of her hands coming to grip mine against her tit. The feeling of her pussy pulsing around me is too much, and I finally let myself tip over the edge.

The pleasure is blinding, so intense that I know I'm sinking my teeth too hard into Gwen's skin, but I can't stop. My blood pounds through my veins, echoing in my ears as I spill into the condom, Gwen still riding the final waves of her orgasm. We're both covered in sweat, our shirts sticking to our bodies and hair to our faces.

When I come back to earth, I release my grip on Gwen, gently holding her as we both try to catch our breath. There's a mark on her neck where my teeth were, and I smooth it over with my thumb.

"Sorry about that," I murmur. She turns her head over her shoulder and I kiss her softly.

"Nothing to apologize for."

We slowly untangle ourselves from each other, cleaning up as best as we can, and Gwen's head rests against my back the entire ride home.

# Acknowledgments

Hi cuties!

Thank you so much for reading my first ever book! This has been such an unbelievable experience, and I'm thankful to everyone who has been involved. So thankful, in fact, I imagine my acknowledgments are going to be the longest chapter in the book.

First and most importantly, thank you to my readers! You're taking a chance on a brand new author that you more than likely found through my flared based TikToks. That's a leap of faith if I've ever heard of one. I'm so honored that you spent your time and energy reading my silly little pegging murder book. Every word of encouragement from all of you has made more of a difference than you'll ever know.

I am certain that it was not an easy experience, being on my team. My alpha, beta, and sensitivity readers, editors, friends, mentors, and confidants were patient, kind, brilliant, and enormously helpful in making this book the best version of itself. So very special thanks to the following beautiful humans:

- Rose Santoriello, my perfect, lovely, delusional developmental editor
- Erica VanNoy and Marissa Bologna, my amazing alpha readers
- Nikki Lincoln and Lo Morales, who provided their

knowledge, lived experience, and expertise to my characters and their journey as sensitivity readers

- Casadi Brendemuehl and Stephanie Sameli, my beautiful beta readers
- Jess Wisecup and Naomi Loud, my "slap you in the face with some tough love and reality" readers
- Everyone who slid into my DMs to support me during the writing process

Love you all to pieces.

A special thank you to R.N. Barbosa (@barbosbooks_) for swooping in at the last second to be my savior proofreader. You are talented and wonderful and I appreciate you so.

Another well-deserved shout out to Amanda Hawkins (@eternalgeekery) for designing my cover. I gave you a Google doc and a dream and you turned it into a vision. I'm so beyond thankful for you and your brilliance.

To my mom and brother, who absolutely should not have read this book. Thank you for supporting every version of me as an author—from writing Christian dystopian YA sci-fi books in high school (unpublished, don't worry) to today.

To Erin, my ride or die, my real-life-best-friend turned book-swag-creator. Thanks for flexing into this weird social media author life I've decided to live, and for creating my adorable stickers. Oh, and for learning to deal with people calling me Rae. Love you.

To Jess Wisecup, for calling me an idiot when I needed to hear it, and pulling me out of my spirals. And for creating that discord group. Not really sure if we'd be here without it.

And to Rose. Thanks for giving me the one brain cell we share long enough for me to write this book. Only we could truly tolerate each other while we write. The [redacted] Podcast has kept me sane over the past six months, and the hours upon hours of voice memos back and forth probably contain 80% of the plot of this book. I could not ask for a better gremlin. I love you.

Charlie and Gwen have meant the world to me. This book has been one of my greatest achievements, mostly because I proved I was brave enough to try. I hope you loved them, and I can't wait to introduce you to Clara and Deniz.

# About the Author

Rae Douglas (they/she/he) is a 30 year old debut author from the San Francisco Bay. They love writing stories about mutual obsession, family trauma, heathy BDSM and kink, and friends who know platonic love is just as valuable as romantic love. They have lived all over the United States, from Los Angeles to D.C. to Branson, and love road tripping as much as possible. In their free time, they can be found in a natural history museum, at a baseball game, or on a whale watching excursion. They can be reached at @seeraewrite on all platforms.